PRAISE FOR UNRAVE[LED]

BY SONDRA UMBERGER

Book 1 ROBBED-Innocence Stolen
Book 2 RIPPED-Lies Exposed
Book 3 RESTORED-Truth Unfolds

A triumphant story based on shocking true events, on how an innocent child, a determined woman, and a Christian counselor, journey for the truth to overcome unimaginable abuse. **Couldn't put the books down**. ~*M.J. Turner, Retired Christian Counselor*

A captivating novel based on actual events. Determined and combating evil with faith-based principles, confrontations ignite, and spiritual weapons discharge, leading to victory! A story of sexual addiction that exposes the hidden lies of many. **Offers hope and restoration**. ~*Jean Christine*

When all feels lost, discover hope, healing, and redemption—**a page-turner**. ~*Genevra Bonati, Author of series: Forgiven and Free: A Halted Heart*

The author of Unraveled-Rewoven pens an excellent trilogy that unmasks the inconceivable abuse and anguish of the brokenhearted. A novel based on true events—a faith-igniting story of perseverance and victory **leaving your eyes wide-open.** ~*Catherine Scholz M.Ed., M.S., LPC*

This riveting novel takes you into the depths of an evil realm swirling with lies, abuse, and sheer terror. Yet faith rises-and light battles against the darkness, finding perseverance, promises, and power. **Based on a true story—A MUST READ.** ~*Anna Wise, Author of Mercy Me www.Anna-Wise.com*

As a retired sergeant major, a police officer, and a public servant, I have seen abuse, violence, and dysfunction on many levels. These novels, inspired by real events, expose subjects that need to be brought to the light while showing healing and redemption that come through faith. A spiritual story of perseverance and purpose. **Eye-opening and captivating**. ~*R.L. Richards* SGM Ret

Unraveled–Rewoven is a trilogy inspired by real events. This story exposes a broken world of unthinkable abuse and trauma. Determined and combating evil with faith-based principles, a spiritual battle erupts, leading to victory! **A wonderful story of hope and restoration**. ~*Healing Heart Ministry, Inc.*

As a victor and overcomer of childhood abuse involving parental dysfunction and addiction, I was able to relate to this compelling trilogy. Unraveled-Rewoven exposes the silent violence of trauma. These books **offer hope, encouragement, and freedom** that comes by unlocking long-buried thoughts and fears. I would **highly recommend** these books. ~*Nicole Zurcher*

The Unraveled – Rewoven Trilogy is a **MUST READ**! In her debut novels, Sondra Umberger grips the reader with the style of a veteran author. Sondra takes us into the dark, dark world where Satan rules. The evil, the abuse, the cruelty she reveals, most of us would prefer not to see. We need not only to see, but we need to take action to stop evil. I pray readers will recognize the truth and act. At the end of this trilogy, Sondra invites you to the greatest remedy of all. One caution: Once you start reading, you won't want to put the book down. This trilogy will cause missed meals, sleeping, and total schedule destruction. ~*J.C. Richards, Author of Shattered Trust www.jchrisrichards.com*

UNRAVELED·REWOVEN

BOOK 2 ❖ A TRILOGY BASED ON TRUE EVENTS

RIPPED

Sondra Umberger

Disclaimers:

For mature audiences. Discretion is advised.

This book deals with child abuse, satanic ritual abuse, sexual assault, domestic violence, pornography addiction, and other forms of abuse and violence. While the author has taken great lengths to ensure the subject matter is dealt with in a compassionate and respectful manner, it may be troubling for some readers.

This book is inspired by real events therefore names, dates, locations, and identifying details have been changed to protect the privacy and safety of individuals.

This book is for informational purposes only. While every precaution has been taken in the preparation of the book, neither the author nor the publisher shall have any liability to any person or entity with respect to any loss or damage caused or alleged to be caused directly or indirectly by the instructions contained in this book.

The information provided in this book is not intended as a substitute for the medical advice of physicians, psychologist, or any other professional. [v8]

ISBN 978-1-953202-01-7

Printed in the United States of America.

In loving memory of my dear friend
and sister in the Lord,
Maria

Maria knew all too well that the unspoken—screams havoc. Because Maria was
unable to use her voice or tell of her abusive story before her passing:

~I am speaking out on her behalf.

~I am speaking out for the countless victims of untold abuse.

~I am speaking out for those who still suffer silently.

Victory and triumph, then and now,
are in our Lord, Jesus Christ.

Maria, I know you are in the presence of God,
embraced in his love. My heart sings with joy,
knowing this truth,
knowing you have freedom,
and knowing we will be together again.

Unraveled-Rewoven is dedicated to those in need!

I have written this series of books to encourage anyone who desires hope and healing to become a truth-seeker, striving for answers that will set you free. After reading this trilogy, I hope the story will inspire and equip you to fight the battles that rage in your life.

Stand firm, each moment, each day, each week, until the passing of time is merely a reminder that you are an overcomer in Christ.

I encourage you to study and apply the Holy Scriptures into your life with the intent of building intimacy with the Lord. I pray your truth journey will take you from victims to victors, Unraveled-Rewoven!

RIPPED

SONDRA UMBERGER

PROLOGUE

Catherine
January 1994

My hands tremble as I grab my Bible off the nightstand. My suitcase sits at the foot of our bed; my clothes neatly packed. Our flights are booked and ticketed. All I have left is to finish loading my book bag.

But what about me? Am I ready?

My husband, Hunter, walks into the room. He leans his muscular frame against the doorjamb; his hands tucked into the front pockets of his jeans. I'm going to miss him.

"Do you have everything?" He rakes his fingers through his blonde hair, pushing it off his forehead, exposing his bright blue eyes.

"I think so. Just a few last-minute things to do."

"Do you have your ID? Your plane ticket?"

I smile, knowing his questions hint at his anxiety about my trip. I know because my own anxiety keeps climbing up my throat. "Both my ID and ticket are in my purse."

"How about your camera and film? You'll want to take a few photos if you make it to Churchill Downs. Have you ever been to the Kentucky Derby?"

Hunter talks as if I'm going on a sightseeing vacation instead of traveling to receive serious memory retrieval counseling. It's his way of covering up his concerns. Perhaps fears?

We're both unnerved by the uncertainty of what will be revealed in Kentucky. I need to know the truth about my past, about those lost years from six to almost nine years old. It's time to solve the mystery of my haunting, recurring nightmare.

"Catherine." Hunter's voice pulls me back into the conversation.

"Huh?" I look up.

"I just asked if you've ever been to the Kentucky Derby."

"Nope," I say, stuffing a notepad in my book bag. "I've never been to the Derby. But it's on my to-do list, as well as trying out a Mint Julep."

"Good luck with that." He forces a chuckle. "It's made with 120 proof Kentucky bourbon." He crossed his arms over his chest. "Hard liquor and strong southern booze don't quite sound like you." He shakes his head. "I don't think you'll like it—at all."

"Oh...bourbon?" I frown. "I thought it was a sweet, minty drink, like chocolate chip, mint ice cream."

"I'm afraid not. But when in Rome? Give it a shot. At least you can say you had a Mint Julep where they run the Kentucky Derby."

The inane conversation centers me—and distracts me. I'm so grateful for a supportive husband.

The doorbell rings. We both look towards the front door. "It's probably Marion. Would you mind answering that while I finish getting my things together?" I check my watch. "We need to leave in about ten minutes. Let her know where you'd like her to park her car while we're gone."

"Sure thing." Hunter turns to walk out of the room.

"Thanks, sweetheart," I shout over my shoulder. My stomach grumbles with nerves.

I whisk my flight itinerary off the top of the dresser. I fold the paper in half, then quarters, and place it inside my purse. I quickly fasten my heavy suitcase and roll it out into the hallway along with my book bag, leaving both at the top of the stairs for Hunter to take to the car.

Marion's waiting in the foyer when I come traipsing down the stairs. A small suitcase, the size of a carryon bag, sits by her feet.

"Hey, I see you've packed light—unlike me."

"Yes, I am a light packer." She tilts her head and offers a small grin. "How are you feeling, Catherine? We will be in Kentucky by noon. Are you emotionally prepared for the day?" Her face lights up with encouragement.

"You mean, other than this early morning flight?" I roll my bloodshot eyes. "I'm doing fine. I've waited a lifetime for this opportunity. I'm ready to solve this mystery. And now…I'm more psyched up than you know." I say, trying to convince myself.

Hunter breezes by, going upstairs to retrieve my things from the hallway. Within seconds, he tromps back down the steps carrying my suitcase and book bag.

"Ready, ladies?" He offers a hopeful smile.

"Yes," we say in unison.

Marion pats Hunter's shoulder. "Thank you so much for making this trip possible. I appreciate the investment you are making into Catherine's life, as well as into my continuing education." Her smile is humble, her eyes compassionate.

"No, Marion, thank you for being Catherine's counselor and for being there to support her…and me. You're our Godsend." He lowers his head, his tone sincere. "Not many people know how to deal with this type of issue."

I turn to them both. "I'm the one blessed to have the two of you in my life."

I lean into Hunter, giving him a big hug. "I'm sure you're ready for the middle-of-the-night screams to stop."

He nods a vigorous yes, and smiles, making light of the fact, but I know we're serious.

Second thoughts arise. Am I opening a Pandora's box? Will I dig up something I don't want to see? Or worse—maybe it's something that should be left buried—forever.

A cold shiver runs through me. I focus on the warmth of Hunter's hand instead of the fear of the unknown shadowing my thoughts.

Marion
Christian Counselor
January 1994

The Denver airport bustles with people either arriving or departing on flights. Suitcases on wheels rumble past us in every direction. A stream of announcements echo throughout the terminal from the loudspeakers.

The three of us navigate to the departing gate. I stand to the side to allow Catherine and Hunter time alone. I gaze in admiration as Hunter releases Catherine from a long protective embrace. Even at a distance, I can hear their conversation. Loyalty and devotion infuse their words as they say goodbye.

"Catherine, God is with you. You can do this. We can do this." He squeezes her hands. "The Lord has made you a fighter. Believe me, I know."

Hunter sends Catherine a reassuring wink and clings to her upper arms appearing reluctant to release his cherished bride.

"Thank you, Honey. I want to believe that you're right and that I'll be fine. I'm just glad that Marion will be with me."

Catherine kisses her husband and pulls him close for one last hug.

God never ceases to amaze me. I marvel at the fact that amid

Catherine's painful journey in search of truth, she has found love. Hunter strengthens her with his support and understanding, encouraging her to fight to unearth her past.

In the midst of her battle—their battle—our battle, I find myself feeling alone and lonely, yearning to obtain the same type of committed relationship for myself someday.

They turn toward me. Catherine and Hunter's smiles appear nervous—forced. She motions for me to join them.

Catherine takes both Hunter's and my hand. Her hand trembles in mine. "Together, we will fight. I know I can count on both of you to be there for me. Thanks for your support. I appreciate your accepting my need to seek answers." She furrows her perfectly waxed, arched eyebrows as if in deep thought. "Not just answers; I need the truth, regardless of what it may bring to light."

At this point, we are all shaking. We part hands. My fear and anguish mix with an awkward excitement of not knowing what lies ahead. I hope for the best. I anxiously spin my watch numerous times before rechecking the time. It has only been three minutes.

As we move into the boarding line, Catherine's words replay in my mind, 'I need the truth, regardless of what it may bring to light.'

We walk past the gate onto the boarding bridge. Before rounding the corner, we turn and see Hunter's silhouette fade out of sight.

I suspect Catherine's past, as Catie, will soon be unveiled and will expose the hidden secrets of her lost years.

Too many clues point to the covert world of the occult.

I prepare myself for the awakening.

And I pray Catherine is ready to give words to the unspoken that screams havoc.

CHAPTER ONE

Marion
January 1994

Violent gusts of wind assault the wings of the aircraft as we approach the Kentucky runway. The airplane pitches fiercely in the turbulence. I clutch the armrest, my fingernails digging deep into the faux leather. My white knuckles expose my unspoken trepidation.

A lingering thought settles upon my mind. Lord, are you warning me? Does this flight parallel with what lies ahead, in excavating young Catie's hidden secrets and grown Catherine's nightmare in search of truth?

I stiffen as twinges of nerves prickle up and down my spine. Catherine's story is all too familiar with what I have researched, describing Satanic Ritual Abuse. Am I ready to dive into what lies ahead?

I glance over at Catherine, who is jostled by the turbulence, yet sound asleep. Her eyes are swollen, shadowed with gray circles from the repetitive loss of sleep. Her color is pale, almost ghostly, with fatigue straining her appearance.

Self doubt assails me. Am I the right counselor for Catherine? Am I qualified, even with this new training? What have I gotten myself into—will I be able to handle what she hopes to uncover?

The force of the hard landing pushes me firmly back into my seat, then jolts me forward. My palm slams over Catherine's hand, waking her. Her eyes spring open with question.

"What happened?"

"We are here. Rough landing." I explain, almost robotically— perspiration beads under my arms. I lift my hand from off of hers. She doesn't notice.

We lean to look out the airplane window. The January sky appears almost black with winter storm clouds. Strong winds whirl debris into the air. Small flakes of snow spit from the sky. I shiver, but not from the weather.

"We are here, Catherine, in Kentucky. Are you ready?" I sense darkness but say nothing of my concerns.

"Umm. Yes, it's time to remember. That's why we're here. I know the memories are all stored somewhere within my brain. I'm trusting God to show me the way—to show us the way."

As we prepare to exit the plane, Catherine secures a sweater around her shoulders, almost as if hugging herself, before she grabs her book bag. Like a frightened soldier knowing a huge battle lies ahead, she pulls her shoulders back and pretends to be brave. "Let's do this, Marion."

I follow her lead. "Yes. Absolutely, Catherine," I say, projecting confidence I do not have.

Unlike my voice, an eerie threat toys within my mind. "Ready or not…here we come."

CHAPTER TWO

Catherine
January 1994

M arion and I pick up the rental car at the airport and drive straight to the hotel. To our delight, our hotel room is warm and cozy, unlike the frigid air outside.

We unpack and then grab a quick bite to eat before heading over to Bethany Taylor's office, who specializes in memory recovery. As we pull up in front of the counseling center, Marion holds up her datebook to confirm the address. Her hand trembles slightly. *Is she nervous or cold?* I glance away, pretending to be unaware.

She closes her datebook and says, "Yes, this is the right place."

One step out of the car, my stomach does a flip. I reassure myself. *This counseling is the opportunity I've been waiting for—waiting for decades. At last, I'm here and can finally search for answers. I can do this.*

Marion points out the beautiful architecture of the old Victorian house with its turrets, dormers, and wide wrap-around porch. "This home makes a beautiful counseling center."

I'm too unnerved to pay attention. I simply mumble, "Uh huh."

Once inside, I walk directly to the reception desk. A young girl in her twenties with a bright, welcoming smile and a sweet southern accent greets us. "Welcome, y'all. You must be Catherine." Her bright blue eyes match her smile. "I have a packet for you with several forms for you to fill out. Please take your time and make yourselves at home." She includes Marion in the conversation. "Would y'all care for some sweet tea while y'all are waiting?"

We both decline.

My fingers squeeze the pen to stop my jitters as I fill out the required paperwork. The receptionist verifies my information and then escorts us into the room where I will receive my counseling.

I take a deep breath and a quick look around, seeing two overstuffed wingback chairs, both cream-colored with a side table in between, and a lamp that softly lights the room. A long sofa and coffee table set across from the chairs. A box of tissue and a writing tablet with a pen lay on the glass tabletop. I take a seat on the couch and cross my legs. I squeeze my thighs tight to keep my legs from bouncing.

The door opens, and in walks a tall, thick-waisted woman of middle-age. Long brunette curls drape around her dark-olive sweater, matched with a pair of black dress slacks. Her soft smile welcomes us. She glides over with her hand extended.

"Hello, Catherine, I'm Bethany."

After introducing herself to Marion as well, Bethany explains in detail the counseling protocol and how we will proceed. I feel a smorgasbord of emotions: anxiety, nervousness, and an awkward excitement about the possibility of what could unfold. Having Marion near, right across from me, soothes my heightened nerves.

While Bethany instructs, Marion jots notes in her spiral notebook.

"Catherine, I see from your paperwork, you've only been married a short time—newlyweds. Is your husband aware that you're receiving counseling?"

"Yes, most definitely." I cock my head. "Aware? Aren't all husbands aware?"

Bethany's eyes crinkle at the corners. She looks like someone who smiles a lot. "You'd be surprised. Sometimes individuals choose to keep their counseling private, often due to…well, an array of reasons. But I'm happy to hear your husband is on board."

She folds her hands, resting them on her lap. Her nails are unpolished but neatly manicured.

"Marion has informed me of your history and that you have a recurring nightmare that has plagued you for some time. For about three decades, correct?"

I nod.

"And that you've connected the dream to what you refer to as *your lost years*. Those were the years when your father was married to a woman named Anna. Is that accurate?"

"Yes," I confirm. "The nightmare jolts me awake, often screaming. It's one stressful issue that my husband, Hunter, and I would like to resolve. I have been upfront with him from the beginning about the mystery of my past."

Bethany's warm eyes have an encouraging glow. "A spouse's awareness and support are very advantageous." She tilts her head. "How old were you when you lived with this stepmother and her family?" She glances down at her notes. "She had two children herself. Close to your age. Is that right?"

Again, I nod and nervously wet my lips before I explain. "Anna came into our lives after my mom died suddenly from a brain aneurysm. I was five years old when my real mom passed away." I swallow the lump in my throat. "My siblings and I met Anna several months later. My father and Anna married the same year after I turned six. Her daughter, Melinda, was a couple of years older than me, and Shawnee was four years old, the same age as my baby brother, Charley." I nervously jabber on. "I also have three older sisters. The oldest is Charlotte, number two is Claudia, and number three is Carolyn. My mom thought it would be fun for all of my siblings to have the same initials," I say to add some lightheartedness to the conversation, but more so to calm myself.

11

"Our mom also taught us how to look after one another." I go down our list of names explaining how the older sibling was to watch the younger, next in line, and how it was my job to watch Charley. My chatter ends with, "Although, I am sure Charlotte always kept an eye on all of us after mom died."

"Hmm…I see."

Bethany jots more notes. Her brow furrows, somewhat studious, reminding me of a science professor contemplating a theory. And the tone of her one-word statement, 'hmm,' unnerves me.

I look over at Marion and gesture with a shift of my head toward Bethany. Marion's quick to read my facial expression and body language. She speaks up.

"Catherine, I mentioned to Bethany over the phone that you are employed as a dental hygienist and attending college—taking counseling courses. The conversation led me to disclose the partial memory that you experienced about a month ago."

Marion turns to address Bethany. "Catherine's experience with this type of memory recovery was at the counseling center, where she attends classes. She was amazed how quickly she entered into a memory, especially a memory she believed was lost." She cocks her head, then finishes her thought with one word. "Suppressed."

Marion redirects her attention back onto me. "I told Bethany about the recollection you had, the memory of when you were attending a wedding?"

I give a quick nod.

Marion continues speaking, "Well, I explained that it was this particular experience, or rather a memory, that was instrumental in bringing us here to Kentucky."

"Yes, that's correct," I say. My back stiffens.

"Why don't you relax and get comfortable." Marion encourages.

Bethany picks up her writing tablet and pen while coaching me to recline on the long couch. A small blanket lays folded over the armrest. I reach for it and drape it over my legs, then lean back. The squared cushions sigh against my weight. I slow my breathing and relax my shoulders.

Bethany starts the session. "Catherine?" I shift my eyes in her direction. "I would like to begin with a prayer."

She bows her head and closes her eyes. Marion and I do the same.

"Dear Heavenly Father, we come to you in the name of your son, Jesus Christ. Lord, we invite the Holy Spirit into this session to lead and guide Catherine into the hidden memories of her lost years. Thank you for your presence and love. We trust you in all things. We ask for your truth to be revealed and to bring healing to Catherine. In Jesus name, we pray. Amen."

The room falls silent. Only the sound of the heat, blowing out the vents, hums inside the room. The hushed tones feel awkward. I don't know what I'm supposed to do, or what will come next.

"Umm...is there anywhere, in particular, I should begin?" I ask.

I need to get started before my fear rises too high, and I chicken out.

Marion speaks up. "How about beginning with something familiar from your recollected memory?" Her voice is soft and supportive, like a protective mother, nudging her child to be brave. "Perhaps your desire and excitement to wear Anna's daughter, Shawnee's, pretty yellow dress?"

I close my eyes, then release a slow sigh. I scan my thoughts, seeing a vivid image of me dancing in a walkway, thrilled that I'm going to be in a wedding.

I focus on the emotions of wearing Shawnee's dress. Excitement. Anticipation. My memory unfolds, taking the same path as previously traveled at the counseling teaching center. I'm giddy with delight to wear the beautiful satin, overlaid with chiffon, but then—

The scene fades and becomes blurry. Fuzzy, like in a dream. There's a winding road. I'm running with beautiful wild horses. I look to a bright blue sky, yet it appears to be wallpapered with child-like, happy images.

I enjoy the memory until I find myself feeling timid—fearful. I slowly enter the mouth of a dark cave, a lava-filled cavern, hot with the presence of evil. Darkness encroaches. I sense it wants to swallow me. I jerk instinctually, swallow hard, and search for the courage to move further into the memory. My heartbeat rises. My chest feels heavy, like it might explode. I push through a darkened, scary wall into a familiar scene....

Catie
Spring 1963

I skip up the cement walkway toward the cellar-like church with Anna. I'm so excited 'bout goin' to my very first weddin'. She nudges me toward a set of steps leadin' down a hill to a side entrance.

"But, Anna, I want to go in the front doors of the church. Why do we have to use these icky cellar steps?" I whine.

"Catie, this is where they perform the weddings. It's a special room for these types of ceremonies. Besides, we are the honored guests. The *special* people are presented through these doors, and we want to make sure everyone sees you in your pretty yellow dress."

I smile and admire my princess dress. Anna looks pretty too in her lavender dress and matchin' hat. She likes to wear dresses that show off her figure. That's what my big sister, Charlotte says.

Anna opens the white doors that smell like fresh paint. We enter the dark, dingy room to another smell. Real bad. Pukey bad. I plug my nose. No one seems to notice the stink, except me. And even though it is warm outside, this dark room feels cold as winter and looks more like a dungeon. I roll the hem of my dress between my fingers.

Two policemen stand guard inside the doors. I recognize the blonde-haired man. I've seen him before, at the 'Little Store' just kitty-corner from our house. I remember him bein' there the day we bought bug spray. We had a bunch of flyin' ants, swarmin' on our front porch. Anna was bein' too friendly with the man—then and now.

She smiles at the two officers. I do the same, wonderin' if they see my pretty yellow dress. They nod. We walk down the hallway. It's icky and dark. There are too many creepy cobwebs here if you ask me. The room has oiled dirt floors that smell like mud and yucky worms.

My eyes take a few minutes to adjust. Granny Ivy walks toward us. She's all dressed up, like Anna. She looks like she has on her Easter clothes with a matchin' light green bonnet.

Torches light up the walls of this big room. Chairs fill both sides of the aisle, also lit by torches on tall poles in the ground. I count them, one, two, three, four…ten hangin' lamps.

In the front of this cellar weddin' church, there are millions of candles.

"It's s-o-o-o-o pretty. I can't wait to see the bride." I whisper, but I'm not sure why. I slowly look at this weddin' room. I want to make sure I see everythin'. I'm over the top 'bout seein' my first weddin'.

Anna and Granny Ivy say, "Catie, we have a surprise for you. Do you want to guess what it is?"

"What? What is it? I love surprises!" I screech with excitement, clappin' my hands.

"You're going to be in the wedding. You will be the virgin princess!"

Granny Ivy claps her hands, and so does Anna. Feelin' happy, I join in and clap along. I'm not sure what a virgin princess does in a weddin', but I'm thinkin' it must be like bein' a flower girl or bridesmaid. Now I know why Anna let me wear this special princess dress.

Charlotte is the oldest of us girls. She told me all about a weddin' she attended. I can't wait to tell her my good news. She'll be tickled pink to hear I get to be in the actual weddin'. I start dancin' and singin' on the spot, "I'm in the weddin'. I'm in the weddin'!" I swish the pretty dress side to side.

Anna and Granny Ivy nod toward their men-friends. Their smiles look tight, like Sylvester, the puddy cat, when he has Tweedy Bird in his mouth. They must have a big secret. Maybe it's another surprise for me. I dance in place and bob my head back and forth in excitement. Everyone smiles at me and seems extra friendly.

Four big men walk up. They're huge, probably real cowboys. They carry some kind of a platter. It's a pretty gold color. Reminds me of a giant turkey platter but even bigger—gigantic. My grandpa would call it a hog platter 'cuz it's big enough to hold a hog. The shiny platter is fastened tight onto a flat leather square with lots of handles on all four sides.

Granny Ivy says those handles are what the men hold on to when they carry, what I call the hog platter, but she calls it a presentation board. She seems thrilled, but I'm not sure why since she's grouchy most all the time.

One of those giant men says, "I know a few ladies I'd like to get on that there bitchin' board."

"So, mister," I tug at the hem of his jacket. "What's a hitchin' board?"

"Huh? What's that you say?" His hand cups his ear.

"I heard you tell your friend you'd like to put some ladies on the board. Why's that?"

Anna scurries over. She quickly comes between the men and me.

"Catie, darling, you shouldn't eavesdrop. Come over here with Granny Ivy and me."

Her arm circles my waist, tuggin' me away from the men. She shows me a small paper cup. "I have some Kool-Aid for you. Hurry and drink up so we can show you the special Presentation Board."

Anna winks at Granny Ivy, and holds the cup to my lips. She puts a napkin underneath to keep me from spillin' any on my dress.

"Anna, there's somethin' wrong with this Kool-Aid. It tastes yucky." I scrape my tongue on my teeth to erase the ickiness.

"Now, stop that, Catie. You're going to mess up Shawnee's dress. There's probably not enough sugar in this batch."

She wipes the spit off my face. Once we're finished, Anna waves the men over.

"These nice gentlemen are going to put you on this board to carry you down the aisle. That way, everyone can see how special and beautiful you are."

They all smile at me.

"Well, if I'm so special and the virgin princess, why can't I just walk down the aisle?"

Granny Ivy speaks up, "Because you're too small, little Catie. You're only five…umm… or six years old.

"I'm almost seven!" I interrupt.

Anna corrects her mother. "Mom, Catie turns seven this summer."

"Oh, that's right, but anyway, we want every person here to see how beautiful you are in this lovely dress." Granny Ivy points to my princess outfit. "But don't you worry your sweet little head." She cups my face into her hands, givin' me a little jiggle. "They will fasten you on tight so that you won't fall."

I don't think I've ever seen Granny Ivy so happy. She smiles at the men and says, "I suppose we could leave one of her hands free so that she can wave at our friends. Don't you think?" She glances at the men and winks. Anna nods in agreement. The biggest man reaches down and pretends to pinch my nose.

He smiles and says, "Catie, that's your name, right?"

"Uh, huh. It sure is." I swish my dress at the man.

"You'll be fine, but tell me if you feel a little shaky. You can also grab onto the side of the platform with your free hand if need be."

They sit me on the platter, then steady me on the board with straps that look like small dog collars. They fasten one around my wrist and the two others on my ankles. Anna arranges my dress, flarin' it over my legs, and tuckin' it under.

"One, two, three…" The four men, two on each side, lift me high into the air.

I let out a cry. "I-I-I'm afraid. It's too high."

I grab onto the extra dog collar with my free hand. I feel too wobbly.

"I want my daddy!" I shout.

Anna rushes to my side. "Catie, your daddy couldn't be here because he had to work. But he told me he is so-o-o-o proud of you. He didn't tell you himself because he didn't want to ruin your big surprise." She pats my hand.

Anna's actin' all syrupy-sweet. Is she puttin' on an act for her friends? I wish she were always this nice.

"You look so beautiful," Anna gushes. "Just between you and me, you look prettier than Shawnee in this dress. It's perfect for you. I told you I'd let you wear this dress for a special occasion *if* you promised to be good. Now—I kept my promise."

She stares into my eyes, then speaks firmly. "So, you must keep your promise! You understand?"

I jut my lower lip into a pout but nod in agreement. Anna, once again, fluffs up the dress.

"Have fun, Catie. Make sure you wave at everyone. You're very special." She smiles at me and then at Granny Ivy.

"You are the one *chosen* to be the virgin princess—*only you*," Anna calls back over her shoulder as she walks away.

They take their seats toward the front of the church. I can barely see them now. My tummy rumbles. The Kool-Aid Anna gave me is makin' me sleepy. I let out a big yawn.

The four men balance me on their shoulders. They walk slow, as they carry me down the center. Both sides of the aisle are full of people, all lookin' at me. They clap, makin' the biggest ruckus like I'm Miss America. I wave like Anna told me, but I don't like bein' up so high. *Why is everyone actin' like I'm so important? Isn't the bride supposed to be the special girl at a weddin'?*

I stare at the crowd. As we get close to the front, Anna glares at me and coaches me to smile extra big. I obey and fake a huge smile. The crowd claps even louder. My head spins like I'm on a merry-go-round.

Six more men includin' a young boy, stand at the front of the church when we finally arrive. They all wear hooded black bathrobes —their faces hidden in the shadows.

Are they all waitin' on me? Where's the bride and groom? They must be comin' real soon.

I stretch my neck to look over the people toward the back of the basement church, and then I glance back to the altar.

The young boy looks up. Yay! It's Gilbert, Granny Ivy and Buck's foster kid. He's my friend. I feel better knowin' he's here. I flash him a quick smile, and by accident, a giggle pops out. I wonder if he sees my pretty princess dress, perfect for a weddin'.

He doesn't smile back.

I squint hard to focus on his bright green eyes. Uh oh...he's been cryin'—his eyes are red and puffy. His cheek is swollen—black and blue. Gilbert looks at me, then at the ground. His fists are clenched.

Was he forced to be here?

A man grabs Gilbert. He yanks him in close with a hard jerk. The man's ugly scowl warns Gilbert not to move.

Wait a minute, aren't weddin's supposed to be happy and fun? Somethin's wrong! Real wrong!

Chills crawl all over me. I feel dizzy and sick to my stomach.

The candles shine bright across the front of the altar. The hooded man in the middle raises his head and steps in front of the other men. The glow from the candles show that it's GG Dean! He's Granny Ivy's Dad; Anna's grandfather, and my step-great grandfather. GG Dean is what I call him. GG stands for great-grandfather. But he doesn't act like a nice granddad. He's the one who does the yucky kissin' stuff!

The four men start to walk again. They carry me to the center of the altar, right where Gilbert and the scary six hooded men stand. All of them lift their heads. The candles light up their faces. They have those creepy black eyes. Gilbert is the only one with color in his eyes.

The air stands still and suddenly feels like winter again—icy cold. I shiver.

Mean Dean uses his ugly boney finger to motion the cowboy-men to lower the hog platter on top of what looks like a small stage. It's kinda like the singin' and actin' stage that my nice grandpa, my real mommy's dad built us in our backyard, but this one is higher and covered in a long, black, satin cloth.

Something feels icky. I twitch.

CHAPTER THREE

Marion
January 1994

My nerves ramp up, and my back stiffens. Tension takes hold of my shoulders as Catherine twitches and thrashes on the sofa. Her face grimaces, unlike the playful, childlike countenance of Catie.

As she tells her story of the wedding, I watch her excitement and innocence leave, replaced by skepticism and fear.

I scribble a quick note to Bethany. *Is she okay? Should we take a break?* My hand trembles.

Bethany shakes her head and writes her answer below my question.

No, she is deep into the memory, and this is where she will find the answers.

I slip the lined notebook paper under my clipboard. I know Bethany is right. My concern for Catherine's pain and her discomfort cloud my reasoning. I remind myself that Catherine has been searching for more than three decades to unlock this mystery. She firmly believes, as do I, this dream reflects suppressed memories from those years her father was married to Anna.

The timeframe is what Catherine refers to as her 'lost years' when she went by the name Catie.

I take a deep breath and tell myself to focus on what is best for my client regardless of what will unfold. I pray silently for truth and healing.

Bethany softens her voice and coaches Catherine to continue telling her recollection....

Catie
Spring 1963

My stomach jerks. I don't like this creepy weddin' church. It looks nothin' like my Grandpa's church that I saw on Easter. They had all sorts of white and pretty things.

GG Dean stands tall at the front of the altar. His eyes look black with yellow snake diamond slits in the middle. I've seen this look before. He's proud and cocky—just like a rooster. He won't change his mind when he gets into one of his stubborn moods, bent on havin' his way. He yells at the four cowboy-men to put the platter on the yucky black satin crooked stage.

"Get going! You heard me. MOVE!" Mean GG Dean hollers.

Together the big, strong men lift the hog plate higher, and then off their shoulders. They walk toward the very front of the church to where GG Dean stands shoutin' orders.

The men lower the fancy board and me onto the stage. The

platter teeters and totters. I grab the side with my free hand and let out a small scream.

"I want my daddy."

Anna stands. She looks straight at me and gives me the stink eye. Granny Ivy remains seated but bobs her head in agreement. It's a warnin' to shut my mouth and be still. I will, sure enough, have a beatin' waitin' for me if I fuss and make Anna or her mother look bad by not obeyin'.

GG Dean steps forward, then raises his hands high. The crowd goes quiet.

"It is with great honor that we are gathered together in celebration of this divine wedding. We have the privilege of having the Honorable Judge with us this evening." His voice is loud and booms across the church.

The crowd cheers as a man stands. GG Dean chatters on about him, but I can't make out what he says. His words sound funny, kinda like he's talkin' in slow motion.

The Kool-Aid Anna and Ivy gave me makes me sleepy and dizzy.

GG Dean sticks his hands out straight and then lowers them, and the people sit.

"We call upon you, oh, great one. We are grateful to have been chosen to serve you. What a privilege to offer this innocent virgin princess unto you, our lord, to become your bride. We hail you, oh sun of the morning!" GG Dean's words echo off the walls, along with the claps of the crowd. My tummy feels sicker.

GG Dean moseys on over next to me, along with his fart-smellin' stench. The smell burns my nose. I want to heave. He puts his face close to mine, then kisses me, one of those icky French kisses.

I gag. Without thinkin', I reach up and dig my fingernails into his face!

His eyes narrow and glare. "Tie this bitch up! How the hell did her wrist come loose?"

WHAM! His hand hits my cheek so hard, it feels like my head will fly off.

CHAPTER FOUR

Marion
January 1994

C atherine flails—her head slams to the backside of the couch as if an invisible entity struck her. A red welt shaped like a handprint rises on the side of her face. I scribble a note to Bethany.

Do you see an impression of a hand on her face? How is that possible?

She writes back.

It's a body memory. Catherine's body is reacting to the pain she's remembering. Body memories are a reliable confirmation that a client is retrieving suppressed memories.

Again, I scrawl and push my note pad into Bethany's view. The note states: *Catherine appears to be in both time spheres, the present, and the past. She is describing and acting out what happened in her childhood when her family called her Catie. Her voice resembles the voice of a six-year-old. Is this normal?*

Bethany jots down a quick answer.

Yes, this is normal. She is not only remembering the past; she's reliving her past through this memory. That's why she's speaking as a child and will probably continue to do so as her suppressed memories surface.

Bethany softly asks Catherine, "What's happening now?"

Catherine describes her memory as if the event is happening at this very moment. She releases a fearful childlike cry. She rubs her cheek as tears stream from her eyes.

"My cheek stings," she whimpers. "I'm gonna slide off. This stage is crooked. It leans to one side. It's broken." Catherine pushes herself back from the edge of the sofa. "I'm gonna fall off."

She stares out into the room, her eyes squinting as if she is looking at someone or something. Bethany encourages her to continue.

"Catherine, I mean Catie, what is it? What are you experiencing?" She pauses and waits for her response.

"One of the hooded men is comin' over. He unfastens my ankles and guides me to lay back. He scoots my legs out from under me and pulls them off the platter. They're danglin', not touchin' the ground. I don't like this." She grimaces.

"I'm afraid! I try to get up, but another man pushes me back and holds me down. Big black things like sling-shots are tied onto my wrist to stretch my arms down next to my sides. They pull so hard, my shoulders hurt.

"A hinged metal thing, shaped like a half-circle or headband, is placed over my forehead and fastened. The mean man is smushin' my head onto the platter. The cowboys tie extra ropes around my shoulders and waist. I can't move. I can't move."

She struggles to move her head but is unable. I can imagine a brace holding her head in place, but to my naked eye, there is nothing visible, yet her lack of movement is vivid.

She murmurs like a child. "I can only move my eyes, so I can't see what they're doin'."

Her closed eyes search from side to side as if looking for help.

"Nothin'. I can't see nothin'. No-one is here to help me. Where's Daddy?" Catherine cries out in Catie's voice. "Daddy. Help me, Daddy."

She kicks her legs into the air.

"OUCH!"

I make a note of Catherine's child-like response. Bethany continues with her questions.

"Catie, why are you kicking?"

"Two men are fastenin' some kind of belts across my belly & bottom. It hurts. It's pinchin' my skin." She screams out into the room, "I want my mommy. Mommy!"

Her body stiffens, and her lower lip juts into a pout.

"Please tell us what you remember, dear," Bethany coaches.

"Anna runs to the front of the church, callin' out, 'I'm coming, Catie. I'm coming.'

"I can't lift my head to see her, but I can hear her. Just the sound of her voice makes me sick. I don't want Anna. She's not my real mommy and never will be! I hate her. She only pretends to care. I know she doesn't care 'cuz real mommies don't do bad stuff like this. She only wants everyone's attention. She picks fights or makes scenes so that everyone will look at her. That's how it always is, just like now. I hate her! She's a big pig, and she's the one who deserves to be on this hog platter. Not me. I hate her!

"Anna snuggles her face next to mine and says, 'I'm so proud of you, Catie. Someday you will thank me, you'll see, this is all for your best.' She turns to the crowd, then raises her voice so everyone can hear. 'My special daughter, Catie, has been chosen to be the bride of the most high, the god called the bright morning star, the powerful, eternal shining star. I couldn't be prouder.'"

Through choked tears, Catherine speaks in a child-like plea. "I'm too young to be a bride. I don't want to get married. I'm too little. Please don't make me. I want my *real* mommy. I want my daddy. Where's Daddy?" She sobs.

"Catie, you are doing an excellent job. Breathe deep, and stay in the memory. What's happening now?" Bethany asks.

"Anna shadows over me, she cups her hand hard over my mouth, smashin' my teeth into my lips. 'You know, Catie, your daddy's working. I'm your mother now!' she snaps at me. 'Now, you better mind and be still!' She grits her teeth. 'Be still!'

25

"My heart sinks. None of this makes sense. No one listens. I can't breathe. My nose is stuffy from lyin' on my back. I can only breathe through my mouth but Anna has it covered.

"GG Dean steps next to Anna and growls under his breath, 'Do your job, Anna. If she doesn't shut up, and I mean it, I'll gag her—right now.'

"If he does, I'll die. Anna puts a tissue to my nose and tells me to blow. I obey and blow as hard as I can. I fight to breathe, gulpin' air with each breath. Even with my arms tied down, I'm still able to grasp the pretty, yellow satin. I run the softness of the dress between my fingers.

"GG Dean stands over me. I look at him. He lifts a shiny brass bowl above his head and shows the people in the room. They roar with excitement. He lowers the container and hands it to Anna, tellin' her to fasten it onto the hog plate.

"She obeys. I feel her hands fumble. She's attachin' it somewhere behind my legs."

Catherine/Catie kicks her right leg into the air. Her arms remain very still from the wrist up. Her hands twist as if she is trying to free her arms.

Bethany gestures and encourages me to enter into the questioning.

"Who or what are you kicking?" I ask.

"I kicked Anna." She whines. "My leg stings. Anna pinched my bottom, and it's barely on the edge of the platter. Anna's grabbin' at my panties. She's tryin' to take them off."

She squirms, twists, and kicks her legs. All of a sudden, her legs jerk and spread. Before either Bethany or myself can question her behavior, she narrates what is happening.

"Two icky men just pulled my legs apart, forcin' them on each side of the crooked stage. I can't move them."

Her upper body squirms slightly, but her thighs remain spread and stiff.

"Now, everyone moves away from me. The crowd of people chant funny words. Words I don't understand. Their voices are gettin' louder and louder.

"Gilbert slowly shuffles toward me. Once he's close, right next to me, lookin' down over me, two men remove his black robe. I can see his bare shoulders, but not much else, 'cuz my head is held in place by the metal headband. He lays on top of me. His face is swollen and bruised. He's taken a hard beatin'.

"Gilbert whispers into my ear, 'I'm so sorry, Catie.' His body shakes. 'I don't want to do this. I don't want to do this, Catie.' Tears pool in his swollen eyes.

"Buck cracks his bullwhip across Gilbert's back. His back arches. He screams. The whip catches my dress. The fabric tears—it's ripped out of my fisted hands.

"*Will Anna beat me 'cuz Shawnee's dress got torn? Why did Buck have to go and ruin the princess dress?*

"Gilbert's warm tears fall on my face. Between sobs, he says, 'I'm sorry, Catie. I'm so sorry.'

"Mean Dean throws a hard slap to his head. 'Stop your talking, boy. I want action! You idiot!' he orders.

"Gilbert fumbles under my dress. A sharp pain rips through me—and fills me.

I scream, "You're hurtin' me. Stop! Stop!" I thrash what little I can.

"Gilbert cries and whimpers. 'Catie, so so-r-ry. I'm s-o sorry.'

"I feel somethin' strange—it's evil, like a monster. I can't see anythin', but I know it's here. It feels big, mean, and much stronger than Gilbert and me put together. It has a huge scary shadow."

I witness Catherine open her eyes wide and then pinch them closed. Her hands clench with white knuckles. Her fingernails dig into her palms. I anticipate seeing droplets of blood in her hands at any second.

"I see it!" she shouts. "Inside the darkness, I see flamin' red and yellow eyes."

Catherine shivers.

An eerie wave of chilled air sweeps through Bethany's office. I hug my arms close to my body.

"I hate him," Catie's child-like voice calls out. "It's evil. Do you feel it, Gilbert?"

"He whispers, 'Yah.'

27

"It's the devil, isn't it?" I ask.

"He nods his head on my cheek. Then he closes his eyes. We both stiffen from the weight and the pukey odor."

"Do you smell that, Gilly?"

"He nods, then says, 'It stinks like something's dead.'"

Catherine chokes out her words. "Cold air surrounds us like a frozen blanket. The stench makes me gag. I squeeze my eyes together. I fight to free myself. An unknown, wicked, gruesome, heaviness smashes onto Gilbert and me."

Her body flails. She gasps for air. It is as if the breath has been knocked out of her!

CHAPTER FIVE

Marion
January 1994

I gasp, but Bethany sits quietly and appears calm. My heart feels heavy, weighed down, like a beast of burden that is carrying too much. I want to take a break, for Catherine's sake, as well as myself. Bethany must sense my tension and concerns. She slips a note in my direction.

This technique is exceptionally effective to unbury suppressed memories, but the client must feel and then follow these intense emotions to where they've felt these particular feelings before. It is the emotional trail that leads to the locked-up memories.

Bethany gestures with her head toward Catherine. She encourages me to be the first to comment.

My voice sounds rough with tension. "I know this memory is

challenging for you, Catherine. You are doing great. If possible, please continue to share with Bethany and myself what you are remembering."

Catherine lays limp but manages to respond. "Gilbert is snatched away. I lie there. Unable to budge, even after the ties and belts are removed. It feels like my life has left me. I don't want to live. I want to be with my mommy in heaven.

"All I can do is stare at the once beautiful yellow dress, stained, ripped, wrecked. That's how I feel inside my heart—wrecked. I clench my hands on the silky fabric. I gather and roll the cloth in my fingers —tighter and tighter. It helps me ignore and blot out the noise, laughter, and cheers of the icky people."

Catherine gives a thin cry, then continues talking like a child. "The judge man takes the bowl and lifts it in the air, again speakin' words that I don't understand. He says the people need to honor him: Satan, that is, the most powerful leader.

"I turn my eyes away from the judge and onto the yellow satin. I keep rollin' the fabric, feelin' its softness, anythin' to take my mind off the man ramblin' on with his lies about the devil. He clanks a metal thing into the bowl, then splashes it onto me. With each pass, I cringe at the wet, warm, and sticky sprinkles fallin' onto my bare arms, legs, and face."

Catherine curls up on the sofa into a fetal position.

"I don't want to be here. I want to hide."

"What's happening now?" Bethany inquires softly.

"I don't like these people. They won't let me go. I don't know how anyone could be happy or celebrate in this dark disgustin' dirt floor room. It's no place for a weddin'. The other bride and her groom must've thought so too 'cuz they never showed up. I don't want to be here anymore, so I'm gonna make-believe I'm playin' in my sandbox at my old house with my nice Grandpa."

C atherine's body relaxes on the couch as if she is sleeping. After a few minutes and for no apparent reason, she catapults straight up. Her eyes bolt open.

"It's too intense! I'm not prepared." She spurts out her words. "I need a minute. No, I need more than a minute."

She compresses her temples with her hands. Her face grimaces, and her voice is gruff, like when startled awake from a deep dream. She slumps back into the couch and uses her arm to shield her eyes. Tears seep down her temples.

Bethany and I remain quiet, giving Catherine the needed time to digest all she has re-lived. After about fifteen minutes, she falls into an exhausted sleep.

We slip out and into an adjacent sitting room to debrief while Catherine rests. We can see her from where we sit through the French-paned doors. We keep our voices low so as not to disturb her.

I begin. "What was she describing? Have you ever heard of anything like that before?"

"Yes, Marion. Unfortunately, I have, many times." Bethany leans in to explain quietly.

"It's a satanic ritual. Referred to as a virgin child dedication. It is a ceremony where a child's innocence is defiled and presented to the devil for an unholy marriage covenant. It's to mark the youth as Satan's—a part of his dark family. The *bitching board* is the word Catie overheard the men using. It is an apparatus used when breeding some types of dogs, hence the term. Sadly a similar but modified version is used to hold down a victim for ..."

She looks at me and says it straight out. "Rape."

I stiffen at the rawness of the word and the comprehension of what has happened to Catie—Catherine.

"The bowl she described is used to collect blood, semen, and often other excretions. The other six men will often contribute their secretions. The fluids are used afterward in a blood communion, to drink amongst the leadership and victims. It's also sprinkled on the altar and onto the virgin as a sign of praise. Based on what she said, it's hard to say if one or all raped Catie—Catherine. Not that it matters, the defilement, the overpowering, and the forced abuse are beyond what anyone should have to endure. Sadly, she will probably revisit this memory many times, and with each time, more details will surface."

Bethany writes several notes in Catherine's file.

"Marion, did she ever mention if her father was involved in the occult?" Bethany asks.

"No, he was not. I asked Catherine after her first recollection of the black wedding. She said, 'No, never.' Her dad worked the midnight shift and sometimes two jobs to support the family. Anna and her parents took advantage of his absence. They lied, wanting Catie to believe her father had given his permission. It was a part of their manipulation and deceptions."

I reach for a tissue, then lower my head to blow my nose and blot my eyes. In my deepest being, I can sense, even smell, what Catherine has gone through as a child. My heart is burdened, overflowing with sorrow. However, I am determined to help her win this war. I know the battle she must fight—it is a battle for her mind. I will teach her how to fight against the lies and replace them with the truth—truth that will set her free.

Catherine stirs. I bolt from my chair and hurry back into the counseling room; Bethany follows. The tension in the room feels like a tightened violin string.

When she finally speaks, her voice sounds deflated. "I had no idea when I promised Anna to be a good girl what it meant. It's clear now. I was bargaining with evil." She lowers her head.

An instant later, Catherine screams into her hands. "NO! NO! NO!"

She shakes her head as if trying to jostle the memory from her mind, and erase it from her new reality.

Catherine continues to vent. "I hate this. I hate those people. Now I know why I didn't want to remember. They were evil. I knew instinctively I didn't want to be a part of Anna and her family."

Her body shakes. She grips her shoulders to still her tremors. She looks from me to Bethany. Her hands move from her shoulders to cover her ears.

She pleads, "Help me, Marion! I keep hearing their words

screaming in my head, 'It's your wedding…you are the virgin princess. A bride to *Satan!*' My skin's crawling. My body hurts."

Catherine rubs her arms like she is erasing a chalkboard. I suspect it is more of an attempt to erase her past.

"Catherine, I'm so sorry. You were only a child. You were and are innocent. It was not your choice." I interject with the hope of calming her.

"I want to believe it never happened," she whimpers, "but I know in my heart…it did. I know it's real. I remember so clearly. I remember the details of the smells, the touch, the voices, and the clarity of that yellow dress. I can still see the evil smiles on their faces; so many hideous faces."

She covers her mouth, and talks through her hands, shouting out muffled questions.

"How do I stop their voices blaring in my head? How do I live with this?"

CHAPTER SIX

Catherine
January 1994

A sound blares. *What is it?* I pull the soft sheets up to my chin. The confusing noise grows stronger. Its loud clamor jolts me awake and thankfully out of my recurring nightmare. My eyes flash open. My body ripples with tension.

The phone on the nightstand is ringing. I'm slow to prop myself up on my elbows. Marion's bed covers are tossed back, and the sound of the shower comes out from the bathroom. I reach for the receiver, not sure of how many times it has rung.

I scrape a disjointed, "Hello," from my throat.

"Hi, honey. How ya doing? Did I wake you up? You sound groggy." Hunter rattles on with his chipper voice.

"I think so. Umm, I'm glad you called. Otherwise, ahh, I'd still be stuck in my nightmare."

"Where's Marion?" His tone is now sharp. "Didn't you tell her to wake you if she sees you thrashing in your sleep?" His words rake into my fogginess. I'm not fully awake, but aware enough to sense a protective tension.

"Yes, she knows." I yawn. "But she's in the shower."

I stretch, attempting to shake off my sleepiness. I'm distracted. Images flash through my mind like a photo-kaleidoscope haunting me of the details from yesterday's session.

What's real? How can it be? Please don't let it...

"Catherine."

Hunter's voice yanks me back into our conversation.

"Yeah."

"How did it go yesterday? I was worried because I hadn't heard from you. I thought you'd call last night."

"Sorry, Honey, yesterday was...uhh, exhausting."

I want to rip the memories from my mind. I squint my eyes; emotional and physical pain pulsates in my skull.

"After dinner, I must have passed out the minute I hit the bed." Looking down confirms it. "I'm guessing Marion covered me up since I'm still dressed, minus my shoes."

"That doesn't sound so good. What happened?"

My eyes sting with tears that puddle and threaten to spill over. Fear rises.

How do I tell him? Will he want to leave me? Of course, he will. And I wouldn't blame him. My life and the memories from yesterday sounds insane. Will Hunter be able to deal with this, or will it be too much?

I carefully choose my words and speak softly, almost in a whisper, in hopes of cushioning the blow.

"It was good and not so good. I had an intense breakthrough...ummm...but..." I choke up. My throat closes from the stress. "Umm...not easy to explain. I might need Marion to help me walk you through what happened. I mean, what was revealed."

"What?" His voice sounds strained. "Why can't you tell me?"

"I'm...I'm afraid. Everything is so crazy." Tears flow down my cheeks. "Ahh, let's just say my worst fears are confirmed. Several memories came back."

"Isn't that good? That you're finally remembering?" He pauses, waiting for my answer.

I shake my head as if he can see me. I stammer weakly, "Yes, I suppose it is good news, but-but-but, unfortunately, it verifies that Anna and her family were a part of the...sa-tan-ic," I place my hand over my mouth, holding back the words, holding back the screams I want to release. "Hunter," I swallow. "Anna and her family were a part of the...sa-tan-ic..."

My voice breaks. I stutter. I push myself to stand tall, my back rigid, like steel. I take a deep breath, then force out the tormenting words.

"They were a part of the satanic occult. Bethany refers to my memories as satanic ritual abuse. SRA for short."

Why did I tell him the abbreviation? Perhaps nerves?

My heart pounds.

What is he thinking?

Silence. The rhythm of his breath sounds through the receiver.

"Hunter, are you still there?"

"Yes, I'm here. I'll always be here. Nothing will ever take me away from you." His words comfort me. "How are you doing, honey? I mean, how are you dealing with all of this?"

"I feel awkward talking about what happened. Somehow saying it out loud makes it hurt even more. It sounds sharp, even sour on my ears. Just hearing the words sounds like fingernails on a chalkboard." I sniffle. "I suppose I've known it my entire life—the memories confirm what I've suspected. I don't want to believe it, but I know it's real and..."

I sob, unable to hold back the tears or the stabbing ache in my heart. Darkness covers me like black tar. My screams catch in my throat.

I saw my innocence stolen. I relived the defilement.

I battle for hope after flashing back to the sickening act. Hopelessness shadows my heart. I can't speak.

How can I possibly make Hunter comprehend such atrocities when even I can't?

"I understand, Sweetie. I'm so sorry, Catherine. I didn't mean to upset you or press you on details. When you're ready, we can talk more. We have a lifetime to talk. No hurry. Just know I love you. I'm here for you. Should I call you later today?"

"S-sure, th-that would be n-nice, maybe this ev-ening."

I breathe deep, trying to compose myself before I continue to talk.

"We won't be finished with our session until five or six p.m. Kentucky time. We'll probably go out to eat afterward, so it might be late."

"It won't be too late," he assures me.

"Thanks." I grip the phone close to my ear, and my eyes squint to suppress more tears. I eke out a parting, "I love you, Hunter."

I hang up the phone just as Marion comes out of the bathroom, dressed and ready for the day.

"How about some coffee?" she says in a perky voice.

I keep my head low to cover up the shame that weighs heavy on me. "Sure, that would be great. I'm going to go into the bathroom to get ready. I'll leave the door unlocked if you don't mind slipping in a cup once it's brewed?"

I scurry into the bathroom without making eye contact. I don't want to pretend that I'm fine, and I don't have the energy to have a cheerful conversation.

———

The local Waffle House smells of cooked bacon, fried eggs, and hash browns. It makes my stomach grumble. I place an order expecting to eat, but once my meal arrives, I stare at the heaping plate of food—my mouth waters, but not from hunger.

The fluorescent lights reflect off the chrome-edged tables in the diner. The bright and sterile room irritates my eyes. I return my focus to Marion.

"Marion, I'm struggling with what I remembered yesterday." I pause, swallowing hard, pushing down the nausea. I look up, seeing her face lined with compassion. "But now, it's as if I've never forgotten."

She allows me to talk.

"I don't know how to live with these memories. I hate Anna and her family. And what they did." I sigh, then quietly speak. "I despise what Dean made Gilbert do to me."

I cradle my forehead in my hands and rest my elbows on the table. "Marion, I don't think I'll ever be able to forgive them."

The clamor of dishes and silverware rake over my frayed nerves. The waitress clears the table next to ours. I reach for my coffee cup, cradling its warmth in both hands. They tremble. I take a deep breath, trying to calm myself.

The lines around Marion's eyes soften. "It will be okay, Catherine. This experience is incredibly hard, but I can see how God is answering your prayers." She reaches out and squeezes my hand. "I am sorry for what they did. It was wrong. You were an innocent child. God knows that healing comes through knowing the truth. Hold fast to the truth."

She adds cream into her freshly poured cup of coffee, then pushes the small pitcher across the table in my direction.

"You need to eat, Catherine. It is important to keep your strength."

She offers a hopeful smile after I butter my toast and take a bite.

Following breakfast, Marion drives us to the counseling office. Upon our arrival, Bethany scans my appearance. Her brows raised with curiosity.

"You look different, Catherine. Quite a change from yesterday."

"I wore my hair up. I'm too tired to be bothered with hot rollers."

I feel a need to explain, yet I wonder why.

"You look, well...dressed up." Bethany's expression looks understanding.

"I guess I am a little." I glance down at my black dress slacks, cream silk blouse piped in black, accessorized with a decorative silk scarf and jewelry.

"Truth be told, I needed to dress up. It makes me feel better." I hold my head high, fighting against the dense weight of shame. "If I look good on the outside, somehow, it soothes the cringing ache of what feels like poison seeping out from within me."

I clear my throat to push down the rising vomit. "I'm referring to the repulsive memories."

I turn my face away, not looking at anything or anyone. I've said more than I intended. Feeling too vulnerable, I inwardly rebuke myself for not filtering my thoughts.

"I hope my outfit will somehow make today's sessions more manageable." I force a weak smile, stand erect, and rein in my emotions. I need to feel in control.

"I understand," Bethany says. I see tenderness within her eyes. I believe she does understand. Maybe more than I know.

"Catherine always dresses nicely, but perhaps today there is a need...umm." Marion seems to be at a loss of words. "How about we start in prayer?"

We lower our heads. Marion leads. She asks God to help us, to help me, to go back into my past—to remember.

Bethany's expertise and training are a great support. She knows her way around the mental obstacles and obstructions that try to block me from remembering. Marion's being trained by Bethany during my sessions. She's more involved today, which gives me comfort.

I'm willing to go deeper to remember the truth—but I'm so afraid. Afraid of where it might take me. My mind and emotions feel as fragile as porcelain. I fight against the sharp cutting lies in my head. Each accusation is a razor-sharp threat that I'm about to go crazy. I won't—no, I can't allow the lies to rip even the smallest opening into my mind.

I remind myself of the scriptures, 'No weapon formed against me will prosper.' 'I can do all things in Christ who strengthens me.' I focus on the comfort of knowing Marion is close, within sight. She's praying for me, praying for us.

Bethany suggests, "Considering yesterday's session, I'd like to propose easing into your past in a pleasant, more comfortable way by sharing an enjoyable memory." Her tone is soft but clear. "How about a recollection during the same time frame, ages six to almost nine years old. We can see where the memory takes us."

My torso aches from sitting as straight as a broom handle. The cushion lets out a swish as I shift my position. The tension leaves my back. After a few head-rolls, my neck and posture relax. I glance at Marion. She smiles and winks.

"Well, let me think." I pause, reflecting on a particular time from my childhood. I decide to share a story that features my grandparents, my real mother's parents. Although they are long gone, their memories are soothing. The recollection comes alive in my mind. I can almost feel their embrace.

I ease back on the couch and into my memory…

"It's Christmas Eve, a cold clear night. My face stings from the bitter air, feeling almost frozen. The broken heater in the car makes us girls and Charley snuggle up to keep warm. It's a short drive. Dad pulls into their driveway before we've had the chance to ask, 'how much further?' We fidget in the back seats, ready and waiting to scramble out of the car.

"Seeing Granny Grunt and Grandpa makes missing my mom easier. I feel closer to her when I'm with them. My Grandpa is a wonderful storyteller. His tales of Mom's funny mishaps, pranks, and all of her fun-loving gags keep her alive in my heart. Grandpa says my mother had personality plus; she was friendly, outgoing, and enjoyed having fun. To hear him tell it, he'd say she was very social and loved parties and was quite the entertainer or a 'lolly-gagger,' as he put it.

"My mom taught us to be fun-loving too. We sang and danced a lot. She loved to hear a good story and was great at telling jokes, just like my sister Claudia."

My shoulders relax, and I allow my arms to rest at my sides, sinking comfortably into the couch. My mind drifts off into a memory with my grandparents. . .

Catie
Winter 1963

I'm seven years old...

The sky looks dark blue with the stars twinklin' like glitter. The stars shine so bright I wonder if I'm lookin' at the floor of heaven. The air feels extra cold, so cold you can see your breath. Charley and I play-act, pertendin' we're smokin' cigarettes. He has another big black eye from one of the many so-called 'accidents' at Poison Ivy's and Buck's farm. We pretend Charley smokes Lucky Strikes cigarettes because the commercial says, "I'd rather fight than switch."

It's a special night, Christmas Eve. We're goin' to Granny Grunts and Grandpa's house. They're so much fun. I love seein' them. I love the smell of Granny's cookin' the second we run through the door. It smells like heaven. And we can eat as much as we want, it's nothin' like Anna's teaspoon portions at meals. Yay! I twist and turn in the backseat and almost break out into a dance 'cuz I'm so excited.

Daddy parks in the driveway. We hop out of the car and run toward their house. The porch lights shine bright so we can see our way to the front steps. Daddy knocks and then presses his arms out like an airplane to hold us back.

Grandpa opens the door. "Come on in and give your Grandpa some sugar," he says with his arms spread wide.

Granny Grunt stands by his side with a big grin, cheek to cheek, on her face, and a large cookin' spoon in her hand. She wears her flour-covered apron. All of us kids tackle them with hugs and kisses. A puff of flour from her apron sprinkles my face. I peek my head from around Granny's waist to see her kitchen table piled high with homemade sweets. I gawk at the fudge, no-bake chocolate oatmeal cookies, Christmas candy, nuts, and one of my favorites—tangerine, squishy, sugared, orange wedge candies.

I tug on her hand, pullin' her toward the kitchen, and shout to the others. "Look in the kitchen! I found the jackpot!"

Granny's as excited 'bout these sweet treats as we are. A giggle bubbles up from her throat. "You kids are my favorite sweets."

She smiles, her cheeks puff up like a chipmunk savin' nuts for the winter, as she watches us eat and lick our sticky fingers.

Every year Granny sews all of us girls new Christmas nightgowns and pajamas for Charley. Each of our nighties are sewn from a different flannel fabric. She also makes us a matchin' stockin' with our names embroidered on the front. That's how we know which gown is ours. Grandpa fills our stockin's full with fruit, nuts, and candy! Christmas Eve is my favorite night of the whole entire year!

Their Christmas tree is beautiful. It's silver with a round rainbow disc next to it that twirls, changin' the tree into four different colors. Red-blue-yellow and green. I love bein' here. I feel safe, loved, and happy—happy to have my belly filled with treats. Yum-yum. I don't want the night to end.

I never ever want to leave my grandparents' house. Still, it's easier on Christmas Eve knowin' Santa will visit our house later tonight. The rule is we need to get home and be asleep before he comes. We can't be late 'cuz I don't want to take a chance of missin' Santa and his reindeers. But, there's a problem; we now have two very naughty girls in our family, my step-sisters, Melinda and Shawnee. They're so bad —bad enough to make Santa fly right over our house. Melinda is two years older than me and should know better than to be naughty, but she doesn't care.

Once home, I hurry to slide into my new, fluffy soft, flannel nightgown. I'm ready for bed, but I have a few minutes before the 'lights off' time 'cuz Melinda and Carolyn are still changin' their clothes.

I peer out the bedroom window searchin' for any glimpses of Santa in his sleigh.

Melinda comes up. "Whatcha doing?"

"Watchin' for Santa." I stare, squintin' deep into the night sky.

She laughs and points her finger at me, and then holds her belly. "You're such a big baby. I can't believe you still believe in Santa

Claus." She lets out another burst of laughter and doubles over. "I haven't believed in that stupid baby stuff for years. Even Shawnee, who's more than two years younger than you, knows it's all make-believe."

There's a creepy ugliness in Melinda's scrunched-up face, the way she wrinkles her nose and frowns her mouth, along with her bulgy bullfrog eyes. She's havin' fun tryin' to hurt me. She's so hateful. I turn away and continue to look out the window.

"Frog Eyes, you don't know everythin'," I sneer.

"I know way more than you—Big Baby. Santa's your parents! That's why we have to be in bed and sleeping before the so-called Santa comes. It's because they don't want us to hear them bringing in all the presents from the car trunk and their other hiding places. That's when they put them under the tree, stupid." Melinda attempts to put her head between mine and the window, then sticks out her tongue at me.

I turn slightly, lookin' at her, and then at Carolyn in disbelief.

"Carolyn?"

Silence. My sister doesn't say a single word. She has a sad look on her face as she crawls into bed. I'm afraid Melinda might be tellin' me the truth. No way, I don't want to believe her.

"Good night, Carolyn. And shut up, fart-face Melinda!" I stick out my tongue back at her.

Marion
January 1994

'I *stick out my tongue…*' I inscribe detailed notes of Catherine's session. She has remembered Christmas Eve with her stepsister, Melinda.

Bethany takes a drink of water, returning the glass to a coaster on the table to her right. "What emotions are you feeling, after having your stepsister tell you Santa isn't real?"

Catherine's face grimaces. Her voice remains as the voice of Catie. "Sad and let down. But what's way worse is knowin' Melinda hates me. She's happy to see me sad. She'd love to wreck my Christmas, but I won't let her see me disappointed." She crosses her arms over her chest. "I can't believe my parents lied to me. Anna yes! But Daddy?"

She holds her head between her hands. "I'm confused. I don't want to believe Frog-eyes. It hurts my heart. I want to believe in Santa Claus."

"This is very good, Catherine, umm...I mean Catie." Bethany catches her misdirected use of names.

Catherine's voice resurfaces. "It's upsetting, painful, disappointing, and so familiar, just...like it's happening...today." Her words crack and are labored with pain.

"Enter into the hurt. Allow yourself to feel those emotions." Bethany affirms.

Catherine's face scowls, which reflects the discomfort and hurt she feels in the memory, confirming she is cooperating with Bethany's request.

Bethany shifts in her chair and continues to encourage her to feel the emotions.

"Thank you, Catherine. You're doing great. Allow yourself to connect to the pain and the disappointment."

Bethany pauses for several seconds, which feels like a lifetime. I hold my breath, waiting with my pen held tightly.

"Would you be willing to follow these emotions to where you have felt them before? Preferably, to where you felt this way for the very *first* time?"

I sit, praying silently, as I jot my notes. I write as fast and as neatly as possible, knowing Catherine will want a copy of my documents. I concentrate on describing her body language, facial expression, as well as her words, and any details she reveals.

Catherine's body rocks back and forth. She gives an account of her feelings as Bethany instructed. I am amazed at how easily she goes into describing yet another memory, however further back in time. I watch her past unravel; however, it does not appear to follow any chronological order. Her mannerism and speech change, again matching those of when she was young Catie…

"It's sometime before Christmas, 'cuz we haven't gone to Granny Grunt's and Grandpa's yet. Anna wakes me *again*. I wish she'd just let me sleep. I want to sleep. It's dark outside. I hate these secret night meetin's. I don't like havin' to keep secrets from Daddy and my sisters."

Her facial expressions and tone mirror those of a whiney, upset child being awakened in the middle of the night.

"But I don't want to get up," she moans. "It's dark and cold. I don't want to go!"

She starts to whimper. She curls up into a fetal position and cuddles herself for warmth as if she longs for the comfort of her bed. I make a mental note: her body language emulates her story.

With purpose, I write my observations onto the lined tablet. This memory is further back in time, a while before Christmas.

My notepad is several pages deep with commentary. I focus intently, as she relives her memories. I wipe the sweat from my palms and listen to her tell the story from a six or seven-year-old point of view.

"Please, Anna, I don't want to get up, I'm tired," she whines, sounding groggy.

Bethany asks, "Will you describe to us what is happening?"

She nods. "Anna's pressin' her hand hard across my lips. She stares at me with her ugly, snake-slit eyes, inches from my face. She shows me her teeth. Her growl is silent, but I know what it means; I have to go. If I give her a hard time, I'll pay for it later. Or worse, they'll hurt Charley."

Catherine/Catie's expression becomes a frown. "It's what they call my rebellion and disobedience. I push away from Anna, but I still obey and force myself out of my bed. I tiptoe not to wake the others. I follow my icky stepmother. All I want is to sleep. Now I'm gonna be so tired in school tomorrow."

"Thank you, Catie. You're doing great." Bethany is careful not to use words that would pull Catherine into the present and out of the memory as young Catie.

"What is happening?" Bethany asks. She leans in, listening to every word, while I concentrate on taking accurate notes.

"Anna forgot our blindfolds this time, and she din't give us the medicine either. It doesn't matter 'cuz we fall fast into a snooze. I hear Charley's voice in the distance cryin' when I break out of my sleep.

"Old Granny Poison Ivy shakes me hard, like a rag doll. I'm afraid she'll shake my head off. When my eyes finally focus, we're at the barn tonight. I hate comin' to this place 'cuz it's always horrible. I hate Anna for bringin' us here. I hate Buck. I extra hate GG Dean for bein' the leader. And I extra, extra, hate the bad things they always do to us. I hate all of them. It would be easier if Anna din't make Charley come."

Catherine pounds her fist against the cushion of the sofa in frustration.

"Mean Dean gathers up all the children, includin' Charley and me, and takes us into the barn. The animals eat their suppers in the stalls. Hay is piled high into the feedin' troughs. In the middle of the barn, there's a cradle, made out of old lumber, with straw stickin' out in all directions. Daddy sometimes calls me a Curious George, and he's right 'cuz my curiosity leads me straight toward the wooden box. To my surprise, there's a small baby layin' in the straw.

"Charley, look!"

Catherine's eyes are tightly closed, yet she points across the room.

"It's a baby!" she says with an excited squeal.

"Charley rubs the sleep from his eyes to get a better look. We stare into the straw-filled trough. Even though I'm seven and Charley's only four and a half, we know this is a nativity scene. I wish my sisters were here to see this. I start my usual dancin' around when I get excited.

"Hey, Charley, I think they might be doin' a play about the story of baby Jesus and Christmas!

"I pull him next to me, huggin' him tight. He pulls back, stretchin' his neck past me, not wantin' to take his eyes off the baby or the animals.

46

"I think of my grandparents: Daddy's mama, Teenage Granny, and Mommy's parents, Granny Grunt and Grandpa, as well as Daddy and my real mommy. They told us the Christmas story. The one 'bout Jesus. And 'bout Santa, too. Teenage Granny told me the Santa part. She said, 'Mr. Claus is a rich man who provides gifts to all the poor children, like us, so that they can celebrate the biggest gift of all—the gift of Jesus.'

"There's a lot to know 'bout Christmas. I can't say I know it all, but what I do know is, God is real, and he had his Son born, Jesus, so we would know that he loves us."

She cups her hand to her mouth and leans forward, mimicking a child whispering into someone's ear. "Remember, Charley, if we believe—someday we will get to go to heaven and be with Jesus. And even extra special for us…we'll see Mommy again!

"Charley jumps straight up and down, 'cuz that's how he dances. I join in with him, even snappin' my fingers to a make-believe beat.

"Mean Dean lets out a loud whistle. We leap to attention. He orders us kids to gather around the baby. Some kids are gabbin' in the back of the circle. We don't know them, but they're breakin' the no talkin' rules. Dean signals Buck and Ivy. I don't bother to turn around, 'cuz I know what's comin'. And I'm right. I hear them scream, followed by Buck yellin', 'Shut your mouths, or I'll shut it for you. Permanently! You know the rules.'

"Out of the corner of my eye, I watch Ivy drag off two kids by their hair, while Buck separates the other boy.

"Mean Dean calls the baby, Jesus, but I know he's not the *real* Baby Jesus. Everybody knows the Christmas story happened back in what Grandpa calls 'the ancient days.' That was way before he or me were ever born. Dean's as old as dirt, and he always lies, so I'm thinkin' this baby is just named Jesus. I don't dare ask, but I wonder it all the same.

"There are lots of kids in the room, but for some reason, Dean focuses on Charley and me.

"'Hey, you two.' He jabs his finger in our direction. 'Get up here!' Dean throws his arms out and motions for everyone to back away so Charley and me can get a good look at the baby. Charley steps back and then crouches behind the legs of a grown-up who's standin' nearby. I wonder why Dean's bein' so nice. He makes me and Charley nervous.

"Dean snuggles up behind me. He kneels onto one knee, pressin' his chest close into my back. I lean against him, not wantin' to get too close to the baby. I'm worried I'll wake him up.

"Dean latches his large hands onto my forearm. His cowhide work gloves have little black, rubbery bumps on them, makin' his grip feel extra tight. So tight that I can't move my hand.

"Somethin' isn't right. It feels wrong; like spiders are crawlin' on me. Mean Dean isn't a good man, not one to be trusted. I wonder, what's he gonna do? I twitch.

"His grasp loosens for a second as he pulls somethin' out of his back pocket.

"Charley shouts, 'No!' His eyes open wide. 'Run, Catie!'

"Ivy yanks Charley over and smacks her hand over his mouth, smotherin' his words.

"Dean circles his arm back around me. Then—I see it!…"

CHAPTER SEVEN

Catie
Winter 1963

Mean old Dean motions to Poison Ivy to keep her hand smashed over Charley's mouth to muffle his cries. My poor baby brother fights, twists, and turns side to side. Twice he lifts his legs and kicks at Poison Ivy, just barely missin' her.

Two grown-up men jump in to help Ivy. Three against one isn't fair. Charley's outnumbered. He finally gives up and slumps.

I pull away from Dean and reach out to Charley, but another adult steps right smack in front of me, blockin' my way. I can't help my brother. I can't do anythin'.

Dean grabs me by my hair, yankin' me close. My back smashes into his chest facin' Charley and the adults. The crazy man pries my fingers open and puts some kind of large and cold handle into my hand.

I turtle my head, stretchin' it out as far as I can to see what he's doin'.

Oh NO! Why is GG Dean forcin' his huntin' knife into my hand? He grips his hand over mine, holdin' my hand too tight. So tight I can't move, not even one finger.

The knife is big and ugly. Dean's hurtin' my hand. I struggle to twist but am able to turn just a little. I glare up at him. My eyes search for an answer.

"Whatcha doin', GG Dean?"

He looks wicked. The color black stares out from his eyes, a piercin' darkness. He looks like a devil. His grip gets stronger. Tighter. His body presses against mine. He nudges me closer. Over baby Jesus. We hover over the little one's cradle. I push back into mean ole Dean's chest. He presses me forward.

Dean commands. "Kill him!"

What? I scream, "NO! NO! NO!"

I twist. I squirm. I wrestle, but I can't move. I can't get away. I'm unable to break away from his hold.

He reminds me, "If you don't do this, we're gonna have to kill your baby brother. Your mommy wouldn't want Charley to have to die on account of *you*!"

His hot breath is on my ear. "If your mom were here, she'd tell you to save Charley."

I look at my baby brother. He trembles and chews on his shirttail. Tears stream down his quiverin' face.

The room spins. I'm gonna be sick.

I sob. "Mommy. Mommy. I want my Mommy."

What would mommy want me to do? I've already lost her. I can't lose Charley, too.

Ivy pipes in, "My darling, Catie, Anna is your mother now."

"I don't want her. I want my real mommy."

"That's just too bad, isn't it?" Granny Ivy grumbles.

Then she shouts at the crowd of people like she's braggin'. "My

Anna saw something she wanted, wanted it real bad, and we were determined to get it for her. Even if we had to make it happen."

Granny Ivy flashes an odd smile and looks at her husband, Buck. A scary smile. "Isn't that right, babe?" Grandpa Buck doesn't smile. He backs away.

I cry out, "Mommy. Help me, Mommy."

"You're just like your mother, Catie. You're hardheaded. You don't listen. She wouldn't listen either. That's why we had to kill her." Poison Ivy raises her voice. "Yes. That's right. We killed her! We killed your precious mommy. We were there that night."

Poison Ivy is nothin' more than a creepy scar-faced Frankenstein-lookin' hag. She leaves Charley with the two adults and slithers around her devil-dad, Dean. She puts her face close to mine, nose to nose. Her hot breath reeks of icky cigarettes and stinky coffee.

"Yes, darling Catie, we were there. We came in through your mommy's and daddy's bedroom window. We waited in their closet until *your mommy* came down the hallway toward her bedroom. She'd just finished serving you kids corned beef and hash for dinner."

Ivy scrunches up her nose and gives me a straight-lipped smile, mockin' me. "We grabbed her just outside the bathroom."

She pauses to make a huge smile. "You heard her scream. Didn't you, Catie?"

One of our friends put chloroform over her mouth. It knocked her out cold. Then...."

Ivy lets out an evil laugh, just like her husband, Buck, and father, Mean Dean. "We stuck a needle right into her neck. Your stupid mother didn't even realize what we'd done." Ivy pretends that she has a needle. She presses her finger into the back of my neck and says, "Real easy. Nothing to it. We quickly hid in the bedroom closet and waited."

She laughs her ugly laugh again. "And while the house was full of neighbors, we quietly snuck out through the window without anyone being the wiser."

The small group of people gather around the baby. They cheer and clap for Granny Poison Ivy.

As my icky step-grandmother tells her story, I recall the exact details of the night Mommy screamed. It was Daddy's bowlin' night, and he was gone. It was also the last time I saw Mommy. I think back and remember the corned beef hash she cooked. The glass of milk I drank. Then came the scary screams from the hallway. Cries so loud, they sliced the air like a big butcher knife. I remember Charlotte runnin' to help Mommy. She shouted from the hallway and told Claudia and Carolyn to keep Charley and me in the kitchen, away from Mommy. Then Charlotte ordered my sisters to go for help, leavin' Charley and me alone. We were scared stiff, not knowin' what to do.

Just like now—I don't know what to do. Why would Anna and her friends kill Mommy?

The room spins again. I feel heavy. Can't breathe. Sweat stings my eyes. I blink it away.

Ivy sneers. She stares at me the entire time, then moves next to Charley. Buck inches closer on his other side.

Charley's trapped! His eyes are wide—filled with terror. He looks to his right, then to his left. Then he looks at me.

"Help me, Catie! Help me!" he begs.

We both shake. We're scared to death. Charley closes his eyes and starts suckin' his thumb, somethin' he hasn't done since the night Mommy went to bowl with God.

Ivy's voice is soft, yet creepy. "Your mommy would want you to save your baby brother, Catie." She playfully tussles the top of Charley's hair.

"She wouldn't want us to have to kill him, now would she?"

Granny Ivy's eyes seem to plead. And then her voice changes, into a shriek, "On account of you!"

She rips at Charley's hair. Hard. He yelps, but keeps his eyes closed. Ivy glares at me and raises her voice. "You can stop this. It's really up to you, Catie."

They killed my mommy, and now they're gonna kill Charley! They killed my mommy, and now they're gonna kill Charley! They killed Mommy and now Charley!

I tremble. My mind whirls. Can't think. I have to save Charley. I can't lose my baby brother too. *It takes my breath. I panic.* I push hard, away from Dean.

The room spins. A new girl, about my age, jumps into the crowd in front of Mean Dean and me. And right in the nick of time. It's the first time I've seen her. She's a cute teensy-weeny little thing—a blonde version of the television star, Shirley Temple. She has big beautiful blue eyes, a smile on her face, and seems precious and bouncy. She looks like her name would be Barbie. I like her 'cuz she's tryin' to distract Dean.

She says, "Oh, Uncle Dean, you don't want to do this. Babies are so-o-o-o sweet. You know how much I like to play with them." She tilts her head, flirtin' with Dean. "Babies are so much better than dolls." She twirls her curls, bats her eyelashes, and pleads with her big blue eyes.

"Uncle Dean, you know I will love you extra bunches *if only* you would just let this little-bitty baby sleep and not hurt him. There are other babies; you don't have to hurt this one. Can he be mine?" Barbie raises her eyebrows. "I would love to have him as my Christmas present. Please, Uncle Dean? Pretty please, with sugar on top?"

I keep my eyes on her and Dean as she begs and pleads.

His eyes remain dark—hard—determined. He pushes her, hard and off to the side. She stumbles and falls into some poopy straw.

Dean shoves me, then punches me in my stomach. *It takes my breath. I panic.*

He laughs his devil laugh. The old man loves torturin' kids. Actually, he loves to torture anyone—everyone. I hate him.

A husky boy tromps out from within the straw patch where Barbie landed. He doesn't seem afraid of Dean. Not one bit. He squares his shoulders and stacks his hands on his hips, challengin' Dean with a gruff voice.

"You're the biggest *butthole* of all. You only pick on kids. Why don't you pick on someone your own age? You're nothing better than a fart-smellin', booger eater! When I get bigger, I'm gonna tear your head off. You hear me old man?" He steps closer and has the nerve to glare at Dean, givin' him the stink eye. "Leave Catie, and Charley, alone!"

Dean spits out a laugh and ignores the boy. I don't understand why he isn't mean to Barbie and this boy, the way he is to Charley and me? I've named the spunky boy, GI Joe, 'cuz he's strong and fearless like a soldier. Mean Dean moves between us, so I can't see the soldier boy anymore.

Dean grabs me. He yanks me up real close, then tightens his grip. Sweat covers me like a wet towel. With his one hand around my waist, the other over my hand and wrist, he makes sure to hold the blade in place. The handle feels warm and wet against my hand. He lifts me slightly and scoots us over toward the baby.

What can I do? What would Mommy want me to do? I can't lose Charley.

Can't think. Can't breathe. I can't kill the baby. I won't kill the baby!

Dean positions our arms. His hand squeezes over my hand. The knife points straight down. He aims at the innocent baby boy.

Oh no! Oh no! Oh no! Dean's too strong. I can't hold back our hands. He pushes our hands down, movin' the knife closer. His muscles are too big; his strength overpowers me.

I feel hopeless. Helpless. I resist with all my strength. I squirm— kick—bite and scream, hopin' someone, anyone will help me. My muscles burn. I shut my eyes and shake my head.

"NO, NO, NO!" I beg.

Sweat, snot, and tears run down my face. My vision blurs. I hope this is one of those bad dreams Anna's always talkin' 'bout.

I shake my head to wake myself up, but nothin' happens. Nothin' happens 'cuz it's not…it's not a dream…it's not a dream!

The baby opens his eyes and begins to whimper. The poor little boy is scared. Me too!

"Look what you've done, Catie! Shut the hell up!" Dean's scratchy whiskers press hard against my cheek. He forces my head to where I can see Charley.

Buck holds my brother in a headlock. Charley's fightin' as hard as he can. Ivy covers his mouth. I hear his muffled screams.

"You have to kill him. YOU must do it!" GG Dean orders me.

"No way. I'm not gonna do it. I don't care what you say." I twist

54

and turn my head to face him the best I can, then muster up enough courage to spit in his face.

His eyes narrow. His hand clamps down even harder onto my hand. His muscles are so much bigger than mine. I fight back, but it does no good. It's not fair.

He moves our hands closer to the baby. I see the knife in our hands, his hand over mine. Closer and closer, it inches toward the little infant.

I hear a small cry.

I pee in my pants.

RED!

I squeeze my eyes shut.

CHAPTER EIGHT

Marion
January 1994

I watch Catherine as Catie screams like an injured animal. She wails, "Red! Red! Red!" The color drains from her face. She thrashes, then rears her head back.

"He's a liar. I didn't do it! Dean did it. His hand was on my hand. He did it. He did it. I don't care what he says. I swear. I promise. I didn't do it!"

I yearn to go to Catherine. Bethany motions for me to stay in my chair. I fear Catherine is going to pass out. Her breathing is labored. She gasps. Bethany perches on the edge of her chair and speaks very calmly.

"What is Dean saying to you?"

Catherine lies limp on the couch. She mimics his words.

"'Catie, look at what you've done! You're a wicked girl! Catie, you are just plain evil. You deserve to die for what you did!'"

Catherine shakes. She lies straight and rigid, covering the full length of the couch. Her body trembles, seemingly out of control. She clutches the sides of the cushions, but her body still quakes.

"What happened next?" Bethany encourages her. "Stay in the memory."

Catherine covers her face and talks through her hands. "I collapse to the ground. My body feels like rubber. I can't move. I'm numb. All I can do is to look up at him and holler back, 'I did nothin'. You did it. You're a monster, Dean. You did it!' "

Catherine continues describing the moment. "Dean argues. He asks the crowd of adults in the circle, 'Whose hands were on the knife?' The grown-ups chant, 'It was Catie's hands on the knife. It was Catie's hands.'

"I can still hear their lies echoin' in my head—they chant it over and over. I can't make it stop."

Catherine uncovers her face only to move her hands over her ears as if trying to silence their words. Her childlike expressions show panic mixed with determination.

Her lower lip juts out in a pout. "I'm telling you, Dean, it was your hand, over my hand. And you know it! You did it!"

Catherine/Catie looks up. She searches my face, yet it appears she is staring right through me.

"He says it's the person's hands on the knife who's at fault. The mean old man says he was only tryin' to stop me from doin' the evil deed."

Her facial expression reflects confusion in her attempt to reason. She stumbles over her words.

"I told them all…I wasn't the one…but everyone keeps sayin' I did it. It wasn't me! I swear. It wasn't me!"

She sits and cups her head between her hands, then plummets over in ear-piercing sobs. She wails.

"They say I killed Baby Jesus. They say the police will believe them 'cuz my fingerprints are on the knife. It was my hand on the knife!

"The two policemen standin' in the shadows come forward. Each takes their place next to Dean. They're in uniforms. The taller one rests his hand on his gun holster and says, 'They're right, Miss. Catie, it will be your fingerprints on the knife.'

"Dean lifts his hands, showin' the crowd and me his gloves. I look at my hand and forearm. The bumps from his gloves are imprinted onto my skin."

Catherine stiffens and then opens her eyes.

"I can't think." She shakes her head. "Their words. Horrible lies. Their words hurt. I want it to stop. I need it to stop! I don't know how to end this nightmare." She pulls her hands to her chest as if the stabbing accusations pierce her heart.

Bethany interjects, "Catherine, stay in the memory as Catie. Please close your eyes and try to return to the memory."

Catherine immediately obeys, and Catie's voice comes forth at a deafening volume.

"It wasn't me. It was Dean's hand. He forced my hand." She points her finger as if addressing a swarm of people. "And you all know! But you'll lie to make sure that no one ever believes me. Even the police 'cuz you're all liars. You'll twist the truth and say it was my hand on the knife."

Bethany leans in. "What happens next?"

"*It takes my breath. I panic.* I'm afraid I'll faint but right then a child, the one I named GI Joe, barges up again. Wham, a hard kick lands right smack into Dean's shin. The dirty tennis shoe leaves a footprint on his jeans. GI Joes yells, 'You've done your dirty business. Let it alone, Dean.'

"Dean looks down at the scruffy little kid standin' with one hand on a hip, and the other hand clenched into a tight fist. With a puffed out small chest, my soldier friend blocks the hateful man from gettin' near me. The young boy's stance says that me and Charley are gonna be protected. I can breathe.

"Dean rubs his chin as if he's amused and admires the kid's spunk. The crowd laughs.

"Dean ruffles the young lad's hair and says, 'Whatever you say, little buddy.' He turns and walks away with Buck and Ivy. The crowd follows.

"Since we aren't supposed to know anyone's real name, my little rescuer turns out to be okay with the name I made up: GI Joe. The kid says it's a great name since the little rascal wants to be a soldier. I guessed right. We're the same age, but GI Joe has a lot more courage, strength, and fight than I do.

"I collapse on the ground with Charley, who sits at my side. Barbie comes over and comforts me. GI Joe stands in front of us. On guard. He makes sure that Dean and the other adults don't come back. The grown-ups clear out of the barn takin' the bundled baby with them. They turn the lights off.

"The moonlight shines through the upper barn window. There's enough light for us to see each other. We huddle close and rest.

"Charley whispers, 'Dean, Buck, and Ivy said if I tell anyone what they did, anyone at all, they'll kill me, the way they killed Mommy. What should we do, Catie? Should we tell Granny Grunt and Grandpa, when we visit this week?' His lower lip and chin quiver. 'Do you think they'll really kill me?'

"I immediately lie and tell him, 'No! And besides, we can't air our dirty laundry, or they'll definitely take us away from Daddy. I'll protect you, buddy. Besides, I don't want us to be stuck in one of those foster homes or worse, the orphanage.'"

"I'm so afraid that I shake, but I don't tell Charley that I'm really more worried 'bout them goin' through with killin' him.

"'I'm not sure what to do, Charley...I can't think right now. I just want to forget,' I mumble."

Catherine brings her knees to her chest, hugging her arms over her shins. She lets out a lifeless sigh. She hides her face, burying it against her thighs.

I can no longer resist going over to Catherine. I jump up and spring to her side. She sits, as still as death. I hand her some tissues and a glass of water. She slowly accepts both into her shaking hands.

"Oh, Marion. Thank you for being here." Her words sound weak.

I sit with her on the sofa. "I am here, dear." My heart aches for her and for what has been uncovered. My compassion stirs from the exposed malevolence.

We wait for several minutes in undisturbed quietness, allowing Catherine to rest.

Several minutes pass before Bethany asks, "Catherine, would you care to freshen up or use the bathroom?"

She gives her directions to the restroom. Catherine stands, then staggers out of the room, appearing to be in an exhausted fog.

While she is gone, Bethany confirms the memories point to the satanic occult—to ritual abuse. She informs me there are three levels of abuse; all of which are horrific.

"Marion, many victims of this type of abuse don't live through it. Those that do often end up in a mental facility. Some commit suicide. For those who do make it, some struggle to function. There are many emotional scars to overcome. Depending on the individual's core strengths and level of abuse, they have the potential to become perpetrators. This type of counseling is and will be an intense spiritual battle—a journey for some time to come."

"Oh my goodness, Bethany, you have been exposed to a world that few know exists. Why isn't this publicized? Why are we not hearing of these things on the news?" I shake my head, perplexed.

"Marion, unfortunately, I have been exposed to such wickedness and more. The world turns a blind eye to this type of abuse; the sexual and psychological abuse of innocent children." A sadness covers her face. "I suspect there are important people involved who have the money, power, and connections to keep it quiet. This type of abuse has been around for ages."

"Unbelievable," is all I can say.

"I know. Such secrets are easily refuted because most people, nice decent people, like yourself, have a hard time looking at such evil. Denial is a common reaction that the occult and the sinister forces behind these crimes use to their benefit. Just suppose that respected and important people were to swear and demand that such atrocities do not exist. In that case, most people will believe there isn't a problem. People do not want to know about such abuse. And with that mindset, there is nothing to address or resolve. All the while, such crimes continue to be committed. You wouldn't believe the money that changes hands at the expense of these innocent kids."

"What?"

"Yes, profits are made. It is more organized and evil than what most people can wrap their minds around."

My words stick in my throat. I choke out, "What can I do?"

"Exactly what you are doing, Marion. We may not be able to fight the huge organization of the occult individually. Still, we can offer truth and hope to the victims of such atrocities. The fact that you are being trained in this type of counseling will benefit not only Catherine but also other individuals that the Lord will bring to you along the way."

I thank God for protecting Catherine. "Bethany, I suspect Catherine was exposed to such mistreatment and harm from six to close to nine years old."

"The timeframe of only a couple of years may have saved her life and was definitely to her advantage. It's a shorter duration from the many I've worked with over the years. Catherine seems to be strong, a fighter, but the stuff the occult does to its victims is so evil. It's hard to accept people can be so evil. Dark. Malicious. Disturbed." Bethany shakes her head.

"Trust me, Marion, I've worked with SRA victims—it's a hard road. But be encouraged; the Lord is greater. I've had the privilege to share in the healing process of many who've recovered from SRA."

"Do most people heal?" I ask, thinking of Catherine and Charley.

"Not all, but each case is unique. There are many factors. I approach each client, trusting God to guide and lead. Counseling definitely offers healing, but some things are extremely hard to move beyond."

"Bethany, what about a timeline? Do the memories come back in any order?"

"No, there isn't any timeline. The memories come back when your client chooses to remember them. It's quite random. The only way to attach a time frame to any memory is if the client remembers how old they are in the memory. This case will be easier because you know when Catherine lived with this stepparent. Six to almost nine years old. Right?" She writes a note in Catherine's file.

"Yes." I nod.

"With some clients, it's harder to say because the abuse may have lasted a lifetime, meaning well into their adulthood before they finally escape. The perpetrators of some victims are their neighbors or even their parents. You never know. Trying to pin down an age or timeline can be all across the board."

I wipe my sweaty hands on the sides of my slacks. "Catherine is highly functional and very intelligent. With each learned truth, she absorbs its healing like a sponge. I hope and pray that this will continue as we enter the battle that lies ahead."

Bethany offers a soft smile and an encouraging nod.

Catherine walks into the room, holding a wet cloth to the back of her neck.

"I hope you don't mind, Bethany, but I asked your receptionist for a washcloth. I'm not feeling so great. The cool water helps the pounding in my head."

"That is perfectly fine, sweetheart. Come in. Please, have a seat."

Bethany reiterates similar facts about the occult with Catherine. She does not seem surprised, as if she already knows.

Bethany tells Catherine, "God is merciful. He allowed you to have your special friends to help you endure and survive the abuse. I trust the Lord in all things. I see the little kids who tried to help you out of an impossible circumstance as a gift from God. Small comforts can mean a lot in such duress. Why the names Barbie and GI Joe?"

"I made them up. We weren't allowed to know anyone's real names. So, I made up names based on whoever they reminded me of, like GI Joe, who acted like a soldier." She shrugs. "The only real person's name I knew was Ivy and Buck's foster kid, Gilbert, but I didn't know his last name. And who knows? 'Gilbert' could have been a made-up name they had given him."

I move toward Bethany to shake her hand. "Thank you for today.

I think it is time to take Catherine to dinner, then back to the hotel for some much-needed rest. It has been a hard and challenging few days."

I turn and look at Catherine. She does not speak. Her head hangs low, and her eyes downcast. She only nods in agreement.

CHAPTER NINE

Catherine
February 1994

I'm grateful I agreed to go to Kentucky in January. Since returning three weeks ago, Hunter and I have spent time together doing the things we love. It has been a great distraction. He picked Marion and me up at the airport with flowers, which melted my heart. Yesterday was a fun-filled day of skiing at Winter Park. I love beautiful scenery and crisp air. It makes me feel alive. Hunter's smile was so big it puffed his cheeks, which added to our laughter.

Still, like this morning, I find myself heavy and burdened with the memories when I've any time alone. I've been pacing, matting down the bedroom carpet's fibers with a steady walk back and forth.

The more I walk, the more it relieves the numbness—this dull lack of consciousness that has been with me since childhood, as far back as six years old. It's as if the blood was cut off, anesthetizing my brain and my past into a deep sleep.

However, now my mind is slowly awakening like a numb foot stimulated with the sensations of sparklers. I'm finally waking up with feelings and flashes of light—sparks of scenes from my past's buried secrets.

There's a force burning inside me, pressing me to visit those feelings and confront my childhood memories. I appreciate my sessions with Marion. My memories are coming back, not in any particular order, but coming back just the same. And more easily than I had imagined.

I stop in my tracks and stand perfectly still. It's that urging voice again, a voice, deep inside me, saying, "Catherine, it's time to wake up the past. Dig up those memories, and exhume them into the light."

Is that you, Holy Spirit?

I jerk awake. Hunter is rustling my shoulders. Once again, I realize my nightmare, along with my blood-curdling screams, have awakened my husband. My breath races, and my heart thumps wildly against my chest.

Hunter sits up in bed and rubs his eyes. Even though it's hours before either of us needs to get up for work, he slides out of bed.

"I'm going downstairs to read. You rest."

I fluff the pillow and roll over but don't dare fall back to sleep, fearful the nightmare will return. Falling back into the nightmare a second time is always more fierce. After a few minutes, I give up on rest and crawl out of bed, heading for the shower.

The warmth of the water feels dull as it spills over my body. I scrub my body, scouring away the recent revelations. My vigorous cleansing is uncomfortable, yet I feel more alive.

How do I live with this? How could Dad not know? Why didn't my siblings protect me? And why me? Why Charley? What happened to Gilbert?

Wicked images circle my mind, like a flock of vultures, moving in closer—tighter. The ugliness from those childhood years attack my thoughts. My head hurts as a battle rages within my mind.

I step out of the shower and towel off the beads of water. A new memory flashes across my mind like a streak of lightning. My eyelids squeeze together, but I still see the images of Gilbert and me as Dean's braided, black leather bullwhip soars through the air and cracks above our heads. Startled, we jump and then cower. A second crack sounds. This time it slashes across Gilbert's back. His screams echo. The stinging whip hits my hand and snags the satin fabric, ripping the beautiful yellow dress.

My chest aches. Stress, shame, defilement, grief, and fear...all torment me. The weight of the emotions press in all around me. My feelings appear to have talons that lurk in the darkness of my mind. Each one lies waiting, hovering, circling closer, refusing to leave, and looking for any chance to devour me.

I slump onto the edge of the tub—exhausted. Knowing I must dress, I force myself to put on my dental hygiene uniform. I grab my makeup bag along with my journal and trudge over to the vanity mirror. I remove and unfold the paper with typed scriptures Marion gave me. I place it next to the sink.

I read aloud Ephesians 6:12. "For we do not wrestle against flesh and blood, but against principalities, against powers, against the rulers of the darkness of this age, against spiritual hosts of wickedness in the heavenly places."

The demonic influences and wickedness of Anna and her family still haunt me, even decades removed.

What about Barbie? GI Joe? Does God indeed send special friends?

While brushing my hair, I walk the entire length of the bedroom and back.

How can people get away with such atrocities? Should I go to the police? Are those people even alive? I don't know any real names or where they live. Where did they take us? There were so many places other than Ivy and Buck's barn. How can I prove anything?

I stride four more lengths before stopping at the nightstand to set down my brush. My scalp is taking a beating. I stare at my family photo, along with two wedding pictures.

How deeply networked is this occult? Do they know where I am after all these years? Will they come after me or go after my family? My family—should I tell them? How can I? What good could possibly come out of telling them? Shivers of fear slither up my spine.

I recall Marion's words, 'Your family should remember their own memories in their own time. What you and Charley experienced will be different. Your sisters were not present in your recent memories.'

My memories…am I crazy? How can this be real?

My focus moves onto our wedding photos. Hunter looks so handsome. He seemed happy and content.

What will he think about this unfolding mess? What would I do if I were him? How long before his patience runs out? How could Hunter or anyone understand?

Unanswered questions gnaw at my mind like a dog chomping on a bone. With each question, the bite of fear takes its toll on my nerves. My skin crawls with the possibility of the occult members knowing my whereabouts and my family's location.

Am I opening a can of worms? If they find out I'm remembering, will they finish the job? KILL ME? What am I exposing? Memories of a six, or seven, or eight-year-old? Heck, I don't even know the exact age I was at the time. Everything's scrambled up in my mind. And if I tell, what good will it do?

I grasp my head and press, holding it tight in an attempt to stop my thoughts from spinning out of control. I return to the vanity, focusing on applying my makeup, from moisturizer to lipstick. Looking at the clock, I have an hour before needing to leave for work.

The bombarding thoughts retake flight.

What will happen if I expose what they have done? Years—decades have passed. Dean, Buck, and Ivy must be long dead. Anna? Anna who? I heard she'd remarried. Once? Twice? Her kids, Melinda and Shawnee? Probably married. No last names.

Waves of helplessness crash upon me—pummeling me. The sessions in Kentucky, although intense, had brought results. Truth and answers—yet, I still struggle to process my thoughts. I shake my head to rid myself of doubt. I gasp for air, sucking in all the hope I can muster, relying on my faith.

My mind flashes to Marion. Thank God for her willingness to

research the process of memory retrieval. I don't know what I'd do without her dedication and encouragement. She helps me find the courage to unearth my past. My upcoming session creates anxiety, knowing the recollections feel like returning into the pit of hell. I shudder, anticipating what awaits. Conflicting thoughts slap at me.

Why would Marion want to help me after knowing what I've done?

My concerns move on to Baby Jesse, the name I gave to 'Baby Jesus.' Condemnation. Guilt. Worthlessness. Another slam of emotions, like waves crashing against a rocky coast.

I fall to my knees and rock, pressing my hands hard against my skull. I fear my brain is about to explode.

I call out, "They killed the baby! They killed my mom!"

My body shakes uncontrollably. Pain from the stress and tension rip through me, saturating my core: body, soul, and spirit. I lie on the floor and intertwine my fingers into the carpet to ground myself.

I can't take this. If I cry anymore, I'll surely go crazy. I can't handle this pain. It's too much!

My mind spins, tornadoing, out of control. Fear strikes me.

I hate Dean. I hate Anna. I hate all of them! What if I go crazy? Or worse —what if I'm already there?

With great purpose, I speak aloud, "Stop crying. Stop crying. Breathe. Breathe deep—deeper."

I obey my words. I suck in my tears, stifle my sniffles, and breathe deep as I search for calmness and peace, but all that comes is a familiar numbness. A familiar numbness that I've grown to detest. However, today I welcome it—I no longer want to feel. I stand and walk to my bed. The stress is all too much. I need time. I need sleep. My words slowly die down and are replaced with deep breaths.

Hunter taps me on the shoulder. I jump.

"Catherine, sweetheart, sorry, I startled you. Why don't you come into the kitchen for some coffee?"

Catie
Spring 1963

My teacher taps me on my shoulder. "Catie, wake up, sweetheart."

Startled, I lift my head off my desk and peer at her. "I'm sorry, Miss Anderson. I guess I fell asleep."

I take a quick look around to see if my classmates are lookin'. I'm relieved to see they're all busy with their school projects.

"Catie, you're taking quite a few naps in class lately. Are you sleeping well?"

"Not really." I keep my eyes down.

"Why is that? Don't you have a bedtime?"

"Uh, huh…" I slowly nod. "It's at eight o'clock, Miss Anderson."

"Perhaps you need to be in bed by seven, so you can stay awake in class. Do I need to call your parents?"

I glance up quickly and then lower my head in silence.

I wish my teacher would call Daddy, but Anna always answers the telephone. If she tells her I've been sleepin' in class, I'll only get another beatin', but it will be worth it if Daddy knows.

It is time for baths, toothbrushin', and the last drink of water before bed.

I've been thinkin' all day 'bout how I can get more sleep, so Miss Andersen doesn't tell Anna I've been nappin' at school. I figure I can save time and sleep longer if I don't have to make my bed.

I wait till Carolyn and Melinda are fast asleep. I wish I could sleep as soundly as my sisters. They sleep through the night when Anna sneaks us out of the house. For bein' such good sleepers, my sisters seem as sleepy as me the next mornin'. Melinda and Shawnee not so much. They're always wide awake.

I slide out of my bed and onto the floor, making sure not to mess up my bedspread. I climb up on my dresser and stretch out for a good night's sleep. But my feet dangle off one end. The wood is hard. And it's not as wide as my bed, so I have to be extra careful turnin' onto my side.

I don't know what time it is when I wake up, but I'm cold and uncomfortable. My teeth chatter. My plan isn't workin' at all. I crawl into bed.

It seems like only minutes before I hear Carolyn. "Time to get up, Catie."

I open my eyes; the bright mornin' light shines through the window. I'm tired and disappointed that my plan failed.

Tonight I'll try my second plan. It has to work, 'cuz I don't have a third plan.

I'm nestled comfortably underneath my warm blankets after the lights are out. Once again, when my sisters are asleep, I push back my covers and tiptoe into my closet. The streetlamp glows enough for me to see my white cotton blouse and navy blue pleated skirt hangin' where I placed them earlier.

I shimmy out of my nightgown and put on my school clothes. If I can save time by not havin' to get dressed, I can sleep till the very last minute, pull the blanket neatly in place, and then run downstairs, ready for breakfast. Sleepin' in my clothes should buy me a good ten or fifteen minutes. Providin' Anna doesn't shake me awake for one of her secret trips. These are my last thoughts before I drift off into a much-needed deep sleep.

I wake up happy to hear Carolyn and Melinda arguin', 'cuz it means I slept the whole entire night. I stretch, yawn, and then throw my covers back, thrilled that I'm already dressed for school. I jump up and quickly make my bed. As I walk into the bathroom, my head jerks backward. Anna yanks a fistful of my hair.

"Ouch!"

"Catie Kay! What have you done to your clothes?" Anna screeches. I follow her angry eyes. She stares at my outfit. Lookin' down, I see my crumpled pleated skirt and wrinkled blouse.

"I'm sorry, Anna. I was tryin' to save time so that I could sleep longer. I'm tired at school 'cuz of our secret trips."

She slaps her hand across my mouth so hard that my head slams against the bathroom door. WHAM! It makes a big racket. So loud that Charlotte, Claudia, Carolyn, and Melinda run out of their bedrooms into the hallway.

"What in the world is going on?" My oldest sister, Charlotte, demands. The rest of the girls all gawk at my clothes.

Anna yells, "I spent hours ironing those clothes, and she sleeps in them so that she can sleep longer." Her long boney finger points at me. "Catie, you deserve more...," her eyes narrow, "...much more than a little slap."

I stand frozen in place, too afraid to speak. Or move. I'm disappointed, again. And now I have a real beatin' comin'. But at least school will be out for the summer at the end of the month, so I won't have to worry 'bout fallin' asleep in class.

Claudia steps forward. "Anna, I'll take her and help her change her clothes." She puts her arm around my shoulder and motions me toward my bedroom. I rubbed the goose egg knot on the back of my head.

Carolyn snarls and mouths off to Anna. "What good does it do to knock her in the head over some stupid clothes?"

Melinda talks behind my back. "Only stupid babies do dumb things like sleep in their school clothes."

Marion
May 1994

I slept on and off last night. The morning came quicker than I had hoped. I sip my morning coffee while preparing for today's appointments.

Since our Kentucky trip back in January, Bethany Taylor has remained an excellent educator, mentor, and coach. She too inquired about my speech, in that I do not use contractions. I explained my parents had their quirks about language and saw combining words, as in contractions, as a form of laziness. I started talking when I was about one-year-old, and by the time I went to school, it had become my speech pattern. Bethany, as well as my parents, say it makes me sound professional and educated. I am not sure if that is true; however, Bethany's instruction has been an invaluable education and asset as I advise Catherine (Williams) Stone.

Her appointment is this evening. I grasp her file—worn, tattered, and thick with papers. Since 1992, Catherine has had numerous challenging revelations concerning her past. She continues to persevere in search of freedom from her recurring nightmare and her mysterious lost years.

As her memories surface, Catherine's emotions, or sometimes lack of emotions, come in random, unpredictable waves. Her recollections confirm verbal, emotional, physical, and sexual abuse, which mirror other documented occult victims.

I savor the freshly brewed coffee. This morning I find myself depending on caffeine to help my mind focus. I slowly move my finger down the appointment book, stopping on each name to confirm I have the files for today's sessions. My day is in order.

I lower my head and pray, "Lord, please give me guidance and direction for each person on my schedule, to help them to find your truth and healing…"

In a blink of an eye, I find myself reaching for the last file on my desk.

I am grateful for the new clients the Lord has brought my way. All have various types of abusive backgrounds. I have not minded the extra time needed to study this counseling technique. I have become proficient in working through distracting obstacles and exposing belief systems, which have proven to be mostly lies or twisted perceptions.

I take full advantage of instructing my clients on seeking truth and healing by applying biblical principles. How incredible to see how God, through his word and his commanding presence, sets people free.

Prior to my experience with Catherine, I thought I was aware of evil. Still, I had only heard about such occult rituals secondhand, basically hearsay, but from reliable sources. However, my firsthand experience with Catherine has confirmed the reality of the satanic occult.

A smile comes to my face as I thank the Lord for Catherine's continual growth and hunger to learn. Nevertheless, unlocking and dealing with trauma has been a challenging process for Catherine. Time has been our friend.

I look forward to seeing her this evening. She has only recently returned from vacation, a trip Hunter earned at work.

Catherine walks into the office, her hands full with two thermal coffee cups. She holds them up. "Hey, Marion, I brought you some specialty coffee. 100% Kona—straight from Hawaii."

She sets the mugs on the coffee table, sliding one in my direction. She takes a seat on the couch and slips a brightly-packaged container of coffee from her purse and hands it to me.

"I bought this coffee for you on vacation and brewed a batch before leaving the house so you could preview the taste." She grins and raises her eyebrows along with her cup. A tinge of light burgundy lipstick stains the rim.

"Umm...it's so rich. Try it." Catherine tips her head toward the mug in front of me.

"Thank you." I bring the cup to my mouth, inhaling the full aroma before taking a sip. I glance over at her.

"Oh," I say, offering a big smile. "You are right. This coffee is great." I take a couple more sips. "What? No book bags or the other things you normally carry?" I tease. "Are you traveling light today?"

"Yes, it's my day off. My other stuff is in my car." She raises her shoulders. "I admit it. I'm a bag lady. I have a bag for everything." She reclines and makes herself comfortable. "Are you ready to get started?"

"Is there anything in particular on your mind you would like to discuss, Catherine?"

"Yes. My MIND, that's the issue." The corner of her mouth tilts upward. Her lips are defined with neatly applied lipstick.

"I have good days and not-so-good days. When I speak out the scriptures of how God sees me, it fires me up. I picture myself as a soldier and tell the enemy to leave and shut up in the name of Jesus. Those are my best days, and when I feel the strongest."

Her smile fades. "But then I have days when I'm full of doubt. I feel like the scum of the earth. Days when I hate myself."

She lowers her head. "I feel so ashamed. Angry. Alone. Sometimes I'm furious at God for not stopping what happened to me!"

She raises her hands and continues to fire questions. "How do I deal with such anger—outrage?"

"Catherine, you are discerning correctly. You are at war. A spiritual battle warring within your mind. Your anger is a normal response. However, it is how you handle your emotions that will determine the outcome. You have reason to be angry, but I need to clarify, it was not God's will for such atrocities to have happened to you. Those were the personal choices of your perpetrators, not to be confused with God's choices."

Catherine shakes her head in frustration. "Sometimes, I lose sight of that fact."

"The Bible is very clear about anger in Ephesians 4:26-27."

She lifts her Bible off the coffee table. I give her time to look up the scripture before reading it aloud. "'*Be angry, and do not sin, do not let the sun go down on your anger, nor give place to the devil.*' God's word warns us of Satan. He is our enemy, a liar, deceiver, our adversary, and seeks whom he may devour. He is a thief who comes to kill, steal, and destroy. The enemy wants to use displaced anger to rouse and activate doubt as a way to diminish your faith. He is the tempter behind your doubt."

"It's hard to face my past. Sometimes, I think I was better off when I kept it suppressed." She taps a finger against her chest. "Why is the enemy after me?" she asks, followed by a deep sigh.

"Because of who you are. The verses are very explicit about your identity. You are the Lord's child and a precious daughter whom he dearly loves. The devil despises the Lord's adoration and loyalty for his children, and he hates you for that very reason. God has given you everything you need to overcome the enemy and live a godly life." I lean in, making direct eye contact.

"Listen closely. I have always taught you the truth, Catherine. *Straight up*, as you call it. Today is no different. In many ways, as a child, you were thrown into the arena with lions! And you survived!"

A car honks outside in the parking lot. It distracts my attention, but Catherine barely blinks. I allow her time to rummage through her thoughts. Finally, I say, "You do not have the luxury of toying with vacillation and denial, unlike people who pretend the devil and evil do not exist."

She leans forward, her elbows on her knees, gesturing her permission for me to keep explaining.

"And yes, you will be challenged with great uncertainty and may even question your beliefs. However, you must choose to war against the temptations of the enemy. Most importantly, do not allow evil to use your anger to doubt the Lord. It is in your best interest to direct your righteous anger toward those responsible: Anna and her family."

Catherine gives a sharp nod. "You're right, Marion. I know what you're saying is true. It's just that sometimes I struggle with… indecision, wariness, and plain and simple…doubt."

She lowers her head. I observe Catherine's fatigue but press forward. "Do you remember the story in the Bible where evil spirits were tormenting a man's son? His father went to Jesus, asking for help." I read aloud. "'… *these evil spirits often throw him into fire or water to kill him. But if you can do anything, take pity on us and help us. If you can?'*"

"*'If I can?' said Jesus. "Everything is possible for him who believes." Immediately the boy's father exclaimed, "I do believe; help me overcome my unbelief!"*"

"Marion, where is that in the Bible?"

"In the book of Mark. You will find it in chapter nine, verses twenty-two and twenty-three. Catherine, we all have questions and doubts, and as the man requested help with his unbelief, we too must ask the Lord to help us build our faith." I speak firmly and directly. "We are all facing a spiritual war. I am here to train you to fight—to fight like you have never fought. You have been enlisted in this spiritual war, whether you like it or not. And it is my job to equip you to win."

The room suddenly feels cold—frigid. I shiver and sense something ominous has entered my office. Caution stirs my heart.

CHAPTER TEN

Catie
Spring 1963

Anna is cold-hearted. Her heart must be frozen. She couldn't care less that I'm always tired at school. It turns out I picked the wrong outfit. I din't know cotton and pleated skirts wrinkled so easy. She kept her promise and gave me a beatin'. At least this time, the beatin' wasn't too bad. Probably 'cuz my sisters were at home. This time there were no bruises. Only another big goose egg on the top of my head from her hittin' me with the heel of her shoe. That's two lumps in one day. One on the back of my head from her slammin' me into the door and now this one.

I'd like to show them to my teacher and even ask her to feel 'em, but I'm afraid to tell her. I'm scared 'cuz if Anna and her ugly fat family find out, they'll kill Charley.

I feel lucky to have my sisters around to protect me. Most of the time, they're nice to me, but sometimes I can tell they're tired of havin' me around. They think I'm too little to talk 'bout boy-stuff, makeup, and fashion. I don't understand why they don't include me. It's not like any of them even have a boyfriend, wear makeup, or have any fancy outfits. After all, our clothes come from Goodwill. None of them look anythin' like the glamorous outfits in those magazines they're always sneakin' to read.

Maybe they don't want me around 'cuz I look so different. I'm the only brunette with eyes shaped like an elephant—small and sad lookin'—kinda like Daddy and Teenage Granny but a different color. My eyes are the same turquoise color as our refrigerator, only darker. To hear my sisters talk, they say I don't look like anyone in our family. Not Daddy. Not Mommy. Nobody. That's why they say I'm adopted. Even though Daddy says, it isn't true. But I still wonder.

What they don't know is that I'd love to have their eyes. All of them have big, round, light blue eyes. And they're tow-headed, blondes, with soft curls. It doesn't seem fair. I feel short-changed, as Grandpa would say.

At one time, I wanted to tell them how pretty they are with their beautiful blonde hair. Carolyn has the thickest hair. Her ponytail is twice as thick as mine. I've thought about tellin' them how I wished the Cinderella Fairy Mother would change my eyes to look like theirs. Especially Charlotte, who has Cleopatra eyes. But not anymore—not after they started makin' fun of me, by callin' me Squint Eyes. I'm keepin' my thoughts to myself. They think I'm ugly, 'cuz that's what squint eyes *really* means. Sometimes my sisters even narrow their eyes like they're starin' into the sun and say, 'Look. We look like Squint Eyes, Catie.' I don't laugh. It's not funny, not at all.

F rom around the corner, I hear the rusty gate squeak. Someone's comin' into the backyard.

Daddy calls out, "Why are you sitting outside all by yourself? Where are your sisters?"

I look up at Daddy through blurry-eyed tears.

"Oh, Catie, why are you crying? Is this about you getting a spanking for wearing your school clothes to bed?"

I look down and stare at my boots. "No, that was bunches of hours ago. I'm sad 'cuz everyone says I'm ugly. They say I have *squint eyes*. I've been out in the backyard *all by myself*, and no one cares. They din't even check on me."

My tears come out like a leaky faucet. I wipe the snot from my nose with the back of my hand. "It hurts my heart when the girls call me names. And today more than ever, I miss Mommy." I drop my head, starin' at the stick I've been usin' to dig into the ground.

Daddy squats and zips up my jacket, then hugs my shiverin' shoulders.

"Do you know why your sister's call you Squint Eyes? He puts his finger under my chin and tips my head back.

I wipe my cheeks and answer. "It's 'cuz they don't want me around. I bug 'em. They *never* want me around. They're always tellin' me to go away and play." I gulp to catch my breath between sobs.

"Well, I know exactly why they call you that name." Daddy nestles in, right in front of the orange crate where I sit. He looks straight into my small eyes.

"You do?" I cock my head to the side—surprised and curious.

"Yes." He brings me closer. "It's because they're jealous."

"Jealous of me?" I shrug my shoulders. "Why?"

"Because they know you are the only one…out of all my girls who…."

I sit up straight, eager to hear more. "Who what?" I bounce up and down on the orange crate.

"Who has princess eyes. "

"PRINCESS EYES?" I jump to a stand. "I have princess eyes?"

"Yes! And they all know it too. You have my eyes, your daddy's eyes. And I am the king in this family." He cocks his head, makes a firm nod, and points his finger at me. "And you are the only one of my daughters to inherit princess eyes! Your sisters are just jealous, plain and simple."

That has to be it. My sisters have such beautiful eyes, and blonde, shiny hair,

79

but they don't have princess eyes—so why else would they call me names? Or even care?

"That has to be the answer! Daddy, you're so smart." I wrap my arms around his neck and squeeze tight. My heart sings. I skip away, excited to tell my sisters that I know the truth.

I let the screen door slam shut as I run into the house and call out to them. "Charlotte, Claudia, Carolyn!" As I round the corner, I see Charley comin' up the hallway carryin' a few green army men.

"You wanna play, Catie?" he asks.

"In a minute, Charley. First, I have somethin' to tell the girls. Daddy told me the secret."

"What secret?" He stops in his tracks, eager to listen.

"Why the girls call me Squint Eyes."

"Why they call you that?" He tucks one of his army men into his front pants pocket.

I grab his hand and tug him along. We sprint around the corner and barge into the bedroom, not botherin' to knock or say hello. Charlotte is readin' out loud from a magazine, but I dint wait for her to notice me. I march up and get right in front of their faces. I feel pretty proud of my princess eyes. I put my hands on my hips and spout off. "I know why you call me Squint Eyes. Daddy told me the *real* reason."

All three of my sisters peek over the top of the magazine, *True Confessions*.

"Huh?" all three ask at the same time.

"You're just jealous, 'cuz you know I'm the *only one* out of all us girls who has *princess eyes*."

After a long pause, they wrinkle up their foreheads, scrunch up their noses, and squint their eyes as if they have no idea what I'm sayin'. I square my shoulders and stand my ground. They're not foolin' me by actin' puzzled.

"Daddy says you girls are just jealous 'cuz I am the ONLY one out of all of us girls who inherited princess eyes." I flutter my eyelashes like I've seen Anna do when she's around handsome men.

Carolyn is the first to speak. "Well, your pug nose has nothing to do with your eyes. What do you have to say about that—*Pug-Nose 38?*"

"Huh? What? What does that mean?" Confused, I look at my oldest sister.

Charlotte explains, "Oh, Catie, Carolyn's teasing you. Pug-Nose 38 is a play on words referring to a small revolver. It's a gun that policemen carry. They call it a Detective Special, Snub-Nose 38. It's because the barrel is short. And because your nose is short, and turns up a little, like when you were a baby…" She scrunches her nose. "…and it hasn't changed, so Carolyn changed your nickname from Squint Eyes to Pug-Nose 38."

Charlotte lets out a soft snicker, lookin' back at my other sisters. Carolyn laughs real loud. Claudia gives her the stink eye for bein' mean to me.

"Come on, Charley, let's go play army." I turn around, talkin' to Carolyn over my shoulder. "Snub-Nosed 38 Detective Special, huh?" I pause, thinkin' 'bout it. "You can call me Pug-Nose 38. I like it."

I smile and walk out.

It isn't my fault that my nose hasn't grown up, but there's time.

My sisters don't call me Squint Eyes anymore. And I don't feel bad about my small, sad, turquoise eyes that favor an elephant's eyes, like Teenage Granny's and Daddy's. 'cuz now I know that my eyes are truly *princess eyes!*

Catherine
May 1994

I bolt awake, sitting straight up in bed. It's the same tormenting nightmare. My eyes flash to the light coming from the clock. It's only ten minutes before my alarm is set to go off.

I look over to an empty bed, relieved that Hunter is already up. I'm grateful this is one time I didn't wake him with my screaming.

Painful and ugly memories bombard my mind. My thoughts, like a whirling hailstorm, pelt me with accusations. My heart stings. Numerous questions arise, but there are no answers. When will this end?

I press my palms hard against my temples to offset the tension. Harder and harder I press as if to smash these unwanted images, but it doesn't work. I cover my face and let out a desperate moan.

Why would God let me go through such abuse? Something must be wrong with me. Did I deserve such cruelty? What kind of a person am I? Was it my fault? Am I responsible for the evil done to me?

I want to curl up in a fetal position and hide. Pretend it isn't real. Clips of Marion's words sound within my mind. *'You need to fight. It is important to remember. You must unearth the past, the lies. Search for the truth and speak it out. Then your rest and peace will follow.'*

I cling to her encouraging words. I muster enough strength to cry out, "Help me, Lord. Help me! Within the nearness of my mind, I hear God's words. *'The truth will set you free.'*

A calmness slowly settles over me. My shoulders relax. My mind quiets.

Is that you, Lord?

Somewhere I find the determination to climb out of bed. I walk into the bathroom, turn on the faucet, and let the cold water run over a clean washcloth. I hold the frigid, wet cloth to my eyes, forcing myself to focus on the cold instead of the nightmare.

I empty my cosmetic bag onto the vanity. The contents spill out in all directions. A tube of lipstick rolls to the far side of the marble top, landing on several 3 x 5 index cards inscribed with Bible verses. I pick up the card and read it silently.

2 Corinthians 10:3-5 For though we walk in the flesh, we do not war according to the flesh. For the weapons of our warfare are not carnal but mighty in God for pulling down strongholds, casting down arguments and every high thing that exalts itself against the knowledge of God, bringing every thought into captivity to the obedience of Christ.

My fingers trace each word. I grab another card and speak the words aloud.

"'Luke 10:17-19. *"Then the seventy returned with joy, saying, "Lord, even the demons are subject to us in Your name." And Jesus said to them, "I saw Satan fall like lightning from heaven. Behold, I give you the authority to trample on serpents and scorpions, and over all the power of the enemy, and nothing shall by any means hurt you. Nevertheless, do not rejoice in this, that the spirits are subject to you, but rather rejoice because your names are written in heaven."'*

God's word resonates with something deep inside of me—my spirit, perhaps? Either way, I understand. My mind *is* the battleground. It's so simple…and it seems so obvious. The enemy: *principalities, powers, rulers of the darkness, spiritual hosts of wickedness* are different ranks of the demonic forces, all on assignment, whispering lies and deceit, that somehow make their way into my thoughts. It's as if they're speaking outside of my head. I must recognize and then debunk the doubts, accusations, and lies. Lies spoken in first person, as if they're my own thoughts, opinions, and beliefs.

My understanding comes together like a light bulb has clicked on, leaving my mind clear. I get it! The enemy is at work, wanting me to believe the lies he plants, hoping I won't question the source. He wants me to assume the thoughts are mine. That's why God tells us to take every thought captive, to examine what we're thinking. He warns us to question every thought. Whose is it? Mine? The enemy's? Or the skewed opinions of a darkened world?

I remember Marion's words, 'You must expose the lies and replace them with the truth. Anything that is not true, command it to leave.'

I speak out into the room. "In the name of Jesus Christ, any demonic influences must leave now—be gone!"

The heaviness lifts. My mind calms. I slide down the front of the vanity onto the floor. I take hold of my study cards, reading each aloud. Quietly at first, but with each pass, I paraphrase the verses. I raise my volume until I'm shouting. I sit erect. "I can do all things through Christ who strengthens me. You, Lord, will never leave or forsake me. I am *your* child, God. And you are always with me. Even if I don't understand what has happened or why…you are always there. I'm alive. You have given me a wonderful life. I am more than a conqueror in you, Lord."

My words sing out his truth, a beautiful melody that brings comfort, like soothing salve to my soul. I stand, proclaiming the power in God's words. "Any evil on assignment, you must leave now, in the name of Jesus Christ. SHUT UP and GO!" I punch my fist into the air.

I am relieved. Strengthened. Refreshed.

———

After readying myself for work, I shuffle down the stairs at an energetic pace. I dart around the corner in search of a much-needed cup of coffee.

"Sounds like you're having a loud morning." Hunter raises his brows in question.

"Yes, I was." I offer a quick nod.

He continues to blend a smoothie for breakfast. "Catherine, I can tell you aren't sleeping well. The restlessness is becoming a pattern. This can't be good for you."

"I agree. I'm sorry that I'm keeping you awake." I muster an apologetic smile. His words feel like a jab. Suddenly, the confidence I felt just seconds ago begins to crumble. The words, 'I don't think I can deal with any more pressure,' sound within my mind. I push down the fears and remind myself that God did not give me a spirit of fear, but of power, love, and a sound mind.

"Your eyes, they're puffy. And now…you have dark circles." He looks over the top of the blender as he's pouring his breakfast drink into a large glass.

"I put extra makeup on this morning. I guess it isn't hiding that I'm sleep-deprived."

"You might want to add some more of that putty stuff."

I laugh lightly, amused at his sweet way of telling me I'm not looking so great.

"I'll touch it up in the car. Thanks, Sweetie. I've got to run. See you tonight." I place a quick kiss on his cheek. He pulls me in for a hug and lingering kiss.

The clock reads 6:45 a.m. when I drive into the parking lot at work. I love my job, and I'm thankful to have something else to concentrate on other than my haunting memories.

Diane looks up from the front desk with her usual upbeat smile as I walk through the door with my arms full.

"Hey, let me give you a hand." She takes a couple of bags from me and carries them into my hygiene room. "Catherine, you have a busy load today. I've taped your schedule on the wall and brought in your patient's files." She points to the folders on the countertop.

"Thanks a million, Diane. You're the best." I smile and send her a wink. "Is the coffee brewed yet?"

"Sure is. I've already poured my first cup." She lifts her coffee and then pauses in mid-air and frowns. She locks her eyes on mine.

"Catherine, you don't look right." She gives me a studied look. "Is everything okay?

Her question feels awkward. Does Diane think I'm hiding something? I almost chuckle, thinking I'm paranoid. However, it dawns on me. I am concealing something. It's a secret, encrypted within my soul, shrouding my lost years and recurring nightmare. Secrets buried so deeply that even I don't know the answers.

I give Diane my best dental white smile. "No. Everything is fine— it's all good." I wave a hand over my darkened eyes. "I'm just dealing with some allergies, that's all." I turn on my heels, forgoing the coffee, and head toward the X-ray room, feeling the weight of Diane's concern—and her intuitive eyes boring into my back.

Marion
May 1994

C atherine runs into the office. "Sorry I'm late, Marion. My last patient arrived late, so my work ran over a little." Her voice is slightly distressed, and her breathing labored.

She takes out her journal. A host of papers fall to the floor. She scoops them up.

"You are late, but we are only ten minutes behind schedule. I understand delays can happen sometimes." I gesture a hand toward the love seat. "Please sit down and relax."

After a few minutes of small talk, we settle into conversation with our Bibles open.

"First and foremost, let us turn to 2 Peter 1: 2-4." We read it silently to ourselves, and then I ask Catherine to read it aloud.

I summarize, "These verses mean God has given you everything, meaning everything, to live an honest and productive life." I pause and point at the verse. "This next point is important; the Bible specifies that *everything* comes through the *knowledge* of God. If you are unaware of what you have been given, how can you possibly use those things?"

She shrugs her shoulders. "I can't."

"Exactly. That is why I am here to help you obtain a strong awareness of God's word and his promises to you."

I shift around in my chair. The ache in my lower back reminds me that I need to buy a new lumbar pillow for the office. I scribble 'back support cushion' on a small sticky note to make sure to add it to my shopping list.

"Catherine, today, we will touch base on the book of Ephesians.

"I genuinely understand your anger. It is expected and reasonable. However, it is crucial to direct your anger properly and not at innocent people or God. The Lord loves us so much he gave us all a free will to make choices. Unfortunately, your stepfamily chose an evil path. They deeply hurt you, and for that, I am genuinely sorry." I place my hand over my heart to show my sincerity.

"It is essential to understand that their choices were not God's choices. I believe the Lord protected you and Charley. The fact that you are still alive is proof.

"Do not be dismayed. God Almighty will make them answer for their evil choices. Just as he will make you answer for your choices." I offer a soft smile to encourage her.

"So, Catherine, it is okay to be angry, as we have discussed many times. The key is that you do not let anger drive you to sin as the word instructs in Ephesians 4:26-27."

Catherine purses her lips. "I'm not doing so well with that. Part of me wants those slime balls to pay for what they've done." She crumples a tissue tightly in her hand. "When I think of them, sometimes I get so enraged. I don't dare repeat my thoughts; it only ramps up my emotions." She tosses the tissue into the basket near the wall.

"I believe I understand how you might feel…"

I know all too well and would never share my sinful thoughts of wanting Anna and her family to pay for their evil.

"Umm…And I also understand where such intense emotions may lead. I will explain, but first, please turn to John 10:10."

Catherine searches for the verse. I lean forward and wait. The pause allows me a moment to push down my own anger and say a silent prayer.

Lord, may your will be done in the lives of Anna and her family for their choices. I give my indignation and frustrations about them over to you. Please help me stay focused on assisting Catherine to find the truth and not get swept away with anger and revenge. Please forgive me, for I know vengeance is yours and yours alone.

I clear my throat. "God's word warns us that the enemy is a thief who comes to steal, kill, and destroy. Satan would love to use your anger to steal the joy from your life. In that very verse, Jesus promises us life to the fullest. So, be aware and do not let the devil or his demons, manipulate you into grumbling or cause you to see yourself as a victim, spending useless time in pity parties. Instead, be wise and focus on what Philippians 4:6-9, says..."

Catherine flips through the pages until she finds the passage. She places a bookmark to hold her spot, and quickly jots down a few words on her note pad before laying it on the seat. In unison, we read together.

"'Do not be anxious about anything, but in everything, by prayer and petition, with thanksgiving, present your requests to God. And the peace of God, which transcends all understanding, will guard your hearts and your minds in Christ Jesus. Finally, whatever is true, whatever is noble, whatever is right, whatever is pure, whatever is lovely, whatever is admirable—if anything is excellent or praiseworthy—think about such things. Whatever you have learned or received or heard from me, or seen in me—put it into practice. And the God of peace will be with you.'"

Catherine leans over the coffee table, "Thank you, Marion. I love the practical ways you're teaching me to war. I know the battle is for my mind. I can clearly see how the enemy starts jabbering negative self-talk all around me, making it sound like my voice. Sometimes I'm still blindsided into thinking it's my own thoughts. But not as often. I used to be easily duped and distracted by the enemy." She lifts her finger and makes a twirling motion as if pointing out the trail of a bumblebee flying around her head, causing great distraction. "But now I'm choosing to fight back. Satan and his minions are such deceivers." She crinkles her nose and then offers a sweet smile. "I mean big buttholes." She winks, bringing humor and lightness into our conversation.

I delight in hearing Catie's words collide into Catherine's description. We burst into belly-busting laughter.

I sense God alongside us, pleased to see joy in the room and the strength that is growing inside of Catherine's soul.

CHAPTER ELEVEN

Catherine
June 1994

"Catherine. Catherine. Wake up!"

I hear my name. His voice is near—yet far. My body—jostles. Deep sleep has a death-grip hold on me. I can't move, but somehow I manage to open my eyes. A man's shadow covers me. His form is blurred—unfocused. His hands grasp my shoulders. He won't let me go. Heaviness holds me captive. Tension rips through my body.

He's dragging me back to them. I don't want to go! I must find a way to get away—to run. Where's Charley? I thrash my head side to side, looking for him. All I see is darkness. I can't find Charley! I hear a loud voice...

"Catherine, Catherine...wake up! Can you hear me? Wake up."

A face comes in and out of focus. I gasp!

"What? What's wrong?" In confusion, I plead, "Where am I?"

After multiple blinks, my vision clears. It's Hunter. He shakes me again.

"Oh, Honey." I lunge forward and wrap my arms around his neck and pull him close.

"It's okay, Catherine. I'm here." He looks deep into my eyes. "I've been calling your name. I've been shaking you, but you weren't waking up." He frowns. Worry lines crease his face. "Are you okay?"

"No!" The word comes out in a shriek. I clamp my lips together. "I mean," I suck in a deep breath to attempt to conceal and control the keyed-up emotions that are bolting through me like a live sparking wire.

"I'll be...okay...just give me a minute."

I cling to him. My fingers clench his t-shirt in an unrelenting hold as if he were a life jacket. The dimly lit room looks as foggy as the thoughts inside my head. What is real, and what is not?

Hunter speaks into my ear. His words bring me back into the moment. "Catherine, how long will I have to continue to wake you?"

His remark feels more like an accusation, indicating that I'm a burden. The thought brings an ache to my heart. I lean back enough to glimpse his face, to see his eyes. If words were written on his face, Hunter's expression would read perplexed, frustrated, and even a twinge of irritation and anger.

His questions continue, "Shouldn't this dream be getting easier? I mean, with you knowing what some of it means?" The tightness in his tone cuts the air like scissors.

Feeling hurt, I want to scream out my frustrations. Instead, I squeeze my hands into fists to hold back my thoughts. My nails press deeply into my palms.

Please stop pressuring me. I just woke up. How am I to know when this dream is going to get easier? What am I? I'm not some chart to be engineered into a specific timetable. I'm your wife, a real person with real feelings. I've no idea when this crazy dream will end—if ever.

I gather my thoughts before speaking. "Hunter, I'm trying to understand the things you're saying, but actually—to answer your questions—NO—it's not getting any better. In fact, it's getting much worse! I hate it. Every time the dream comes, it unnerves me. Also, now I'm struggling to wake myself. I feel like I'm losing it—losing control."

I reach for the bedcovers and pull them close to my chest. "Don't you see, Hunter? I'm getting stuck in this same nightmare, over and over again. It's wearing me out."

I push my bangs back, wiping the sweat with my fingers.

"Do you think I like having to depend upon you to wake me? Especially with demands like these?" I rub my damp hand on the sheet. "Before my recalls, the entire nightmare was just a big riddle," I say. "And yes, I do understand parts of the dream. However, the unsolved parts—are what haunt me. I'm tired, frustrated, and afraid."

The skin under Hunter's eyes is dark and puffy. He also looks tired and weary—even more, defeated. He lowers his head.

"I need for you to understand," I say. "I fight daily to address this mystery. In some ways, I want to solve it, and in some ways, I don't." A sob catches in my throat.

Hunter reaches for my hands and gently folds my fingers into his. My skin almost stings; I cringe from being touched. My mind flashes to Dean's hands over my hands! My chest rises as I fight for air. I jerk my hands away and cry out.

"NO! Unraveling this dream isn't helping! Seeing all these old images in my mind are painful. My emotions thrash and claw at my consciousness like the memories have become alive and are back to taunt me—to destroy me!"

I cover my face with my hands. "I hate Dean. I hate myself! And I hate the horrifying scenes that plague me."

I shake my head and kick the covers as hard as I can, as if kicking at Dean, Anna, and their evil bunch.

Hunter says nothing. He leans away and gives me time to vent.

My voice rises, "And the yellow satin dress..." I lean forward and grab my stomach as it cramps and heaves.

I bellow, "That yellow dress, the same dress I've seen in my dream for the last thirty years. That dress was once only a mystery, but now I understand its meaning."

I twine my fingers in my hair and pull on the long strands. It hurts, but the pain keeps me focused and stops me from returning to my pattern of emotional numbness.

"That very yellow satin dress is a depressing reminder of my black wedding. And my defilement!" I drop my head. "I hate the men, all the sickening men clawing and pawing at me. Their manipulation and overpowering to control…" I gag. "I was only a little girl."

"I want to scream! I want to cry! I want this all to stop! But what I *don't* want is to start my weekend in anger and aggravation!"

The tension between us twists at my already tight muscles, like a taut rope. My shoulders rise almost to my ears. I feel like I've been hung on a clothesline with wooden clothespins digging into my flesh. I roll my neck to ease the stress.

Hunter's eyes water. "It hurts me seeing you like this. And not being able to fix this," he pounds his fist into his palm. "It's driving me crazy! I want to go and kill all of those…."

The muscles in his clenched jaw twitch. "And as far as you know, they're probably already dead. So I can't even do that." He grits his teeth. "I don't care if they're dead. I hope they're alive enough to *feel* themselves burning in hell."

Hunter rakes his fingers through his hair.

I knead the bed linen so tightly that it hurts my knuckles and cuts off the circulation to my fingers. The clock on the nightstand ticks loudly in the strained silence.

I'm the first to speak. "I know you want to help me, Hunter. I realize it's been a long time, and you're tired, but you can't fix this. I, too, am weary. I feel pressured and guilty when you say things like, 'shouldn't this be getting easier or better?'" I mimic his words in a nagging, sarcastic voice. "I've suppressed these memories for over three decades. Marion says I'm doing great, and these things take time. I don't know what more I can do." I turn away. "I can't take any more stress."

Hunter scoots closer to hold me. "I'm sorry, Catherine. I'm not sleeping well either. And yes, I'm tired. I didn't mean anything by what I said. It just came out wrong. It seems like everything I say anymore always comes out wrong. It's frustrating, and I feel powerless. I can't seem to say or do anything right anymore."

Wrapping my arms around him, we embrace, both letting out long sighs. I force a smile and toss the covers back and reach for my robe.

"Let's go downstairs and pretend we're having a normal Saturday morning. A new day, a day without nightmares, no lack of sleep, and no craziness." I fasten my robe around my waist.

Hunter offers a straight-lip smile.

I walk toward the door and look back over my shoulder. "How about I make us a big breakfast, like normal people? Bacon, eggs, and toast?" I act perky in the hope of changing the mood.

He nods. "Sure, sounds great. I'll start the coffee and pour some orange juice."

As we head down the steps toward the kitchen, Hunter stops. "Oh, just a minute. I'll be down in a few." He runs back upstairs to his office.

I get busy with preparations and set the table. Opening the window allows crisp air into the room. I need some form of freshness in my life, especially this morning. I focus on the sweet things in our life, like Hunter rubbing my aching feet every night. He knows how to make them feel so much better. My heart goes out to him, knowing he wants to help and accepting he can't change my past. I just wish he wasn't so frustrated about trying to fix everything.

When the food is ready, I run up the stairs to get some exercise and fetch my husband. As soon as I sprint into the office, Hunter turns around. Seeing me, he jerks, as if startled. With a quick slam, he shuts off the computer.

"Catherine, honey, umm…ahh…is breakfast ready?" His brow furrows.

My back stiffens. *He looks tense. Guilty? Uncomfortable? What's he hiding?*

"Yes, I came up to tell you. What are you looking at on the

computer?" I lean in over his shoulder only to see a darkened screen. Blank. Black.

"Oh nothing, just killing some time," he says with a nervous smile.
Is he lying? Why?
"I'll get the orange juice."
What doesn't he want me to see?
Hunter stands and jets out of the office toward the kitchen.

Marion
June 1994

I am heading for the kitchen break room when Catherine enters. Her stride is quick, and her hands are full. She carries a book bag, purse, a cup of coffee, and a thick journal tucked under her arm.

"Hello dear, please make yourself comfortable while I quickly refresh my coffee. Would you care for anything to drink?"

"I'm good." She lifts her cup.

My new diet with limited calories has rendered me fatigued. I pour a steaming hot cup of java and head back to the counseling room. I hook my foot on the break room door and tug. It bangs shut.

"I am sorry for the noise, Catherine. The door closed a little harder than I had planned."

I find her already seated with her arms and legs crossed with a steady bounce of one foot. Her journal and pen lie on the cushion next to her.

I tilt my head to capture a glimpse of her facial expression. She is not her usual chatty self.

I begin our session with a question. "Please tell me, Catherine, how are you doing?"

"Not so good. It's been one of those days when everything feels difficult. I woke up late. I must've slept through my alarm. I broke a cup and splashed coffee on my clothes and had to change after I cleaned up the glass scattered all over the floor." She rolls her eyes. "I dove into my car only to see my gas tank was on fumes. I had to go back home because I forgot my books for class. And, well, here I am." Her pen rolls off her lap and onto the floor. She lifts her hands as if not surprised.

"Marion, I'm still struggling with the nightmare. And, Hunter's frustrated having to wake me. I'm sure it's unnerving to him." She unfolds her arms and drums her fingers on the armrest. "It's wearing on both of our nerves.

She squirms in her seat. Once again, she firmly crosses her arms. "What the man doesn't understand is I don't need him to fix it for me. In fact, he can't fix this. I only want him to listen."

She throws her hands up and lets them drop back to her lap. "What is it with men thinking they have to fix everything?"

I cup my hand over my mouth to stifle a soft chuckle. I am amused, yet understand Catherine's exasperation with the differences between men and women.

"Have you considered telling your husband what it is that you need from him? You may try saying, 'I am not asking you to fix my problems; what I need from you is to simply listen.'" I cock my head to the side and wait for her answer.

"I think I have, but maybe I haven't. She crosses her eyes. Her tone changes to playful. "Why didn't I think of that myself? Duh! Probably because it's so easy and straightforward. I need to write that down on my things-to-do list." She lets out a small giggle.

"Asking him to listen is simple." Her serious expression returns. "It's remembering my past that's overwhelming. Honestly, this whole mess makes me want to scream. I feel pressured. If I could snap my fingers and have this all behind me," she briskly nods her head, "Ohhh, believe me, I would. I told my husband I didn't know what more to do. This stuff is hard enough to revisit, much less to process. It's painful, and I'm attending our sessions at a pace I can handle."

Her cheeks flush pink and deepen in color, the more she expresses her complaints and concerns.

"Catherine, Hunter wants nothing more than to protect you. He desires to be your rescuer and to go to battle for you."

"I wish he could, but my battle isn't physical. It's spiritual." Her mouth twists into a scowl.

Catherine returns to her seat and immediately thumbs to a particular page in her Bible. "My battle is supernatural, just like this verse says, *'For our struggle is not against flesh and blood, but against the rulers, against the authorities, against the powers of this dark world and against the spiritual forces of evil in the heavenly realms.'*" She looks up.

I am pleased to hear Catherine refer to scripture to describe her challenges.

"The supernatural world involves demonic attacks and deceptions as well as angelic provision and protection," I add.

She continues, "Believe me, I know. I'm battling first-hand with such things. I'm always warring against the lies inside my mind and trying to overcome all the crazy dysfunction that the world says is normal." She grits her teeth and shakes her head.

"Yes, Catherine, the battle for our minds is a reality we all must face. You know this personally, even if the world denies the existence of demonic influences. Secular culture may think dysfunctions are normal because everyone faces such chaos. However, such things are not normal or right. They are simply common."

I encourage Catherine to continue to vent. I pay close attention, as I know listening to her struggles validates and affirms her value. I allow her to speak the words she would not dare share with anyone else. The effects of fatigue shadow Catherine's face, revealing her disheartenment and emotional exhaustion.

"Hunter has no idea what I'm going through." She dabs the corners of her eyes and continues. "I don't fault him for not understanding. I mean, who would?"

She lowers her head and pulls up her legs, then wraps her arms around her shins.

"Marion, I want to believe that my husband only wants to help me, but it seems like the more I tell him—his anger becomes worse. I feel his distance. I suppose he's fighting his own battles."

She sniffles and puts a tissue to her nose.

"I admit that counseling was my idea. I wanted—no, I needed to remember—but I had no idea how hard it would be to live with all this guilt and shame. I need Hunter's reassurance now—more than ever."

"Yes, I appreciate how you are feeling. A couple needs to uplift one another during times of challenges. I wish I could give you an easy answer," I say. "Nevertheless, you are going to have to continue to fight. The doubts, fears, and lies will continue until you identify them and their source. Once you recognize and replace those false beliefs with truth, then you will be able to stand firm. Eventually, your emotions will line up with the truth."

I lean forward, then fold my hands in my lap.

"It takes time, Catherine. You are rewiring your brain with godly truth."

"I know, you're right. After I explain to Hunter that I need him to listen, then maybe I'll be able to explain this mind battle more clearly. I hope we can get on the same page. It will help to take off some of the pressure. I hate being so edgy."

She grabs the hem of her denim skirt and rolls it up. Tight. Her knuckles blanch.

"Marion, coming here isn't easy, but it helps to know you understand. I don't have anyone else that comprehends this disgusting stuff. At times, I feel very alone. I know it's best not to tell my family, but I wish I could." She sighs deeply. "Thanks for being here for me."

"Catherine, I'm always here for you. Someday when the time is right and with God's leading, he may direct you to share this with your family. However, at this moment, the best way I can assist you is to continue to teach you faith-based truths and how to engage and overcome this spiritual war."

"Marion, there's something I've wanted to ask you."

"Yes, what is on your mind?"

"What do you know about spiritual gifts? I'm referring to discerning of spirits in particular. I've brought it up before. You know

I see things—spiritual things that others can't see. Or if they do, they don't talk about it. I suppose they're afraid, like me, fearing others will think they're crazy."

"To what exactly are you referring? What do you see, Catherine?"

"It started with Buck, Dean, and Anna's crazy family. I could see darkness in them. Especially in their eyes, as if something evil was looking back at me. Their eyes would change from their normal color to black and some snake-like, diamond-shaped pupils. Even the corners of their eyes would sometimes turn up, like their eyes were smiling in a mocking sort of way." She shivers. "It's hard to explain."

She twists her bracelet several times. "I've even smelled evil. There's a stench, a decaying, reeking odor. And sometimes the temperature will change, dropping fast, instantly cold. I can sense good and evil. I don't know how I'm able to comprehend such things exactly. It's similar to ordinary senses, but I must have an extra set of spiritual insights. I can see, hear, smell, feel, and even taste in the spiritual realm. With certain people, I'll get a bad taste in my mouth. Not to mention, I also see supernatural light, like angels."

"The gift you are describing is the discerning of spirits, which is the ability to distinguish the supernatural realm. I know several people who also have this gifting. I believe God allowed you to perceive this dimension to equip you for what you were and are up against. The Lord has given his children additional gifts. I am referring to the full armor of God, which prepares us for war and so much more." I shuffle through a file looking for a particular handout.

"Based on conversations with Hunter, I believe your husband wants to fight for you. However, you may be accurate in saying he does not know how to address spiritual warfare. Nevertheless, God has thought of everything." I smile.

I take out a drawing of an English suit of armor, designed to protect the entire body.

I hold it up. "Catherine, this is how I imagine Hunter sees himself, as your Prince Charming willing to go to war for you. In this case, this armor of steel plates is not the answer. However, his loving desire to protect you may be where his frustrations come from, not with you, but from within himself. Is it possible that he may feel, in some way, that he is letting you down?"

"Well, maybe, you might be right," she says, sounding almost swayed. "I like visual aids. It helps me to understand things—even my husband."

I point back to the drawing.

"The reason I am showing you this drawing is to introduce another kind of armor. It is a type of protection God provides, armor for the soul, as in the warring we mentioned earlier. Turn to Ephesian 6:10."

We shuffle through the pages to find the verse. Catherine reads aloud. "*Finally, be strong in the Lord and in his mighty power. Put on the full armor of God so that you can take your stand against the devil's schemes.*"

She keeps a finger on the page as she scrutinizes the verses, pausing to make notes.

"Think about it this way." I nod, careful to stress my next words. "It is not an armor made of steel plates; instead, *you are* the full armor."

"Huh?" She cocks her head sideways.

"You see, this type of armor is not only a blessing from God, but it is also a reflection of who we are as the Lord's children, his family. For some, it might sound scary, the terms; battle and armor, but this is something *we* do together with the Lord. The Holy Spirit never leaves us. He is always here. As you will see, this gift defines our identity and the power and authority the Lord has given us. You will find that understanding this concept will render you more courageous.

"Umm...I think that makes sense. It reminds me of a time when I was a little girl and how I was able to overcome my fear because of my sisters. In a way, we faced or battled it together."

Catherine wraps her arms around a throw pillow, giving it a little squeeze as she tells her story during her days as Catie. "I was only four years old, and my real mom was still alive..."

Catie
Summer 1959

"Yes, Charlotte, I wanna go down Mr. Golden's slide, but it is so-o-o-o tall. I've only been on a slide with three or four steps." I look up and count. I stop at ten 'cuz I can't count any higher, and there are more stairs to count. My tummy starts knottin' up into one of those fear knots. I lower my head and kick my tennis shoe in the dirt.

Claudia, Carolyn, and a few other neighbor kids run into Mr. Golden's backyard. One of the older boys scurries up the tall ladder and swoops down, whoopin' and hollerin' 'whoopee' all the way. His legs are long enough to jump to a stand at the end of the slide.

Timmy, from across the street, runs up and starts givin' me instructions. "Catie, it's tall, alright, but after a few times, you'll love it." He wipes his drippy nose on his sleeve. "I'm heading home to get some wax paper."

I tilt my head. "How come? What do you need wax paper for?"

"'Cuz it's extra hot today, and that slide is super-duper hot. It will burn you if you don't have long pants on but keep your knees bent in those pedal pushers, and you'll be fine."

"But what about the waxed paper? Does it make the slide less hot?" I ask, still curious.

"No, not really, but if you put it under your bottom before you slide down, it waxes the slide making it even faster!" Timmy runs off in a jiffy to get home.

Charlotte says, "That's a great idea! Hey, Claudia, Carolyn, come over here and talk to Catie. She's scared of going down the slide. She thinks it's too tall. Talk some sense in her head while I run home to get some waxed paper."

Claudia walks over and puts her arm around me. "It's okay, Catie.

I was scared the first time or two I went down as well. It just takes some getting used to."

Carolyn joins in. "I'll go down first, and you can watch me, and then you won't be afraid."

Charlotte runs up swingin' several pieces of waxed paper over her head. I'm thinkin' I don't want a sheet. I don't want to go down the dumb thing in the first place, and I double don't want it to be any faster.

Carolyn is the first up the ladder, with me right behind. Claudia follows givin' me several nudges to keep climbin' higher. Charlotte stands at the base of the ladder waitin' for her turn.

I look to the ground and immediately shut my eyes. I whimper, "This is too high. I don't think Mommy would want me on this giant slide."

Claudia comes up right behind me with her arms on both sides of the railin' makin' sure I don't fall. I bite my lower lip to keep from burstin' out into tears. I mouth to my big sister, "I'm scared."

Timmy yells from the ground. "Catie, you're next…You'll love it. You're the C family. You guys aren't afraid of anything. You don't let anything stop you."

I can't move. I'm too afraid to go up, and Claudia won't let me go down. And just when I'm 'bout to scream for my mommy, Claudia whispers into my ear. "Catie, you don't have to go down alone. I'll go with you. I'll put you on my lap, and we can slide down together. I'll keep you safe. Timmy's right; we are the C family. We don't let anything stop us."

Timmy only said that 'cuz all our names start with a C, but my fears are somehow gone. The bugs bitin' inside my tummy left. I grin, knowin' I have my sisters here to help me.

Carolyn waves from the bottom and yells up to me. "You can do this, Catie. It's scary, but don't let that stop you. It's fun." I snuggle into Claudia's lap. Charlotte is now at the top on the ladder waitin' for her turn. She's next after we go down. My big sister smiles and shouts, "Claudia, hang on tight to Catie. She's gonna love this." Claudia wraps her arms around my waist, lockin' her hands together, and I cling tight to her wrists.

Swoosh! We are off flyin' in the air.

We land sprawled out at the bottom on the slide. My eyes are as big as saucers, as Grandpa would say. Charlotte is flyin' down the slide straight towards us. She lands on her feet. We all break out into giggles. I stand brushin' the dirt off my pedal pushers and yell, "Whoopee!"

I spend the rest of the afternoon flyin' down the slide with my sisters. By the end of the day, I find the courage to go all by myself. Timmy says I'm brave 'cuz it took him two whole days of goin' down with an older neighborhood boy before he found the guts to go by himself. I smile, but I know my courage came from knowin' my sisters, my family was there to help. Mommy and Daddy are goin' to be so proud of me.

CHAPTER TWELVE

Marion
June 1994

I am as proud as a parent of Catherine's eagerness to learn. "What a remarkable story about you, as Catie, finding the gift of family courage. The armor is a gift from our Father God, and as you will see, this gift defines our identity and the power and authority the Lord has given us. Just like your example, you used the protection of your family and were able to war against your fears.

"The full armor of God is similar. It is something that we put on with the Holy Spirit but also something we can do together with other believers; our family."

"I think that makes sense, but could you give me some examples?" Catherine picks up her pen, ready to take notes.

"It might be best if we both stand while I demonstrate."

"Well, I did say that I liked visual aids." She moves her journal and pen to the side and stands. "I'm ready."

"For the sake of memory, I am going to demonstrate the armor from the top down, like getting dressed." I wave my hand down from my head to my toes. "It makes it easier to remember; however, the order in which the armor is listed is a fascinating study, perhaps for another time. We will start from the top by putting on the helmet of salvation."

I lift my hands and pretend to put on a helmet. "I find this component interesting because it covers your head, or better said your mind. You have experiential knowledge with the battle for your mind. You understand how the enemy tries to take away your truth, hope, and anything else he can steal. He is a thief. That is why this piece of armor is called the helmet of salvation. Salvation is the very thing the enemy cannot take away from you."

"Trust me," Catherine says. "I know that one all too well." She mimics me by placing a helmet on top of her head. "The enemy is always taunting my thoughts."

I look at Catherine and can imagine her as Catie, eager to learn and follow instructions. Then and now, she is searching for ways to overcome her battles and fears.

I move my hands down as if attaching another article of armor. "The breastplate of righteousness is a reminder that we have been made righteous through Christ. Jesus paid the price for our sins. His death reconciled us. Another way to say it is that he made us right with God."

Catherine places her hand on her chest. "Oooh, I like this one. It covers the heart." She closes her eyes, grinning. "It warms my heart, knowing I'm good with God. You know—in right standing, not that I deserve anything."

"That is correct; we are undeserving. God's sacrifice is about what he has done for us and not about anything we have done."

I wait for Catherine to open her eyes. I then move my hand down to my waist, sucking in my stomach as if tightening an imaginary belt. "I wish this belt was more like a corset to conceal my extra belly." I smirk.

"Oh, Marion, you look fine. You're your worst critic. I could say you need to apply Philippians 4:8 and focus on your blessings..." She winks. "...but I won't."

"You are right. It sounds as if the counseling classes you are taking are paying off. Touché."

We both exchange playful laughs and then continue.

"This is called the belt of truth. Some versions of the Bible say to gird your loins with truth. The loins of a warrior are quite vulnerable. This area of the body reproduces physical children, and in this case, it also refers to reproducing spiritual children. Another way of putting it is, as followers of Christ, we are to share our faith, in the hope that others will become believers and children of God."

Catherine follows along, simulating, putting on every piece of armor.

"Why don't people talk about this? I can't believe I'm the only person who battles with negative self-talk, fears, and demonic influence."

"Catherine, unfortunately, people do not want to admit that they lack knowledge about how to deal with their struggles. It makes them feel awkward and uncomfortable."

"I understand, but in the long run, isn't it better to eat some humble pie and be honest about your difficulties? After all, everyone has problems."

I grin on the inside, picturing Catie asking the common-sense questions of a curious child. An obvious reality flashes across my mind. Catie is Catherine, still curious, and fighting her way to overcome the obstacles in pursuit of truth—truth that will set her free.

With a small soft smile still in place, I answer her inquiry. "Challenges are a part of life and are never-ending. The enemy takes advantage of people who try to maneuver life alone without the help of others. Especially those individuals who isolate and keep their issues private. The demonic will pelt and hurl all sorts of lies and false beliefs about anyone and everyone, which brings me to the next piece of armor: The Shield of Faith." I push my arm out with force. "This shield is used to block the lies, deceptions, false accusations, and temptations of the enemy. This attack is one of the enemies' areas of expertise."

"Oh, that's a fact. I know that all too well." She raises her voice. "Satan knows how to get under the skin of so many people."

I circle my arm as I raise my mighty spiritual sword into the air. "And Catherine, this is your battle stance." I pose as a warrior on the battlefield with my shield extended, covering my torso, and my sword is aimed. "The sword of the Spirit is the Word of God. You use it by speaking aloud the very verses you have been memorizing. Proclaiming God's word is how you war against the battle for your mind and do combat against the demonic influences."

Catherine slashes her imaginary weapon into the air. My mind flashes to Catie and how brave she was to try to battle against Anna and her family. She was too young to comprehend a spiritual war, yet on other levels, she understood all too well. My eyes well up with tears. I lower my head so Catherine does not see. I wipe my eyes. She continues to swipe her sword and speak her proclamations.

"I am no longer going to listen to doubts and fears because the Lord didn't give me a spirit of fear. And," she says, her eyes looking upward. "I can do all things through Christ who strengthens me."

"You speak the truth." I nod in her direction. "The full armor of God reflects your identity, as well as the power and authority the Lord has given you to war spiritually. You must use these abilities to command the enemy to leave, in the name of Jesus Christ. Submit to God and stand firm, resist the devil, and he will flee. However, be aware, the world will always throw judgments, criticisms, and blows at you because they are, unfortunately, deceived and lost. They do not know God personally or his truth."

"So what you're saying is, they don't know what they don't know?"

"Correct. It is our commission and purpose to go and tell the world about Jesus and the hope we have in him. That, Catherine, my warrior, my soldier girl, is how we love God, love ourselves, and love others. Someday you will tell of your battles to help others fight in similar spiritual wars, which may include your family and even Charley.

"Remember, the enemy's most effective weapon is convincing

people that he does not exist. Your personal experience tells an entirely different story. It tells the truth about the enemy and how he tried to take you out by unraveling your world, but God has another plan. You are being rewoven by our Almighty Creator and Lord!"

M y eyes scan the open page of the file on my desk when a light knock sounds before the office door swings open. I peer over the top of my reading glasses as Catherine sashays into the room, a bounce in her step, wearing a cute floral print dress with a pair of sandals and a light cotton sweater.

"The way you are dressed, I surmise it is nice outside."

"Yes, finally. Colorado can go either way, hot or cold, but today is warm. The temperature gauge in my car said it was 82 degrees. I'm ready for some fun in the sun. I'm also excited because Hunter and I are going to the Buell theater tonight to see a play. We both love the theater."

Catherine takes a seat and quickly pulls out a piece of paper from her book bag and plops it on my desk.

I adjust my glasses to see the diagram and break into a big grin. It is the suit of armor I had given her at our last session. On the sides, she has written many notes and numerous references to scriptures.

"Marion," she says, an energy in her voice, "this last session was awesome. I've been studying the armor of God all week. And I have to say—it works. How do I know?" she says, with confidence, "Because the battle for my mind has quieted."

She rubs her palms together, eager to share her story.

"Here's what I've been practicing, Marion. Any time a *negative* thought tries to surface, I immediately tell it to shut up. I tell it to leave, in the name of Jesus Christ. Oh, and Hunter couldn't be more pleased because I've stopped entertaining the nit-picky thoughts I've had about him. You know, I'm nipping them in the bud, so to speak."

She smiles as if proud of herself.

I smile back. "That is great news, Catherine. I can see you have been hard at work." I hand the paper to her and say, "I'm sure your husband is enjoying the rewards of your endeavors."

"I have to admit, there has been less tension between us. When I hear anything in my mind that isn't true, I paraphrase one of the scriptures and say it out loud."

She cracks her journal and points to the 3-by-5 cards she has neatly tucked inside the pages. "These are my verses." Catherine fans the cards she has put to memory.

"Why do you think people refuse to look at the proven facts about Jesus and the Bible? For instance, one of my relatives said to me once, 'I don't want to hear about all that scuttlebutt and religious stuff. It's all a bunch of hearsay.' Don't they realize they're betting their lives on something they don't know much about?"

Catherine tosses her long soft curls over her shoulder, then lowers her brow.

"If my cousin would have been willing to check it out, she would have found that the Bible has been proven correct historically, archaeologically, scientifically, and prophetically. When I asked her to tell me an example of the 'scuttlebutt hearsay,' she backpedaled and said it was just something she had heard. It's a shame; so many lost souls parrot false beliefs without even studying the Bible themselves. What do you think, Marion?"

"There is one principle I believe that will always keep people in darkness," I say. "That is contempt—prior to investigation."

"Wow, Marion, you have such a way of giving clear meaning and zest to words. It's as if you speak with cardiac zapper paddles. Your words bring the truth to life."

"Speaking of truth and life, I don't believe we have discussed when you came to understand the truth of salvation? How old were you when you became a believer?" I ask.

Catherine's eyes light up with the look of a young child. "Oh, you bet, I remember. It's a long story. I was seven years old..."

Catie
Summer 1963

My eyes open. Yay! I slept through the night. I stretch, long and hard, then toss off the covers, full of energy. I'm sleepin' through the night, but only 'cuz Daddy has Friday and Saturday nights off now since we started goin' to church. He says he has enough seniority to make such a request, but he still has to work on Sunday nights. I don't mind, 'cuz he leaves after our bedtime.

I hurry to get ready for church. I'm much faster gettin' ready for church than I am for school. There's somethin' special 'bout this church and my Sunday school class.

After Mommy moved to heaven, Daddy and us kids din't go to church as much. I'm not sure why, but I sure missed it. I loved the singin' part best. I've never heard an angel sing, but everyone says Mommy sounded just like one when she sang in the gospel band with her family.

Daddy told me we needed to go back to church. He says it'll help our families grow closer and get along better. I know he means Anna and Melinda, 'cuz they're the only ones who don't get along. Shawnee's okay, but her mom and sister are startin' to rub off on her, but in a bad way. I bet Daddy's thinkin' a good dose of God might take some of the meanness out of Anna and her daughters. I hope he's right. But I'm pretty sure Daddy doesn't know they favor the devil over God.

We've been goin' to the same church for a while. All of June, July, and most of August. So far—no real changes, except for when we're actually there. Anna pretends to be sweet. She's really friendly with all the church folks, but I know she's just one big fat phony. She lies straight through her teeth to the ladies at church. She says things like, 'We would absolutely love to go on a picnic and have the children play together sometime.' She smiles politely then walks away actin' all concerned for us kids, like a hen gatherin' her chicks.

And today, like always, as soon as the church ladies are out of hearin' distance, Anna trashes them while we walk to the car.

"Did you see those clothes? Straight from the Goodwill." She rolls her eyes in disgust.

I don't want a busted lip, so I hold my tongue. After all, I could point out that my family's clothes are from Goodwill. But not Anna and her daughters. They wear rich people outfits.

Anna complains, non-stop. She mumbles underneath her breath till she gets cornered again by another mom invitin' her to do somethin'. I ignore them and skip ahead.

I climb into the back seat of our car to play the string game, Cat's Cradle, with Carolyn. Charlotte and Claudia do the same. Charley takes a turn here and there, 'cuz he's still learnin' to play.

A cool breeze blows through the open car doors. Melinda runs up and jumps into the car sayin' it's her turn to sit in the front seat, *again*. She leans her head over the back of the front seat and butts in on what we're doin'.

"Oh, the string game. Yuck." She wrinkles her nose and says, "That game's for sissies." She starts singin'. "Charley is a sissy. Charley is a sissy."

She chants on, givin' her best shot to bug him.

Charley gives it right back to her. "Melinda, what would you know about being a sissy or a girl? You're nothing more than a two-ton-Tessa. There's nothing girly about a huge whale like you."

He laughs at the look on her face. We join him, snickerin' till Anna makes her way to the car.

"These women are unbelievable. I had to pull myself away. I thought I'd never get out of the parking lot," she says.

Angry Anna lets out a huff and then slams the car door shut shakin' her head.

"Like I have time to listen to those *boring* women with all their casserole recipes and unsolicited suggestions on how to raise kids."

We sit still and silent, like squirrels being spied out by a dog. We watch and wait for Daddy. He shuffles across the parkin' lot.

Carolyn leans over and whispers. "No blow-ups, at least not yet."

I say under my breath, "That's 'cuz we're still in the parkin' lot where people can see her."

We double-cross our fingers hopin' we can get through the day without Anna goin' off her rocker. Especially today. We're supposed to have lunch at Granny Grunts and Grandpas. I love to see 'em. They take us to church sometimes too. My favorite days are when Grandpa gets to preach. Also, when they give us candy. Sucker days are special Sundays. It's when the visitin' children receive their height in suckers. I make sure to visit my grandparents' church on that day.

Granny Grunt says Grandpa would've had his own church if he hadn't broken his back workin' in the factory years ago. After that, I guess he only has enough energy for one job. But I don't think they count the farm and the garden. That must be his hobby.

I like their orchard trees the best, 'cuz we can eat as much fruit as we want. They have apple trees, peach trees, and cherry trees. One time Granny Grunt had to make a whole bunch of apple crisp dessert 'cuz when Charley was only two or three years old, back when Mommy was alive, he took just one bite out of every apple in the bushel basket. I was glad 'cuz apple crisp tastes even better than a plain old apple.

Charley said he tasted every one of those apples, 'cuz he wanted to see if all the apples tasted the same. Which they din't. He said some were sweet, and some were sour. The sour ones made Charley spit. But when Granny Grunt made the crisp apple dessert, she'd used all the apples. Even the sour ones. Granny always says, if you use enough sugar, everythin' turns sweet. Too bad she couldn't sweeten the likes of Anna.

As soon as Daddy slides into the front seat, Anna turns as sour as vinegar. If only I could spit her out, the way Charley did those apples. If I could, I would roll down the car window and spit her as far as the moon. Then we could drive home without Anna and her bratty kids.

CHAPTER THIRTEEN

Catie
Summer 1963

Another Sunday, and I bet today will be no different. Daddy pulls into the church parkin' lot. Anna sits next to her daughter in the front seat, bein' her usual sour-apple self. We all hustle out of the car, skippin' up the sidewalk.

Me and Carolyn bet Claudia a piece of cinnamon candy that Anna will pretend to be nice to all the church folks, as usual. *How can grown-ups be so blind? Can't they see that Anna's nothin' more than a big fat phony-bologna?*

Inside the sanctuary, Daddy motions for us to sit in our usual pew on the right side. We file in, youngest to the oldest. Charley shuffles in followed by Shawnee, then me, Melinda, Carolyn, Claudia, and

Charlotte. Our family takes up an entire row, with Daddy and Anna on the end next to the aisle.

I have to sit between Anna's two snotty daughters. They never seem to tire out of bein' big, annoyin' brats. They watch and scheme against me—even at church. I ask Charley to change seats with Shawnee so he can sit next to me.

The wood of the pine pews match the knotty wood on the ceilin' and it smells like we're in the forest. The songbooks must've been here forever, 'cuz they smell like Grandpa's basement, old and musty. It's a familiar scent, that makes me feel at home.

The pastor sprints up the three steps to the front of the altar. He takes the microphone in one hand, and his Bible is in the other. He sings the last of the chorus with the rest of the congregation.

His voice booms, but he doesn't sound like an angel—at all, and not anythin' like my real mommy when she used to sing. And I'm not sure why he has such a big smile on his face. Maybe he's happy 'cuz it's his favorite song. Or maybe he thinks it's funny to have such a sour voice. Only Claudia and me seem to notice. She peeks at me, then pinches her nose, indicatin' the preacher's voice is a real stinker. I giggle and cross my eyes back at her. She would know 'cuz she has such a pretty voice, like our real mommy.

Melinda reaches over and pinches me hard on the thigh. She points her finger at me like she's my boss. I crinkle up my nose and stick out my tongue. Usually, we would continue fightin', but my attention is jerked away to what the preacher is sayin'.

"Today, I'm going to be talking about the fall of Lucifer. He was one of the archangels, who at one time lived in the heavens. Lucifer wanted to raise his throne above God's throne. And if you can believe it, that foolish angel picked a fight with the one and only God Almighty, the Creator of the Universe!"

The pastor laughs.

"God's not someone to pick a power struggle with; needless to say, God, being all-powerful—won. He kicked Lucifer out of heaven. The Lord Almighty sent him tumbling to earth."

Pastor B.T. slams his foot hard onto the floor, makin' a big kaboom. He pretends it's the sound the archangel made when he hit the ground.

"After his fall, Lucifer took on many names: Satan, the devil, the serpent of old, the deceiver, the tempter, the liar, and the father of lies."

The preacher opens his Bible and lays it upon the pulpit.

"Please turn to Genesis 3:1-24."

I whisper to Charley. "Can you believe it? The devil used to be an angel? And God is the all-powerful one!"

I wrinkle up my nose and glare at Anna.

"I knew it, Charley! Anna and her family are all liars, just like Satan. And did you hear him? The pastor says that Satan is the father of lies."

We both bounce in our seats. I can't wait to hear more.

Melinda gnarls up her face and whispers, "You know none of this really matters."

"Shh. Shh. Shut up, Melinda, I can't hear the preacher." I speak loud enough for Daddy to hear. It works. He stretches his neck, and gives her *the look*.

I missed some of the Bible readin'. But I'm pretty sure he said Satan went into Adam and Eve's neighborhood. They lived with God in some beautiful garden. A serpent, who was actually the devil in disguise, talked Eve into eatin' a fruit from the one tree they weren't allowed.

I look at Charley, who's also listenin' to the pastor's every word. He leans over and whispers real quiet-like, "Uh-oh...she's in trouble now."

I'm thinkin' it musta been real temptin', like a wet paint or a do-not-touch sign, it just makes you want to touch the thing. For me, it's my curiosity that gets me in trouble—Eve musta been curious too. Adam as well,' cuz he also ate the fruit. I wonder how it tasted.

I listen on. Uh-oh! They're in double trouble now. They got kicked out of the magic garden that gave free groceries. Now they have to work hard for their food, like Grandpa on his farm. Satan's nothin' more than a big butthole, makin' promises he can't keep. Now he's gone and wrecked Adam and Eve's friendship with God. They're all sad, but God told the devil their fight wasn't over.

"Yikes," I turn to Charley, who's wide-eyed. We both know a threat when we hear one.

He asks, "Is God mean?"

I'm not sure, so I keep quiet.

Pastor B. T. lifts his Bible into the air, pointin' to a page. "No, the Lord didn't forget about us. Right here in Genesis 3:15, he made us a promise."

He reads on sayin' some big words, I ain't got a clue what they mean. And just when I scratch my head, the pastor says he's gonna explain it. Whew, I sit up, lean forward, and rest my elbows on the pew in front of me. I listen as hard as I can and try to ignore Melinda, who's pullin' on the hem of my dress.

"To put it simply," the pastor says, "we've inherited the condition of Adam and Eve. We start our lives separated from God. But the good news is God had a plan to restore our friendship with him. That plan was and is Jesus!"

The pastor stops, then looks up at the cross on the wall behind him. He slams his hand on his chest.

I jerk in my seat. *Is the preacher havin' a heart attack?*

I suck in a big breath and wait. Nope. He starts talkin' again. I let my air out, and it must've been loud, 'cuz my dumb, mean, step-sister hits me in my arm. I know she's tryin' to bug me. I ain't gonna let her make me miss out on what the pastor's preachin', but if he were singin', I'd slug her right back."

In a soft voice, Pastor B. T. says, "Jesus, God's dearly beloved son, was sent to live on earth. Jesus was crucified on a cross, shedding his blood, in order to pay the price for our sins and our rebellion. He was buried in a tomb and miraculously rose from the dead on the third day!"

The congregation claps, and some of the people even yell, "Hallelujah! Hallelujah! Praise the Lord!"

I stand up and look around at the ruckus. The pastor raises his hands in the air again, then slowly lowers them. As he does, the people sit down, includin' me.

"Yes. Jesus rose from the dead! His resurrection proved his deity and his power over death. Proving he was and is the Messiah. The Savior. And the Son of God!"

The pastor's words boom again. His shoutin' voice sounds much better than his singin' voice. It gives me goosebumps. I sit on the edge of my seat and hang on to the pew, listenin' to his each and every word.

I heard it—plain as day. Jesus is the most powerful. He has power over death! I can't wait to tell mean old Dean. I look around at all the people. The crowd is as excited as I am. I look to see if my family is hearin' this. My sisters and Daddy look straight ahead at the preacher, all wide-eyed.

Melinda pouts, as usual. She looks just like Anna, their hands crossed over their chests, like twins. Charley and Shawnee have sleepy eyes and lean on one another's shoulders. That's okay. I'll tell Charley later.

Pastor B. T. paces the stage. He marches from one end to the other.

"Jesus ascended into heaven and is seated next to God, speaking on our behalf."

Huh? What's ascended? That must mean he flew.

"Little ones," he pauses and looks in the direction of where me and my family sit. "Now, don't you be disappointed in Jesus leaving. There is a crucial reason."

Pastor B. T. looks right into my eyes. I twitch a little. It's so quiet you cudda heard a church mouse run across the floor. He pauses.

"Now listen up. Jesus' reason for leaving earth was to provide the way for us to be reunited with God. God, the father, sent his son, Jesus, to pay for our sins. And now God will send the Holy Spirit to live inside and empower those *who believe*. As his children, we can war against Satan's lies. His temptations. His deceptions." He pounds his fist into his palm in rhythm to his words. His voice is even stronger.

"As believers in Jesus Christ, we are no longer victims, but victors!"

I turn to Charley. "What does that mean? There are three of them? God is three?"

Charley shrugs his shoulders, not knowin' what the pastor's talkin 'bout either. He snuggles back up to Shawnee and closes his eyes.

Charlotte hears my question. She mouths, "Yes, it is called the trinity, meaning three. I'll explain it to you later."

Anna elbows her. She jumps in her seat. Claudia nods, assurin' me that they'll tell me later.

A chubby old church lady waddles up to the piano. She plays a slow song and sings the words like an angel. The preacher should let her sing all the time.

"Just as I am without one plea, to live for God who died for me…"

Pastor talks right over the church lady who's singin', but it doesn't sound like he's interruptin' her. Some of the other people join in and sing real quiet-like.

I know for a fact, everythin' the preacher says 'bout Satan is true, so I figure what he's sayin' 'bout Jesus must be true too! The only thing the pastor forgot to talk 'bout was the folks who follow Satan— the devil lovers. The people like Anna and her family. They're all big buttholes and are as mean as rattlesnakes. Maybe the preacher can't talk 'bout mean butthole people in church.

I wiggle in my seat, excited to hear more about Jesus, and the Holy Spirit. But I'm not sure 'bout Father God. He seems selfish to me. After all, he took Mommy to heaven to have someone to bowl with him. I don't like that part, but I love the part 'bout Jesus payin' for my sins and sendin' me a friend, the Holy Spirit.

I sit still in my seat and think hard 'bout what the preacher said. He musta read my mind, 'cuz I sure need Jesus to save Charley and me from Satan and his followers: Devil Dean, Buck, Poison Ivy, Anna, and the rest of the bunch.

Pastor B. T. lowers his voice and talks real soft.

"Now, while this music is playing, if there's anyone who would like to receive Jesus into their heart and life, you just make your way to the front of the altar, and I will lead you in a prayer to do so."

I jump in excitement. *Is it that simple?* All I have to do is go down to the pastor? That's what I needed to hear.

I peer at the aisle, like a cat watchin' a fish. I have to get past my family. Mainly, Anna. I'm afraid to excuse myself politely, sayin'

117

please, pardon me, and so on. That'll never work. Anna will snatch me up, tellin' me I'm too young, or some other phony excuse to keep me from gettin' to the pastor.

The music keeps playin'. The church lady sings. *'Just as I am, though tossed about. With many a conflict, many a doubt, Fightings and fears within, without, O Lamb of God, I come, I come.'*

My heart hurts. I want the pastor to understand that I need Jesus.

I need a plan to get to the preacher. I figure it out, I'll pretend I'm playin' red-rover, red-rover, then I can get by everyone, 'cuz I'm fast and quicker than anyone in my neighborhood. I take a deep breath, and then I make a mad-dash-run. I scram and run by everyone in my family.

Tears swell in my eyes, makin' the aisle blurry, but I make it to the front. When I reach the preacher, I'm out of breath, but that doesn't keep me from blurtin' out.

"I need Jesus to save my family and me. Especially me and my baby brother, Charley. I need Jesus to rescue me..." I take a deep breath. "Rescue us from the wickedness of the devil."

From the corner of my eye, I can see Anna talkin' to Daddy. She's tryin' to get out into the aisle—to get to me. I can't tell what she's sayin'. But she doesn't take her eyes off of me. We watch each other. Neither of us blinks.

I talk fast. The pastor kneels and places his arm around me. He leans in to hear me.

"Now slow down, little one. Slow down. I can't understand you. Okay, now what is it you were saying?"

Anna's in the aisle. She's comin' my way! Fast!

"I need Jesus in my life and to save my family and me from Satan. And the devil lovers."

The microphone tumbles off the stand. It squeals as it falls to the floor.

"Sorry, young lady."

He picks up the contraption and clicks it off.

"What..."

I don't wait for him to ask. All I can get out is, "I want Jesus in my life to save my family and me..."

Anna marches fast like a soldier and makes it to the front. She stands right next to me before I can finish. She slides her arm around my waist, under my cardigan sweater. She hides her hand from the pastor. She pinches me—hard. Anna looks directly into my eyes with threats only I recognize. The others only notice her big smile and not the deceivin' words that come out of her mouth.

"Darling, you don't need to bother Brother B. T. with all of your wishes. Jesus knows what's on your sweet mind and heart. Let the pastor pray with the others as well. It's not polite to take up such an important man's time."

I pull away and turn to face the pastor.

"But wait. How do I get Jesus in my life? Help me do it, Pastor B. T. !"

My voice cracks, and my fear rises. I grab the preacher's hand with a death-hold. I'm not lettin' go—come hell or high water, as Teenage Granny would say. There's a tap on my shoulder. I peak to see who it is. It's Daddy with all my sisters and Charley. Still, I won't let go of the pastor's hand.

"Well, Brother Forest, it looks like your whole family is here to ask Jesus into their hearts. Oh, what a glorious day it is." Pastor B. T. 's smile is as big as when he was singin'.

We all gather together holdin' hands. I have the preacher's hand on one side and Daddy on the other. Pastor B. T. leads us in a prayer, which we all repeat. It is simple and to the point.

"Lord Jesus, thank you for dying on the cross to pay the price for my sins. Thank you for forgiving me. Please send the Holy Spirit to come to live in my heart and life. I now receive the Holy Spirit and the power to live the life you ask of me. Thank you. In Jesus Christ's name, Amen."

The pastor's attention moves on to Anna, who's flirtin' with him. She compliments him on what an important spiritual man he is, usin' her slitherin' phony words. *Can't he see she doesn't mean a word of it?* She's only sayin' those things to distract him. She has to make sure to get him away from me.

I'm thinkin' I might be able to read Anna's mind just like the pastor was readin' mine earlier. She thinks he's an idiot—so easy to play. Well, maybe he is. I watch her thank him.

"Oh, pastor, we are so very thankful to have you in our lives. Our family depends on you to help us follow the Lord. You don't know how much we need to hear your wonderful preaching to strengthen our family. It's so tiring to be a mother of seven. I try so hard to be a good mother to these poor children."

Anna bats her eyes and twirls a curl from her blonde locks.

"You know, Pastor,…the children lost their mother?"

She makes a sad face, actin' like she's brokenhearted.

I feel sick.

Anna gushes on, "I need Jesus' help to carry this heavy burden."

She leans into the pastor's embrace as he prays, "Lord, please give Anna the grace and patience to be the loving mother she desires to be."

I could puke! It's always 'bout Anna. She makes sure she gets all the attention and looks like a saint. *And he believes her?* I scream on the inside. I wish I could make myself fart on command like Charley. I would rip off a big one right next to them.

CHAPTER FOURTEEN

Catie
Summer 1963

Claudia skips up the sidewalk to catch up with me. "Catie, isn't this a great day? We all have Jesus in our hearts. Mom would be so thrilled. I know Granny Grunt and Grandpa will be happy too. I'm gonna telephone them when I get home."

She wraps her arms around her shoulders like she's pretendin' our grandparents are huggin' her. Her smile is bright like the sun. Right then, it hit me. I'd invited Jesus into my heart. My jaw drops at the thought. That means he's on my side!

A warm feelin' spreads through my chest, kinda like Vicks Vapor Rub, but on the inside. I think back to what the preacher said. I'm not sure 'bout the power Pastor B. T. was talkin' bout, but I figure since the Holy Ghost is livin' in me, he'll let me know.

Once we're loaded up in the car, Daddy explains. "We'll all be baptized next week after church in the local river."

"What does that mean?" I ask.

Carolyn speaks up. "It's where they dunk you in the river, so your salvation takes. So it sticks and doesn't wear off. You know, the water washes off your sins."

Charlotte interrupts, "No, it doesn't. They do dunk you under the water, but you were saved when you accepted Jesus into your heart. When the preacher prayed for you."

"This is gettin' confusin', Daddy, What do they do? And why?"

"Peanut, baptism is where you're lowered into the water and then lifted back out. It is similar to Jesus dying, being buried, and rising from the dead. We acknowledge God and his love by doing this as an act of faith and appreciation." Daddy glances at me in the rearview mirror. "Understand?"

"I think so. We're sayin' thanks. And when we get dunked, it's like you're dead and buried, and when we come up from the water, it's like Jesus comin' up from the grave, right?"

"Hey...how did you get so smart?" He looks surprised at my answer.

I giggle. "When you explained it, I remembered I'd heard 'bout it last month at Grandpa's church on candy day."

The river is runnin' slow. Several leaves float on top of the water. I take a second to look around before I head down to the river in a mad-dash. Dirt puffs from under my feet as I skid down the path to join Pastor B. T. on the bank. My sisters shuffle down with ease. Daddy has Charley in tow. Anna lags behind actin' all timid 'bout what she pretends to be a steep slope.

I look up at Anna, lolly-gagin' at the top of the path. I shout to her, "This isn't hard, Anna. You've been down deeper ditches at your mother's farm. This path is nothin'."

She glares at me and gives me the stink eye warnin' me without words to shut up if I know what's good for me.

I stare back at her white blouse and her wrap-around blue seersucker skirt. I told her this mornin' that the preacher said to wear a dark-colored t-shirt with dark shorts or pedal pushers. She told me to mind my own business. I know what she's up to—and it's no good. I saw her put on a pretty see-through lacy bra under that white blouse. Anna has to make everythin' all 'bout her.

I clap while each of my sisters are bein' baptized. When it's my turn, I jump up and down in the dirt on the side of the bank. "Come on out, Catie." The preacher waves me over.

I wade into the river. It's as cold as ice water. My little piggies are squealin'. The mucky bottom feels icky, but Pastor B. T. wraps his arm around me and steadies me in the river. My toes sink deeper. Yuck.

"Do you understand why you are here today, Miss Catie?" he asks. It takes my attention off the muck and back to why I'm here.

"I sure do. I'm bein' baptized as a symbol of my salvation in Jesus Christ. When you dunk me, it represents Jesus' death, and when I come up, it's 'bout him bein' raised from the dead. Daddy and Grandpa call it his res-er-wreck-sun."

He smiles. "Yes, that's right, Catie. Resurrection."

"On last Sunday, when I prayed and asked Jesus to save me and my family from the devil, is that when I got the power of the Holy Ghost to win against evil and Satan? And is that why they call it born again, 'cuz you get a new spirit? A holy one, instead of the bad one I had before I asked Jesus into my life?" I wiggle with excitement.

He pinches my cheek. "Well, I don't believe I could have said it any better. Yes, Miss Catie, you were born again when you first believed in Jesus and what he has done for us. And the Holy Spirit that is now living inside of you," he points to my heart. "will provide you the power to live a godly life, just as God created you to do."

He turns to Daddy. "Forest, this daughter of yours, has a unique understanding of spiritual things. She's quite intuitive. I wouldn't be surprised if the Lord doesn't call her into ministry. How old is she?"

I answer for Daddy. "I'm seven."

"Okay, Miss Catie, who's seven. Are you ready to be baptized?"

"Yes sir, but do you think you should dunk me twice? My sister says the water washes off my sins, and I have one, for sure, that's really bad." My mind goes to baby Jesse.

He smiles lettin' out a soft chuckle.

"Catie, Jesus paid the price for all of your sins. One time is enough."

"Okay. I'm ready then." I smile as big as I can, then nod yes.

"I baptize you in the name of the Father, the Son, and the Holy Spirit."

I pinch my nose and take a deep breath. He places his handkerchief over my mouth and dunks me under the water. As I'm comin' up, my siblin's clap.

Daddy carries Charley into the water. The pastor moves closer to the shore 'cuz my brother is so short. Pastor B. T. reaches out for Charley. As soon as he is finished bein' dunked, Daddy realizes he forgot the towels in the car. He hurries to the bank to fetch them; all the while, he's pullin' Charley through the water.

Charley laughs and shouts, "Hey, everybody, look at me. I'm swimming."

We waddle up the bank like little ducklin's followin' Daddy onto the grassy area where the rest of the church families wait for their turns to be baptized. The cool mornin' air makes us shiver in our wet clothes. Daddy hands Charley off to Charlotte and runs to the car.

Anna wades into the water. She makes all sorts of ohh's and ahh's to grab the attention of the families standin' on the bank of the river. I frown and give her a dirty look behind her back. She holds her hands in the air actin' all weak and helpless and in need of the pastor's assistance. She's as helpless as a—I can't think of anythin' that's helpless right now, but Anna is anythin' but weak or powerless.

The pastor's mouth moves, but I can't hear what he's sayin'. With his arm across Anna's back and his hanky over her mouth, he lowers her into the water. The other families watch from the bank. They wait for Anna to come up out of the water so they can cheer and clap.

Anna stands tall, but no one cheers. The whole crowd goes dead silent. Anna slowly dawdles through the water to the bank in her see-through blouse. I knew I was right. She's showin' off her lacy bra and breasts for all to see.

The pastor looks over at Anna and realizes what's happenin'. He runs through the water and up the bank to grab his sports coat. He moves so fast he beats Anna to the shore, who purposely takes her good sweet time.

"Oh, my goodness," she says lookin' down at her chest as if unaware and so embarrassed—yet never once covers herself. Are you kiddin' me? Does she think her pretendin' is foolin' anyone?

I pray quietly. "Dear Jesus, please, don't let Pastor B. T. or any of the other husbands look at Anna. She's just like the devil she follows."

I watch her twist, shakin' side to side like she's tryin' to splash off the water, lookin' like the dog that she is. She pulls at her blouse, attemptin' to lift the wet sticky fabric off her skin. Anyone knows the best way to cover up is to cross your arms over your chest.

The pastor lays his jacket on Anna's front, like a blanket. Of course, Anna wants more attention. She takes it off.

"Oh, Pastor, I don't want to get your nice sport coat all wet."

Daddy hustles down the path with the towels. Carolyn runs up and grabs one. She wads it up and throws it right into Anna's head. Daddy sees what's happenin'. He quickly walks in front of Anna, blockin' the view from all of those who are gawkin'.

"Woman, what were you thinking? Cover yourself up!" His voice is firm.

I run over and stand next to him and Anna. "Daddy, I told her this mornin' the pastor said dark t-shirts."

Anna sends me a dirty look. To my surprise, I send her one right back and then tug on my daddy's shirttail. "It's your turn." I point to the water. "The pastor is waitin' on you."

I clap extra loud when he comes up out of the water. I feel different—light. I'm not afraid. I know for sure, if anythin' happens, Daddy and my sisters will be goin' to heaven to be with Jesus and Mommy. I'm especially excited for me and Charley havin' tickets to heaven, 'cuz we may be goin' there sooner than the rest of our family.

125

Marion
September 1994

S leep and rest last night was less than heavenly. My first cup of coffee this morning is a necessity, as I endeavor to wake up completely and start the day. Notebook in hand, I curl in my wing-backed armchair near my office window to jot my impressions from my recent sessions with Catherine.

The last several months have been moving along in a positive direction with Catherine. She remembers quite readily. The memories are flowing, and she is able to identify her false perceptions. Her trust in the Lord is enabling her to find the truth.

These recollections are answered prayers. There have been some highs and lows within her emotions, but that is to be expected. Catherine continues to persevere with reasonable reactions to her past being unearthed and exposed.

The ink skips, leaving out several letters in my notes. I am unable to finish writing the last words in Catherine's file. I vigorously push hard on the pen, scribbling circles. A few specks of ink emerge until it scrapes empty along the paper. I toss the pen in the metal wastebasket under my desk. It clanks as it bounces off the side into the bottom of the empty basket. I grab another pen from my desk and finish my final entry, September.

I say a prayer for my client and then set the folder on the top of the pile. I am prepared for my day.

C atherine arrives on time, as usual, for her Friday afternoon appointment. She seems on edge, tapping her foot, and distracted. I place my finger to my lips, thinking.

"Catherine, it seems that you are experiencing some significant tension."

She twists her hips from side to side, appearing uncomfortable. Her foot tapping is even faster. "I feel super stressed out today." She scans the office as if looking for something. "I've been coming to this office for two years now. Not that it isn't beautiful, which it is but, can I make a...perhaps an unusual request?"

"You are always free to speak your mind, Catherine," I say, puzzled by her question.

"Can we go outside or maybe even go for a walk instead of having our session here? I need a change of scenery. The fresh air and sunshine help me when I feel stressed."

I ponder her suggestion, wondering if conducting her appointment outside would pose any problems. "I am fine with your idea; however, with the understanding and agreement that I cannot guaranty privacy." I raise my brow in question. "I have no control over what is heard in a public setting. Of course, if you agree, I will use the utmost discretion when needed."

"I know, Marion. I'm in total agreement and will take full responsibility. I'm cool with getting out of this office and appreciate you moving out of your comfort zone with the proper protocol."

Catherine and I are more than a counselor and client. We have become trusted friends, which is rare but not unheard of with faith-based counseling.

"This will be fine for today and on occasion, but you do realize this would never work for memory work."

"Of course, no worries." She scoots to the edge of the love seat.

"Well, okay then, Catherine. Besides, a walk could do my body some good in the weight loss department." I stand to gather my coat and supplies.

"Great, I could really use the distraction. Thanks, Marion. I'm sure the crisp air will help clear my head."

I insert a small writing tablet, my miniature-size Bible, and pen into my pocket. After zipping my jacket against the cooler fall air, we set out toward the west-side of campus. A few early fallen leaves crunch under our feet as we take in the mountains' breathtaking views in the distance.

I purposely make small talk for a while, and then we stroll in silence for a bit. Catherine's hands are jammed into her pockets, and she stares at the sidewalk as we progress. Finally, she breaks the silence.

"Marion, I hate to say it, but unfortunately, things are tense at home. Hunter and I are like two ships passing in the night. He's always busy in the office most evenings if he's not at some meeting or group thing. He's constantly doing something but not with me. Something's off with us. I'm afraid we're drifting apart."

Catherine squints her eyes against the late afternoon sun. I wonder if she is in deep thought or perhaps has a headache.

"Let us sit for a moment on the bench over here." The bench looks inviting, shaded by a brilliantly colored tree. After we settle, I pause to give her time. "Did you have a fight?" I inquire after a few minutes.

"No. We get along okay when we're together. We're just not together very often. Even when he's home, Hunter doesn't feel present. I can tell something's askew."

She stares off towards the mountains for a moment and rubs one of her knuckles absentmindedly. "It reminds me of Edward. It's hard to put my finger on it, but I feel an emotional distance."

She closes her eyes as if thinking it through. I allow her as much time as she needs, gazing at the Colorado blue sky interspersed with wispy clouds. When she is ready, she turns back to me. "When I've tried to bring the subject up, Hunter denies any distance between us. He becomes defensive. He says everything's fine. On the surface, everything looks the same. But it's not. I sense something isn't right. It unnerves me."

I rub my finger over the edge of the wooden bench. "Relationships can be complicated with legitimate concerns. Has Hunter said anything about there being a problem between the two of you? Do you have any proof or concrete reasons for your suspicion?"

She rolls her shoulders and stretches her neck, side to side. "No, not really. Maybe it's nothing." Catherine shrugs half-heartedly. "Maybe I'm just paranoid?"

I pull out my pocket Bible. "I suggest you take a look at 2 Timothy 1:7." I hold the book out so she can read it.

She reads the verse slowly, concentrating on each word.

"'For God has not given us a spirit of fear, but of power and of love and of a sound mind.'"

I explain. "The enemy and his cohorts use fear to bring strife and division. God's word states the truth in plain English. God did not give you a spirit of fear. So if God did not give you the spirit of fear, who did?"

Catherine draws her brows together. "The enemy? If the spirit is from the enemy, it must be demonic. Right?"

"Putting valid fears aside, like being robbed or threatened for your life. Yes, there is a demonic realm within our reality that can influence us, especially when dealing with unmerited fears. When you are afraid, worried, anxious, distracted with fear…do you feel powerful?"

"No, not at all. I feel the opposite. Powerless, weak, and timid."

"Do you feel loved?" I arch an eyebrow, encouraging an answer.

"No, I struggle with feeling valued, loved, or cherished. I feel alone and lonely in my own house. Especially lately." She frowns and looks down. The soft breeze teases a tendril of loose hair.

"And what about your mind, does it feel sound?"

"Are you kidding?" she smirks, twisting her fingers together. "No! I'm a wreck. Complaining doesn't seem to help. I feel frightened, doubtful, powerless, and unloved. My mind whirls around like a tornado, looking for a place to collide."

She tips her face to the sky for a few seconds.

"Catherine, my dear, that type of fear is not of the Lord, but from the enemy. Remember, when fear comes knocking at your door, ask yourself, whose thoughts are these? Also, ask, why am I feeling such emotions? If you determine it is not a realistic fear and not from the Lord, then take authority over the thoughts. Command the fear to leave, in the name of Jesus Christ."

She looks at me, doubtfully.

"Catherine," I say, my voice straightforward. "Remember, God promises us power and authority over evil."

She blows out a long breath and nods her head in agreement. I suspect she is feeling an array of emotions, one of which may be that she needs a break.

I stretch the ache in my back as I stand. "How about we stop at the campus coffee shop for a cup of your favorite drink? Then we can discuss this more. Coffee and cocoa, right?"

"Yes, that would be great. Thanks, Marion." Catherine stands and stretches, and we turn in the direction of the student center.

The coffee shop feels cozy after the crisp fall air outside. The décor is made from old barn wood, accented with antiques giving it a farmhouse feel. The rich smell of coffee brings everything up a notch.

I carry a tray with one cup of black coffee and one cup of her special order, half coffee and half cocoa. I make room for a plate of sweet, shortbread cookies that looked so decadent in the display case. My stomach growls, desperately craving a treat. I tell myself, NO, determined not to break my diet. The floor creaks under my feet as I walk across the coffee shop carrying the tray. Catherine looks up.

"Oh, yum. I'm always hungry for cookies." She selects a cookie and dips the shortbread into the mocha mixture. Placing it to her lips, she sighs. "Umm. That is heavenly."

It does not seem fair that Catherine can eat whatever she wants and maintain her slim figure. I even look at a cookie and swell up ten pounds. I push those thoughts aside, realizing I must maintain self-control over my own choices and not compare my metabolism with others. This diet and proper nutrition is my battle; no one else's.

While Catherine munches, she thumbs through her journal and scrolls her finger down the page as if speed-reading. She stops at a particular section.

"Marion, what you just told me backs up the verse in Luke 10:17-19. The verse where Jesus sent out the seventy men to do ministry."

Catherine reads aloud. "Listen to this. 'Then the seventy returned with joy, saying, "Lord, even the demons are subject to us in Your name." And Jesus said to them, "I saw Satan fall like lightning from heaven. Behold, I give you the authority to trample on serpents and scorpions, and over all the power of the enemy, and nothing shall by any means hurt you.'

"This is starting to make sense." She gives a careful nod. "I've been tormented by fear, worried about Hunter pulling away, and possibly even leaving. I'm stressed out because of the impact my memories have had on us and our marriage. You know how he hates conflict." She raises both palms. "Unfortunately for him, resolve and confrontation could be my middle name. I can't tell you how many times I've entertained thoughts of him regretting marrying me."

She lifts her eyebrows and gives a weak smile. A crumb of shortbread clings to her lower lip.

"Marion, what I hear you saying is, I don't have to give in to the fear or shame about Anna and her family, as well as my fears about Hunter's love. I need to accept the truth and receive the forgiveness God offers me. I never realized how much my struggles interlink with the spiritual realm."

She pushes up her sleeves to her elbows. "Again, it comes back to the battle for my mind." She swipes her hand through the air, emphasizing the unseen.

I allow Catherine time to reflect on this new revelation. I catch a brief look at the clock. Our session is coming to a close. "This is why scripture tells us our battle is not with flesh and blood, but against spiritual wickedness." I finish the last sip of my coffee. "The word instructs us to take every thought captive, so we are not paralyzed by fear. This is a war, a battle for your mind. So it is high time to use the shield of faith against the fiery darts of lies and deceptive accusations of the enemy."

"You're so right, Marion."

The tense expression she had when she arrived has vanished, yet a sudden coldness hits me at my core. Nervousness settles in my stomach. I discern a valid concern for Catherine's suspicions as we walk to the door.

CHAPTER FIFTEEN

Catherine
December 1994

The doorbell rings. Hunter sprints to answer the front door. I follow. I'm nervous yet excited to have time with my in-laws. We make a point to see them several times a year, but living in different states makes our visits even more precious.

The Christmas season is a wonderful time to spend with family, yet it makes me miss my family even more.

We open the door and say, "Hello" in unison. Hunter and his father, Jefferson, hug, followed by high-pitched verbal squeaks. Since childhood, he and his father have been making such sounds at each other, a strange but sweet endearment.

Jefferson is a quiet man, reserved, and picks his words carefully; that is when he speaks. But he always has a warm smile for me, which speaks louder than words. He is a full head shorter than Hunter. His mother says Hunter gets his height and blonde hair from her father.

Like Hunter, Marie is friendly and always wants to make sure everyone is having a good time. But today, her usual warm bear hug is absent, and she feels rigid and cold. I sense her distance as she immediately pulls away.

Looking behind her, I search for Hunter's two sisters: Lee, who is a year and a half older, and Harriet, who is a year and a half younger. No one is there. "Where are the girls and Harriet's boyfriend, Barry? Aren't they coming?"

Hunter's mother spits out a stiff, "No!"

Hunter, who consistently avoids conflict, nervously speaks up. "Hey, Dad, do you want to go into the garage to see my ongoing projects?"

Really? He's leaving me to fend on my own. Alone. Abandoned in the middle of whatever is brewing within his mom? Unbelievable.

"Marie, let me take your coat."

She peels it off her arms and hands me her jacket.

I force an awkward smile. "How about we go into the kitchen for a cup of coffee?"

She nods. The tension is thick, like cold molasses.

"Any sweets? I have cookies, Danish, or some biscotti."

"No. Thank you."

Her short-snipped answers make my nerves dance on edge. *If there's a problem, just say it. Come on. I can't read your mind.* If she were in my family, that's what I'd say, but Hunter says his folks never discuss problems.

Instead, they prefer to run off and hide—like an ostrich, putting their heads in the sand. I hate beating around the bush. Why can't she say what's bugging her? *Breathe. Talk to her with gentleness and respect. Maybe she doesn't know how to be open about her concerns.*

"Marie, is something wrong?" I pause. Silence. "Has something happened?"

Marie perches on a barstool at the kitchen island. She picks up a spoon and stirs her coffee; the spoon clanks loudly against the sides.

She usually is a sweet, kind, and caring person, but not today. Her coldness, plus lack of words, bothers me.

I lean in close; my hands press against the island. "I can sense that you're upset."

She sips her coffee, her eyes cast downward.

"If you're uncomfortable discussing it, I understand. I only want to make sure you're not upset with me. Or Hunter."

She glances down and fumbles with her napkin. "Well…" She clears her throat. "Harriet told me…YOU said…her boyfriend wasn't welcome…ummm, in your home."

She looks up for a second, searches my face for an answer, and then lowers her eyes and continues to stir her coffee.

I'm taken off guard. I'm instantly skeptical of Harriet, Hunter's sister. I suspect she is using this blatant lie to cause strife and division. Is Harriet blame-shifting? Why?

"Wow," is the only word I can manage.

My emotions race—igniting my triggers. My mind flashes back to a time where I was blamed for something I hadn't done. Dean's voice rings in my ears, tormenting me. 'It was your hand on the knife. Your hand! Your hand!' This haunting memory sends me in a whirl.

Breathe deep, breathe deep. That's the past. It's over. Don't go numb, don't do it, talk calmly. Hunter's mother is a kind and loving woman. She only needs more information.

"Marie, I assure you I never said any such thing. I haven't spoken to Harriet in months. Last week, however, I did overhear a conversation between her and Hunter about her boyfriend coming for Christmas. Hunter didn't say the man wasn't welcome." I take my time, making sure to talk slow and precise, to prevent any misunderstandings.

"Harriet told Hunter that she preferred to have Lee stay at our home along with you and Jefferson. That way, she could be alone with her boyfriend at her house. Hunter wouldn't agree."

I lean in towards Marie until she looks at me. "He's a protective brother. He merely said their sister should stay at Harriet's house as a chaperone since the man is still married."

"Going through a divorce," Marie interjects.

134

I know all too well about married men dating before they're divorced. An irritation rises within me toward Harriet for dating a married man. I know it isn't over until it's over, and even then, it's not necessarily over. I put those thoughts aside and continue.

"I know Hunter's heart is to protect Harriet from being the rebound girl. He doesn't want Barry to use her or hurt her."

Marie scrunches her brow. She looks away. I lean toward her to make eye contact. "Why would Harriet make up such a story? Why would she lie?"

Silence. Marie stirs her coffee. Her lips are tight.

Hunter shuffles into the kitchen, along with Jefferson, both wearing big smiles. "So, what's to drink, Catherine?" Hunter asks.

I force a smile. "What would you like?"

Marie looks relieved to have her husband and son back in the room. Her face softens. She smiles and straight away asks Hunter and Jefferson what they were doing in the garage. The three of them get lost in conversation.

I prepare hot coffee for all and add a splash of cocoa in Hunter's and my cups. I pour Marie a refill then busy myself around the kitchen.

"Hey Catherine, it looks like my sister, Lee, and Barry aren't coming," Hunter blurts out as if it's just a matter of fact. He turns toward his father. "So, Dad, is Harriet still planning on going downtown to see the Christmas lights?"

"Yep. She should be here shortly."

His mother doesn't speak a word. I'm unnerved by the awkwardness. How can his family simply pretend there isn't an issue? Talk about the elephant in the room. I hate being accused of something I haven't done. And even more, not being allowed to resolve the issue. My chest tightens like a fist, and my resentment rises.

I know Hunter senses my uneasiness. I tried to bring it up. I was in the middle of saying, 'It appears that Harriet has misled your mother about her boyfriend's visit—' He cuts me off. His brief scowl tells me he expects me to write it off, whatever it is that's bothering me. He wants me to start fresh, like turning the page to a clean sheet of paper —in other words, pretend nothing is wrong.

Marion
December 1994

I write page two in the upper right-hand corner of a fresh piece of paper. As needed, I continue to make notes as I listen to Catherine.

A few stray snowflakes hit my office window, but my space heater keeps it toasty inside. Definitely warmer than the Christmas visit Catherine just endured.

"What I hear you say is that your husband's sister lied to his mother about you. And when he dismissed your concerns in front of his family, you did not feel protected. Was it because he did not intervene on your behalf?" I say, glancing up. "It must have been disappointing to have Hunter ignore the problem within his family. I understand you were upset about being blamed for something you had not done."

I slide the tissue box in her direction.

"Marion, you see, undeserved blame triggers me. I hadn't done anything wrong with his sister, yet she blamed me, and Hunter allowed it by not speaking up for me. The emotions were intense—I flashed back to feeling unprotected, like when I was a child. As an adult, I know my dad and siblings didn't have a clue as to what was happening. But I wonder why? How could they not know?"

She leans forward, the ends of her teal silk scarf swinging. "And why doesn't Hunter notice? This is not the first conflict his sister has instigated. Can't he see the mistreatment? Why doesn't my husband protect me? Why does he pretend there isn't a conflict? Why does he avoid confrontation? Especially when it affects me? Especially when it triggers me in such a deep and painful way."

She makes a deep throaty sound and tosses her hands up. "Sometimes, I feel invisible to Hunter, as if I don't matter. I feel small, insignificant, and not important."

Catherine falls back into the sofa. Her shoulders droop, her spine bows. She stares at the wadded tissue in her hand, and her lower lip quakes.

I take advantage of the moment to minister counseling.

"Catherine, please allow yourself to feel these emotions. Embrace your awareness of feeling small, insignificant, and unimportant. Permit yourself to follow the emotional trail of when you have previously felt this way."

Catherine leans back into the cushion and closes her eyes.

"Focus on feeling unprotected and allow yourself to remember when you felt this way before, preferably the very first time you felt these emotions."

I watch the movement of her eyes under closed lids. Red blotches appear on her cheeks, and tears stream down the side of her face.

Catherine slowly speaks. "It was a bright, sunny Sunday…"

Catie
Indian Summer
1963

It's a bright, sunny Sunday after church. It's September, but what people call an Indian summer. Daddy says they call it that 'cuz the weather is warm well into autumn, and the Indians would stay longer before movin' to their winter homes. Sometimes they would help themselves to the Pilgrims' groceries without askin'. But I like it 'cuz it's still sunny and hot so we can still go swimmin'.

A mild breeze blows, like Teenage Granny's window fan that keeps me cool when I'm at her house. We take our assigned seats in the car, thrilled to be on the way to the lake. I love lake days, playin' on the beach, diggin' in the sand, and splashin' in the water. We've packed our buckets and shovels. Daddy promises us unlimited time to play in the water and build sandcastles.

"Well, kids, it's going to be a bluebird day," he says from the front seat. The wind blows through his shiny brown hair.

I watch out the window and search the clear sky for any bluebirds. Not a one. "Daddy, there aren't any bluebirds. The only bird I've seen so far is a black crow."

Daddy chuckles slow and easy. "A bluebird day has nothing to do with bluebirds; it's just a way to describe a pretty blue sky."

"So why don't you just say it's a pretty blue sky?"

My sisters' giggles, snorts, and laughs come from all directions. They're makin' fun of me. Even Charley kicks his little legs up and down in the seat and laughs too. I don't like bein' made fun of, not one bit. I sit back, cross my arms over my chest, and stay quiet in the backseat of our blue station wagon.

Daddy looks at me in the rearview mirror. "Catie Kay, you better stop pouting, or one of those bluebirds might just land on your lower lip that's sticking out like a perch."

I suck in my lip to avoid any more teasin', but my brows remain scrunched, with a look strong enough to kill if anyone says one more word about those stupid bluebirds. It's not my fault that adults, especially my dad and Teenage Granny, say things that don't make sense. Like the elephant in the room, and now the bluebird day. Sometimes I feel like I can never win. It seems like someone's always pesterin' me.

We pull up to the gate at the lake. A short man with black-framed glasses, like the singer, Buddy Holly, trots over to Daddy's window.

"A park-pass for the day, sir?" He takes a quick peek into our car.

"Yes, I'm taking the kids to the lake for the day. You can't beat these Indian summers going clear into September. I'm hoping my kids can burn off some of their rowdy energy." He smiles at the man. "And I can relax a bit. Maybe even get some shuteye. I work the graveyard shift."

Daddy pulls a dollar from his wallet to pay the man.

"That's rough. Good luck to you, mister." The man tips his head.

We drive up to a perfect parkin' place right near the sandy beach. I'm itchin' to get to the water but have to do my share of carryin' all the stuff we brought. Daddy fills my arms with towels. The other kids carry toys, blankets, and a sack of popcorn for our snack.

Daddy holds my elbow, then motions for Charlotte to grab Charley's hand. We all start walkin' to find our spot on the lake.

Goody-goody-gumdrops, I'm glad Anna din't come, 'cuz she and Melinda always wreck our fun. Shawnee's okay if Melinda's not around, but today Anna and her two brats went to Poison Ivy's house.

W e arrive home before the streetlights come on. The sun gave a rosy shine to my nose, on the tops of my shoulders, and across my back. I don't mind the sunburn. It's well worth it. Soon, it'll be peelin'. Then, we'll be like monkeys peelin' off each other's dead skin. We like to see who can get the biggest piece.

I hear Anna callin' from downstairs.

"It's dinnertime. Come on down."

I gobble up my macaroni and cheese with sliced hot dogs. Bein' the first one up the stairs, I'm the first to take a bath. I'm extra tired when I crawl into bed. I drift off into dreamland.

The door creaks. I don't know the exact time, only that it's dark outside when someone comes into the bedroom. I feel my shoulders bein' shaken. I hope it's one of my sisters. I slowly peek out of one eye.

Uh, oh, it's Anna!

CHAPTER SIXTEEN

Catherine
December 1994

Hunter and I peek out the window as his sister pulls up to the curb, parks, and stomps up the driveway. The door flings open, and Harriet bolts through, without even a hello to her brother or me. She makes a beeline to her mother and father to embrace them with an overly long and needy hug. She begins a conversation, asking about their drive to Denver, completely ignoring Hunter and me.

Harriet's rudeness dumbfounds me, and my anger burns. *How dare she lie about me. And what nerve she has to come into our home and treat us like we don't exist.*

I step forward to confront her. My husband takes my arm and gently pulls me back. He speaks up. "Hey, everybody, how about we get in the car to go see the Denver Christmas lights and have some dessert and cocoa? Mom, Dad, do you remember me telling you about the great pastry shop on the Sixteenth Street Mall?"

"Sure do," Jefferson pipes in and then fetches their coats. He helps Marie with hers, and they head to the car.

I hang back to shut off the lights and lock up. When I walk out the door, Hunter has pulled the car out of the garage.

Hunter and his parents have seated themselves in the front seats. *My seat.* It appears they have conveniently left room for me to sit in the back seat with Harriet. *Cowards.*

I climb into the SUV and notice Harriet is without a coat. "Hey, where's your coat? Did you forget it in the house or your car?"

"I didn't wear one." She stares straight ahead.

"No worries, I have several. I'll hop out and get you one of mine."

"No. I don't need a coat." Still, she stares straight ahead.

"Are you sure? It's freezing outside! Walking around downtown Denver without a coat would be miserable. I really don't mind lending you one of mine." I open my door to slip out. "It'll only take me a minute."

Harriet screams as if I've slammed the door on her fingers. Her face trembles. "I said, I DO NOT NEED A COAT!"

Not only is she loud, but she's also leaning toward me and in my space. My eyes widen. I clench my teeth in anger, and my pulse races.

Who does she think she is yelling at me when I'm just trying to help her?

"Just get into the car, Catherine." Hunter rolls his eyes at his sister.

I pause, unwilling to let it go. "What? Come on, Harriet. You forgot your coat in the dead of winter? Are you for real? You've lived in Colorado for years. What's this all about?" My sarcasm and volume increase as I go on. I stare into her eyes, demanding an answer.

Is this her plan to sabotage the evening? Oh, I can see through her tactics. Poor pitiful Harriet doesn't have a coat, so everyone has to change their plans.

Hunter clears his throat to attract my attention. I look at him in the rearview mirror. His eyes cut toward his parents. I'm making them uncomfortable.

I don't believe this. Hunter and his parents put up with her crap. That's ridiculous! Unbelievable! So, we're going to pretend the elephant isn't in the room?

No one speaks. The silence screams, shhh! They all look forward like rigid, wooden nutcrackers. *Chickens.*

Catie
Indian Summer
1963

I slowly open my eyes. Anna's finger is on her lips, meanin' I'm not to speak. I lay stiff, like wood, and wait. A small light shines in from the hallway. She motions for me to get movin'. If I weren't such a *chicken*, I'd scream and wake my sisters. But I obey and slip out of bed. I squint to see my way out of my bedroom, makin' sure not to wake anyone.

Once downstairs, I see Anna has my jacket and extra clothes laid out on the arm of the sofa. Charley's bundled in his summer windbreaker. His small fists rub at his eyes. I open my mouth to ask a question, but Anna covers my lips, givin' me the shhh sign. Once we were in the car, I ask, "Where are we goin'?"

"Since you and Charley had such a fun time at the lake today, I have a special surprise for the two of you."

Charley asks, "But, Anna, where are the other kids? Don't they want to go? And how about Dad?"

"Your Dad already left for the night shift. The other kids didn't want to come."

"She's lyin'," I say under my breath. "I like surprises, but would rather be surprised by gettin' to sleep."

"Don't you start, Catie Kay!" Anna sneers. Turnin' in the seat, she takes the bottle of medicine from her handbag and pours each of us a big spoonful. We both gulp it down. She throws the blindfolds at us. "Put these hankies on each other." We've done this so many times that we don't ask why anymore. We know the routine.

"Charley put Catie's on first."

Charley does as she orders. I lift the cloth from one eye so I can see to tie his in a firm bow.

"Now lay down in the back seat. We'll be at your surprise before you know it." She lets out a playful giggle.

I fall off to sleep. How long? I don't know. It seems like only seconds before Anna wakes us. Jerkin', shakin', and yellin'.

"Get up! Come on. Let's go! Let's go!"

Swiftly, she hurries us out of the car. It takes a minute for my eyes to focus. We're in some parkin' lot. I see the familiar white church in the distance. We never get to go inside through the front doors. I remember the steep steps leadin' down the hill. We're always ushered to the back cellar door and its creepy dark dirt floors.

The foul smells of evil reek inside my nose. My stomach lurches at the familiar stench that smells like decayin' maggots in a garbage can. I smell it whenever I'm with this bunch. They all have those black eyes too. But not everyone has the same devil eyes and wicked laughs like Buck and Devil Dean. Their eyes match their wicked hateful hearts. Somehow I know they're worse, more horrible than the others.

Once inside, Anna stands behind us. She shoves another spoonful of medicine at us. I'm grateful that it's not the bitter syrup she gave us in the car. It's the cherry-flavored stuff. Yummy.

"Swallow this. It will keep you from feeling sick."

"The only thing that makes me feel sick is the smell." I plug my nose.

Charley nods. "What's that stink?"

"I have no idea what you're talking about, but if you want to have another fun beach day, you'll need to take this sweet syrup because the sun isn't out. I don't want you to catch colds from playing in the water."

Anna points at somethin' on the other side of the room. We twist our heads and see large barrels and troughs of water. My eyes fix on the colorful buckets and shovels lyin' on the floor next to a pile of sand. Maybe Anna means it.

"Can we go play? Really?" I cock my head, hopin' for her permission.

"Sure. Have fun, but first, another teaspoon of the medicine."

She lifts the brown glass bottle. We obey, gulpin' down the cherry liquid, then skip off to make sandcastles. Anna calls out, "Catie, now you look after Charley."

We mosey over to the toys. A bunch of kids skip up to the sand pile at the same time. Charley's shy around strangers. He hangs on to my arm and shirt, anythin' to keep us connected. I smile to calm him and pat his hand. We want to play, but we're afraid to speak, 'cuz of the no talkin' rule. Dean and Buck stare at us like vultures, just waitin' to pounce. Lookin' for any reason to be mean.

We peek at each other, not sure if we can play or not. We focus on the toys with bright eyes and excitement.

"Hi, I'm Cha—"

I pinch Charley's hand—another rule.

"NO names!" I mouth to my brother.

The other kids act like they din't notice. No one wants trouble. Thankfully, Charley's back is to the vultures. They din't see or hear him speak.

A tall boy makes the first move towards the play area. We follow close behind. We sit and immediately dig in the dirt with our shovels. We build sandcastles like at the beach. A few kids, includin' Charley and me, fill small rainbow-colored containers with water and sand to drizzle decorations onto our sandcastles.

One of the boys slaps the water in a nearby trough. A big splash sends cold water down our backs. We spring up and join in a fun water fight. There are so many little hands slappin' and gigglin' with each splash. We're all wet and havin' the best time. Everyone is mostly our ages, four to eight years old. We form a circle then run and dance around the trough. It's like a game of musical chairs, without sittin' down.

Granny Poison Ivy's husband, Buck, calls out to all of us. His boomin' voice quiets the room. "Attention, everyone. Attention. Gather around to hear what we'll be doing tonight."

We sit on the floor at Buck's feet. The other adults, includin' Anna stand nearby.

"It's movie time!" Buck shouts, throwin' his arms wide with a big smile.

Charley and me look at each other, shocked. They allowed us to have fun. And now we get to see a movie?

Buck points to the movie projector aimed toward a white blanket thing hung on the wall. The first reel is a short, fun cartoon. We squeal seein' our favorite two mice. While the second reel is bein' set up, they pass out small bags of popcorn. Charley and me dance in a circle holdin' hands. I whisper, "This is like the drive-in and the beach all in one day."

We wrap in dry towels to keep warm. They start the second feature. I hope it's another cartoon. After the movie starts, I look at Charley and whisper, "This movie doesn't make sense."

He shakes his head and mouths, "It looks like a grown-up movie."

The scenes change too quickly. First, we see kids playin' on the beach. Then it switches to waves.

"You thinkin' those are ocean waves? They're as big as giants," I say, real quiet.

"Don't know. Never seen de ocean. You ever?"

"Nope. But I'm thinkin' it might be."

"Shhh! Catie! Charley! You know the rules." Ivy snaps.

She raises a large wooden plank in the air. We button our lips, puttin' our heads low to the ground. I use my fingers to squiggle out a message in our secret code for Charley to be quiet and only to whisper when no one is watchin'.

We lift our heads as the movie flickers. There's no talkin' yet, only sounds and noises. It goes on and on—seems like forever. I try to watch it, but it hurts my eyes. It flips too fast. Changin' from children to water, to swimmin'. Then back to children playin'. This stupid movie is all about water. Now it flashes to kids in bathtubs and keeps changin' to show more kinds of water. I'm tired and dizzy.

Charley whispers, "My tummy feels sick. I'm spinny." I cross my eyes tellin' him I feel sick too.

Keepin' my head still, I pretend to watch, but all the while, I look around the candlelit room. I can make my eyes look to the far side without movin' my head. It helps with the dizziness. I see the grown-ups off to the side. They're talkin' and laughin' havin' their own drive-in beach party.

I move my eyes back to the other kids sittin' near us. They're swayin'. Gilbert leans into the boy next to him, askin' if he feels okay. All the kids whisper that the movie is makin' them sick.

The movie slows, changin' into a new story 'bout children bein' baptized with shimmery Christmas decorations in the background. I don't recognize anyone. It's a homemade movie, like the ones I've seen at Grandpa's and Granny Grunt's.

The story starts with a family at church. This one has voices. The daddy and mommy tell the good children if they believe in Jesus, they'll go to heaven, but first, they have to be baptized 'cuz that's the way to show you're a good kid. Then the movin' pictures show bunches of kids bein' dunked in troughs, like the ones in the room. They also show a cute, itty, bitty baby dunked in a barrel of water. Then the movie stops.

The bright light glares on the white blanket. We cover our eyes.

Buck barks out orders. Dean stands behind him and points at anyone who's not payin' attention. Buck's voice gets louder. "Come on, …stand up. Make a circle around the barrels and troughs. Divide up into groups of four."

Charley and me walk over to the barrels that we'd been playin' at earlier. Two redheaded kids skip over to be in our group. They look like brother and sister, both with freckles across their noses and red curly hair. The girl seems sweet, but I don't dare talk. She giggles a lot. I like that about her. I smile at the new girl. She smiles back.

Buck snaps at Granny Ivy. "Woman, turn that projector light off."

The room darkens. With only candlelight, it's hard to see. Buck and Dean stand in the middle of the room.

"Okay, you kids, listen up. Pay attention. You know the rules. No talking—no names. OR ELSE!"

We know what that means. The redheaded boy snickers. Poison

Ivy walks away from the projector. She grabs a leather strap on her way.

Wham! She slaps the kid in the side of the head. His ear turns bright red. The boy cries out in pain. Everyone remains silent, includin' me and Charley. We're afraid we'll get walloped if we say a word or even look the boy's way. I pull Charley in close.

A new lady that we are to call Miss Bee brings a sweet baby in a diaper to the barrel of water. Anna and Granny Ivy tell us they baptize babies different 'cuz they're so small. Miss Bee shows us the different ways. First, she sprinkles drops of water on its head. Then, she takes a cup and pours water over the little one's forehead. It whimpers with a bit of a wiggle. She tells us she's now gonna dunk the baby in the water like we'd seen in the movie.

This baby is gonna grow up to be extra, extra, good, havin' three different types of baptisms.

Miss Bee gently pushes the baby under the water. You can see the partin' of the water as the baby goes down, and the water floods over its face. I wait for her to bring the baby up. I'm afraid 'cuz she's takin' her good time.

"Excuse me, Miss Bee, don't you think you should bring the baby up now?" I say.

Suddenly somebody behind grabs and yanks my hair. Pain rips through my head. I can't see who it is, but his voice screams into my ear. My head rings.

"It's none of your damn business! You'd better keep your mouth shut if you want to keep your teeth."

He flings my head forward. I grab the barrel's edge to steady myself from goin' into the water on top of the baby. Bubbles rise to the top. I cry from the pain in my head and for the sweet baby.

My heart beats so fast my chest hurts. I'm afraid. Anna's family and the devil bunch have dunked me in one of those horse troughs many times. I know what it's like to be held under the water too long. I've taken in a big gulp a time or two, and it hurts, plus it's scary. This baby is bein' held under the water a lot longer than me and Charley ever were.

I start countin' to myself. One, two, three, …. I know how long I can hold my breath underwater in the bathtub. I've been practicin' for when Anna and her creepy family dunk us again. My limit is forty-six seconds. Fifty-three. Fifty-four. Fifty-five. I feel like I'm gonna faint. I blow out, needin' to catch my breath. I look at the lady. She's still holdin' the baby underwater. I scan the room to see what the adults are doin'. Nothin'. Just watchin'. I look at the other kids and see the fear on their faces.

Devil Dean warns us. "Don't even think about tellin' anyone unless you want what just happened to the baby to happen to you!" His words sting my ears. "And all you crybabies, if I hear one peep out of any of you…you'll be the next one *baptized.*" He splashes water out from one of those large troughs. "I dare ya. Come on. Let me hear just one whimper."

Charley looks up at me with big eyes. Tears stream down his cheeks. He holds back any and every sound. My head pounds. I'm torn between screamin', cryin', or reachin' in for the baby, and runnin' away with Charley. I don't know what to do. I stand stiff, frozen with fear. *It takes my breath. I panic.*

Someone tugs on my arm. I look to see GI Joe and Barbie.

"Hey!" I reach out and give them both a hug and pull Charley into the circle. "Do you think they've drowned the baby?" I mouth the words. I know the answer, but I need GI Joe to tell me the truth.

The stocky soldier boy nods his head, meanin' the worst. Anger rises in my chest. GI Joe pushes past me. Right up to the lady at the barrel. She's still holdin' the baby underwater.

WHAM! He kicks her in the shin and extra hard too.

"You like pickin' on children, or an innocent baby, who can't fight back. You're a coward! A green-belly coward. If I were bigger, I'd dunk your head in that barrel. You remember me. Look at me! Someday when I'm a big strong soldier, I'll be back. Then, you'll have to deal with me."

I'm ready to jump in when someone holds somethin' over my nose and mouth. I feel Charley's hand slippin' away. The room turns black.

I wake up and find myself in my bed. My head pounds and everythin' seems a little blurry. I blink several times to clear my eyes. I look over to Carolyn, who's conked out on her bed. She lifts her head. Her eyes look extra sleepy.

"Why are you so sleepy, Carolyn?" I question.

"Not sure. Some days, I just wake up feeling groggy, like I'm still sleeping." She yawns. "Charlotte & Claudia say they have trouble waking up sometimes too."

Anna suddenly scurries into my bedroom and asks, "How are you feeling, Catie?"

I glare at her.

"I've been so worried about you. You have had such a high fever. I tried everything to bring your temperature down. I could tell by the way you were thrashing. You had a bad dream. I brought you downstairs with me for most of the night."

She's lying. I squint my eyes at her. She's such a liar, but a part of me wants to believe it's just a horrible dream. But Anna's just makin' up a fib to cover her tracks 'cuz Carolyn musta woken up and din't see me in my bed.

We all know we're not allowed to go into Daddy and Anna's room. Their room is off-limits. You only have to do it once. Your beatin' will remind you never to do it again. Anna says it's 'cuz parents need privacy. But I know better. It's more about her gettin' away with all her sneakin'. She sneaks us out of the house, and she thinks I don't know, but she also sneaks men visitors into her bedroom.

"What about Charley? Is he sick too?" I say loud enough for my sisters to hear.

She narrows her eyes.

Marion
December 1994

C atherine sashays into my office. She plops down on the love seat before stretching out her legs. She narrows her eyes slightly and lets out a small grunt.

"What is wrong?"

She looks up. "With my legs? Oh, just a little twinge. Hunter and I have been taking swing dance lessons. I don't know which muscles are sorer, the ones in my body or my face from laughing so hard."

She smiles, but it soon fades. Her hair and clothes disheveled, unlike her usual put-together appearance. She blows out a frustrated breath.

"Marion, I'm trying so hard to be upbeat for Hunter and be grateful for all the wonderful things in our life. But I feel like a ping-pong. I don't know how long I'm going to be able to take these horrific memories. I feel as helpless now as I did before we began. The emotional pain is crushing at times."

We rehash the details of her recent memory from our last session. She cringes at the realization of the secret, midnight beach party, and how she, Charley, and the other children were forced to watch movies, leaving them ill; all the while purposely leading to the drowning of the baby.

"Marion, after this last memory, I did some research on the occult and found some articles stating they used brainwashing techniques on their victims. It mentions several techniques, but the part that caught my eye was the use of films with flashing lights." She tilts her head. "Do you know anything about that?"

"Catherine, I am sorry for the pain this memory has brought upon you. I do not want to add to or intensify your heartache."

I choose my words carefully, making sure not to mention anything about the occult practices that she has not remembered.

"To answer your question, yes, I do know a little on that subject. I surmise the splicing of the homemade movies were intended to tire and confuse the mind. Television was fairly new in the early sixties. At that time, television programs were filmed with one camera, maybe two sometime later. Flashing from scene to scene overstimulates the brain, and makes it hard to focus, concentrate, and difficult to remember. It is part of a brainwashing technique used by the Nazis who experimented on their victims. A vicious doctor, referred to as Dr. Death, used these methods to fragment minds and disrupt their subjects' thinking ability. It was a strategic tactic to control them." My voice stays calm, even though the details disturb me greatly.

"The occult adopted the Nazi techniques in the sixties and seventies. History shows the occult testing these methods on children, which may explain the likelihood of why you felt tired, confused, and sick while watching the movie."

Catherine runs her finger through her hair, pushing her bangs off her face. She wheezes out a big sigh.

"How do I fight against such an organized evil group? It feels too big. Overwhelming." Her face grows tense. "Marion, I've seen so much. Too much! Each memory confirms why I didn't want to remember. I feel like I've opened Pandora's Box. Memories are flowing out regularly, at home, and here." She sniffs and reaches for a tissue.

"Every time I see a milk carton with a missing child, I wonder if it's the occult behind the abduction. Snatching some innocent toddler or schoolchild on the playground. Do you know how they do this?"

I'm not sure if I want to know, but Catherine needs me to listen.

"They tag team. One distracts the parent, while the other steals the kid. Or they pick up some teenager hitchhiking—never to be returned."

She twists her head back and forth. "It makes me physically ill. I'm so overwrought with…sh…shame, guilt, and h…hatred."

Her voice cracks. "Sometimes, Marion, I find it even hard to breathe."

I position myself in my chair, squared off in front of Catherine. I need her undivided attention to help settle her thoughts and emotions.

"Catherine. Look at me." My voice is firm, intending to grab her awareness. "First of all, you are *not* responsible for the occult's choices and actions. You were an innocent child, only six years old when you met Anna. You did not have the physical, mental, or emotional capability to overcome them. You were instinctually trying to survive and protect your brother. Yes, you did some things, but not out of real choices. You were obedient to their demands to save Charley's life—and your own. Fear is a powerful weapon. They used fear and threats to control you and keep you quiet. However, a large portion of the heaviness you are struggling with is unforgiveness."

I lean in closer, staring into her eyes. "I am referring to forgiving them…and forgiving yourself."

Her eyes widen.

I continue talking, "It's one thing to forgive someone who has made a mistake or used poor judgment or unintentionally has hurt you. But how do you forgive someone who has contrived to bring harm strategically?"

CHAPTER SEVENTEEN

Catherine
December 1994

Hunter strategically pulls the car curbside in front of the pastry shop in downtown Denver, so his folks don't have to walk too far. "Mom, Dad, would you mind finding us some seats while I park the car?"

Harriet shoves her door wide open, muttering, "I'll go inside, too."

I climb out of the back seat of the car and walk around to the passenger side.

Jefferson glances at me. "How about you, Catherine? You coming in?"

"No, thanks." I smile. "You go on. I'll ride with Hunter and walk back with him. We did come downtown to see the Christmas decorations."

"Sure, okay." I notice Jefferson's perplexed expression as he watches Harriet hug her shivering body against the cold. He tips his hat in my direction and shakes his head. I now know he disapproves of his daughter's decision not to wear a coat.

After we park the car, Hunter speaks before I have a chance to complain about his sister. "Let it go, Catherine. I want to make the best of the evening. Don't allow my sister to steal the fun from our time with my folks." There is a pleading in his eyes. I know he's right. I hold back my frustrations and nod in agreement.

We walk briskly back to the pastry shop. With my gloved hands tucked inside my heavy coat pockets and my wool scarf covering my neck, I feel warm against the cold. Hunter puts his arm around me, and together we take in the storefronts, the Christmas lights, and all the beautiful decorations. My festive mood returns.

As soon as Hunter and I arrive, we all place our orders at the bakery counter. The variety of cakes, cookies, pastries, and sweetbreads make my mouth water. In my experience, sweet desserts have a way of putting everyone in good spirits, even those in the foulest of moods. But glancing around, I'm not so sure about this group.

We follow Jefferson to a table. An uncomfortable silence hovers over Hunter's family. They appear to be dry-mouthed from the unspoken edginess. They gulp water to choke down their desserts, but not Hunter and me. I savor each bite of my Crème Brûlée, licking my spoon clean. My husband finishes off his triple chocolate flourless cake, and his yummy moans speak for themselves. I delight in every sip of hot chocolate, determined to have a good time and not let Harriet rain on my parade, or better said, sleet on our parade.

With my warm mug cradled in my hands, I decide to stir up conversation. "Why don't we all share a favorite Christmas memory? Or a fun family tradition?"

I go first in hopes that the others will join in. I talk about my memories of Christmas Eve at my grandparents' house. The baked goods, the matching pajamas for all my siblings, the Christmas songs we sang together as a family.

Hunter is eager to share his Christmas story of receiving a pair of Pony six-shooter cap guns and holster. Marie's face lights up as she listens. The more Hunter and I share, the more Harriet's jaw tightens. Her left eye twitches. She refuses to speak and remains tight-lipped, stewing in her pent-up anger.

Both Hunter and his parents say nothing about her snarled-up face and occasional huff and puff.

Jefferson, a generous man, pays the check and then hems and haws trying to get his question out.

"Uh...would you mind driving us to see the festive decorations and lights, Hunter? I know you had something else planned, but I don't think Harriet thought it through in not wearing a coat."

It's an awkward moment. I want to roll my eyes in disgust at Harriet. I figure she definitely thought her little hissy fit through, with the intent to wreck our plans. *But why?* Jefferson firmly looks at Harriet, then back to me, letting his eyes fall to the ground with an apologetic gaze.

I feel sorry for him, but Hunter responds, sounding nervous before I have a chance to speak. "Sure, Dad, we don't mind." He pats his stomach. "Now that I have my belly full of that great chocolate cake. I'm sugared up and ready to go."

We drive around in downtown Denver. This time, I'm comfortable in the front seat snuggled between Hunter and Jefferson. It is a magical winter wonderland. White lights illuminate the town: restaurants, hotels, and the towering Christmas trees covered with colorful ornaments and ribbons.

Hunter and I share our ooh's and ahh's over the beautiful lights. Only Jefferson joins us with an occasional smile and positive comment.

Harriet and Marie sit in the back seat, completely mute.

When we arrive home, Harriet jumps out of our SUV and marches straight to her car without a single goodbye, much less a thank you.

I can't wait to see Marion. I need to share my unvented frustration about how having Hunter's parents and his youngest sister over for the holidays has brought tension into his family.

I sigh. What is worse is the tension between us.

I open the door to Marion's office. Marion sits in her wingback chair. Before taking a seat, I start spewing out my update. I feel like I'm about to burst.

"You're not going to believe the Christmas I had with the ostrich family. Talk about anxiety."

Marion stays quiet for a moment. "Catherine, I can just about see the anxiety and frustration rolling off you. May I suggest something?"

I bite my lip and nod.

"I would not normally propose this, but I know how a change of scenery has such a calming effect on you. Why don't we go for a drive around the campus and continue talking? I think a change of scenery might do us both some good. It is the end of the day, and there is something I would like to show you."

After scanning the four familiar walls of the office, I have to agree. We head out to Marion's car, a compact, blue Honda, parked in the staff lot. Marion suggests that she drive since my agitation might not make me the safest driver.

Once buckled, we leave the lot, and Marion suggests I watch the scenery for a bit before speaking. She turns onto a winding street toward the back of the campus. Adorable, decorated bungalows, sugar-dusted with the recent snowfall are visible through the trees. I feel my tension lessen as the twinkling Christmas lights soothe me.

"Do you want to tell me about your frustration?" Marion murmurs.

A deep sigh escapes, but at least I'm not pulling out my hair like I wanted to earlier. "You know, Marion, dealing with Hunter's family feels like trying to pry the lid off a tin can with my bare hands. They are unbelievably stoic. It's downright frustrating. Here I am trying to sort out my own challenges, and now…" I pause to pull off my gloves. "I don't mind dealing with Hunter and his family, but how do you resolve problems if they're unwilling to admit there's an issue? It's a hot mess."

"Not only that, Marion, but the recurring dream continues. I think Hunter's getting used to it, but that probably isn't a healthy thing."

I massage my temples, trying to thwart off an oncoming headache.

"But now I'm revisiting the recovered memories in my dreams, making them more like nightmares."

Marion glances over at me, her back leaning comfortably against the driver's seat. Not me, I lean against the seatbelt, my leg nervously jiggling as I spout my aggravation.

"It breaks my heart and physically hurts my chest to carry unresolved conflict. Especially when all it takes is a simple, honest conversation."

Marion adjusts the heater and clears her throat. "Catherine, let me start with the dreams." Her voice is steady, her smile soft. "God can use dreams to communicate. They can bring clarity, allowing our subconscious to sort through beliefs and information. So, it is not uncommon to revisit recollections in our dreams. It is a way the mind can reflect memory."

She turns the car onto a smaller lane that curves into one of the college's open spaces. The late afternoon sun makes the snow sparkle. "Catherine, while in Switzerland, you remembered the first time your nightmare began. You were nine years old. Your mind has repeated that dream ever since. I believe it was a way of preserving the past until you were ready to investigate what it represents."

Marion clicks on her right blinker and makes the turn.

"Now, if you have no questions, I would like to discuss your in-laws."

I shake my head in agreement. "I don't have any questions about my dream, but I can't wait to hear your take on Hunter's family dynamics."

Marion pulls into a parking area at the open space. A beautiful snow-covered hill stands before us, framed by stately evergreens. She shifts the car into park but leaves the engine running for the heat.

Marion leans her head on the headrest. She gestures with her eyes for me to look to my right.

I rub the condensation from my window, peering at a sweet nativity scene. Marion knows the promises of God are wrapped up in this very powerful message. The sight of the baby Jesus brings hope to my heart. "Aww…how soothing."

"I knew you would appreciate its beauty. I drive by here every evening on my way home."

We both sit quietly, watching the sunlight disappear behind the mountains. The nativity lights sparkle brightly against the approaching darkness.

"Catherine, I would like to give you a brighter perspective. When I met with your husband earlier this week, we discussed how his parents dealt with family issues. During our conversation, Hunter gave me permission to share with you whatever I think is of value. Although I have only met with him a few times over the last year, the good news is, he is willing to meet as often as necessary. Your husband desires to become a good communicator. I would say you have been a good influence on him, in that matter. The fact that Hunter spoke freely on the phone with his sister is something he said was new for him. That is a step in the right direction."

I release my seatbelt so I can turn towards Marion. "Well, if he told you anything about his family," I say, almost scoffing, "you'll know that was a huge move for Hunter."

Marion offers an understanding nod.

"According to Hunter," she explains, "his parents never fought nor had any disagreements in front of him or his sisters. As a result, he and his siblings do not know how to resolve conflict."

"Umm-hmm." I give several brisk nods.

"Hunter said he believed any display of anger was unacceptable and interpreted anger as a defect in himself or the other person. 'A weakness,' is the term he used."

Marion tilts her head to the side, squinting at the scenery. "Hunter's belief systems are why he tends to conceal his emotions, especially those associated with anger. Catherine, the fact that Hunter admitted to stuffing his emotions is a good sign and is the first step of coming out of denial."

Marion reaches for her bag in the back seat and removes a sheet of paper.

"I counseled Hunter about 'active listening' or 'drive-through talking'. I believe this will be helpful for the two of you."

I reach out to accept the paper from her.

"The rules are similar to placing an order at a drive-through restaurant."

She counts out the rules, one on each finger. "First, you place your order. Second, the listening person repeats back what they heard. And thirdly, you respond by confirming, clarifying, or pointing out any mistakes or miscommunication."

Marion turns in her seat to act out the scene.

"For example," Marion pretends she's lowering the car window to place her order. "I would like to order a hamburger with onion rings and a chocolate shake."

She changes her voice as she banters back and forth with the pretend employee.

"Thank you, Miss. I have a cheeseburger, onion rings and I didn't get your drink. What beverage did you want to order?

"I said, I wanted a hamburger, not a cheeseburger, onion rings, and a chocolate shake."

"Okay, that's a hamburger, onion rings, and chocolate shake. Right?"

Marion breaks character and leans back in her seat.

"I know this may seem like a silly exercise, but there is a lot to learn. Did you notice only one person speaks at a time?" Marion glances at me, eyebrows raised.

I nod.

"The purpose is to improve communication. One person is to talk for two to three minutes without any interruption. The other person may take notes and may comment, but only when it is their turn, and not before. You will be surprised at how much is assumed that is never spoken. Making assumptions can lead to conflict."

"Hunter mentioned something about this," I say. "He called it fast-food-talking." We chuckle.

"By the way, while Hunter was here for his session, he referred to you as Peanut. How did you come by that nickname?"

"It's a sweet childhood memory. One of my favorites…"

Catie
Autumn 1963

"Daddy! Daddy! Daddy's home!" He walks through the front door. I giggle and run to him, dancin' and bouncin' in place.

"I'm home!" He shouts toward the kitchen where Anna is cookin' dinner. Daddy reaches down to give me a big hug. He walks over to the sofa, plops down, and lets out a long, 'Awww.'

Before he has a chance to speak, I pounce on his lap.

"Tell me how I got the nickname Peanut."

He chuckles. "I've told you that tale a million times, Catie. Don't you get tired of hearing that story?"

"Nope. Tell me again. Please. Pretty please." I crinkle my nose, smile as big as I can, and cuddle close, ready to hear my story.

"Okay." Daddy nuzzles me in under his arm. "Mommy and I were at the photographer's studio having your first baby picture made. There was a big fluffy pillow on the table covered in a pretty silky fabric your mommy loved. The photographer asked us to lay you on the pillow."

He tickles me. I laugh from the tickle, but also 'cuz I know what's comin'—the part about my pretty dress.

"Mommy dressed you in a beautiful delicate dress with booties to match."

"What color was it, Daddy? Even the little flowers on the collar."

"A pretty, pale pink with rosebuds on the lace collar."

"What happened next?"

"We laid you on the pillow, then moved aside, out of the photographer's way. Once behind the photographer, we looked back at the pillow. To our surprise, the cameraman asked, 'Where is she?'" Daddy shrugs his shoulders.

"You were gone! Mommy and I ran over, afraid you might have fallen off the table. You weren't on the floor. You weren't on the table. You were gone."

Daddy pretends he's scared. He raises his arms in the air like he's amazed and puzzled.

I giggle. "Then what?"

"Mommy was in a panic until she found you. You had sunk deep into the pillow. I put my hand under the pillow to push you up, so your first baby picture could be taken.

"The photographer said, 'Well, she's no bigger than a peanut.' And the name stuck, Catie." He brushes his finger over my nose. "You've been Daddy's little peanut ever since.

"Did you know then that I had princess eyes?"

"I sure did. So did your mother."

"So did Mommy?"

"Uh, huh." Daddy's eyes leak.

"I wish Mommy was still here."

CHAPTER EIGHTEEN

Catie
Autumn 1963

My first wish is that Mommy was still here with us. My second biggest wish is to be able to stay in my bed all night. I never know when Anna's gonna wake me up in the middle of the night. I hate havin' to go to all those creepy places. But if I have to go, at least Charley and I get to see our friend, Gilbert. That's if Anna takes us to Buck and Poison Ivy's barn.

Tonight is different; my sisters are spendin' the night at someone's house. And Melinda and Shawnee got woke up too. That's 'cuz it's a Friday night, and we just started back in school. Anna wouldn't want her angels to have to miss sleep during the week.

As we walk into the barn, I see a nurse Lady is here. I hope she's nice, unlike most of Anna's family's friends.

"Come on, kids, gather around." She motions the children to come close.

We all bunch up around her in a half-circle. She has the cow roped to the stall behind her.

I chatter with Charley and our friend Gilbert. "Bessie's a nice cow. She squirts out warm milk. I've milked her a time or two with Buck and Dean's help. It's fun."

Gilbert says, "You wouldn't think so if it was your job. Milking time for Bessie comes every morning before the sun comes up, and at night too." He yawns and rubs his eyes. "Not to mention all the other chores involved in cleaning up after her." He yawns a second time.

"You tired, Gilly?" I understand 'bout not gettin' enough sleep.

The nurse lady yells. "You three!" She points her finger at us. "Stop that talking, or I'll have Buck tan your hides. You hear me?"

Gilbert, Charley, and me, all jerk to attention. We look around to see if Buck and Dean are anywhere near. If she tells on us, it means a beatin'. I cross my fingers behind my back.

Miss Nurse continues, "Gather around, children. Come. Get closer." She encourages us to shuffle in tighter.

She announces, "We're going to have a health class to learn about farm living and what happens in nature."

She jabbers on about birds and bees, but it doesn't make sense bein' they have a cow and some horses. We've seen birds and bees here before, durin' the day, but now it's dark outside.

Miss Nurse acts all excited. "You are all so lucky to learn about nature at such a young age."

She hands a stack of papers to her assistant.

"Children, look at the photos, then pass them on to the child next to you."

I take one of the papers and glance down. "Ick. These pictures are of all kinds of animals makin' babies. It's bunches of different animals and more than just dogs. I don't like it."

"Yuck." Charley pushes the paper away.

Miss Nurse snaps. "Everyone must take a turn looking at the pictures. Including you three!"

Her long finger points straight at us. We nod, then put our heads down. Gilbert slowly backs away and goes into his bunkhouse without any adults noticin'.

I whisper, "Charley, let's try to figure out what type of animals are in the pictures."

We recognize dogs, horses, goats, and lambs, but as for the others, we're not sure. The nurse lady passes out some new photos. They're of bare-naked people! And they're in the same position as the animals. Yuck!

I wrinkle up my nose and look up at Anna, who's now standin' next to me. I tug her sleeve. "This is embarrassin'. And I think Charley and me are too young to see this icky stuff."

Anna gives me one of her syrupy answers like she does to Daddy when she wants her way. "You both need to be comfortable with nature. This class is educational. Now, Catie, you mustn't be disrespectful. Pay attention." She points to the front where Miss Nurse stands.

I raise my hand. Miss Nurse points to me. "Yes, what do you want to ask?"

"I don't have a question, but I have somethin' to say, Miss Nurse."

She nods her head.

"I saw two dogs doin' it once. But they got stuck together."

Melinda and Shawnee burst into laughter. They bend over and hold their bellies and laugh at me. "Catie, you're so stupid. You're the stupidest and don't know nothing."

The children glare and make fun of me. They make me feel dumb. I can feel my face turnin' red, and my ears burn. I look down and kick at the straw on the ground.

Poison Ivy comes over and wallops me on my fanny. "Pay attention! If you're gonna visit this farm, you'd better understand what goes on in nature." Her voice is gruff.

"I thought I was," I say.

I give Granny Poison Ivy a dirty stare. She's just lookin' for an excuse to hit me.

"I'm gonna ask my daddy 'bout what you're doin'." I add, lowerin' my voice.

Poison Ivy pinches me on my shoulder so hard it burns. I look up.

Her eyes have turned dark, black. Somethin' evil lives inside her too. It looks out at me. I tense up at the sight.

Anna looks at her mother. They share one of those puzzlin' looks. It's like code without sayin' a word. They're up to somethin'.

"If Catie here would just learn to mind and quit being so mouthy, I wouldn't need to tell her father she's nothing more than a smart-aleck, in need of a butt beating." Poison Ivy continues pinchin' my shoulder—hard. Tears well up in my eyes.

Anna leans over, "We don't have to tell your dad about you being disrespectful. Now, do we? She pets the tops of my head with gentle strokes.

I shake my head no and look back at Miss Nurse.

The nurse talks smoothly. "This is all-natural and is how every one of us got here. People and animals all make babies. Sometimes we need to practice things when we are little, so we are ready for when we are older."

She smiles real big and looks into each of our faces.

"You will be smarter than any of the other kids at your school."

Some of the kids smile and laugh 'cuz they're happy 'bout bein' called smart.

Melinda holds Shawnee's hand and says, "We're already smart, so now we will be the smartest of all the kids."

I whisper into Charley's ear, "They aren't smart. They're stupid buttholes since they like lookin' at all of these animals' buttholes. They're butthole lovers."

We burst out laughin', but no one hears us over the other kids gigglin' at the photos.

"Children, now children, listen." The nurse shouts to gather our attention.

"God made animals and human bodies in a very similar way. He made the things of nature to feel good. It is God's way of letting us know *it's good because it feels good.*" Her voice sounds excited again.

Ivy brings over a photo of a girl's private part. She says a bunch of stuff 'bout how God made these special parts feel good when touched. And it's the same with animals. She passes the photo around the group.

Another lady wearin' a nurse's uniform, hands Miss Nurse a baby in a diaper. She lifts the itsy-bitsy baby so Ole Bessie-Cow can sniff her.

"You see kids; animals love little babies, kids, and adults. Animals are our friends. And we are their friends."

She cradles the baby in one arm while she scratches the cow's head. You can tell Bessie-Cow likes the scratchin', 'cuz she lifts her head side to side like she's tryin' to say to Miss Nurse where she has an itch. We all giggle.

"You see, God put animals on the earth to help us. I'm going to read from the Bible where God says we have dominion over all the animals. That means we are their boss and can tell them what to do."

She returns the baby to her helper, then reads from a brown leather book.

The helper takes the baby's diaper off. Miss Nurse lets Bessie-Cow take another sniff. The baby must taste good, 'cuz Bessie starts lickin' her. And the nurse lets Bessie-Cow lick the baby's privates too! The baby seems to like it since she din't cry and lets out a bunch of coos like it tickles.

"You see, children?" Miss Nurse laughs and cuddles the baby. "See —she loves this, and you will too."

The lady stares right at me!

I don't like how she's lookin' my way. I instantly have the creeps. I look down and rub my tennis shoes in the dirt, but I can still hear her talkin'.

"This is all so natural and beautiful. Beautiful, just like all of you. Thank you all for being such good students. You're all dismissed to go play in the yard."

The kids cheer and run out of the barn into the grassy area. I reach out and grab Charley's hand, and we start to run away, but it's too late. Mean Dean and Buck jump in our pathway. They stand in front of us with their arms spread out to block our way.

"Yuen's ain't goin' anywhere!"

Marion
January 1995

I listen to Catherine unfold her past as Catie. After hearing the details, I view her desire to forget such painful memories as a reasonable response. I would also want to forget.

My mind refocuses on the underlying subject of forgiveness. I have my concerns for Catherine. I know that unresolved offense, especially ones harbored for years, are dangerous, causing more damage than most can understand. In Catherine's situation, it has been decades.

Unforgiveness and holding on to transgressions or wrongdoings acts like an invasive cancer that breeds hardness of heart, rage, defensiveness, strife, unrest, stress, and so much more. Clinging to offenses stimulates an unending list of emotions and attitudes that steal joy and peace from our very lives. Catherine has had so much loss, and I do not wish more due to her lack of understanding about forgiveness. I share my concerns.

"Forgiveness?" Her brow furrows, and she clenches her teeth. Her jaw muscles flex as she briefly closes her eyes. Her chest rises and falls with each deep breath. Tears pool in her eyes. "I'm not sure I want to…and for that matter if I can forgive them." Catherine stares unfocused out into the room. She pulls her knees up and hugs her legs close to her chest.

"Forgiveness? Forgive them? I don't know if I've made it clear about Anna and her family. There's more, so much more…"

CHAPTER NINETEEN

Catie
Autumn 1963

The nurse dismisses us kids from the so-called health class. Charley and me try to make a fast dash into the yard\ but Mean Dean and Buck spread their arms to block us.

Gilbert walks out of his bunkhouse, right behind them. I use our made-up sign language to ask him what's happenin'. Why are they stoppin' us from goin' outside? He rolls his eyes and shrugs his shoulders.

Dang, he doesn't know either.

Charley and me move, as slow as snails, backin' up into the shadows. I smell trouble. And it's comin' straight from Dean and Buck. It's that yucky smell again. It reeks. Smells super bad—even worse than the cow, Ole Bessie.

"Hey, you brats, get back over here. I see you trying to hide," Buck orders.

Me and Charley instantly freeze. We look over at Gilbert. All three of us are as stiff as sticks. We dare not look their way. I stare down at the ground and cross my fingers hopin' they're not talkin' to us.

"Catie, Charley—NOW!"

I grip Charley's hand tighter and walk as slow as I can toward Miss Nurse, her assistant, Dean, and Buck. Gilbert follows.

"These here nurses are tryin' to teach you kids a health class about the body and how it responds. Our bodies have nerves that react to things that feel good, and things that feel bad."

Dean takes a set of needle-nosed pliers from the top pocket of his farmer-overalls. He glares his black eyes at me.

"You know about how pliers can hurt, isn't that right, Catie?" He snarls.

My skin crawls 'cuz I do remember, just like it was yesterday. I nod my head, feeling shaky.

SMACK!

Mean Dean backhands me across my mouth. I taste blood.

"What have I told you about speaking up when spoken to?"

I hold back my tears. The lump in my throat grows so big it hurts.

"I see your eyes welling up. If you start blubbering like a baby, I'll give you something to cry about. You hear me?"

I mumble, "Yes, sir."

"That's more like it, Catie. Now you get over here and lay on this bale of hay. But, take them britches off first."

I look right at Dean to question him with my eyes since I'm too afraid to speak. He raises his hand to backhand me across the face, again. I flinch, waitin' for the blow.

Buck speaks up and starts givin' orders, "Charley, you come over here. You're a young-en, but you need to watch. Gilbert is gonna do to Catie what Bessie-Cow did to that baby."

Buck's tryin' to be the next big boss. I'm guessin' he thinks he's gonna take Dean's place in the devil-club. Of course, that probably won't be till Dean drops dead. If that old man died right now, that would be just fine with me. He's nothin' more than a big stinky fart-fink.

"Now, Charley, you best get moving, or I'll have to…" Buck raises his hand. Charley crouches.

Dean walks up next to Buck and nods in agreement.

Charley steps back. "But, Mr. Buck, that cow was licking that baby's private parts. Why would anyone want to watch that? That's nasty." He wrinkles up his nose. "That's where you pee."

"Gilbert, you get up here. And don't tell me you don't know how 'cuz I know you do. You show Charley. Make sure the boy watches."

"But Buck…Charley's—Charley is Catie's brother."

Buck punches his fist straight into Gilbert's face. The blow sends him flyin' to the ground. Dirt and straw stir up a cloud around Gilbert.

"I know he's her brother!" Buck barks. "And I don't need you mouthing off. Keep your damn mouth shut if you know what's good for you."

Mean ole Buck kicks dirt into Gilbert's face. The poor boy cowers on the ground. He slowly reaches up to wipe the dirty dust from his waterin' eyes.

Dean strolls up. He smiles at the goose egg lump Buck has made on Gilbert's cheek.

The devil-boss Dean turns toward the nurses, and says, "Ladies, continue with your class. You know what to do. And if these kids give you any problems, you know where to find me."

I wait till Buck and Dean leave before I ask if someone else can do the nasty stuff. I have everythin' crossed; my fingers, arms, and legs, hopin' she won't make me.

Miss Nurse answers, "Catie, that isn't up to me. Dean and Buck make those decisions. And they said you're the one. If you cry or throw a fit, I'll have to call them back, and then our class will be on how the body responds to pain, instead of pleasure."

She stoops, so we are face to face. "Do you understand?"

I understand all too well 'bout the hidden places, where pinchers and pokers can be used to hurt me.

"Yes. Yes, ma'am," My words crack.

She gently pets my hair and then motions me toward the bale.

"However, if you lay still, you'll see, this will feel very pleasurable." She gives me a fake smile.

Our attention turns toward the baby, who's fussin'. Miss Nurse looks around for the other nurse lady, her helper, who isn't anywhere to be found.

Gilbert speaks up, "I saw Dean take your friend toward the bunkhouse."

Sadie, Buck's dog, gives me a doggy kiss. She's such a precious pup. Her warm licks on my hand make me feel like she understands. Sadie might be as sad as me. She stares at me with her beautiful brown eyes. I squat and pet her sweet little brown head and floppy black ears.

The baby starts cryin' really hard and kicks its feet. It's probably from the scratchy straw on her bare skin. Miss Nurse picks her up and wraps her in a blanket covered in cute little bunnies. I watch her cuddle the baby close and kiss her forehead. She notices me watchin'.

"Catie get undressed like Buck said and lay on the straw. You wait until I get back, and we'll all get started." She walks away to look for her assistant.

Sadie scampers off. I shuffle over to the bale and do as I'm told. I shut my eyes tight, 'cuz I don't want to see Gilbert and Charley starin' at my bare bottom. My embarrassment picks and pokes at my heart like the straw picks and pokes at my bare-naked skin. I squirm. *Why do I have to do this? I hate them. I hate all of these devil people. What are they goin' to make Gilbert do?*

I'm so afraid. My body shakes so hard it takes my breath. I panic.

Someone taps me on the shoulder. I open my eyes. It's a girl, and she's small, smaller than me. She was probably a tiny baby too, like me, when I got the nickname, Peanut. Funny enough, this girl's hair is the color of peanut butter, as well as the freckles across her nose.

She seems nice enough, but I still pull away 'cuz I've never seen her before. She musta snuck in from the yard. She crouches on the other side of the straw bale.

"Psst, psst…" She raises her head just enough to whisper in my ear. "The best way to do this is to hide your emotions. Don't let them know how you feel. They like it when you're sad, afraid, or embarrassed. So you have to stow away your feelings. They like doing the things you hate, and they'll use it against you."

I nod and whisper back. "How do you do that?"

"Stow them away. Don't let Dirty Dean and his bunch know they're getting to you."

I keep my head still and stare straight up on the barn ceilin'. I like that she has nicknames for Dean too.

"How do you stow away your emotions? Do you mean smush your feelin's deep down inside, like hide 'em? Like maybe inside a peanut shell?" I turn my head pretendin' to look off into ole Bessie-Cow's stall. I quickly check to see what Charley and Gilbert are doin'. They have their backs turned. I don't want anyone to notice us breakin' the talkin' rule.

She's quick to answer. "Yes, a shell is fine, but it should be more like a bombshell to keep them safe. Dirty Dean and Buck are mean, evil, devil workers, and are straight from hell! After you hide your feelings, then pretend you're doing something else, something you like to do. You know, like daydreaming. Also, keep your eyes closed. It makes it easier."

"Okay, I like to make-believe. I'll pretend I'm with my mommy. She always kept me safe and happy. I already do that sometimes, but I've never tried it durin' yucky times. I think, umm, I can do it. I'll give it a try. What's a bombshell? Is it like a shell for a bomb, kinda like a peanut who lives in a shell?"

"Yes, kinda. It's a place to hide things. It will keep you and your feelings safe." We hear voices in the back of the barn. They're comin' closer. The smart, brown-haired girl ducks into the shadows and scurries out of the barn before Miss Nurse gets back.

I decide I'm gonna call her Peanut, 'cuz she's small just like me and her hair is the color of peanut butter. She's sweet and told me how to hide my icky emotions. I'm gonna make my feelin's small, just like her, and smush them into a peanut bombshell while I daydream 'bout Mommy. My feelin's will be safe in the shell, so Anna and the evil bunch won't be able to use them against me, just like the new girl said.

It's not even one whole minute before the nurse lady returns. I have my plan, so I don't bother listenin' to what she says to Gilbert and Charley.

I wish Mommy were here to protect me, but she's not, so I close my eyes, really tight, just like Peanut told me. I make-believe about the time when I learned to ride my very first two-wheeler bike. I drift off, rememberin' a happy time in the past with Mommy and Daddy.

CHAPTER TWENTY

Catie
Summer 1960

We have a family bike. Well, we only have one bike, but everyone shares it. That means the bike belongs to the whole family. It's tall and dark green. My older sisters can ride the bike super good.

I'm four years old, soon to be five! My birthday is at the end of the summer, right before school starts. I'll be goin' to kindergarten. Mommy says I have to know a few things before they'll let me in: my name, phone number, and address. That's easy. Plus, I already know Granny Grunt's and Grandpa's phone number and Teenage Granny's too.

I have to be able to count, know my a-b-c-'s, and tie my shoes. I can do it all. But I'm addin' this to my list: to ride a two-wheeler bike.

I hop on the family bike every day and practice long and hard. I've had a few spills, but I've figured out that I need to wear long sleeves and pants for protection.

I'm not allowed to wear my dressy clothes unless Mommy gets them out for me. And that's only for special times, like goin' to church. My clothes are hand-me-downs, but I'm lucky 'cuz Mommy promises to sew me a new dress of my very own, for my first day of school. I've seen the fabric. It's white with little red hearts, and she's gonna trim it all in pretty red lace.

Since most of my play clothes have holes, I'm gonna have to be extra careful and aim to fall in the grass. Even if I get skinned up, I'll have me a crusty scab to pick later.

I scurry out of our house and yell to Carolyn, "It's my turn. It's *my* turn."

She hands me the bike. I climb on but start wobbly. My problem is I can't see. When I push the pedal down, the handlebars block my view, but I can see over them when the pedal comes up. I try leanin' side to side, but it makes the bike even more wobbly.

Timmy, a neighborhood boy, shouts as I pass by, "Catie, you look like a drunk Indian."

"Huh?" I yell back.

What Timmy said din't make sense, so I keep on ridin'. I'm more interested in figurin' out this ridin' bike stuff to add it to my pre-kindergarten checklist. So what if I wobble side to side? I can still see and stay up without fallin'. My smile grows bigger with each pass by my house.

Back & forth, I ride up and down the sidewalk, only goin' as far as the house of the neighbor whose cat died. Then back up to the man's house with the big slide in the backyard. That's a good long way— eight or nine house lengths. After several swipes, I'm able to coast at a fast speed.

As I glide by my house, I shout in delight, "Look at me. Look at *me!*"

All the kids yell back, "Great job, Catie."

I yell to Charlotte. "Go get Mommy, so she can see me ride!"

On the next pass, I look at the house, then the front step, and the driveway, but Mommy's not outside. One more pass—still no Mommy.

I pedal up to the house and toss the bike on the ground, 'cuz there's no kickstand. I charge toward the house to tell Mommy I can ride a two-wheeler, *all—by—myself.*

As I run through the grass—WHAM! Somethin' sharp sticks in my foot.

"Ouch! Ouch! Ouch!"

I can't walk, so I hop on one foot to the porch, then crawl up the four steps.

"Mommy!" I cry out in between sobs.

Mommy runs out the front door. "What's wrong? What's wrong, Catie?"

All I can do is hang onto my foot and screech. I rock back and forth, holdin' onto my foot. Mommy and Daddy are always tellin' me to stop my screechin', but I can't help it now.

"It won't stop hurtin'."

Mommy looks at my foot, and right between my big toe (Market, and The Piggy who stayed home) is a big fat black bee stinger. It's deep! Mommy can't get her fingers ahold of what feels like a sharp needle in between my toes. My foot is swellin' fast.

"Charley, move out of Mommy's way so I can carry Catie to the kitchen table." She sits me right on top of the table like she's servin' me for dinner.

"Catie, stay put while I make up a special paste to draw out the stinger."

I watch her mix up water with baking soda and something else, then place a little circle of the white stuff over the bee stinger. She blows softly on the wet paste.

"This will feel cool, but don't you pick at it. It has to dry before I can take it off. So don't touch it, sweetie."

"Can I look at it?"

"Yes, look, but don't touch," Mommy says with a little laugh. She wags her finger at me.

Charley climbs up on a kitchen chair. "I thought you said no kids on the kitchen table."

"This is different, buddy. Mommy has to have Catie up high, so I can see to remove her bee stinger."

He stretches his neck to see the white stuff. We both stare and wait for the paste-like patch to dry.

Mommy slowly lifts the hardened patch. The stinger comes out on the first try. I stare with curiosity.

"Catie, you are inquisitive and fascinated by the most unusual things."

"Can I keep it? To show my friends?" I bob my head, excited about my new show and tell.

"Yes, darling, but don't let them touch it, or it will crumble."

Mommy places my stinger pointin' straight up on top of a cotton ball. She puts it in a small box—for all to see.

"Now, Catie, your foot is too swollen to play right now, so you'll have to sit on the porch for a while. I'll place some ice-cold rags on your foot to bring down the swelling."

I proudly show all my friends, my cool bee stinger. I can't wait for Daddy to get home so that I can show him.

I lean back against the house and smile. I've had a *great day*. I can ride a two-wheeler, and I'm only four. Mommy says I can ride my bike for her and Daddy on another day when my foot's better.

I look up as Daddy pulls his tootin' and pootin' car into the driveway.

"Daddy, Daddy, come look at my bee stinger."

He moseys over my way with his lunch bucket swingin' by his side.

"Well, what do we have here, Peanut?"

Charley and Gilbert shake my arms. I open my eyes. *I'm still in the barn. Yuck!*

"Come on, Catie, get up."

I look around. "Is Miss Nurse gone?"

Charley and Gilbert nod.

I ask Gilbert, "Are we done?"

"Yeah." He looks down at his feet. "Sorry, Catie." He spits and wipes his mouth on his shirtsleeve.

Charley pipes up. "Yeah, I'm sorry too, Catie." He looks at the ground and kicks at the straw. "Buck and Dean are crazy wanting me to watch that kinda icky stuff. Gilbert told me to stand in front of the nurse lady and to keep my chin up the whole time but to look down with my eyes. We tricked 'em. I promise, Catie, I looked at my tennis shoes, just like Gilly said."

I look out of the corner of my eye and spot Peanut walkin' through the barnyard. She turns and waves. I give her a quick hidden wink.

"Hey, Charley, how 'bout I teach you how to ride a two-wheeler bike this week?"

"Really, sis?" He gives a sweet toothy smile and bounces from foot to foot.

Marion
February 1995

"Your baby brother sounded so sweet and tender. He seemed to have a spunky side as well," I say.

Catherine smiles as she shares Charley's excitement about the opportunity to learn to ride a bike. Her smile fades into a frown. She lowers her head and picks at her chipped and marred nail polish. A fleck of rust-colored polish falls to her lap. She places the chip in a tissue.

"You talk about my brother, my baby brother, and have heard about the things they did to him. And to me! Then how—" She raises her hands in the air. "How could I ever...ever...forgive them? What they did?" She shakes her head. "Forgiveness?"

Catherine lets out a long, drawn-out huff. "They don't deserve forgiveness." She folds her arms across her chest.

"And for that matter, I'm not sure I want to forgive them." Her brow furrows. "Much less forgive me. I don't deserve forgiveness, either. What happened was so awful. It's...it's unforgivable," she says and ends almost in a mumble.

"You know, Catherine, I think it is time for a short field trip since we are not working on memory work today." I stand and reach for my coat and purse, slipping my pocket Bible inside.

"Where are we going?" she asks, reaching for her coat.

"You will see."

We stroll across the campus, our breath frosting the air. Before long, we arrive at the campus chapel. After stomping off the snow on our boots, we enter the quiet sanctuary. The afternoon sun streams through the beautiful stained glass windows, puddling pools of colored light on the floor.

I lead Catherine toward one window in particular. The image of Joseph and his coat of many colors.

"Do you remember the events that happened to Joseph before he became second in Egypt's command?" I ask.

"Well," Catherine counts on her fingers. "His brothers made fun of him, threw him into an empty cistern with plans of leaving him to die, but decided to sell him into slavery. And if that wasn't bad enough, his master's wife falsely accused him, and he ended up in prison. And even though he helped others by interpreting their dreams, they also forgot about him—for years." She tilts her head. "I think I may know where you're going with this."

We settle on the pew near the image of Joseph. The air in the chapel is still and quiet.

"Catherine, it is evident to me that you do not understand forgiveness. Although none are deserving, we can receive absolution or a pardon based on what the Bible says in John 3:16.

"Jesus willingly died, making it possible for ALL to receive forgiveness for their sins—including *yours.*" I point my finger at Catherine. "It is not about what you have or have not done. It is about what Christ has done on your behalf. You received his gift of salvation and forgiveness the moment you believed. At that moment, you became a cherished daughter of the Lord."

I shift position and gather my thoughts.

"During your years as Catie, God not only saved you, spiritually. He also protected your life from Anna and her venomous family. This truth may be hard to hear, but *if* your perpetrators were to believe in Christ and sincerely repent, God would forgive them."

"I doubt if that will ever happen." Catherine rolls her eyes. "I can't imagine that bunch having any sincere regret or remorse about their dirty deeds. They celebrated their evil tasks. To break all of the Ten Commandments was considered a noble and respected goal. Talk about repulsive. They purposely sucked me into their evil club. I hate them! And I find it hard to live with such disgusting memories and on account of them." She sets her jaw.

"Nevertheless, dear, we are to forgive." I bob my head with each word and raise my brows to emphasize the point. "I suspect you are struggling with the enemy's false accusations. He may be enticing you to believe that somehow your sins are worse than most, but not quite as bad as Anna and those in the occult. Both claims are lies straight from the enemy. Accepting this falsehood prohibits you from giving or receiving the benefits and the tremendous freedom forgiveness brings. Sin is sin, and Jesus died for *all* our sins. We need to repent and ask for the remission of our sins."

Catherine stares beyond me and off into space. She appears lost and alone, sitting deathly still. I press on to explain the benefits of being pardoned. Still no response.

Righteous anger bubbles up, like a shaken soda. I raise my voice to garner her attention. "I will not have you checking out. Do you understand me?"

My pointing finger bobs as if the digit has a mind of its own. I am surprised at myself, as much as Catherine appears to be taken back by my response. She jumps slightly, flinches, and her eyes widen at my scolding.

"Yes, Marion. But you see…I'm not sure…at times like these, my emotions are too intense to handle, so I find myself going numb."

She fans her hands out and shrugs her shoulders. "When that happens, it's almost impossible to measure or weigh my emotions. I'm unable to balance what I feel or believe."

"Truth is the only measurement, Catherine. Emotions can be reactive. Your feelings can be all over the board, like shattered glass with sharp edges, painful and cutting. Our emotions based on beliefs are *not necessarily the truth*. Do you remember us talking about how our beliefs create our emotions? Followed by our actions?"

She nods and retains eye contact.

"You have believed many erroneous things, which you *now know* are lies. When you believed those lies, your emotions may have felt accurate, but they were not. However, once you understood the truth, it was the truth that brought you healing and set you free. Joseph could have believed what his brothers said about him, or what his master's wife or the prison warden said.

"As Christians, we are to be truth-seekers, searching God's word and confirmation from the Lord. Truth brings godly emotions, followed by godly actions."

"Okay, but how do I forgive? I don't know how. Believe me, Marion, I've tried." She curls her upper lip into a snarl.

"Many people don't comprehend how to forgive because they misunderstand its meaning." I cross my legs. "I'm going to ask you some questions. I'll give you a handout with the same questions back in the office."

She sits up straight, looking interested.

"Catherine, would you agree someone has hurt you? Yesterday? A year ago? Or perhaps a lifetime ago?"

She nods, her face solemn. Sadness appears to tug the corners of her eyes.

"Did you deserve it? Are you struggling to forget? Does the pain continue? Do you feel stuck, like anchored in concrete? Have you told yourself you are going to forgive the person and even forgive yourself?"

I lean in and squint to focus on her response to my upcoming question. "When you think it is all over, done, and finished, does it crop back up again?"

She nods yes to every question. Tears pool in her eyes and her lips pinch tight.

"Perhaps when you hear their name or see them again, does it trigger you? Do those things stir the memory and pain within your heart all over again?"

She squeezes her arms tighter against her chest.

"Do your beliefs, emotions, and actions come rushing back into your mind? Those vivid, detailed memories that leave you questioning if you have sincerely forgiven that person?"

Catherine lowers her head.

I will not take silence for an answer. "Can you relate to this scenario? Does it at all sound familiar?" I press and ask firmly.

"Yes!" she answers right away. "I'm no stranger to wrestling with forgiveness, unforgiveness, or whatever you want to call it. You should know that by now, Marion. When I try to forgive, it's like a boomerang, I throw it out there, and it comes right back. For me, forgiveness doesn't stick."

"Trust me, Catherine, you are not alone. Many people struggle with this subject. I refer to it as 'Blanket Forgiveness.' It is as if we throw a blanket over the issue. We want to forgive, and we say, 'I forgive so-and-so' and tuck it away. Out of sight, out of mind, right?" I tilt my head, gesturing for an answer.

"It doesn't work, and the painful memories don't go away."

"Because we have not thoroughly dealt with the underlying offenses. The Bible is clear: we are to forgive, and it is to our advantage." I recite the Lord's prayer emphasizing, 'forgive us our debts, trespasses, and sins as we forgive others.' "Catherine, do you understand holding on to grudges, revenge, and bitterness is tormenting and causes *you* harm? You may think somehow hanging on to your offense hurts the other person, *and it may, somewhat.* However, the damage to yourself is far more costly—more than you realize."

I pull my Bible from my purse. "Let us look in Matthew 18:21-27."

Catherine leans over my shoulder as I flip the pages. I paraphrase the story.

"There was a king who wanted to forgive or settle the accounts with his servant. However, before he could, he needed to be aware of the debt to be forgiven."

I look up at her. "To say it another way: Forgiveness requires taking an account."

"What do you mean? What's an account?" Catherine asks.

"It is a tally, or list of the offenses, the hurt, the wound, the damages, the loss, and the debt. It is acknowledging there was an offense. Until we are *willing* to look at the events in our lives and take an account, we cannot forgive or release the offender or ourselves. We lose out on the liberation that is found in forgiveness."

Catherine clears her throat. "So Marion, does that mean I need to remember every little detail about the hurts done to me? And all the wounds I have caused?" She raises her eyebrows. "Do I have to write pages and pages describing *everything*?" Frustration and irritation resonate from her words. Her frown resembles a child pouting.

"No, you do not have to list volumes, only write enough words to be clear on what has happened and what debt needs to be canceled, for the person and yourself."

Unlike my previous scolding, I playfully wag my finger and smile. "So, do not try to wiggle out of this task. You can use shorthand, code, or abbreviations. It doesn't have to be torture. It only needs to be a simple commitment to make a list."

I offer a small laugh, followed by a big smile of encouragement.

She smirks. "Okay. I think I can do that. But you can bet I'm going to reward myself after completing this assignment." She rubs her hands together. "Umm-hmm...chocolate cake sounds good."

"Now, do not torment me. You know I'm on a diet."

Again, I playfully shake my finger and erase the chocolate cake image from my mind.

"Keep it simple, Catherine. This information is for you—no one else. Be honest with yourself. What you perceive as someone's intent may not be true, but you must take ownership if you hold a grievance in your heart. That is a part of what you will be forgiving or releasing. Are you in agreement to start with a list?"

"Sure thing, Marion, I'll get right on it. Do I have a choice?" Catherine jokes.

CHAPTER TWENTY-ONE

Catherine
March 1995

A loud buzzing jolts me awake. I don't want to get up, but it's not like I have a choice. I reach out into the darkness and slam the button on the alarm, not wanting to wake Hunter. The room falls silent, the air stale and dark. I roll over and stretch wide in the bed. The space next to me is empty. It's only then I remember Hunter had an early morning appointment.

He must have been wiped out. We had friends over last night to play cards. We were having such a good time laughing and cutting up that we were up late, way after midnight.

I yawn deep and long, my eyes sluggish and tired. I throw back the duvet and roll out of bed. My day is only beginning, and I don't have the energy to make the bed.

I study the gray skies and harsh winds blowing outside our bedroom window. The storm outside matches the storm brewing inside my head, darkening my mood.

How long can I go on like this? Struggling with my nightmare and disruptive sleep has been chasing me for over three decades. My body feels drained from the demands of work, counseling classes, housecleaning, laundry, groceries, and my unending list of projects.

I rest my hands on my knees. I feel breathless as if slugged in the stomach, sucker-punched by life. Haunting thoughts swirl inside my head. I question their meaning. Am I dealing with the present or the past? Or just plain overreacting?

I walk into the bathroom and spot several verses on the marble countertop; they're a part of Marion's mind renewal assignment. I leave the three-by-five cards accessible on purpose as a reminder to start my day reading God's word.

I pick up the top card and recite Philippians 4:13 aloud. "I can do all things through Christ who strengthens me."

I want to believe the words, but my thoughts, fueled by my emotions, scream the complete opposite. *Strengthen me? I'd need a miracle. I'm not sure God has the time for all my mess.* I shake my head to focus. *Shut up with all the negative self-talk.*

I reach into the linen closet, grab a towel and washcloth, and then turn on the shower.

Romans 8:28 is on the second card. "And we know that all things work together for good to those who love God, to those who are called according to His purpose."

I repeat the words several times to drown out the negative chatter in my head, allowing the words to sink deeper. Teenage Granny often said I was hardheaded. Perhaps she was right, and that's why it's taking forever to memorize these scriptures. I shuffle to the last card, Hebrews 4:16.

"Let us, therefore, come boldly to the throne of grace that we may obtain mercy and find grace to help in time of need."

I mumble under my breath, "I'm in need all right. I need all the mercy and grace I can get, plus the ability to talk to my husband."

While gathering my shampoo and conditioner, I recalled the

heated conversation last night before our company arrived. We are still arguing over what happened months ago at Christmas, probably because his sister continues to be rude.

'I don't feel protected by you,' I told him. 'Especially when your sister acts out.' I draw an imaginary line across my forehead. 'I've had my fill of her crazy. I would never allow any of my siblings to scream at you or manipulate an entire preplanned evening. She has made it clear that she doesn't accept me into your family.'

I stacked my hands on my hips and cocked my head. 'Why didn't you tell Harriet to shut up? To grow up? And to put on a coat if she wanted to join us?'

I fired questions without pause. 'Why did you allow her to treat me with such disrespect?" I raise my hands. "Why didn't you stick up for me? I am your WIFE.'

Hunter's face was blank except for a slight twinge in his eyes. He said he was tired of putting up with his sister. He ignores her because he doesn't want to make waves. He reasoned it was too hard on his parents. He pointed out that his folks were getting older and didn't know how to handle their forty-five-year-old grown child's immaturity.

Hunter reminded me once *again; his* parents never exhibited any conflict in front of him—*ever.* Only once had he heard them arguing from the basement when he was about ten. The discord scared him. He confessed that he is uncomfortable with confrontation and doesn't know how to resolve conflict, so he avoids clashes at all costs.

I step into the warm water and rehash my comments to Hunter. 'Confrontation isn't anything more than giving or receiving more information, which usually resolves most issues. Being raised differently, I'm comfortable with working out snags. What bothers me is having all this unresolved, stuffed, buried, and unaddressed tension in the air. I don't understand how you can live like this.'

My husband rolled his eyes. He didn't appreciate my advice and made his point by pinching his lips and not speaking—a common reaction with Hunter.

Needing a resolution, I pushed him further. His rebuttal was, 'Yes, I know, Catherine, my family and I sweep everything under the rug.

And *not* to my delight, the good Lord gave me a wife who's a rug shaker.'

The warm water runs down my back, soothing the tension in my neck and shoulders.

I've always hated the pretend game. Teenage Granny was right, and it is like the elephant in the room.

My mind continues to spin, and thoughts of condemnation taunt me. *Who am I to complain? After all, life with me must be horrible. I have such unpredictable sleep, which stresses Hunter out, regardless of what he says. I can't seem to get a grip on my emotions. I'm either grieving one minute or numb the next. I hate being such a burden.*

Shame engulfs me like the steam in the shower. I wrestle with the heaviness. Grabbing the soap, I lather up and remind myself to shut up with the negativity, only to find my mind immersed in the list of my unending faults.

Why can't I believe that I'm valued? Loved? Or that I'm cherished? I just read the scriptures. What's wrong with me?

After turning off the faucet, I reach for the towel. Warm steam escapes into the bathroom. I pat myself dry, allowing the cold air to stimulate my senses. While dressing, more questions bombard my mind.

Why do I have to second-guess everything? Am I overly sensitive? Do I overreact to certain situations? And why am I bothered by circumstances that Hunter doesn't see as a big deal? Like his sister lying and being so mean to me?

My nerves feel raw. My heart aches with doubt. I think about how all of this conflict and unrest affects my husband. *Poor Hunter. Who am I to point fingers?*

Maybe I'm a little more like Harriet than I want to admit. My new name could be *Crazy Catherine*. I wouldn't blame Hunter for pulling away. Then a thought hits me, *Is that what Hunter's doing? Is he pulling away?*

My pity party has stolen most of the morning, leaving me only enough time for a quick cup of coffee. I pass by the office on my way to the kitchen. Something grabs my attention. Did I see something? Someone? Was it real or my imagination? The room remains dark and empty.

The aroma of fresh coffee greets me when I hurry into the kitchen. Hunter must've brewed a pot before he left. After pouring coffee into a to-go cup, I take a quick sip. The warmth moves down into my empty stomach. Emptiness—I know that feeling well.

I open the door to set off for my busy day at work, to be followed by a class, and shopping for groceries.

Oh crud, I forgot to put something in the crockpot.

My back stiffens, but I make a point to push back against feeling overwhelmed.

Oh, Lord, help me. I must overcome this battle for my mind. I can do all things through Christ who strengthens me. Let me come boldly before you, Lord, that I may obtain mercy and find grace to help in my time of need. I trust you, God, to work all this out to the good because I do love you. And Hunter, please be with him today.

I close the door behind me and head to my car.

Catie
Winter 1963

The front door swings open. I am the first to look up.

"Yay! Daddy's home from work!" I shout to my sisters and Charley. We don't see him much 'cuz he works most of the time. Sometimes, if I'm lucky, I'll see him before I leave for school, but not often. Daddy says havin' a family with seven kids requires lots of money. That's why I have to wait for the weekends—my favorite days —to spend time with Daddy. He makes us breakfast and watches cartoons with us afterward.

I'm hopin' for a fun game time tonight. Candy Land. Pick-up Sticks. Tinker Toys. And cards too. Daddy likes the same games as me, not like Anna and her spooky games. And since she's in one of her moods, raisin' all kinds of stink, I'm beginnin' to doubt if we're gonna get to play any games tonight.

Complainin' is how Anna picks most of her fights. If you ask me, she loves to stir up trouble. She's a lot like her mom, Poison Ivy. And I don't blame Daddy when he ignores Anna, like when he reads the newspaper or watches the television. Sometimes, he even tunes her out when he talks with us kids. Poor Daddy, he looks worn out from Anna's constant fault-findin' with everyone. 'Specially him.

Anna says it infuriates her when Daddy doesn't pay her attention. Then again, Anna's always irritated and agitated. She sure has a short fuse. It doesn't take much to set her off. She's just a mean witchy woman, and I mean the *real* kind of witch.

Some people might wonder how a seven year old, almost eight, would know such big words like irritate, agitate, and infuriate. Well, I heard Daddy's sister, Aunt Jean, tell Teenage Granny all 'bout Anna's hissy fits. She used those big words. I'm not sure exactly what they mean, but if it means gettin' so mad that your face turns red hot like it's gonna burst into flames, then irritate, agitate, and infuriate all describe Anna.

Daddy sometimes misses the signs of her next eruption. Or maybe he pretends not to notice. Us kids can tell when there's gonna be another uproar. That's Charley's favorite word to describe Anna. *Uproar.* Every time he says it, he makes the sound of a lion roarin'. He says it behind her back, but Claudia says it's disrespectful and that Charley shouldn't.

I often wonder why Daddy would pick such a mean woman to marry. It's not like he doesn't know how to choose a good woman; after all, he picked Mommy. I don't ever remember them fightin', well maybe arguin' a couple of times, but never fightin' like Anna and Daddy.

Anna fights like the cowboys on the television set. She likes to duke it out, with her fists a-flyin'. Daddy has to hold her wrists so she can't hit him, but still, that doesn't always stop her. I've seen her back up against the wall, pull her legs up high, and kick him. He's learned to turn to the side. Otherwise, she kicks or knees him in his private parts.

I've learned to scram when the fightin' starts. I pray that Daddy pins her down before he gets too hurt.

Anna goes ape—often. Even hisses and spits on him. Then the horrible bad words come out of her mouth. Words I can't repeat. There's not enough soap in the world to wash out Anna's mouth.

If Daddy ever asks me, I'll tell him. "Just knock her lights out and then lock her in the basement with the ghost that Anna says lives down there."

But, he never asks what I think. I did tell my sisters and Charley my ideas. They all agreed. 'Specially, Charlotte and Carolyn.

I've had my fair share of meanness when it comes to Anna. I don't dare tell Daddy or anyone, 'cuz they'll kill Charley. They've already hurt him with the pincher pliers and pokey needle things. They say it's my fault, all 'cuz I won't do the things they want me to do. So Charley has to take my punishment and vice-a-versa. It's their rules. They promised they're gonna kill him if I don't start mindin'.

A nna yells, "Dinner's almost ready. Get your damn kids out of this kitchen so that I can get this food on the table!"

Yep, she's in one of her bad moods. She stirs a pot of peas. The steam from the pot looks like it's comin' out of her ears.

"Watch your language in front of the kids," Daddy barks back.

Anna cuts her eyes at Daddy like she wants to cut his throat, and shouts at Charlotte. "Hand me a platter for the meatloaf."

"Okay, Anna." Charlotte opens the lower cupboard to get Anna the dish. "Come on, everyone, go wash up for dinner." Charlotte tells us kids and then hands the large plate to Anna.

With nine of us, washin' hands can take some time. We split into two groups. Some of us go into the bathroom, while others use the kitchen sink. Sometimes, I just wipe my hands on the damp towel. I figure my hands are gonna get messy from dinner anyway.

As we pass to and from the sinks, we sense Anna's temper flarin', gettin' hotter by the minute. She doesn't hide her huffs and puffs. She's like the wolf in the three little pigs, revvin' up enough breath to blow the whole house down.

Claudia walks by just when she erupts. Anna grabs the pot of scaldin' peas off the stove and as quick as lightnin', she flings the pan across the kitchen. A loud shriek echoes from my sister. We all gawk with our mouths open and eyes wide.

Claudia screams bloody murder! She's covered in scaldin' peas!

In a flash, Claudia opens the kitchen door and jumps from the stoop into a snowbank.

She screams and cries so hard that I can hardly hear Daddy tell her to come back inside.

"No, Daddy. My skin's on fire. I'm burnin' up, and the snow makes it feel better."

Anna shouts, "It's your fault, Forest. I didn't see her. I was aiming for you."

I tug on Daddy's shirttail. "Will Claudia be okay?"

I'm afraid for my sister. We push our heads out the side door, starin' at Claudia. We look between Daddy and Anna. We must look like a bunch of frozen squirrels. Too afraid to move or ask questions.

Daddy sends a fiery glare at Anna. "YOU have crossed the line, woman!" His face is red hot and the veins in his forehead bulge. He looks like a volcano that's 'bout to blow. Maybe lava will come out of his ears.

Daddy means business. Anna steps back. She'd better be quiet if she knows what's best. Daddy's never hit Anna before, but I'm hopin', fingers crossed behind my back, he'll pop her a big one. Just like she lets Buck and Dean do to Charley and me. Then let's see if she likes bein' hit. I'd love to see her with a big black shiner.

They glare at each other. No words. Jaws tight. Teeth clenched. This is a new look from Daddy. Him standin' up to her gives me hope. I'm glad Aunt Jean told Teenage Granny all about Anna's temper tantrums.

Keepin' his eyes on Anna, Daddy walks across the kitchen floor. We make way as he walks out the door and down the steps to Claudia. He carries her back into the kitchen and snuggles her in his arms. She muffles her cries as she presses her face into Daddy's neck, not once lookin' at Anna, who din't seem to care that she'd hurt Claudia.

Charlotte follows Daddy and Claudia upstairs. "I'll help you, Dad. I'll get the ointment." Charlotte snarls at Anna as they leave the room.

Sometime later, the stairs creak, and Claudia comes down the stairs with Charlotte walkin' close to her, like they're glued together. Everyone's real quiet till Daddy speaks up.

"She'll be fine. The burns are red, but not blistered."

We're grateful but hungry. Dinner is late once again, minus the peas, 'cuz of Anna's hissy fit. We eat in silence. Daddy stares across the table at Anna. I hope she feels terrible for what she's done, but I'm not sure 'cuz *never once* did she say she was sorry.

Teenage Granny would've said that there's a massive elephant in the room, with everyone pretendin' nothin's wrong. There ain't anythin' that's gonna keep me from tellin' Teenage Granny what Anna did to Claudia. I'll ask Granny to say she overheard it. Otherwise, they'll hurt Charley, as a payback on 'count of me airin' our dirty laundry. Maybe if I tell Teenage Granny, she can help.

Us kids can't take the quiet, so we began jibber-jabberin'. I lean across Carolyn and whisper to Claudia.

"I think you're so-o-o-o smart and cool to think of goin' out into the snow. It's a good thing we had an early snowstorm this month." I smile.

Claudia's eye is swollen and red, matchin' the splotches on her arms, and left cheek. She smiles back 'cuz I called her smart.

Carolyn doesn't care what Anna thinks, and she doesn't whisper like I do. She speaks right up. "You're wicked just like your crazy family." Her eyes send daggers at Anna with each word. Maybe Carolyn has somehow figured out that Anna is a witch, a real witch.

The others join in tellin' Claudia how great she is bein' a *genius* to roll in the snow. Even Charley pipes up. "Claudia, you were as fast as a rocket ship, speeding through the kitchen and out the door! Whoosh." He waves his little hand through the air. "Do your boo-boo's hurt?"

She nods and looks at all of us, but not at Anna. Daddy reaches over and gives her a side hug and a kiss on her forehead.

"Claudia's going to be fine. Aren't you, sweetheart?"

She nods again.

We all trot up the stairs to brush our teeth and get ready for bed. Daddy is gonna tuck us in tonight. Although Claudia's burns hurt, she loves the attention we're givin' her.

Melinda and Shawnee are still downstairs with their mom. Bedtime isn't for another hour, but we can play in our bedrooms till it's time for lights out.

I'm the first to finish brushin' my teeth. I head to my room to check inside my dresser drawer to see if my Christmas nightgown is clean. I'm in luck.

Daddy comes through the door as I finish pullin' my soft flannel nighty over my head.

He slowly trudges over and sits on my bed. The look on his droopy face tells me that he needs a hug. I give him my biggest and bestest hug in the whole wide world.

"Daddy, havin' you and my sisters and Charley here are the only things that make livin' with Anna, umm, well just okay, but not so good. When will you have this house paid for, so you don't have to be gone all the time workin'? How long are Anna and her kids gonna be livin' with us?"

His eyes begin to leak. He shakes his head side-to-side.

"Why can't she just leave, Daddy? Does God have to take her to heaven, like Mommy, before we can get rid of her?"

He lowers his head.

"Daddy. Do you know she's mean? I mean extra mean and a real witch?"

"Peanut, Daddy's really tired. We're going to have to talk another time. The best thing you can do right now is to continue to be my sweet little girl. When all my kids are good and well behaved, it makes things better for all of us."

His eyes are leakin' full blast. I would say he's cryin', but Daddy says men don't cry.

"Goodnight, Daddy. I love you."

He stands and walks to the door.

"I love you too, darlin'."

I want to say that Anna has learned her lesson and has stopped throwin' things, but that's not the case. Not too long after, Claudia got it again. This time it was boilin' water down the front of her wraparound jumper.

Charlotte and Carolyn say Anna doesn't deserve any forgiveness, even though Claudia says she thinks Mommy would want us to forgive. I'm not sure what forgiveness means. Charley ain't got a clue either.

Marion
March 1995

My coffee mug warms my fingers as I get comfortable at a coffee shop near campus. Catherine and I have agreed to meet here, as I have begun renovations at my office. The 'Java Bar' décor is mountain-themed and quite cozy.

Catherine prances into the shop, and before she sits down, she blurts, "Marion, I've been working on my forgiveness list." She waves some papers in the air.

"Oh, that is wonderful, Catherine. I would like to hear what you have written."

"I'm not sure if I did it right, but I kept it simple like you said. I used all the W's: who, what, when, and where. Oh yes, I even added the letter H for how it made me feel." She almost smiles, staring at her written words.

"I have to admit, Marion, it was freeing jotting it down on paper. It affirmed my memories and emotions. Does that sound weird?"

"No, not at all. Forgiveness brings freedom." I take a sip of water to clear my scratchy throat. *I hope I'm not coming down with a cold.*

"Did you bring your notes from our last session?" I ask.

"Yes. They're right here."

She pulls out the ruffled paper. Every inch is covered in her handwriting of various colors of ink and highlighted lines. She turns the paper to the flip side.

"I made notes on the areas where I'm struggling." She looks down at the full pages of notes and then shrugs her shoulders. "It's mostly about the black wedding, but there are other issues as well. I guess I need more time to process." She bats her eyes, seeming nervous. "I can't imagine ever having to speak to them again. Anna and those people. Those—those monsters." Her voice quivers. "Just the thought of seeing them gives me the willies." A startled look clouds her face, like a lost child who is afraid her rescue will never occur.

I wish I could scoop her up, embrace her, and make her feel safe. Nevertheless, the Holy Spirit reminds me that at this present time, Catherine's comfort should come from God, and God only.

"Listen to me carefully, Catherine. Forgiveness should not be confused with reconciliation. That is one bridge we do not have to cross right now. It may never occur."

She nervously spins her wedding ring several times around her jittery finger before she offers a forced nod.

"Catherine, frequently, as in your case with Anna and her family, the offenses may be too great for reconciliation ever to occur. The purpose of forgiveness is to release yourself and the offender from the offense or the debt. Forgiveness is a choice. Your choice. Letting go of your bitterness, resentment, and the fear to trust will release you and bring you peace. Like I have said, there are significant benefits to this truth."

"Th-that's, good to hear, Marion," she says, clenching her hands tightly. "But I'm going to need more counseling and prayer to work through the memories. The black wedding memory for one, as well as the others. They're haunting."

She buries her face in her hands. Several deep breaths later, she says, "Marion?"

I wait for her question. She sits silently and stares at the floor.

I finally ask, "What is it, Catherine?"

"What if I can't forgive them?"

I set Catherine's file aside and lean forward. "Forgiveness is an act of the will, a legal requirement to pardon based on God's command. However, the emotional aspect may require varying lengths of time, depending on the offense."

"No, that's not what I'm saying." She stares into my eyes with a determined glare. "What if I don't want to forgive them? What if I want them to pay?"

She grinds her fist into her hand. "Really pay, for what they've done."

CHAPTER TWENTY-TWO

Catherine
June 1995

I grind through my fears and force myself to focus on moving forward in my counseling. After shifting the car into park and shutting off the engine, I close my eyes and try to let go of the tension I've brought from home. I climb out and shut the car door with resolve, pushing my taunting thoughts aside. I look at Marion's new office sign.

I breeze into Marion's office, eager to see how it's been remodeled. Marion calls out from the back room.

"Hey Catherine, you are early. I am finishing up a file, and I will be out directly. Please make yourself comfortable."

I scan the surroundings, seeing the new design for the first time. I love the colors she's picked; warm creamy walls with gold, burgundy, and deep olive accent colors in the fabrics, pillows, and area rug. It feels warm, cozy, and safe, like Marion.

The cherry sofa table displays multiple photos, all in unique luxurious frames that depict a brief look into Marion's life—full of friends, family, and fun. I'm fond of her tenderness, matched well with her warrior's heart, truly a gift from God.

Her shoes click on the hardwood floor. She stands with her arms wide open. We embrace, and I relax instantly, sinking into one of Marion's big bear hugs.

"The office looks wonderful!" I beam. "Now I can see why it took so long. The decor came out beautifully."

"Yes, I agree. I am happy with the results." Marion smiles as we take our seats.

"I have to admit these last few months have allowed more time to process and accept my past's ugliness. Even with new memories surfacing, I don't feel quite so raw. But truth be told, I missed seeing you."

"That is an encouraging report. Time has a way of soothing wounds, especially when you seek the Lord to expose the lies and replace them with the truth. I have thought about you often, Catherine, and have prayed for you as the Lord led. I figured you were well since you did not contact me."

Marion picks up my file. "I'm fine with scheduling appointments to bi-monthly or monthly as per your request…for now anyway." She raises her brows and offers a soft, compassionate smile. "I am trusting that your healing journey will be in God's timing. Agreed?"

I nod. "My schedule is challenging—juggling work, school, marriage, and counseling all at once. However, I'm thrilled to see you and to get caught up…"

"So, Catherine, tell me about your recent vacation. Did you climb Devils Tower and make it to the passion play with Hunter's folks?"

"We had a blast in South Dakota. The funniest thing happened, in hindsight, I should say. Hunter called the ranger station to ask how long it would take to climb the tower. The guy at the station said about five hours. We planned on seven, being it was a new climb for us." I hand her a postcard of the volcanic core. "When we finished *twelve hours* later!" I pause. "We realized the ranger was being quite literal. He was referring to the climb up and not the descent and rappel, which was another five hours."

Marion's eyes widen. "Oh no, did you make the play?"

"Yes, we did, but barely. We arrived with five minutes to spare. Hunter and I had just enough time to shower. We went with wet hair, and his precious mom made us peanut butter and jelly sandwiches in the back seat."

I wink and giggle slightly. "So…Marion, that's enough about me. How's the dating world going?"

"I admit I am frequently keeping an eye open for any single men. The problem is they are quite difficult to find." A small sigh escapes from behind her hand that covers her mouth. Her eyes briefly glaze, and she looks at the floor.

I set my book bag on the sofa and pull out my journal and pen. "Marion? Would you consider dating ads?" I don't pause for her answer because I want to encourage her to consider the possibilities.

"Have you seen the movie with Tom Hanks and Meg Ryan? It's called something about having mail. Hunter and I rented the movie last week. It's been out a couple of years. I thought it was cute. It's about getting to know someone through letters, like in the olden days of pen-pals, but only now it's writing letters online through email. I hear a lot of people are meeting this way."

Marion wrings her hands and nods with a pensive look. I think she might be considering my suggestion.

"I will think it over. It can only help, right?" She chuckles and blushes. "Catherine, shall we get started?"

"Sure. I'm ready, but Marion, is this normal to have so many conflicting emotions during a counseling session? One minute I'm up, the next I plummet, then I'm back up again. Depending on the memories, I can go from feeling peaceful to feeling like I'm drowning in fear. It's exhausting and frightening."

Marion smiles. "Yes, this is perfectly normal—especially when dealing with trauma and recovering suppressed memories. Your emotions connect to the events in your past. As you engage your emotions, they can easily jump from one extreme to another."

"My appointments cause more motion sickness than an amusement park ride." I make light of what I know lies ahead. "Plus, I often only see random glimpses of my past. It's frustrating."

"Catherine, as a child, your experiences were too much for you to comprehend or process. Often victims of severe trauma suppress memories. Or as Catie would say, you hid the secrets. Your recollections began to resurface while you were living in Switzerland. Correct?"

I nod.

"Memories may come in flashes, segments, or incomplete recollection. However, you do not necessarily have to recall every detail in its entirety to know what has occurred." Marion shifts in her chair. Her voice is soothing and calm. "As an adult, you are better equipped to face your past."

Marion cups her chin in her hand. "Your emotions act as a pathway to the memories. The goal is to expose the belief or falsehood that Anna and her family led you to believe."

"Like them saying my Dad *wanted* me to be a part of the black wedding?" I ask.

"That was a lie they told you, but what did that lie lead you to believe about yourself?"

"That I was not protected, not valued, and that I didn't matter." I hang my head. I remember how painful those beliefs felt.

Marion probes. "And what did those beliefs say about you?"

I instantly blurt out the answer. "That I am unlovable?"

"Catherine, as a child, you thought as a child. However, there are advantages of remembering the past from a child's point of view, as well as seeing it from an adult's point of view. How do you perceive those memories presently?"

"My dad has always loved me. Anna and the bunch lied about him knowing. My father cherishes me, and I am deeply loved." A sense of freedom comes over me, bringing a smile.

Marion points upward, referring to heaven.

"The Lord is faithful to reveal and confirm what was and is true." She pats my file that lays on her lap.

I lie back on the love seat, stretch out, and try to relax while Marion prays.

"Dear Lord, thank you for being here with Catherine and myself. We are grateful that we can depend upon you for all things. We pursue your direction. Holy Spirit, as Catherine wills and seeks your guidance, lead her to truth and healing. We thank you, Lord, for the promise that the truth will indeed set us free. In Jesus Christ's name, Amen."

Marion starts right in. "Catherine, over these last weeks, what new memories and emotions have surfaced?"

"A rush of shame and guilt engulfs me. I feel so responsible like it's all my fault."

Marion responds. "If you are willing, allow yourself to experience this guilt and shame. Identify with the responsibility you believe is your fault. Follow the emotions to where you have felt this way before. Preferably, the first time. Report back whatever comes to your mind."

I squirm deeper into the cushions. I command my body to relax as much as possible. I know the routine. I sense the oncoming emotional rollercoaster, and the battle begins.

"The air feels clammy and cold. Foul air surrounds me, like an infected dog's breath, as if something sinister stands over me, breathing down my neck."

The images surface.

"It's a familiar path—dark. Ugly. It appears that I am inside a human bowel."

Another picture appears. "I see baby parts. Bones tucked in the shadows of nooks and crannies. People are wearing dark cloaks with hoods at some type of altar."

I blink several times, wanting to erase the offensive images. I wrap my arms around my stomach. I feel woozy.

"Oooh, Marion, I know this feeling—the fogginess, the sick stomach—they drugged me."

My head spins, and my belly stirs—waves of nausea rise. I swallow several times to keep from throwing up.

"I recognize the darkness and gloom. It's pressing in, trying to engulf me." I recoil and pull away. "It's evil."

I bite my lip to focus and to stay in the memory. I squirm and then stiffen. "It's too dark." I manage to muster out.

"How are you doing, Catherine? Describe how you are feeling."

Guilty, ashamed, a-afraid, and alone. I sense wickedness. There's an evil presence encroaching. Moving toward me."

"You are doing great, Catherine. You have been here before. Follow your feelings into the memory. Feel the emotions and focus on being alone with evil nearing."

Several minutes pass. "Catherine, what does this memory say about you?"

The answer comes right away. "I'm not valuable. That's why I'm here in this evil place. God doesn't value me because he would've protected me and kept me from harm's way if he did."

Marion questions, "How true does that belief feel? On a scale from one to ten, one being the least true and ten being the absolute truth?"

"Eleven!" My hands clench.

Marion prays, "Lord, tell Catherine what she needs to know about her belief that she is not valued. What is the truth?"

I report to Marion. "His voice is near, present, tender, and soft. God says he values me and has always been with me. Marion, *God, values me!*" His truth suddenly is crystal clear. My excitement rises. "The Lord is now explaining his gift of free will and how he has given everyone the freedom to make their own choices."

I briefly open my eyes and gaze over at Marion. "God has a way of telling me things instantly, but explaining it to you seems to take forever."

"Catherine, what you are experiencing is called a revelation—a divine disclosure from God, bringing truth, knowledge, and understanding at a deeper level. God reveals the truth to you in seconds, which can take minutes, hours, even days to share with someone else. The Lord lives outside of time, so he is not restricted by time. After all, God created time."

I close my eyes to concentrate. Tears stream onto Marion's new pillow.

"What is occurring now? Is the Lord speaking to you?" she asks.

"Yes. He's explaining his love, our will, and our choices. God wants us to choose to love and follow him, but he'll never force us. He allows us to choose out of his love, unlike controlled mindless robots. What we choose is our decision."

I shake my head, side-to-side, feeling my hair rustling against the pillow.

"But I'm having trouble understanding why people choose darkness and evil. Like with Anna and her family." Within my mind, I see their faces.

"Jesus is explaining why he didn't stop Dean, Buck, Ivy, and Anna, and the rest of the evil bunch. He says it's because it would violate the gift of free will." I ponder the Lord's words.

"He's here. I see him. I see Jesus." I say.

My attention shifts onto the Lord's presence. My skin rises with refreshing chills.

"He's standing next to me. Oh, Marion, all of the feelings of being unvalued are gone. Peace is flowing, surrounding me like a soft blanket, warm and hopeful. I feel safe. I'm looking into his eyes, seeing —feeling—sensing so much love and concern."

I tilt my head, trying to decipher more. "There is sadness in Jesus' eyes." I pause and look deeper into the vision. "His sadness is for me."

Again, the Lord's comfort embraces me. I'm compelled to move forward.

"Marion, the emotions are moving in like waves. With each swell, his love feels larger, deeper. It's a love I've never felt before."

Basking in the sensations makes me feel truly loved, valued, safe, and complete. *I never want to leave.*

Suddenly a new vision invades. Words scream within my thoughts, and scenes flash quickly. My feelings instantly shift. Beads of sweat break out on my face. I wipe my brow.

"I'm scared," I shriek. "No, I'm terrified!"

"Catherine, focus. Allow yourself to feel. Permit yourself to remember. What are you believing?"

Marion's words echo, competing with the screams inside my head.

"If I feel, I'll go crazy. It will be too much! I'll go crazy." I dig my nails into the cushion. I suck in a deep breath, searching for air.

Marion interjects. "Lord, please tell Catherine the truth. Will she go crazy if she allows herself to feel and to remember?"

A still quiet voice speaks. *'I am here.'* His word permeates. *'I did not give you a spirit of fear but of power, love, and a sound mind.'*

Calmness overshadows me.

"Marion. He's here. He says, emotions are good, they are a part of my cleansing."

I continue viewing the memories, seeing bits and pieces. I force myself into the fragments, seeing flashes of candles burning, black devil eyes, Anna and Ivy's smiles, and shiny, black satin. My nose fills with a stench. My mouth waters, causing me to swallow repeatedly. I fidget and twist my ring.

Marion questions, "Catherine, where are you? What is occurring?"

The memory sharpens. "I'm standing outside in a dirt parking lot, looking at a church in the distance. Everyone is all dressed up. They're strolling up a walkway." My palms feel sweaty. *"Oh NO!—I know this place!* It's my wedding! I'm there again."

I wipe my shaky, damp palms on the side of my slacks.

"Catherine, encourage yourself to enter into the memory."

I obey her instructions. I push deeper into my past. Deep. Deeper. My body thrashes in reaction to this hellish memory. It's all too familiar. I want to deny it ever happened, but I know without a doubt the reality of what they've done.

"Catherine, what are you feeling? Seeing?" Marion's voice anchors me.

"I'm anxious. Confused. I don't like this place." I squeeze my already closed eyes tighter, trying not to see the images.

"Describe what you see," Marion instructs.

"The room has unfinished dirt floors that have been oiled and packed. Scents of decay, dampness, and wormy earth fill my nose. The candles glow in a warm shimmer throughout the cavern, yet it feels as cold as ice.

"I'm being raised on the presentation platter. My hands grope to find the hem of the satin dress. I rub the cloth through my fingers. I search for comfort but find none, only the softness of the yellow satin fabric."

I know where I'm going. But why? Why must I return?

"NO! NO! NO!" I scream. "I hate this. I hate these people. I don't belong here. I don't want to be here! Why, Lord?"

CHAPTER TWENTY-THREE

Catherine
June 1995

The intensity of emotions catapults me out of the terrifying memory. However, the haunting departing words remain, screaming in my mind, 'It is your wedding! It is your wedding to Satan. You are his!'

My skin crawls. I push myself into the corner of the love seat, pressing tightly against the cushions in a futile attempt to distance myself from what I've just relived.

I cry out, "No. No. No!"

Denial doesn't change my reality. I burst into tears.

"Catherine." Marion's voice redirects me. "Stay in the memory. You are doing great. Keep searching for what it is you believe. What is happening?"

I take a deep gulp to gather my wits and choke out the words. "I'm back at the black wedding. Th-they say...I am the br-bride of Satan."

Hopelessness and all it implies threaten my thoughts. I'm on edge...on the edge of losing my mind. Jagged edges of pain cut deep into my soul.

I cry out, "I can't live with this belief. Who am I? NO! Please, no!"

As panic rises, I suck in air, but there's no relief. I fight for air one breath at a time.

"Catherine, listen to me. Slow your breathing."

I hear Marion's voice and do my best to obey.

"You are doing fine. I am here with you. Take in one long slow breath."

Again, I listen and do as I'm encouraged.

"This is good. You are doing well. Breathe. Yes...long,... slow...breaths."

I calm myself by listening to Marion's instructions.

"Do you wish to go further? It is your choice. I will honor whatever you choose." Marion speaks slowly, her words soft.

I search for the Lord and the needed courage and grit to dive deeper into the memory. I replay God's words within my mind. *'I can do all things through Christ who strengthens me.'* Going deeper, I travel into the memory. Pain. Despair. Hopelessness. The familiar emotions rise. All too familiar...it's more than I can stand. I seek numbness!

Soon I feel nothing. I cling to it. I'm alive, yet I feel dead. Thoughts of being the bride of Satan circle my mind like birds of prey. Over and over the words replay and every time the implications grow closer. The accusations frighten me. Somehow, I know the enemy wants to devour me! I pull my legs to my chest and cower.

"Catherine. Focus. Listen to me." Her voice sounds firm. "Are you willing to hear what the Lord has to say about your belief of being the bride of Satan?"

Unable to speak, I nod. Fear swoops in—it is heavy, suffocating. Terror. Anxious. Raw. The emotions are intense—too intense!

"Please… help me! I can't be—please no—not the bride of Satan. No! No! No!" I thrash my head.

"Lord, please reveal the truth to Catherine. What does she need to know about this black wedding? What did the occult proclaim over her? What is valid?"

Marion's voice lingers. Her questions resound in my mind.

I listen and wait for an answer. Suddenly I see a beautiful vision.

"Marion, I see myself. I'm dressed in a white wedding dress and standing with Jesus. I have an open veil. Jesus is gazing directly at me. There is an incredible deep love in his eyes. His love somehow embraces me."

My tension and fear melt away. I'm immersed in unbelievable peace. *Please, Lord, let me stay here with you forever.*

"The white of my wedding dress is like diamonds; white, clear, and reflecting all the hues of the color spectrum. It's whiter than anything I've ever seen." Even with my eyes shut, I blink in astonishment.

"Jesus stands before me, telling me, 'I am *His* Bride. I am the Bride of Christ. As I hear his words, I'm washed clean of defilement, shame, and death."

Warm tears of joy cascade down my face. A sense of completion, peace, and purity leaves me feeling beautiful, loved, significant, and accepted by the Lord. *I never want to leave. Please, Lord, let me stay.*

I hear Marion's voice in the background. "Father God, is there anything more you want to say or give to Catherine?"

There's a depth of spiritual dimension present I've never experienced. I'm floating in the presence of perfection, yet it feels so natural, fulfilling, and complete. I describe everything to Marion as it happens.

"Jesus extends his arm to reveal a bright shiny ring in the palm of his hand. It's a wedding band made of warm, yellow gold. Jesus caresses my hand and says, 'This ring has no beginning, nor end. It is symbolic of me. *I AM—Eternal Life.*'"

I get it! I understand. "The Lord's telling me, he is Eternal Life, not to be confused with a measurement of time, as in living throughout eternity. He's describing himself. No beginning—no ending." His words flow. "'You are mine. I am in you, as you are in me. This is our covenantal wedding.'"

I hear Marion take in a breath.

"Marion, God is telling me that I received his Spirit inside of me when I believed in him. We became one in a covenantal relationship. It is like his everlasting covenants with Abraham, Moses, David, and marriage.

"I lift my hand as Jesus gently slides the ring onto my third finger. Our eyes meet in an endless second."

Simultaneously, assaulting thoughts crash into my mind. Dark opposing words scream, and cut into my thoughts!

'YOU ARE THE BRIDE OF SATAN. YOUR MARRIAGE AND DEDICATION WERE TO ME! YOUR VOWS STILL STAND.'

I cover my ears. The meaning of the words smash down upon me. The weight of my shame is heavy, too much to bear. I twitch and tremble.

"Catherine, what are you hearing?"

I repeat the accusation and describe the vision to Marion…

My eyes squint, glaring at the congregation of people, separated only by an aisle that leads to an erected satanic altar.

One by one, my emotions rise. Fear. Regret. Defilement. Hopelessness swells like a tsunami. Each wave of emotions is purposed to crash over me and destroy my hope. And ultimately destroy me.

My mind sinks deeper into the memory. I'm tumbled and tossed by the conflicting turbulence that crushes me with despair and doubt.

Marion's prayers encourage me. "Lord, help Catherine to see the battlefield is in her mind. Help her to war against the lies of the demonic and bind your truth to her mind. Remind her of the power and authority she has in you and in your name as your child."

I call out, "Lord, help me! Jesus!"

'I am here.' I know his voice. I search for him within the vision, turning my head frantically in all directions until I find him. He is here. His hands firmly squeeze my hand, my forearm, and pull me up and out of the depths of the scene. I cling onto the Lord's arm with both hands, desperate for my life.

Suddenly, I'm standing next to Jesus. I look down at the dark scene. A wave of fog enters the room. It begins at the back of the altar and moves up and over the crowd. Somehow, I'm able to look intently into each person's face, putting names to some. The fog continues filling the pews until I am unable to see them any longer.

A revelation fills my mind. I'm suddenly aware of their abuse—victims themselves, many trapped and forced into this vileness. Unable to escape. Some have learned to avoid the damage by becoming the abuser. In this world of the occult, your choices are limited. Control or be controlled. Neither are real choices. Both render a life of bondage.

Another wave of emotion topples me, again, hopelessness. The hopelessness I felt as a child. The hopelessness I feel presently. And now the hopelessness I feel for them.

A strange yearning to forgive them comes upon me. My heart fills with compassion and empathy for the very people who had carried out so many evil and brutal acts. I want to separate myself from their entanglement and release them over to God.

But I vacillate. My heart wrestles between hatred, justice, and mercy. Somehow, I perceive they have nothing, only the consequences of their choices! The accountability for their deeds! The guilt of their pending judgment! The responsibility for their actions!

Justice! Yes, justice is what I've long for. Longed for it to the point that my bones ached.

Yet, I hear myself praying, "I forgive them, Father. Help them find hope in you. I forgive then and I release them over to you. I hope someday they will find the freedom I have found in believing in you. In Jesus' name, Amen."

The Lord's soothing voice embraces me. *'I have made propitiation and restitution for you. You are restored through me, and you are my bride.'*

As the fog thickens over the memory, I feel at peace—I'm safe. The fear, the shame, and feelings of being responsible are gone.

In the distance, the fog continues to move as if engulfing a mountain range.

I hear a booming echo of the Lord's voice proclaiming, 'IT IS DONE!'

CHAPTER TWENTY-FOUR

Catherine
Summer 1995

E cstatic about my breakthrough, the Lord's words continue to boom through my mind. I arrive home unable to recall the drive. Before leaving the office, Marion warned me for the umpteenth time to expect a pushback with the battle for my mind. She reminded me of the importance of staying alert and aware of my thoughts, to uproot the lies, and replace them with the truth. The enemy does not like losing ground and most likely will be on the attack.

My false beliefs of not being valued, along with the fear, shame, and feelings of being responsible are gone. All I can do is envision myself in my beautiful bridal gown. My huge grin comes without effort. I would swear I was floating on air. Light. What a night! I'll remember this evening forever. With great enthusiasm, I proclaim aloud. "I'm a Child of God. I'm His Bride. I'm loved and valued!" Finally, my tears are tears of joy.

Before getting out of my car, I promise God and myself that I'll be diligent to continue counseling, and submit to whatever the Lord has for me to remember. No matter what happens.

I quietly enter the house and slip off my shoes, shaking my head with wonder. How is it possible to feel both energized yet exhausted at the same time? Such a strange sensation, but one I like. I tiptoe up the stairs to see the office light is on. I enter.

With a smile, I walk in the office. "Hi, Hunter, I'm home."

He jumps. "Oh, you scared me." He scrambles to shut off his computer, looking disheveled.

"I scared you. Why?" I lean over him to look at the computer screen. It's black. "What were you looking at?"

"Oh nothing, just surfing the web, various subjects. There's a wealth of knowledge on the computer." He spins his chair around directly facing me. "How did your session go?"

A tension scrapes up my spine. Hunter's words sound empty, fake, and redirecting. My suspicions rise.

Why isn't he telling me the whole truth? What's he hiding?

Exhaustion curbs me from probing my husband with questions. I flick on the reading lamp next to the chair and ease myself down onto the soft cushion, grateful for the cradling comfort. I rest my legs on the ottoman, and with little energy left, I rehash a simplified version of my appointment with Marion.

"Tonight's session took me to a place, I...uhh would've never dreamed of going. Um, I found myself, ahh...if you can believe this... wanting to forgive Anna and her family."

My words come out garbled. I trip over my tongue, making a mess of painting an accurate picture of my experience. Although I desire to share and celebrate my miracle with Hunter, I'm distracted with this eerie feeling of distrust.

"It was quite supernatural, surreal even, to ever think I could find compassion or empathy for Anna and her family..."

While Hunter listens, his eyes harden. His brows furrow, skepticism reflects off his expressions. He looks down and picks at his fingernails, never saying a word in response. He seems distant, removed, and I sense he's angry, but I don't know why.

I'm disappointed—and hurt. I cross my arms over my chest and try not to lash out. I hope I'm reading him wrong.

"Well, that's just great, Catherine. I'm glad *you're* able to forgive." Sarcasm spews out in an angry burst. His hands clench into fists. "But if it were up to me, I'd stab them! I'd kill them all!"

Marion
Summary 1995

There. I stab the garden hand trowel into the ground. The last planter of annuals is finished. I sit back and admire my efforts. Two round planters burst with a profusion of red, white, and blue flowers, along with some trailing greenery. They look festive flanking my front door for the coming 4th of July holiday.

My phone rings inside the house. I push to my feet, stripping the gardening gloves as I enter the front door and hurry to the phone.

"Hello?" I sound out of breath. Still need to get into shape.

"Marion? It's Catherine. How are you?"

"I am well. I was just doing some gardening in anticipation of Independence Day in another week." I brush a bit of dirt from my blouse. "How are you doing, Catherine?"

"That's what I wanted to touch base about. I'm a little frustrated." She blows out a breath over the phone. "Do you have a moment to talk?"

"Of course, Catherine."

"Marion, I told Hunter about my last session. You know, the whole forgiveness experience. Here I am finally at a place to forgive, but he didn't seem thrilled about my excitement or freedom, to say the least." Her voice sounds tense. "I don't know, maybe we were both tired, or I didn't explain it right because his reaction was to kill them all."

"It was supernatural when the Lord's presence saturated the room. However, I would contemplate it to be quite difficult to describe the experience to someone who was not present." I smile at the memory, filled with hope for Catherine.

She sighs. "Yes, probably so, but I wanted Hunter to understand that it was beyond *my ability* to forgive those people. And not just to forgive Anna and the bunch, but also to forgive myself. I wanted to share that I had released the lies I'd believed, blaming God for what they had done."

Silence fills the line for a moment before she continues. "Not that God had done anything wrong, but I'd blamed him for not protecting me. This truth—or revelation, as you put it, was such a phenomenon for me! It was absolutely a God thing."

I can feel her excitement over the phone line.

"Catherine, I am thrilled with the revelation and vision the Lord gave you. It is a great and a wonderful springboard. You will find it beneficial to remember this special event as other memories surface. Forgiving Anna and her group may not be a one-time thing. Do you remember what we discussed about forgiveness?"

I pull the phone cord so that I can sit on my armchair, pulling a scratchpad and pen into my lap.

"Yes, I do. Marion, I can see now that my focus was on the pain and the fear of the unknown. I had no idea the freedom that would come. I was over the top about our last session. I saw it as miraculous, but Hunter seemed, well, he reacted defensive and angry. It confused me. I felt like he wasn't on the same page, not rooting for me and—"

"—Maybe as if he was raining on your parade?" I say. "I am not defending him, but perhaps this is the protective side of your husband. Hunter may be experiencing anger and frustration because he is unable to change the past and how it is affecting the present. Perhaps he has misunderstandings about the meaning of forgiveness, or he may need more time to process. You must try to be patient."

I make a note of Catherine's husband's reaction on my pad.

"I'm sure you're right. He probably just needs more time. That's something I can understand."

I wind the phone cord around my finger. "The subjects I am teaching you apply to all problems. A person can bring their challenges to the Lord and apply the same truths found in his word to obtain answers and resolve—as you have," I say as encouragement. "I cannot say what your husband is struggling with, but all personal problems can feel overwhelming and painful. He may have questions or need to discuss whatever is on his mind. He is welcome to schedule an appointment. Ask him to give me a call."

"Thanks, Marion. I appreciate the offer. I'll make sure to tell him."

I hear a soft bang.

"Sorry, Marion, I just opened the cabinet for a cup. I'm so thirsty. I have to say this craziness is hard to accept, even for me. It doesn't make sense to feel sorry and have compassion for the very people who have done so much harm. It must sound even crazier; I mean insane to Hunter."

The sound of running water comes over the line.

"Hunter's reaction bothered me. Whether he needs more time or not, it was odd. I can't put my finger on it, but he seemed agitated when I walked into the office. He turned off the computer—way too fast. It seemed like he was hiding something. It felt off, and my distrust radar rose instantly."

I hear her slurp a drink.

An uneasiness rises within me. "Did you question your husband about what he was viewing?"

She answers after a long pause. "Yes, but he made light of the question. He said he was surfing the web and then redirected to hearing about my session." Another pause. "But I didn't believe him."

"Did you check the history to confirm what he was viewing?"

"Huh? What? I didn't know you could. I'm new with computers. I only know how to do emails and Word documents. Would you show me—I mean how to check a history?"

"Of course, I do not mind showing you, but we can do that when you come in next week."

I make a note on my pad as a reminder, but wonder if investigating the history on Hunter's computer will open a can of worms. I gulp.

"Catherine, I must let you go, but I encourage you to continue remembering, and we will discuss what you have learned next week."

Catie
Winter 1963

Anna says Charley and me must go with her to Granny Ivy's and Buck's house. She pulls into their long driveway. It's bright and sunny, unusual for a winter day. Charley and me hope to catch bugs, but it's harder once it has snowed. Searchin' for insects is just an excuse not to have to go into their house.

We never know what our visits will bring; a fun day or an icky secret day.

We dash out of the car then skip toward the barn to see if Gilbert is in the bunkhouse. Nope. I grab our bug catchin' jars off the workbench and skedaddle out into the barnyard. We catch a glimpse of Gilly with some new kids playin' dodge ball in the field. Charley and me wave and run in their direction.

We din't even ask permission. I don't care anymore 'bout gettin' spankin's 'cuz if this bunch wants to hit me, they will, even if I ain't done nothin' wrong. So, I figure I'm gonna get a beatin', no matter what.

Anna din't seem to notice, 'cuz she has her eyes glued on the cowboy who's hidin' up in the loft of the barn. I saw him send a big smile her way.

He's been at our house before. He pretends to be a fix-it man, but I've never seen him fix anythin' unless it's in Anna and Daddy's bedroom.

However, her favorite visitor is the glass man. It seems like Anna always finds an excuse to have one of her tantrums and throw somethin' through the front picture window. But I know it's 'cuz she wants to see her glass man.

She always shoos us out of the house when her men friends come by. That's fine with me. I'd rather be outside playin' anyway. Plus, it gives me the willies the way those men look at me, and my sisters.

Charley, Gilbert, me, along with the new kids, gather together to decide which team Charley and me will be on. We set our bug jars down, excited to play a game of dodge ball.

Gilbert tells the new kids about the fun we have catchin' bugs together. He points to our jars. "There's a real knack to open up the catcher jar without letting the other bugs out. Catie and Charley are really good at it. But Catie likes the bugs that crawl the best, because the flying ones always find a way of getting into her hair." Gilbert pretends he's me, battin' at pretend bugs and squealin' like a pig. The boys all laugh, but I don't care. I am a girl, and squealin' is just what girls do. I laugh too.

Gilbert tosses me the ball first 'cuz I'm on his team. Charley's on the other team. "Here, Catie, you start. Hey, guys, you better watch out, she's a good aim."

We all run in different directions. I throw the ball and hit the blonde-haired boy right away. "He's out!"

Granny Ivy hollers out into the field, callin' two of the new kids back to the barn. She calls them foster kids, but I bet she's lyin'. *Liar, liar, pants on fire.*

We keep playin'. My team has already won the first game and are playin' our second round when Granny Ivy calls me to the barn. I'm warm from all the runnin', so I stop at the hose for a quick drink. I wipe my mouth on my shirtsleeve then walk into the cool shade of the barn.

The nurse lady is here again, with her mean assistant. She waves me over. They're talkin' with Granny Ivy 'bout somethin'. I see the two fellas I was playin' ball with earlier. They look down, hidin' their red puffy eyes.

Uh oh… they've been cryin'. This can't be good.

They're the same boys who made fun of me for gettin' wigged out over flyin' bugs. I don't mind if they think I'm a sissy 'cuz I'm a girl. But these boys must've had somethin' real bad happen to make them cry. Big boys don't cry, they say.

A stretcher rests on top of two bales of straw. A boy hops down and walks away.

Miss Nurse calls me over. She's not mean like her assistant. Her eyes don't turn black like June bugs either.

I sit on the stretcher. The nurse guides me to lie down and then covers me with a blue cloth from my waist down.

She explains, "Catie, I need to look at your privates."

"Why?"

Poison Ivy, who's as quick as lightnin', yanks on my ear—hard, sayin, "It's none of your business to ask why. Do what you're told." Her face wrinkles up like a prune.

Miss Nurse rubs my leg gently under the blue cloth, where mean old Poison Ivy can't see. Her smile is kind.

"Catie, I need to lower your knee-knockers and panties. I'll make sure the sheet stays over you so no one will see you but me, okay?"

"Uh-huh. Will it hurt?" I whisper.

Granny Ivy spews her poison at Miss Nurse. "You don't ask them for permission. Just do your job!"

Ivy turns a cold shoulder to us and then walks away huffin' in disgust. I'm glad she's gone. I like this nurse lady. She doesn't let Granny Ivy scare her.

I hold still and make sure not to make a fuss as she removes my clothes and neatly sets them to the side on the bale of straw.

"Okay, Catie, I'm going to lift your legs and place each foot on the side of my shoulders."

She scoots me closer to the end of the stretcher and then makes a tent over her head with the blue cloth. It covers both of us. While she touches my privates, she asks questions.

"Does this hurt? Burn?"

I reply sheepishly. "Yah."

Miss Nurse puts somethin' cold inside causin' a giant pinch, followed by what feels like the sharp point of a straight pin. I cry out and jerk to get away. Her assistant pounces hard, holdin' me down.

Miss Nurse assures me, "Catie, please honey, be still. I'll try to be real quick. Do you think you can be brave and hold still for a bit longer?"

I do my very best not to move, but I can't help but wiggle a little. The nurse softly rubs my calf hidden under the tent. When she's finished, she puts my legs down and then pulls out her head and covers me with the cloth.

"I'm sorry, Catie, but I'm going to have to give you a shot. And I won't lie to you. It will hurt, but in no time, your privates won't burn or pain you anymore." She gives me a sad smile.

While her assistant holds me down, Miss Nurse pokes the needle into my fanny. I scream out. Immediately, my mouth is covered. The mean lady's hand smashes my lips into my teeth. The burnin' sting and pressure won't stop. I hold my breath. Now I know why the tough boys were cryin'.

"Okay, Catie, you're done now. You can put your clothes back on. You should feel better soon."

Once dressed, I watch Miss Nurse march across the barn, over to Buck, Devil Dean, and Poison Ivy, who are lookin' into a wooden box.

The nurse lady clears her throat—loud. Her hands are on her hips, and her face is all snarled up.

I sneak over in their direction. I belly crawl, army style, on the opposite side of the bales of straw, and peek over the top to listen in.

"What's going on here?" she yells. "Are you and all your men friends so filthy that you can't wash up and get check-ups for yourselves?"

She stares at Dean, then turns her eyes over to Buck. "All of these kids have the clap!"

Poison Ivy speaks up. "I don't think it's wise for you to be talking to my husband and father like that, Miss Priss—if you know what's good for you."

Miss Nurse ignores Granny Ivy. She leans in closer to the men.

"Well, *what if* one of these kids tells their parents their privates hurt, *huh*? Or their school nurse? Explain *clap* to the parents. Most of these kids are linked back to you."

Miss Nurse cuts her eyes to Ivy. "So, *Miss Priss*, how does a child from three to nine years old contract a venereal disease? Huh?" She glares. "How will you account for that?"

Buck, Dean, and Ivy stand still, quiet, their mouths wide open. I hear a whimperin' sound from the box at their feet. It sounds like puppies. I want to go over and see, but don't dare.

"That's what I thought!" Miss Nurse glares at Granny Poison Ivy like she dares her to say somethin'. Maybe even double dog dares, as she leans face to face with her. I'm hopin' they'll fight and that Ivy will get the daylights knocked out of her. Then Miss Nurse twists and walks away. Dust puffs in the air as she stomps across the dirty, barn floor.

I slowly begin to move. A stick breaks underneath me.

"Who's there?" The three bark out.

I stand slowly, stretch, and then yawn, pretendin' I've been asleep.

"It's just me. I was tired from my shot." I make my eyes look sleepy, then look toward the box. "What's in the box? Sounds like puppies." I bounce my shoulders up and down with excitement.

"Yah, Old Sadie here got herself knocked up again." Dean puffs in disgust. "I thought she'd run off, but we found her this morning in the back of the barn with this here litter of pups. One of the pups ran out, and I almost crushed it under my work boots."

I stretch my neck to get a better look. Three little puppies nestle in close, nursin' on their mommy. Sadie looks happy to have her babies close.

"How old are they?" I kneel. My bottom stings from my shot, but I ignore it and move to the edge of the container. I keep the wooden box between me and creepy Dean.

"I guess about four to six weeks." Buck looks at his wife. "What do you think, Ivy?"

"That sounds about right. I hope they'll be good mousers like their mom."

Mean Dean must've snuck behind me. Without any warnin', he grabs me by my shirt and yanks me up—hard.

"Ouch!" I jerk.

Dean's black devil eyes smile back at me. My skin crawls 'cuz I know he means no good. He twists the neck of my shirt and pushes his fist against my Adam's-apple to choke me. *It takes my breath. I panic.*

Just in the nick of time, Barbie runs through the barn door, out of breath. Her windblown hair and sun-kissed cheeks bring a playfulness and lightness to the room. She looks into the box and squeals.

"Puppies, puppies, puppies! Uncle Dean, Uncle Dean, I heard you had puppies! Can I play with them? Can I? Can I? Please? Pretty please?" She jumps up and down.

Barbie's smooth face looks like a porcelain cupid. I know what porcelain looks like, 'cuz Teenage Granny has a little porcelain figurine. She puts it up high on the knickknack shelf to protect it, 'cuz it's so precious and valuable. She let me touch it once. I made sure to pet it carefully. Porcelain is smooth, like Barbie's face. I stare at her soft pink cheeks, and her cute full baby pucker lips, and bright blue eyes. The kind of eyes that aren't so big that they bulge—like frog-eyes, Melinda. Not too little that they're squinty, like mine. Barbie's eyes are perfect. Her lashes are long and dark, like an older girl who wears makeup, but Barbie doesn't, 'cuz she's only a kid.

I remember seein' her the night of the manger with Baby Jesse. She was there with GI Joe. She must love dresses 'cuz both times she's been wearin' one, the kind pinched in at the waist with a big bow in the back and full at the bottom. I watch her sway back and forth, makin' her dress sail side to side, as she *sweet-talks* Dean 'bout the puppies.

I'd love to have a pretty dress. I feel sad as I look down at my dirty, green, corduroy knee-knockers, with one knee torn open, and covered in dry mud.

Dean moves over, too close to my face. I cringe and squint my eyes.

"Catie, Buck was just sayin' you might like to have one of those puppies for yourself."

I hold my breath so I don't gag from his hot breath stinkin' of tobacco.

"Of course, it has to stay living at the farm, but when you're visiting, you can have one of Sadie's puppies for your very own. Even name it." Dean smiles. His teeth look rotten, the color of dark coffee.

I look over at Barbie, cuddlin' a cute little puppy close to her neck. I nudge closer. She smells so clean. The puppy licks the clean, fresh soapy smell as she tussles the little fellow carefully in her arms.

"Catie, what do you want to name your puppy?" Dean asks as he, Buck, and Ivy, all eyeball me.

I reach into the box and lift out the multi-colored puppy. The little fellow has four white socks and a cute face with brown eyebrows and muzzle. Black spots of all sizes cover his body. He doesn't look anythin' like his mommy, Sadie, who's brown with floppy black ears.

"Hmm. I was thinkin' 'bout callin' the pup, Spot, but on second thought, I think I'll name him, Happy, 'cuz that's how he makes me feel."

I pick up my puppy and bring him close to inhale his sweet puppy smell. His kisses tickle my nose. Barbie and me sit on the ground next to Sadie who watches closely. One of the puppies prances in front of Barbie. She lays her front legs on the ground with her butt up in the air. The little furball lets out several puppy barks. Her tail wags a hundred miles an hour. We name her Angel. I gently play with my pup. I pull Sadie close to me and Happy, so she doesn't feel left out. The mommy dog licks my hands and wags her tail.

Before long, Dean says I need to put Happy down and come with him. I gently place my sweet puppy in the box. Sadie jumps in and snuggles with her babies. The old man takes my hand, then leads me to one of the small stalls.

I know what he wants. It's always the same. I hate it!

My mind wanders. I'm thinkin' 'bout, Happy, so I forget to make-believe that I like Dean's yucky slobbery kisses and rough tuggin' and pushin'. He notices and explodes in anger. His pinches and bites hurt more than where I got my shot.

"I'm sorry, Dean, I was just thinkin 'bout my pup, Happy," I plead, hopin' he will stop. "I'll try to pretend better."

The word 'pretend' accidentally slips out. He slugs me in the stomach. *It takes my breath. I panic.*

An older girl, who I named Lilly, musta heard my cries. She peeks her head into the stall area and then walks right up and stands next to us.

Lilly is tall and slender, somewhere around twelve years old—maybe more. She seems to have figured out all this man stuff. It makes me gag, but she knows how to pretend to enjoy it—a good actress. Unlike me, Lilly smiles and giggles when Dean looks at her. She wrestles playfully with him, and Dean seems to like how the pretty girl acts.

I say we need to give all these men pacifiers. They're just like little babies wantin' to suck all over you. YUCK! But Lilly doesn't seem to mind.

She's beautiful and reminds me of a flower, so that's why I named her Lilly. She wears white and other light colors. She uses her words and whispers to get her way and to stay safe. The men are nice to her, unlike the way they treat the rest of us kids.

Lilly has golden brown, sun-streaked hair with a soft natural loose curl. She doesn't even have to wear pink Spoolie curlers to bed. I imagine she looks like a mermaid with her almond-shaped, green eyes and long eyelashes. Her nose is thin and long, sophisticated, like Charlotte's. Her complexion's clear, with natural pink cheeks. I bet she uses Noxzema Skin Cream 'cuz her face looks just like the ads in my sisters' magazine. Lilly has full lips that look like she's wearin' lipstick, but I know her secret. She bites them to make them look pink. I saw her, and I also saw why they shine, 'cuz Lilly licks her lips—a lot.

Lilly reminds me of Anna. I heard Granny Ivy say that Anna articulates well and uses her eye contact and body language like a pro, whatever that means. Buck says Anna's words, like her body, flow like thick honey. That's probably why the men seem so hungry when they look at her. They also lick their lips. I believe the men stare at Lilly the same way they stare at Anna. She also talks soft and gentle, not hurried or too slow either. She acts just like Anna, but she's nice.

My mind wanders off again, and I can see Barbie and the puppies waitin' for me. I secretly leave to play. Dean doesn't seem to notice.

I feel sad and guilty, 'cuz I called Lilly 'nasty girl' to Barbie. But I'm glad she came into the stall today with 'Dirty Dean,' as my friend, Peanut, calls him. I don't think my mommy would want me to be friends with girls like Lilly.

However, she seems lonely, so when she smiles at me, I'm polite and smile back.

CHAPTER TWENTY-FIVE

Catherine
August 1995

As soon as I put the key into the lock, I hear the phone ringing. I race up the stairs to grab the call.

"Hello, is Hunter there?" A woman's voice.

Breathless, I reply politely, "No, he isn't here right now. May I ask who's calling?"

"Umm...oh...this is Crystal."

Crystal? Did she say Crystal? As in the old girlfriend, Crystal? The one who broke Hunter's heart? The cheater, Crystal? The one who thankfully lives out of the country?

My heart plummets. *Why's she calling?*

"Hello, Crystal. I am Hunter's *wife*, Catherine. And how do you know Hunter?"

"Oh,…umm…hello, Catherine. Hunter and I used to work together. Umm, I'm back in town and was calling him to discuss an investment."

Liar. You never worked with him. You think I don't know who you are. Investments? Yeah, right.

"So, Crystal, you're from out of town? Where do you live these days?"

"Oh, I live in Sweden. I'm here on a short visit."

I knew it was you. Do you actually think Hunter didn't tell me about you and your habitual lying?

"How do you like living in a foreign country? Do you have any plans of moving back to the States?"

"Not presently. It was an adjustment not living in the States, but Sweden is now my home."

"Yes, I understand. I also have lived abroad, in Switzerland, for several years. That is where I lived before moving to Colorado. Hunter and I met only three weeks after I arrived back in the States."

"Well, isn't that nice. I didn't even know Hunter was married."

"Yes. We have been happily married for almost three years now."

Silence.

Finally, she says, "Hmm, I see. Well, will you tell Hunter I called? And have him call me? I'm staying at my mother's home. I'm sure he still has the number."

Why does he still have your number?

I cover the receiver with my palm, not allowing her to hear my sighs of disgust. A rush of adrenaline floods my body. With a hard grip on the phone handle to still my trembling hands, I find a reply.

"Sure, I'll let him know you phoned." I clear my throat. *You bet I'll let him know. As soon as he gets home, I'll give him a good earful about you calling.* "Good-bye, Crystal."

I hang the phone up harder than planned. A thousand questions explode inside my head. Then comes the fireworks of suspicion.

Why did she call the house? Is he with her? Is this her way of spilling the beans? To expose an affair? Would Hunter cheat on me? Never! Never? I thought Edward was loyal, and that turned out to be a cluster of big fat lies.

I lasso in my badgering thoughts of doubt and fear. I tighten the noose around the neck of accusations before I plummet any further.

An image of Crystal flashes before my eyes, looking like a beautiful movie star, perhaps a Sandra Bullock type. I tighten the rope around her pretty little neck. Oh Lord, here I go again. After all, I love Sandra Bullock. Please stop.

I press my temples and speak aloud. "Any evil on assignment, including demonic thoughts, opinions, and negative attitudes, you must shut up, in the name of Jesus Christ. Be gone from me now, in Jesus' name. Amen."

My nerves steady. Calmness settles over me. No matter the outcome, I focus on trusting God. "Thank you, Lord, for the power you have given me over the enemy's lies. Thank you for your word and your truth. I turn skanky Crystal over to you. Please bring any darkness or deceit that needs exposing into the light."

Did I say, skanky? Umm...I didn't mean that. Well...actually, I did. Sorry, God, now I'm lying. You know my heart. Help me Lord, to take my thoughts captive.

A verse comes to my mind. I proclaim it aloud to build my confidence in my husband. "'No weapon formed against me will prosper.' Amen."

I busy myself folding and putting away laundry—check. Homework complete—another check. Work uniform pressed and set out for tomorrow—final check.

Now it's time to relax. After making a cup of hot tea, I pull up a chair at the dining room table with a deck of cards. Another evening alone. Hunter has a meeting and will be out until 8 or 9 p.m. I don't mind alone time to relax, but I do miss snuggling with my husband on the couch. *MY husband, not Crystal's.*

"Oh, here I go again." I give my suspicious thoughts over to the Lord, refusing to chase the negative rabbit trail. My mind wanders back to Hunter.

He has a particular way of making me laugh. I love it when we spend time together. The interests we share make us a good match. I ponder our memories, yearning for more. But now it seems he's gone all the time, busy with work, men's ministry, or his athletic endeavors.

Is he with her?

"Shut up in the name of Jesus," I order.

I shuffle the cards, dealing myself a game of solitaire, which reminds me of Teenage Granny. She spent hours playing cards by herself. *Was she lonely?* I push the thought aside. No way. With five kids to look after and all the messes we made, she didn't have time to be alone, much less lonely.

A second thought arises. Granny's husband died when Dad was in the eighth grade. Poor Teenage Granny had nine kids to raise. Just when she thought she'd finished parenting, we came along, five spunky grandchildren. Her schedule was always full. But then again, you can be surrounded by a multitude of things pulling at you and still feel lonely. I'm juggling many things, and loneliness still tugs at my heart.

I reshuffle the deck, and once again, I attempt to play another game.

Then I think about the phone call from Crystal. The unnecessary lies that spewed from her mouth gnaw at me.

Why would she lie? Why pretend to be a work colleague?

The sound of the garage door interrupts my thoughts, and within seconds, Hunter's footsteps race up the stairs.

"Hey, Catherine, I'm home."

Catie
Winter 1963

"Hey kids, I'm home." Daddy shouts as he walks in the front door. "Are you ready to see the Christmas lights in the neighborhoods on the way to your grandparents' house?"

We're busy listenin' to records. 'There's no place like home for the holidays,' that's what Perry Como sings on his records. But I'm not sure if Daddy's favorite singer has ever been to our house or met Anna.

We all scramble to get our coats. We're lookin' forward to seein' all the bright, colorful lights. I wish we could have more lights on our house, but we *still* don't have enough money for extras.

Daddy said I could ask Santa for lights instead of a doll. Since Frog-Eyes Melinda has already wrecked my belief in Santa, I know what Daddy is really tellin' me. He can only afford one gift per kid, along with the games we'll have to share.

We're all google-eyed with open mouths at the pretty decorated houses on the way to Grandpa and Granny Grunt's for Christmas Eve. Goin' to their home is the best fun. Always.

We arrive back home with our handmade pajamas and matchin' stockin's, brimmin' full with goodies.

Melinda reminds me, *again,* that Santa isn't real. "Only babies and buttholes believe in such fairy tales," she snarls.

"You don't have to believe. You can still pretend," I spout back.

I'm good at pretendin', 'cuz I've learned it makes my life better. Sometimes that's all I have. I pretend Anna, Dean, Buck, and Ivy don't do the horrible things they do. I've been make-believin' real hard for a long time.

I walk by Melinda's bed and send a big fat stinky poot in her direction, on purpose, before crawlin' into my bed. I snicker and hide my smile underneath my covers.

"Did you fart? ICK! I'm tellin' my mom."

I lie still, not peepin' a word, but grin from ear to ear.

Charlotte comes in to turn out the lights. "Happy Christmas Eve. See you all in the morning. Goodnight and don't let the bed bugs bite." She closes the door.

I rub my hand over my new soft nightgown as my eyes fill with tears. I pray. "Dear God, will you please tell Mommy we had a great

Christmas Eve with Granny Grunt and Grandpa? And let her know that they told us funny stories all about her. P.S. And don't forget to tell Mommy that I'm doin' my job babysittin' Charley. And all the girls are doin' their jobs of lookin'' after each other."

I finish up my prayers in the hope that God will deliver my message. I get real comfortable in my bed and then snuggle close to my stuffed puppy, who reminds me of Happy.

Christmas mornin' comes fast. Charley skids around the corner, slidin' across the hardwood floors in his footed PJs.

"Santa was here. Santa was here!" He bounces foot to foot.

I have no idea what time it is, only that it's daylight. Charley takes hold of my blanket and sheet and tugs them off my bed.

"Come on, let's go get Daddy so that we can open presents!"

I rub my eyes. "Are Daddy and Anna awake?"

"Nope, but I'm waking everyone up," he lowers his voice, "except Melinda and Shawnee, 'cuz they'll tell on me. If Daddy hears us all up, maybe then he'll get out of bed."

"Did you knock on their door?"

"Yikes. No way." He shakes his head. "I don't want Anna beatin' me on Christmas. You know how she is about being woke up. Better watch out. She'll knock yer lights out. I sure wish I could do that to her when she comes waking me up in the middle of the night."

"Shhh, Charley." I cover his mouth. "We can't let anyone know 'bout that. If Melinda hears us talkin', she'll tell, and who knows what'll happen."

I look over to see Melinda, snug underneath her covers. Snortin' like the big fat pig that she is. Her eyes bulge even when closed, 'cuz she eats as much as any grown-up, makin' her eyes look like they're 'bout to pop out of her head.

It doesn't take long to get everyone up. Claudia's the first to run down the stairs, not carin' if Anna's up or not. Her voice echoes through the livin' room. She breaks into song.

"*We wish you a Merry Christmas. We wish you a Merry Christmas.* Hey, Dad. Are you up?" She raises her voice. "*We wish you a Merry Christmas and a Happy New Year.*"

Claudia hangs onto the last note, with her arms spread wide.

Their bedroom door cracks open. We gather closer to the tree, hold our breaths, and pray it isn't Anna.

Daddy comes out wearin' a t-shirt with PJ bottoms, with porcupine hair and puffy eyes. He smiles as he combs his hair back. Charley and I clap, relieved. Claudia jumps up and down, still singin'. Charlotte and Carolyn stand next to the tree, lookin' extra sad. I know they're missin' Mommy. I pretend she's in the kitchen makin' warm Cream of Wheat with jelly toast.

Then Anna stomps out of the bedroom, doin' her usual yellin', and my pretend world bursts.

"What in the *hell* time is it?" Anna hollers.

I freeze and pull Charley in close. We look at Daddy.

Claudia springs forward, flingin' her arms in the air. "It's Christmas time!"

Anna sends a slitted-eye glare, her lips pinched. "I don't want to hear it."

Dad takes a step between Claudia and Anna. His eyes plead.

"It's Christmas, Anna, and the kids are excited. Go get yourself a cup of coffee."

"Where are my kids?" She scans the room. "Were you going to have Christmas without my kids? The *hell* you are!"

Before more bad words come out of her mouth, Shawnee walks out of her bedroom, carryin' her small blanket. "Momma, did Santa come?"

Anna hugs Shawnee. "Yes, Sweetie. He sure did. Let Momma get a cup of coffee, and we'll see what he brought my precious, good, little girl."

Boom, boom, boom...Melinda tromps down the stairs, soundin' like thunder. "Wait for me! Wait for me!" she orders.

With warm cups of coffee in their hands, Daddy and Anna come into the livin' room. Anna sets her cup on the table. She then plops on the couch. Daddy sets his cup next to hers and crouches down on one knee to pull out the presents from under the Christmas tree.

Before he hands anyone a present, he announces who each gift is for and that it's from Santa. I'm so excited to see the presents and thrilled to watch everyone open their gifts.

Daddy stretches to hand me a big box. Charley nudges me. "Catie, it's your turn."

I reach for my present. It's the same size as Melinda's and Carolyn's.

"Okay, girls, you can open your gifts."

Melinda tears into her box, rippin' the paper off as fast as she can. Carolyn waits for me so that we can open them together. We all received Nancy Nurse dolls. I lift my doll out of her box and hug her close, smellin' the sweet new plastic. I move her arms and legs up and down to make sure everythin' works. She even has a medical bag, includin' candy pills. I pull back the Christmas paper to see what else is in the big box. A canopy bed!

"Oh my goodness, Daddy." I put my hands to my cheeks. "Canopy beds are for rich girls or princesses. I've never dreamed of ever havin' a canopy bed for myself, much less one for my doll with a matchin' bedspread and canopy. It's a dream come true. It's beautiful. And my new doll, I love her."

Daddy smiles as big as Carolyn and me. He sends us a big wink.

"We all got the same thing," Melinda whines. Her face is frowned up like a prune with big, fake, alligator tears. She's bein' a big fat baby.

She's not to be trusted. I turn away from Melinda and ask Daddy, "Would you write my name on Nancy's foot, so I always know which baby is mine?"

Carolyn stands next to Dad, liftin' her Christmas baby with the same unspoken request. Dad takes a pen and writes our names on our dolls. Melinda makes the most of the moment.

"I won't need my name on my baby since Carolyn and Catie already have their names on their dolls."

As soon as Daddy leaves the room, she shrieks, "You ruined your dolls with all that ink on their foot. They're just junk now. And *I'm* the only one with the best doll."

Anna says nothin' 'bout her daughter's mean remarks. Not only that, Melinda demands her doll's name remain, Nancy, since she was the first to open her doll box and say the name aloud. Anna agrees, *as always*.

How does that make sense? That's not even fair! I'm only a kid and know that's stupid thinkin'.

Anna stands to leave the room. "You girls have fun with your dolls. I'm going to make pancakes for breakfast. How does that sound, Melinda?" She pats her head and smiles.

Melinda's all puffed up. She thinks she's pulled one over on us till she asks our dolls' names.

Carolyn flicks her thick long blonde hair over her shoulders and says, "My doll's name is private, and Catie's doll's name is …well, a, umm…secret."

Melinda cries and pouts. "That's not fair. I want to know your dolls' names. I'm gonna tell my mom you're brats."

We laugh, then pretend to put a key to our lips and lock our mouths. We're not gonna tell Frog Eyes. I wink at Carolyn and snicker to myself, knowin' her doll's named *Pretty Private* and mine, *Sassy Secret*. I make an ugly face at Melinda and call her Frog-Eyes Pig under my breath.

The next day, I bounce up the steps to my bedroom. I look and then look twice. I can't believe my eyes! My brand new beautiful canopy bed is broken. Wrecked. One of the posters is busted off. I search under the doll's bed, then my bed. The post is gone. The canopy caved in onto my baby doll, Sassy!

It had to be Melinda. I run to her side of the bedroom. I look for her doll bed. Huh? I cock my head in wonder 'bout what I'm seein'. There's a piece of black electrical tape on one of the posters. I ease the tape off. Her doll bed is broken as well but taped back together— perfectly. And it holds up the canopy.

I scream from the top of the stairs, "Daddy, come here! Melinda's broken my doll's bed."

Daddy and Anna walk into our bedroom. Melinda hides just outside the door jam. She is quick to peek her head out, wrinkle up her nose at me.

"You broke my doll's bed!" I scream and point at her to make sure Daddy sees her.

"I did not! My doll's bed is broken too!" She stomps her foot.

"You broke your own bed just to make yourself look innocent," I spout back.

Melinda tugs at her mother's shirt and whines, "I'm pretty sure it was Charley, Momma. I saw him running out of our room earlier. He must have done it." She looks to her mom with puppy-dog eyes.

I know she's lyin' to get back at Carolyn and me for not tellin' her our doll's names. Now she'll see to it that Charley gets spanked, *or worse*. And for somethin' he hasn't even done. It's not fair. I hate her! I hate her! I hate her!

Anna sides with Melinda, *as always*.

When Anna isn't lookin', Melinda smiles and mouths, 'nah, nah, nah-nah, nah.' For a second, her eyes turn black like Dean's. Those June-bug devil eyes. I take another look, but she turns away.

Did her eyes turn black?

As soon as our parents leave, she sticks out her tongue. I take a second look. Her eyes look normal now.

When bedtime comes, Daddy has already left for work. We crawl into our beds. Melinda places her doll, Nancy, in her canopy bed for the night, then turns to me.

"Too bad your *nameless* doll has no place to sleep."

"That's okay. I like my baby to be in bed with me so that I can cuddle with her."

I bring Sassy in close to protect her and wonder what mean thing Melinda will do next. I hope it won't be against Charley. Disappointed and tired, before fallin' off to sleep, I cry out to God, *"Dear God, the preacher said you were the most powerful one, so I need you to protect us! Now! Daddy's broke. Can't you give him lots of money so he doesn't need Anna to watch us? Jesus, don't you know that we need to afford a nanny, so we don't have to go live in the orphanage? Please come and get us out of here. Pretty please?"*

Sometime later, I feel my body bein' stirred. I crack open one eye and squint into the darkness. It's Anna....

CHAPTER TWENTY-SIX

Catherine
August 1995

Hunter rounds the corner into the dining room. I squint seeing a big smile on his face. My emotions stir.

"My meeting got out early. How was your night?" He bends down and kisses me on the lips.

"The usual. House cleaning, laundry, homework, setting my things out for work in the morning, and old *girlfriends* calling."

"Huh?"

"Have a seat." I motion to the chair next to me. Hunter pulls off his jacket and drapes it over the back of the chair. He lets out a yawn and plops down.

My heart pounds. "I want to talk to you about a phone call I received today."

"From who?"

"Crystal."

"Crystal? Crystal who?" He stares at me blankly.

"Your ex-girlfriend, Crystal."

I stare into his eyes, searching for nervousness or anything suspicious.

His brow wrinkles. He cocks his head. Puzzlement is all over his face. Then it sinks in.

"Ohh…that Crystal. What did she want? I thought she moved out of the country."

"She wanted to talk to you. Said she was unaware that you are married."

I squint with skepticism and lean in to search his eyes.

A smile breaches his lips. "Are you jealous?" he asks with a soft chuckle. His eyes turn up, twinkling with amusement.

"Should I be?" My words—hard. Serious. Firm.

He scoots his chair back. "No. Not at all. I have no idea why the woman called."

"Well, first of all, she lied to me, saying she was a work colleague. NOT."

I put both hands on my waist, waiting for an explanation.

Hunter says nothing.

"Why would she lie? It's not like I don't expect you to have ex-girlfriends. Why wasn't she upfront and say you used to date? She claims she didn't know you were married. So, why not a congrats? Or did she lie about that too?"

I stand, waving my hands. Still, Hunter says nothing. He has a blank look, like a deer in the headlights.

"I tell you, that woman is up to no good. I can smell a rat a mile away." My anger rises.

How dare she call and lie to me.

Hunter shrugs one shoulder. "How would I know why she called? I'm sure she knows I'm married now. I bet you made *that* very clear." He winks, giving me a side hug. "Don't worry about her, Sweetheart. She's merely an ex. You're my wife. I chose you. You're my forever love." He kisses my cheek, pulling me closer.

His words calm my worries. I let the phone call go and enjoy the rest of our evening.

A few weeks later, Hunter walks into the kitchen while I'm making dinner. He sets the mail on the counter before giving me a big hug.

"Smells great. What's for dinner?"

"Pot roast."

"How'd you prepare a roast after working all day?" He takes a big sniff, searching for the aroma as he heads for the oven.

"I put it in the crockpot this morning before going to work." I tilt my head toward the cupboard where the slow cooker is plugged in.

Hunter removes the lid and takes a peek. "Looks delicious. I'm starved. When will it be ready?"

"It's ready now. I only need to set the table. What would you like to drink?"

"I'll get it. I'm going to have iced tea. Do you want some?" He pours us both a glass. "Oh, by the way, I did talk with Crystal. She and her husband are in town for a few weeks. She said she might stay a little longer to take care of family business."

His words rake across my heart. I stiffen. "What? What did she want?" Neither of us have mentioned her for weeks. As far as I was concerned, it was good riddance.

He lowers the lid onto the crockpot and then says so-matter-of-factly, "Crystal thought it would be nice for the four of us to have dinner. She wants me to meet her husband and to meet you."

I walk over to where he's standing and position myself where I can read his face.

"Are you kidding me? You can't be serious. You are completely out of your mind if you think for a minute I want to go to dinner with her. For one thing, she lied to me. I don't trust her." I pull away from him and slam the silverware on the table.

He shrugs. "I didn't think you'd mind. I thought you might enjoy talking since you both have experience living in a foreign country."

"If that's the case, you aren't thinking right. Have you gone completely insane?"

Hunter wrinkles his brow. "What's the big deal, Catherine?"

"I'll tell you the big deal! Let me give it to you straight, Hunter. Dinner will be a walk down memory lane. She'll spend the entire evening giggling and flirting."

I throw my head back in a fake laugh, then twirl a curl in my hair and bat my eyelashes, mimicking what I imagine she will do and say. "Oh, Hunter, remember this? Remember that?' She'll comment on people you knew, places you've gone, things you've done together. All the while, her husband and I will wonder if you're thinking about when you slept together." My lips tighten into a thin line. "NO! I am not going to dinner with her. And if you go…you'll regret it."

"Wow. I didn't think this would upset you."

"Well, it does. What about our agreement? We promised to leave our past relationships, *like her,* in the past. How would you like to have dinner with Edward?" My hands grip my hips. Knuckles white.

"Oh…okay. I don't care if I see her or not. I'll tell her we can't make it."

"No, Hunter. You will tell her the promise you made to me. And that you will NOT be having any type of a relationship with her."

He nods. We sit at the table for dinner, but my appetite is gone.

Marion
August 1995

The air conditioner hums and groans as it filters the late-summer heat. My philodendron nearby vibrates in the stream of air from the vent.

Catherine fidgets on the sofa, not unlike my plant. She shares her disappointment about Hunter's lackadaisical response to her being upset about his ex-girlfriend trying to move back into his life.

"Trust me, Marion, this girl is trouble. And that's all I need. I find it unbelievable that Hunter could be that naive." She rolls her eyes. "And what's more, I feel like I have to fight to see him. His busy schedule always seems to cut into our time."

She goes on to describe her husband as being spread thin with all his involvements and becoming more stoic and distant. She feels he is not there for her. I listen intently and document her concerns in her file.

Catherine changes the subject, moving on to the conflict with Hunter's sister, Harriet. She says his sister's immaturity and jealousy manifest whenever Hunter's parents pay her any attention.

"Marion, she's a grown woman after all. If you can believe this, she huffs and puffs, even rolls her eyes at me when her mother and I try to have a conversation. During our last visit, she interrupted us and said, 'Mom, come on, let's go outside and work in the garden together.' She totally disregarded me, treated me as if I were invisible."

"Have you chosen to forgive her?"

Catherine sighs. "A million times. If she'd stop being so rude, I wouldn't have to keep forgiving her. It's not like she's sorry or anything."

I click the end of my pen. "Your forgiveness or releasing her from the offense may never have an impact on Harriet. She may never change or have a change of heart towards you. Forgiveness is not about expectations."

"I have no expectations of her. Well, except I'd love to see her take ownership of her actions. And maybe an occasional apology."

"Sometimes, people may want to hang onto resentment and hold a grudge."

Catherine bites her lower lip. "I see where you're going with this. I've done it myself." She tilts her head to the side and raises her shoulders. "Somehow, hanging onto my grievance feels like it protects my heart from being hurt or disappointed again."

I nod. "I understand. I wonder if somehow Harriet views her actions as a way of protecting herself or something that she values?"

I plant a seed of thought and move on to my next question.

"What did Hunter's mother say about her behavior?"

"Nothing. I was the one who spoke up. I pointed out that Marie and I were *trying* to have a conversation. Harriet just ignored me and walked toward the back door, after motioning for her mother to follow. Marie gave me an apologetic look. She seemed embarrassed and uncertain as to what to do or say. It was awkward."

"How did that make you feel?" I question.

"I felt disregarded, not valued, alone, and somewhat betrayed. Well, maybe betrayed is too harsh of a word. Perhaps unprotected is a better way of describing my feelings, I'm not sure. All I can say for sure is I was frustrated. It felt unfair for her to disrespect me. Harriet is such…" She closes her mouth to stop short of finishing her words.

"Hunter and I discussed the strife and division that occurs at his parents' home whenever Harriet comes along. Being we all live in Denver, we have driven down together." She smiles. "I truly love his parents. We have a great time with his folks when his sister isn't there. I'm willing to see Hunter's mom and dad anytime. Family means a lot to me. However, I refuse to go with Harriet any longer. I told him I just couldn't do it anymore. She makes a point of wrecking every holiday. Trying to wade through all her dysfunction is exhausting."

I pull my blouse away from my chest to let some cool air in. "I would imagine the conflict takes away from everyone's holiday. I am sorry Hunter's sister struggles to accept you as his family. Forgiving Harriet or releasing her from the offense or debt doesn't remove the natural consequences. What has happened between you and Harriet is hopefully something you can work through over time."

"I hope so, but I doubt that will ever happen. Marion, when I first heard Hunter had a sister in town, I was thrilled. I imagined we would be the best of friends and have Sunday family dinners."

She splays out her hands. "You get the picture. I was taken aback by her coldness from the very first hug, or better said, lack of hug. It felt like I was embracing a broom handle. Hunter discouraged me from getting my hopes up of having a close relationship with her. He knows how close I am to my sisters. But I was determined."

Catherine shakes her head. "It's partly my fault. I believed I could make her warm up to me. The more I tried, the worse it got. She went out of her way to let me know she didn't like me, and in her opinion, I didn't belong in *her* family. If it were up to her, I would remain an outsider."

"Yes, I know, Catherine. Hunter has mentioned his sister's reaction to you over the years. Even so, it is essential to trust the Lord on his word, which is to forgive."

Catherine looks up with her pen in her hand. "Are you saying, me not wanting to be around Harriet anymore could be considered a natural consequence?"

"Possibly. What does Hunter say about your concerns and choice?"

"He agrees. However, he asked if I would still go on Christmas so he could be together with his whole family. Hunter promises to protect me from his sister. He said he would let his parents know we wouldn't be visiting with Harriet anymore, other than Christmas."

I discern Catherine's present emotions involving Harriet are being sparked and intensified by past unresolved childhood issues. I flip back a couple of dates to compare the emotions. Her current feelings aligned with what she felt when Melinda broke Sassy Secret's doll bed. I jot down: Vulnerable. Unprotected. Unjust. Betrayed. Attacked. And disregarded.

I ask, "Catherine, would you be willing to go back to the memory of when Melinda broke your doll bed?"

She agrees.

"So, Catherine, based on my notes, you had the last words with Melinda before falling asleep. I recall Charley being wrongly blamed and spanked for damaging the doll beds. What happened next?

Catherine reclines on the love seat. She closes her eyes to focus on the memory. Her face turns red, her teeth bear down, and her eyes crease with tension. The strain intensifies as she goes deeper into the memory. She tosses her head from side to side as if wanting to avoid whatever it is that she is remembering.

Catherine relives the memory as if sent back in time. She unfolds her story in Catie's voice...

"No! No! No!" she screams.

CHAPTER TWENTY-SEVEN

Catie
Winter 1963

"**N**o! No! No!"

  Anna slams her hand over my mouth to muffle my screams.

Oh no, she's wakin' me up—again!

Anna drives Charley and me to the farm, but this time there's no medicine. No blindfolds. Anna din't mince her words. Me and Charley are gonna get punished in *a big* way over upsettin' her precious Melinda.

I hate goin' to Poison Ivy's and Buck's stupid house. I want to forget what happened when they had the nativity scene set up. Dean was the one who did the horrible thing to baby Jesse. He said it was me, but Charley and me know it ain't true. Mean Dean is just a big liar.

Charley tugs on my shirt. He nudges me down to whisper in my ear. "You think they're gonna do to us what they did to that sweet baby in the manger?"

"Not sure, McFudd, but stay close," I say his nickname. "I don't trust 'em, but we need to start prayin' for Jesus to help us."

I scoot next to him in the backseat. We both shake, but it's not from the cold.

When we arrive, the whole ugly bunch are waitin' for us: Buck, Mean Dean, and Poison Ivy. Anna yanks us by our coat hoods and drags us toward the barn. My tummy hurts and not a sweet butterfly feelin'. More like bitin' cockroaches gnawin' on my innards, like Grandpa would say.

"These brats ruined *my* Christmas. And poor Melinda's." Anna points at us. "Charley broke two of the new doll's canopy beds and Catie blamed it on *my* sweet daughter. She upset our entire day."

Anna spins around and raises her voice. "I tell you, I won't let this defiant behavior go on any longer. They need to learn! Punished in a way that they'll remember. You know I mean business!" Anna turns to Dean and Buck. "Grandpa Dean, Buck, you know what to do."

Dean snarls at Anna. "Well, Miss Anna, when it *serves you*, you're all right with power and punishment." He lets out a big huff.

Buck chuckles at Dean. Poison Ivy gives her husband a dirty look. Anna rolls her eyes and waves her hand at her grandfather, Dean.

"Well, get on with it!" she orders.

Devil Dean eases his way up to Charley and me. My baby brother's small fingers squeeze my hand. The hateful man grabs Charley and yanks our hands apart. Ivy pulls me off to the side. Buck leaves the room but quickly comes back carryin' a wooden box.

Three puppies—Happy, Angel, and a third pup—stand with their front paws on the box's edge. They're yippin' and excited to see us kids. Sadie wags her tail as she follows Buck's every step. She won't take her eyes off her puppies.

Awww, so cute, 'specially my puppy, Happy.

I look up at Buck. Uh-oh! He has that look—the one with the black June bug eyes. He lowers the box and sets it on the dirt floor.

Charley and me exchange looks. I can't hide my fear.

Buck's up to no good. Not sure what he's gonna do, but I know it'll be awful. He's tryin' to prove he's man enough to take Granny Poison Ivy's dad's place as the big boss. GG Dean calls himself the high priest. I don't know what that means exactly, but I'm thinkin' Buck's tryin' to take Mean Dean's job as the head devil preacher. Seems to me they're competin' for who can be the meanest.

My heart races.

BOOM. The blast ricochets through the barn. Pain rips through my ears, followed by the echo of gunfire.

Buck stands over Sadie.

She's DEAD!

Her puppies shake and whimper, huddled in the corner of the wooden box.

"NO! NO! NO!" All I can do is scream. "NO! NO! NO!"

I'm determined to wake up the entire county with my blood curdlin' howls. Ivy slams her hand over my mouth.

I bite her! I chomp down hard, and I won't let go. Even after tastin' blood in my mouth—her blood.

Buck holsters his gun and runs to his wife.

"Catie, you let go of her, you hear me?" he yells into my face—spit flyin'.

I shake my head side to side. I rip harder into Ivy's hand with each deliberate turn of my head.

Poison Ivy cries out. "Pry her damn teeth off me. NOW! I don't care if you have to bash 'em out! Hurry up!"

Her face is gnarled up in pain. I'm glad.

I see Charley in the distance. His eyes are wide. I remember all they've done to my baby brother. I bite harder.

"Buck squeezes his finger and thumb into each side of my mouth. He smashes my cheeks into my teeth. It feels like he's gonna break my teeth off, 'specially my two loose baby molars.

My eyes spot poor Sadie. Her blood soaks into the ground. That dog din't hurt a soul. Now her puppies are left without a mommy. Orphans. Why'd Buck have to go and kill her?

Then I remember poor baby Jesse in the manger. That was the same night mean ole Poison Ivy was braggin' 'bout killin' my mommy and leavin' us orphans. I feel her boney fingers between my teeth and chomp harder. This one's for Sadie, Baby Jesse, and my mommy. My head trembles as I dig my teeth deeper.

Buck's fingers press harder until his strength overpowers my bite. He pulls Ivy's bloody hand free, then throws me to the ground. He hovers over Ivy, examinin' the damage. She moans and groans.

Anna runs over with a dishtowel and water that foams when she pours it over Poison Ivy's wound.

I'm glad she's bleedin'. I wish I could bite Buck, Anna, and Devil Dean too.

All four of them turn. The whole bunch stare at me. Their eyes are piercin'. I don't even bother to wipe the blood from my mouth or face.

Happy lets out a small bark. I look down at his cute spots. My puppy gives me an excited, full-body wag. The other two pups cower in the corner of the box.

Dean has an elbow grip on Charley's neck. He squeezes. Charley cries out. In the blink of an eye, while lookin' at Charley, Buck grabs my puppy by his scruff, danglin' him in the air. His pitiful little cries get louder and louder and turn into deafenin' shrills as Buck tightens his grip. He's gonna kill my puppy. I can't take it....

It takes my breath. I panic.

There's a racket comin' from the adjacent bunkhouse. All of a sudden, GI Joe busts through the door, talkin' a mile a minute.

"What the heck's goin' on here? You wanna wake up everyone in the bunkhouse? Who shot the gun?" GI Joe cuts his eyes to the ground. "Dog-darn it. Who killed Sadie?"

He looks around and sees Buck's gun holstered to his waist.

"You sick puke, you. Instead of pickin' on helpless children, now you're shootin' innocent dogs? You're wicked at best. Even your own dog? Somethin's definitely wrong with you, old man."

GI Joe looks at Ivy's hand wrapped in a bloodstained cloth, then back at me.

Catie, I saw you from my bunk. Good job. Sadie would have bitten her if she could've. That dog would've been proud of you."

Buck backhands me with his free hand, sendin' me flyin' to the floor.

"Hey, man, knock it off, if you know what's good for you," GI Joe threatens.

I wish I could be as brave as GI Joe. Good thing he's my friend and on my side.

Happy continues to squeal.

"Please don't hurt my puppy, Buck. Why do you have to be so mean?" I plead.

"That would be too easy of a punishment for you, Catie."

Buck rubs his chin like he's thinkin' real hard. His eyes—black and evil.

"I'm not going to hurt Happy...." He belts out his order, "YOU ARE!"

Buck throws Happy to the ground. He lands with a thud, followed by a sharp ongoin' yelp.

I lunge for Happy and take him into my arms. He screams louder as I lift him. I know he's hurt—hurt bad. I gently lower him to the ground and lean over him to protect him as best I can. I turn to GI Joe, who kneels next to me.

"Looks like his back leg is busted."

Happy rallies and tries to run away on three legs, carryin' his back paw up in the air.

Buck steps in his path to stop him from hidin'. He kicks my puppy back in my direction.

I scurry over to Happy. I hold my puppy, careful not to touch his hurt leg. Happy licks a tear from my face. I feel helpless.

Buck pulls out his big huntin' knife from the sheath on his belt. He meanders over. I'm afraid of what he's gonna do next.

GI Joe says somethin'. I can't make it out over my own heavy breathin'.

Buck shouts at me. "Kill the pup, or we'll kill Charley!"

My eyes cut back to Mean Dean, who's squeezin' Charley by the throat, cuttin' off his air. He gasps for breaths. Snot and tears run down his face. He squeaks out two muffled words.

"Help me!"

Buck throws the knife to the ground. It lands right next to me.

My little soldier friend grabs the knife. "I'll do it for you, Catie!" He slips my puppy from my arms. "Sorry, Catie, you heard Buck. It's either Happy or Charley."

He places Happy on his side. My puppy wiggles, tryin' to get away. GI Joe raises the knife.

"I can't do it. I can't do it!" A loud hollow cry comes from GI Joe.

I look at Happy and then back at Charley.

Charley's turnin' blue around his mouth.

I scream, I beg. "Somebody help me!"

Again, it takes my breath. I panic.

A large boy, as big as a man, comes into the barn from the bunkhouse.

"Is that you, GI Joe, I heard hollering?"

GI tumbles over. The knife drops at his side. He hides his tears as he kneels at Happy's side and shouts. "Catie, this dude is my friend. I call him Ice Man, 'cuz he can do the hard stuff. He's a much braver soldier than me." GI Joe sniffs back his tears.

Ice Man takes the knife off the ground. He gently motions to me and GI Joe to step off to the side. I stare in terror at Charley. Bubbles come out of his nose. His struggle is dyin' off. He's barely movin'.

"I scream. 'Hurry! They're killing him!'"

Ice Man takes the knife, lifts it into the air, and brings it down. Again, again and again.

Marion
August 1995

C atherine lies trembling on the couch. We are making progress but at such a cost. With each memory, difficult emotions manifest, making Catherine's life a struggle.

"Out of all the memories, the killing of the mother dog and my puppy is the most tormenting. It haunts me." Catherine moans. "All my rage, resentment, and hatred instantly come back. The pain is so deep. I can still picture the entire scene, especially my little brother's blue lips."

Her hand presses against her heart, and she grimaces, reflecting her physical and emotional pain.

"It makes me feel like I've never forgiven them. Nor do I want to forgive that evil bunch. I want Anna and her family, and all of those devil-worshiping crazed people to pay for what they've done. Why should they get away with their viciousness? They did it all on purpose. They meant to hurt me, and...." She gulps back her cries. "They intended to kill poor Charley and those innocent little dogs."

Catherine's tears of grief flow. She bends over; her arms cradled her stomach as she rocks herself and weeps.

I take a few seconds to master my own emotions. "Catherine, forgiveness doesn't declare what was done was right or okay. It doesn't minimize the offense or excuse it. What happened was wrong and evil. Forgiveness is releasing the person, as well as yourself, from the offense, *not* the accountability or the consequences of that sin. Everyone will answer to God for their choices, all of them; the good, bad, and the ugly."

"What about myself? I hate myself. It's unforgivable—"

"You were a child. You were outnumbered, overpowered, and did not have any real options. It was a form of blackmail," I reason, picking up my coffee cup with a shaking hand.

"That's just it. I realize I didn't have a choice with Baby Jesse. They forced me. But with my puppy, it felt different. I did have a choice. I chose Charley, so the blood is on my hands for Happy. I'm nothing more than a murderer."

"Catherine, that is what they wanted you to believe. That type of manipulation was a part of their grooming and intended to make you feel shame, condemnation, and self-loathing. Their purpose was to make you believe that you were a killer, a murderer." I pause, gripping the coffee cup tight. "Oh dear Catherine, please unravel the lies and realize that it is not the truth."

"How can I not feel that way? I have dreams where I see the knife stabbing through the air, killing Happy. I see it over and over again. Blood spattering everywhere." She squeezes her eyes. "I chose for Happy to be the one to die. So how am I any different from Buck who betrayed and shot his own dog, Sadie?"

I swallow and gather my thoughts. "I see you are upset. I am truly sorry that you are in such pain and grief. However, healing comes from the truth. I can tell you it was not your fault, but it does not seem to stick in your heart. I believe you are still seeing the death of the pups from a child's point of view. We need to pray and ask God to reveal what truly happened concerning Sadie and Happy."

We bow our heads, and I lead, "Dear Lord, Catherine needs to hear the truth about what happened in the barn. Did she have a choice? Speak to her and help her find truth and freedom. In Jesus Christ name, Amen."

I sit quietly and watch Catherine. Her body language and facial expressions tell me she is back in the memory, listening intently. Her eyes dart back and forth as if searching for something. Then I witness her face soften.

I ask, "What did you hear the Lord say?"

Through tears and broken words, Catherine replies. "He said, my choice would have been for Charley, Sadie, and Happy all to live. I would have chosen only good things. Buck and the bunch purposely put me into that situation to break me, to burden me with unbearable guilt and shame. What they chose to do was evil and brutal because they don't have the Lord and can't see beyond the blackness of their darkened souls."

Her shoulders lower. She leans back and grieves the loss of Happy —and her childhood.

"It wasn't my fault." She confesses in a weak, crackling voice.

After hearing Catherine's proclamation, the tension in my back releases. Relieved, I lean forward and place the coffee cup onto the table. My cramping fingers relax.

"Catherine, let your tears flow. You have suffered a great loss. Please allow yourself to grieve. You should have never been put into such a grave situation to decide between Happy or Charley. Such a burden is too much for any child or adult to bear."

I stand and walk over to Catherine. I sit next to her on the love seat and offer an encouraging smile.

"The enemy wants you to hold on to unforgiveness because it gives the offense *power* over your life." I shift my position to make firm eye contact. "Forgiveness *removes* that power."

I gently pat her hand. "Let Jesus cleanse your heart of the despair. He is always here for you. Forgiveness will help relieve the heartache and the torment you are carrying. Give the Lord your pain. Forgive and release Anna, her family, and the occult members over to God. He is willing and able to take on your anguish, because...." Taking hold of her hand and squeezing softly, I say, "because Jesus loves you so much."

I quietly step away to give Catherine time to ponder my words. I know she must grieve and spend time with the Lord. I pray silently, asking the Lord to help her forgive.

I am concerned about how the killing of her pup will affect her trust. Such a deep and twisted betrayal. There were no real choices. She was forced to betray her puppy's trust to save her brother.

"Lord, please bring healing to Catherine's broken heart."

CHAPTER TWENTY-EIGHT

Catie
Winter 1964

Buck telephoned this mornin' to talk with Daddy. He told him that all the dogs got out of the barn last night and ran out into the street, killin' Sadie and Happy. He asked Daddy to break the news to me, addin' he had made a beautiful grave and marker for my puppy, next to the back of the barn. He told Daddy they hoped I'd like it. He even had the nerve to ask Daddy to ask me if I wanted one of the other pups. NO WAY!

It should've never happened. I miss Happy. I gag several times and almost throw up after hearin' Buck's lies. My tears are as red hot as my anger. I hate their stinkin' rotten guts and hope they get what they deserve.

Daddy's face looks sad and worried. He brushes my tears off my cheeks. Anna stands behind Daddy and sends her glares, threatenin' me with dagger eyes, not to speak, or else! I run into Daddy's arms and cry as hard as I can. I can't tell him why I'm really cryin'. Buckets of tears run down my face.

L ater that mornin', I run through the house searchin' for Daddy. No luck. Carolyn stops me and asks, "Who are you looking for in such a hurry?"

"Daddy. Have you seen him?"

"Yeah, I saw him in the garage."

In a flash, I make my way toward the side door, just as Daddy opens it and walks into the kitchen holdin' one of my brother's toy cars that he has repaired. Charley follows, carryin' more cars in his hands. Both shake the snow from their winter hats. Charley's wearin' a turtleneck under his coat. I wonder if his poor neck is red or bruised. I suspect Anna set out the shirt and told him what he was to wear today.

"Hey, Catie, all my cars are fixed!" He raises his hands. I look at his cars but say nothin' 'cuz I have a bigger problem on my mind.

"Daddy, Anna says I have to go with her to Granny Ivy's. I don't want to go over to her house. PLEASE don't make me. I can't go there," I beg.

Charley doesn't say a word. He runs off into his bedroom and shuts the door. I bet he's hidin' under his bed so he won't have to go to Anna's folks' house.

I press my palms together in prayer hands and beg. "Can't you let me stay home with you and the rest of the kids? Saturday and Sunday are the only days I get to see you. Please let me stay home with you."

Anna meanders close enough to pinch my back—hard. "Catie, darling, you know how much you love going to the farm. You always have such fun. You haven't come home without a tear in your clothes, a cut, or a scrape, from having such a good time. Don't you and Charley always say you have a 'great rough and tough time?' You're the best fun-loving tomboy." She turns to Daddy. "Forest, you know how much Catie likes to play hard."

"It's okay, darlin. Daddy worked all night and needs to sleep now anyway. I'll be up and awake when you get back. Have some fun at your grandmother's farm. And tell Gilbert hello for me."

I scrunch up my nose and squint my eyes. I hate goin' to that house. 'Specially the barn. It's always bad. And I can't stand the thought of even lookin' at Poison Ivy, Buck, or Devil Dean after what they've done to Happy and Sadie.

C harley was nowhere to be found when Anna and me left to go to yucky Poison Ivy's house. Melinda and Shawnee are with their dad, Daddy Douglas, this weekend, so I'm the unlucky one who has to go with Anna. When we arrive, I refuse to speak to any of them. *Do they really think I've forgotten what happened to Sadie and Happy?*

As soon as Ivy comes near me, I turn my head. I won't even look at her. I hope her bandaged hand hurts somethin' fierce.

Buck sneaks up from behind and scares the livin' daylights out of me. He laughs his evil laugh and then smacks me hard on the back of my head, so hard—it makes me spin dizzy. I stumble forward but catch myself just in time from fallin'. I can't see right. Everythin' looks funny—blurry. I blink several times to clear my eyes. No luck. My head pounds with pain. Buck raises his hand, ready to hit me again. I suck in air. *It takes my breath. I panic.*

That's when I spot the girl I met in the barn durin' our icky boy-girl education class with the yucky pictures. I named her Peanut because she taught me how to hide my feelin's by puttin' them in a peanut bombshell and then tryin' to daydream 'bout happy things.

She's in the laundry room doin' somethin' for Poison Ivy. I give her a quick wave. She sends me a big smile, then looks back down, not wantin' to get in trouble for talkin' to me.

Poison Ivy asks, as if it's a request, "Catie, dear, would you like to go along with me on a car ride to run a few errands?"

I don't dare say no. I stand still and say nothin'.

"If you're good, I'll buy you some candy. Anything you want and all for yourself. You won't have to share it with anyone."

I try not to get excited 'cuz Poison Ivy says a lot of things but doesn't keep her promises.

We drive for a very, very, very, long time. I musta fallen asleep 'cuz Granny Ivy calls out my name and I jump in my seat.

"Hey, sleepyhead, wake up," she orders.

"Huh?" I rub my eyes to wake up and then look out the window at all the stores. There's a grocery market on the right. While at a traffic light, I watch a woman gently place her baby into a shoppin' cart. Granny Ivy sees her as well.

"What a cute little infant, Catie. It's so tiny. I'm guessin' only a few weeks old. I think we'll stop in here."

Ivy turns into the parkin' lot and slows the car as we pass by the lady and her sweet baby. I stretch my neck to see them a little better.

As we walk into the store, I figure if I offer to help, maybe Ivy will keep her promise. All I want is candy.

"What do you need to buy? I can help you find your groceries and put them in the cart for you."

"I'm not sure yet. If I get something, it will only be a few things. We won't need a cart."

We walked up the aisles to do our shoppin'. The lady with the sweet baby is in front of us. I point them out.

"Oh, there's that cute baby. Can I go and see it?"

"No, you shouldn't bother them," Ivy says a little too politely. "She's probably tired. Babies are a lot of work. Let them be."

We continue walkin'. It isn't like Poison Ivy to be so considerate of others. I don't know what to think since she's keepin' our pace so slow, 'bout a half an aisle away from the lady and her sweet baby. It seems to me Poison Ivy is keepin' a keen eye on them. Almost like spyin'.

Since we're not really buyin' anythin', I run my hands across the cans and count as I go. "One, two, three…"

All Poison Ivy does is pick up a can, look at it, and then slides it back on the shelf. I wish we were by the candy aisle. The woman ahead of us does the same thing, but at least she's puttin' a few things into her cart. She stops, scans the cans, and walks toward the end of the aisle.

The pretty lady leaves her baby and her groceries to walk further down the way. I see her glance around as if she's lookin' for some help from a store worker. She turns the corner.

Uh-oh. The familiar odor like a dead mouse fills my nose. The same yucky smell that always comes whenever they're up to no good. I pinch my nose and pull my coat closed and hug my arms around me. I shiver. *Did someone open the door?*

Ivy clenches my hand and starts walkin' as if we're hurryin' to catch a bus. Now we're almost runnin'. She yanks my arm and drags me along. We're right next to the sleepin' baby.

She reaches out....

CHAPTER TWENTY-NINE

Catie
January 1964

Granny Poison Ivy strikes like a robin at a worm. She snatches the baby out of the shoppin' cart: bouncy seat and all. I look at the baby, still sound asleep. I'm wide awake now. *What's goin' on? What's happenin'?*

Ivy tightens her hold onto my arm and forces me to move faster. More like stiff-legged runnin', away from the shoppin' cart and away from the mother. Straight toward the front door.

With wide eyes, I stare at her. "What are ya doin'?"

"WALK, and walk fast!" she says through clenched teeth. "Don't say a word, if you know what's good for you!" Her arm clenches my shoulder. She digs into my skin. Hard. The whole time she smiles and coos at the little baby girl that she carries in her bouncy seat toward the door.

We are out of the store and into the car before I know it. I din't hear any commotion behind us. I glance toward the storefront. *Is anyone comin' to fetch the baby from Icky Poison Ivy?*

A whimper comes from the baby girl in the back seat. She's so very tiny and beautiful. Her mommy has her dressed in a pretty pink dress with flowers and trimmed in ruffles. Her booties are so small they would fit my Sassy Secret nurse doll. I reach into the back seat and cover her with her warm bunny baby blanket.

When the car moves, I jerk around. Ivy pulls out of the parkin' space.

"We need to take this baby back!" I shout. "What's wrong with you? She isn't yours. She'll miss her mommy! And her mommy will be worried sick about where her baby's gone." I break into sobs.

She looks at me with her evil black eyes. "Shut your damn mouth!" she says, spit flyin'.

"And you best stop the whining and crying, or I'll give you something to cry about." She grits her teeth and squeezes the steerin' wheel.

I gulp back tears. My heart pounds so fast that it's hard to breathe.

What Poison Ivy is doin' is wrong. I cry for the baby. I cry for her mother. I cry for myself. How can any grandmother be so mean and evil? I hate her.

I kneel and look out through the rear window, starin' at the grocery store, hopin' and prayin' someone will run out, so I can wave to let them know Icky Poison Ivy has the baby.

No one comes. I feel helpless. I feel hopeless.

I turn to her. "P-please, let's take the baby back. Please! You know it's the right thing to do. What if she were Anna? Wouldn't you want her back? What about Melinda or Shawnee?"

WHAM! The sting of the back side of her hand slaps across my face and into my nose. Warm blood runs down my nose onto my lips.

She looks at me, smiles, and says, "I told you I'd give you

something to cry about. Now get my handkerchief out of the glove compartment. And don't you dare get any blood on *my* car. You hear me?"

I do as I'm told.

"And you better stop crying or else."

She stops the car at the traffic light. She shoves me in my shoulder. "Catie. You pick. Charley or this baby?"

I say nothin'. There's no real choice. I hold my tears inside.

This must have been her plan all along. There was never goin' to be any candy. Poison Ivy din't decide to go to the grocery store till *after* she saw the lady with the baby. She was shoppin' alright, but not for groceries.

I understand now. I see right through that horrible woman. The only reason she wanted me to go was to use me as a decoy. Like Grandpa's duck decoys. It was all fake. She din't want anyone lookin' at her. She pretended she was shoppin' with her two grandchildren as we left the store, like it was a typical day. There's nothin' typical or normal 'bout this hag.

I sit quietly in the front seat. *Has she done this before?* Then I remember. Baby Jesse at the Christmas manger. And the babies at the baptism. Where did they get these babies? I shiver.

The icky smell of a dead mouse reeks from Poison Ivy, and my tummy turns sour. What will happen to this baby? I fear the worst. I hate myself for bein' here—a part of this wickedness.

Why din't I say somethin'? Why din't I scream? Why din't I run away from Poison Ivy and tell the mommy we had her baby? Why did I do what I was told? I deserve everythin' Anna and her bunch does to me. *But not Charley and not this precious baby.*

I keep my head down to hide my tears. I'm ashamed. It's my fault. I know all too well what it feels like to want your mommy, and she never comes to you. I hear the baby cry. I hate myself.

Marion
October 1995

W hen I arrive at the café, I spot Catherine at a cozy window table for two. I glance around the restaurant. The décor has a cozy mountain feel with lots of wood accents and golden lighting. Catherine has chosen a table in the far corner and shielded from the main room by a tall plant. Her head is bent over her well-worn journal, and her pen moves furiously.

"Hello, Catherine," I say as I approach. "You have chosen a wonderful location. I have never been here before."

She looks up with a serious expression. "I needed to see you, but not in the office. I think my body tenses up in the office because I associate it with the bad memories. But today, I just need a sounding board."

"That is what I am here for," I respond, smiling.

The waitress approaches with glasses of ice water and straws. She takes our orders: a ham and cheese panini for Catherine and a bowl of pumpkin bisque soup for me. Once the waitress departs, I glance at Catherine and note her anxious expression.

Before I can ask her what is wrong, she begins talking, crumpling the straw wrapper in her fingers.

"Marion, I need to talk with you about a conversation I had with a close friend about the baby at the grocery store. I was surprised and taken aback at her response."

I take a sip of my water. "How did her response upset you?

"She was angry. She told me that I needed to go straight to the police to report what had happened all those years ago."

"I see, and what do you think?"

She takes a moment to gaze out the window. Golden Aspen leaves swirl in little clusters along the sidewalk. "Honestly, I'm confused.

Unsure. Keep in mind; I don't know where I was. We had driven a long time, so long I fell asleep. As far as I know, we could have been in another city or another state. And I have no idea who the lady was. I can only guess at the year. Sometime between 1963 and 1965, when I was six to eight or nine years old. I doubt my exact age because I can't say for sure." Catherine shakes her head and covers her face.

"I do not expect you to remember the exact dates. When the memories come back, they are not in any chronological order. Suppressed events return when you are ready to remember and not necessarily with all the details. God is merciful. He allows us to recall what we can grasp. And what we can handle, with his help."

I take another sip of my water. "I have noticed when you remember a childhood memory, one of your coping mechanism is to shut your eyes. Sometimes even covering your face, like you are doing now."

"I know." Catherine uncovers her eyes then tilts her head. "I still do. Like at the movies if I see something that's too intense. Some things are too hard to face. I close my eyes or cover them instinctively."

"How do you feel about the idea of going to the police?"

"Marion, even the thought of going to the police makes me physically shake." She extends her trembling hands across the table. "I don't think I could. NO. I know I can't handle opening up my past to the police. Not now, anyway. I've kept these secrets suppressed for over thirty years. I'm afraid the occult will come after me. I'm afraid for my life. I'm afraid for my family's life."

She begins to rock. Her hands tightly seize the edge of the chair.

"I've thought about it and rehearsed it in my head. I can only imagine how crazy I would sound, trying to describe my story to an officer. 'I just recently had some childhood memories return. Bits and pieces of memories, that is, but I'm hoping to remember more. Well, you see, officer, there was an older woman, I called her Granny Poison Ivy, who is most likely already dead. She took a baby from a grocery store. When, where, and from whom, I don't know. She and her family were a part of the Satanic occult. I don't know any of their last names. And as far as that goes, I'm not sure I even knew their real first names.' End of story."

She shakes her head as though trying to rid herself of the memories. "And what good would it do? The mother of that baby is probably well into her sixties or older, maybe even her seventies. I can't bring her child back. If pressed, I would guess they sacrificed the child during an occult ritual. And if I ever found the lady, it would break her heart all over again."

The waitress delivers our meals. We pause for a prayer of thanks. The smooth pumpkin flavor on my tongue hits the spot.

Catherine pushes up the sleeves of her sweater and takes a bite of her cheesy panini. How I wish my diet didn't restrict me so much.

After she swallows, Catherine continues. "My friend said it would give the mother closure." She cocks her head to the side. "Closure? To find out that your infant was possibly murdered by the occult! What kind of closure is that? That would be more like a nightmare that would haunt her for the rest of her life. I think it would cause more harm than good." She swallows hard and blots the sweat from her upper lip with her napkin.

I set down my spoon, making eye contact. "I understand your concerns, confusion, and fears. Perhaps you may need to give it some time. Maybe you will remember more details."

Catherine nods, picking at the crust of her sandwich. "When I think about the baby in the grocery store, I loathe myself for being too shocked to act. So unprepared. I wish I would've kicked Ivy, then jumped out of the car and ran to the store manager once I'd figured out what she was doing." She squeezes her arms close to her chest."

"I wish I would have done a lot of things differently, but I didn't. I believed and knew they'd kill Charley. They would've said it was an accident. Right now, just talking about the past makes me anxious— stressed—raw. I feel so fragile."

Catherine cradles her head and rocks. "I feel like I'm about to go crazy from the guilt and shame. I don't know what to do. Somehow, I'll have to learn how to live with this mess." She looks around, probably wondering if people are watching.

"Do not worry. You chose a very private table," I say. "One of the ways to overcome trauma is to continue to explore the memories by following your emotions. As you know, the emotions lead you to the beliefs buried in the memories. The Holy Spirit has been gracious to expose the lies and reveal the truth."

Catherine looks at me through her tired eyes. She offers a hopeful smile.

"Many individuals choose to dwell on the trauma of being a victim, but I encourage you to focus on being victorious and a victor. You have overcome so much, and I believe with the Lord's guidance, you will continue to overcome even more."

I recite Psalm 6:1 to encourage Catherine as well as myself. "'For the Lord knows the way of the righteous, but the way of the wicked will perish.' This verse gives me hope that it will all work out in the end."

Catherine's smile grows a little stronger. "You're right, Marion. Although these memories are horrific, the upside is that I find another truth. It has been like putting together a jigsaw puzzle. God is honoring my prayers by bringing me answers and healing."

"Remember your revelation; the one with you in a wedding dress with Jesus?" I raise my brows. "Do you recall the freedom you felt not so long ago? You were able to feel forgiveness and compassion for many of those involved in the occult. I warned you to expect a pushback from the enemy. It is a normal process to feel unforgiveness as memories are stirred."

She nods an encouraging yes, but it looks forced.

"Catherine, continue to journal about the events, your emotions, and the people you need to forgive. After you have taken your notes into account, ask God to confirm what is true. This method will help you to persevere through the forgiveness process. I believe that someday you will be able to release these individuals completely over to the Lord."

I nod my head to encourage her before I add, "There are many people you will have to choose to forgive. And my dear, just as a reminder, *your name* needs to be added to the list."

She looks up. The sun shining through the window reflects off the single tear on her cheek. It reminds me of the light and hope we have in Christ's love. Her betrayals and disappointments run deep within her soul. I pray for her healing.

Catherine
October 1995

"I'll be ready in a minute; I'm putting on my makeup. I thought you said we didn't have to leave until 8:00 a.m. It's only 7:45. I still have 15 minutes."

Hunter walks by slowly and lets out a frustrated huff. "I said, around eight. What do you have to do to finish? I'm running this car race today and have a lot to do. Can you hurry?"

Air blows from my nose like a bull giving a warning snort. Even so, I pick up my speed. I throw my cosmetics into my makeup case. When Hunter gives me a time and then changes it, I get irritated. *That's not fair.* What's worse is when he hovers over me while I'm doing my finishing touches. I spray my hair and add lip gloss over my lipstick.

I walk into the kitchen. "I need my road cup of coffee, and then I'll be ready."

And sure enough, at the stroke of eight, I glide into the garage just as I'd planned. I'm not late, but Hunter acts as if being on time isn't good enough. He's itching to go. There is nothing like spoiling a good morning by being impatient. I shut the car door, hard.

We pull into the racetrack parking lot at 8:20 a.m. We made great time having little to no traffic. It's surprising for a Saturday morning. Hunter's especially pleased at our early arrival. As we exit the truck, Hunter checks on the trailer towing his car.

The brisk October morning air swoops all around me and chills me to the bone. I look for the sun in hopes that it will be warm soon, standing with my arms crossed. I'm cold and irritated with the hurry-up-and-then-wait pattern.

Hunter scurries off while I join the ladies who are snuggled in sweatshirts, sipping coffee. They hold onto their cups to warm their hands. We kill time catching up on each other's latest news while we wait for the rest of the folks to arrive.

All drivers are required to walk the racetrack. I gulp coffee to warm myself. I join the group of drivers to begin the walk. *It's going to be a long day.*

Hunter leans over and gives me a big kiss. "Catherine, that was a delicious picnic lunch. Exactly what I needed, body fuel." He winks and is up on his feet, heading to the pit area to make announcements.

Hunter's voice blares over the bullhorn, "The next session will be slow laps for beginner drivers. The event will start in twenty minutes."

I make a quick stop in the port-a-potty and then hustle back to the pit area. I overhear Hunter talking to Wayne, one of his good buddies.

"Yeah. I hadn't heard from this chick in years, man. Then all of a sudden, she pops back into my life. I'd heard she was back in town. She had the nerve to call the house." Hunter takes off his hat, pushes his hair back, and puts his hat back on.

"Wow. How did that go over?" Wayne lifts his chin in curiosity.

"Catherine saw right through her. Immediately! She tried to feed her some line about us working together and wanting to make an investment. All lies, of course."

Wayne slaps his hand on his thigh and laughs. "Not much gets by Catherine. She's a smart cookie."

"Yeah. I know. She told me right away that Crystal was bad news, and she didn't trust her. She had some strong words about the whole thing. Turns out, she was right. Crystal did come on to me."

"How'd you handle that?"

"I told her the truth. I said I was married now, and I'd promised

Catherine we would keep our past in the past. Meaning, old girlfriends."

"That's wise. Did the woman accept it?"

"Yes and no. At first, she played the, 'can we still be friends' card. When I refused, she asked if I could at least be her broker for investments."

"Eww. That chick is a tricky one." Wayne slowly shakes his head side to side.

"Yeah, I'm not the old fool I use to be. I haven't forgotten our history. She cheated on me and was constantly dishonest. Not much has changed. I feel sorry for her husband."

"Good thing you listened to your wife. You dodged a bullet with that chick. She sounds like trouble. Hey man, don't screw up. Catherine's a keeper." He punches Hunter in the arm. "From my point of view, you married up, man."

They both bust out in laughter. I use the break in the conversation to make my approach. I'm pleased to hear Hunter set Crystal straight. He had told me so, but I didn't know the details. I smile.

"Hey, Wayne. It's a good day for a track event. Hunter is finally letting me drive his prize possession."

"Is that right, dude?" He looks at Hunter.

Hunter makes a face, biting down on his fingers as if terrorized. We laugh.

Wayne spouts, "I don't know of too many people who wouldn't be thrilled to drive an original 1964 AC Cobra. Hunter doesn't let anyone drive this car. Except me. And that was just once." He extends me a high five.

I smack his palm with enthusiasm and smile. "See you later, Wayne." I turn and walk to the car.

I gear up, tighten my helmet, and fasten the five-point safety belt harness. Hunter climbs into the passenger seat, grinning ear to ear.

I cautiously turn my head both ways, making sure I have clearance onto the raceway. My stomach's alive, dancing with butterflies. I'm excited but nervous, being behind the wheel of such a fast sports car.

I depress the accelerator and gain speed. The wind swoops up and over my helmet. My body rumbles from the vibration of the engine. I grasp the steering wheel—my knuckles white. I navigate the first apex of turn one and shift into second gear. The car builds momentum, executing turn two flawlessly. The straightaway approaches. I turn to Hunter, looking for affirmation and approval for being cautious with his cherished vehicle.

"Catherine, you haven't even gotten out of second gear." He shouts through his helmet and over the roaring engine. "If you go any slower, the turtles will pass us."

I yell back, "What? Are you kidding me?" Embarrassment rises, followed by anger. "I'm trying to be so careful, and you insult me!"

I punch the gas pedal. Ripping through the gears, the g's (gravity force) press us into the seats. The car jumps into action. The speedometer reads 100 mph. And climbing. My husband's eyes are wide.

"Slow down, Catherine!" His foot presses hard upon the invisible brake pedal in the passenger foot box.

Laughter fills the living room as Hunter and I rehash our driving adventure on the track.

"Man, I'll never do that again. You slammed on the gas. All I meant was to speed up a little, but believe me, I've learned to pick my words carefully."

"Turtle, huh?" I cock my head to the left and arch my brows.

"I stand corrected." We flash smiles at each other, followed by a long kiss.

CHAPTER THIRTY

Catie
Spring 1964

The tall grass scratches against my ankles. I move turtle slow and stomp extra hard in case there are snakes sliverin' around in this dark field. Why do these devil-people always want to do things in the middle of the night? Tonight is horrible, extra dark. And icy cold.

I don't like bein' up this late—not like I have a choice. My nose runs from the cold. We follow the flashlight as it slashes through the darkness. There's barely enough light to show us the way 'cuz it's pitch black outside. Shadows creep around me and give me the heebie-jeebies. Feels like evil is here and wants to swallow me up.

All of these grown-ups are cautious not to be noticed by neighbors or passin' cars on this country road. These evenin' meetin's are always yucky. Dean hasn't said what we're doin' out here, but you can bet

270

that I'm not gonna ask. I've learned that not mindin' my own business only leads to trouble.

I've been practicin' hidin' my feelin's, like Peanut taught me. It's tough. Particularly when I'm doin' somethin' like walkin' in the dead of night. I look out into the trees. Spooky shadows follow us. My head swings side to side. It's too dark to see.

I search the blackness till I'm able to see the stars. I hope I'm lookin' at the bottom of heaven. I enjoy the night sky with all sorts of twinklin' stars. *Twinkle, twinkle, little star. How I wonder what you are?* That's what I like 'bout the country; the stars go on forever, unlike the city where the streetlights make it hard to see anythin'. I gaze at the stars and inhale the smell of fresh spring grass that reminds me of corn on the cob.

A knot grows in my tummy. Somethin' bad's comin', You can pretty much count on crummy stuff happenin' with this bunch. The whole time we walk, I hide my belly knot and my heebie-jeebies in the peanut shell so Dean and Buck can't use them against me. It's odd, not feelin' anythin'. Ice Man says it's learnin' to go numb. GI Joe says it helps, and not to let these buttholes get to me. I'm glad Charley's not here tonight.

SMACK! Her hard fist stings the side of my head. "Pay attention! Quit gawking at the stars. You're going to trip." An ornery older woman growls at me. She grabs my hand as we walk up a hill.

I pull away from her. "I'm not a baby. I don't need your help," I snarl back.

She leaves me alone.

At the top of the hill, the grown-ups stand around, just outside a barn. I don't know who owns this barn. It seems like all these devil worshipers like barns. Their flashlights point downward. A small but deep hole has been dug in the ground. I know what deep holes mean. Puke rises in my throat, and I fight to hold it down.

In the distance, I hear feet scurryin' on the dirt path towards the group. Out of the blackness, I see the shapes of three grown-ups runnin' towards us. The one in the middle has long hair and holds a bundle to her chest. The woman bends down with her arms full. As the light shines upon her, I see a baby blanket with little bunnies and some kind of stains. I blink, tryin' to figure out the stains. The light flickers on and off the blanket and the three adults.

I move to the front to see what she's holdin'. My eyes squint. I watch and wait for the light to rest on the bundle. I gasp. The stains are blood! It's a tiny baby. My heart hurts. My tummy cramps, formin' a huge fear-knot.

My bottom lip trembles. Hot tears stream down my cheeks. I try with all my strength to shove all my feelin's into the peanut bombshell, but they come too fast. I suck in the cold air. *It takes my breath. I panic.* My mouth waters, and I'm pretty sure I'm goin' to puke.

Suddenly, Peanut, with GI Joe and Ice Man, motion me off to the side. They don't have to say a word; I know what to do. I breathe deep and stuff all my pain, fear, and sadness inside the peanut bombshell before I close it up tight. I go numb.

Buck comes from behind. He pushes me close to the front. So close, I think I'm gonna fall in the hole. The flashlight shines on the woman. She tilts her head. It's Poison Ivy. She's holdin' onto the sweet, tiny child. Her eyes shine black as the night—evil eyes that threaten death. She glares at me. Before I can think, much less say a single word, she yells at me.

"Shut up, Catie! Don't you dare say a word, or there'll be another hole for you. Damn brat!"

I swallow hard and stand firm, grittin' my teeth. I don't blink. Only stare at Ivy. I suspect it's the baby from the grocery store, but I don't want to believe it. I've learned from too many beatin's not to ask questions. I hate these people. They're worse than monsters.

Ivy places the stiff baby in the hole.

Dean slithers to the front of the group, then bends over and scoops up a handful of dirt. He throws it into the grave, over the baby. Buck follows, then Ivy. While each grown-up throws dirt into the hole, Dean speaks. "You are a part of this. You are responsible. You are credited for this act."

The people repeat the same words but usin' the word, 'I'. Hearin' them reminds me of the chants Anna used when she taught us levitation.

The adults proudly chant the words and toss dirt into the hole.

The children follow the grown-ups, repeatin' the same chant. Their small hands throw the black dirt into the darkness of the baby's grave.

Without a doubt, I know I'm expected to participate. When it's my turn, Buck makes his way through the crowd and comes up close. He barks his orders. "Hold out your hand, Catie."

I stuff my hands into my pockets. He jerks my hand out and shoves dirt into my palm. I throw it in the opposite direction.

SLAP! Buck backhands me across the face.

I was expectin' it. I taste blood but feel nothin'.

"Catie, I'm not gonna tell you again. Throw dirt into the damn hole!"

I say nothin', but stare into his devil eyes, determined not to obey him. I'm not sure I'd be so brave if Charley were here. Sometimes, I wish it wasn't my job to babysit my brother. These creeps make my job triple extra hard.

Ivy walks over and puts her face right close to mine. Her hot breath feels warm on my cheeks. She yells, "So, Catie, you think you're just the little smarty pants defying Buck. Huh? Well, you'll be sorry for this mistake." She jabs her boney finger into my chest.

Devil Dean pushes Buck aside and grumbles at him. "Unbelievable, such incompetence. It's pathetic. You're unable to control even a puny child."

Poison Ivy scurries to stand between her husband and her father. I'm guessin' she's worried that fists are gonna start flyin'.

Dean gives his daughter the stink eye before he makes his threats. "I promise this little brat here, and *any of you* who thinks you can defy me, that I won't sleep another day before I kill your loved ones..." Then he shouts, "...and when you least expect it."

His wicked eyes scan the group. His glare rests on me. I shiver, and my teeth chatter. There's a bitter coldness in this night, the same bitter coldness that's in Dean's black eyes.

"And *you, Catie,* out of all people, should know I'll do it. After all, didn't we kill your *mommy?* And we made sure your sweet little *Happy* is dead as well?" Mean Dean takes credit for Buck's and Ivy's evil doin'. She pats her husband's arm to calm him.

273

I push my fear into the peanut bombshell before it can rise any further and sputter, "NO! I'm n-not g-gonna do it!"

Ivy jerks me by the arm and yanks me in close. "You'll be sorry, Catie. You'll see. You're gonna be real sorry."

The crowd stays dead silent. White powder billows out of the grave, like a hauntin' ghost, as Dean pours a big sack of powder, or chemical, as he calls it, over the baby. I wonder if the chemical is a poison? Then he tosses in a few more handfuls of dirt—minus mine. The floatin' powder makes me cough.

Several men scramble to fill the hole with dirt, completely coverin' it, before they pack it down—firm. They beat the ground with shovels and then sprinkle the top with black soil. Within a few minutes, they cover the ground with a patch of grass that had been cut and rolled back. Before we leave the grave, the same men use several large waterin' cans to douse the grassy area.

Dean and Buck inspect the ground, makin' sure there are no tell-tale signs. It's as if the baby never existed.

I gaze at the stars and plead out a silent message. *Mommy, please help. If you're not too busy in heaven, will you look after this baby so that it won't miss its mommy and daddy too much?*

After we leave the gravesite, Ivy shoves me down the stairs of someone's house and forces me into the cellar. All these basements look the same: oiled down dirt floors with brick or cement walls, but some have hard floors too. The ceilin's are low; the adults' heads almost touch the wooden rafters, but I'm short, so it doesn't matter.

A white casket sits in the back of the room. I've heard stories from some of the other kids that whenever anyone misbehaves, they locked them inside one of these death boxes. They call it a coffin, but Teenage Granny told me the proper word is casket.

My mommy had a pretty casket. It was silver, lined with matchin' satin. Daddy dressed her in a beautiful pink satin and chiffon nightgown. Mommy looked like she was sleepin'. I miss her so much, and I can't even remember how she smells anymore. Charlotte has a few drops left of her perfume. She lets us smell it once in a while. We have to keep it a secret, or Anna will destroy it, like Mommy's tea set.

Anna dropped me off earlier and told her mother she'd be back later to pick me up. As bad luck would have it, she arrives right as Poison Ivy pushes me toward the casket.

Anna marches straight over to us. "Catie Kay, what have you done now?" She huffs in disgust. "Won't you ever learn?"

I turn to Anna and put my back to Poison Ivy. "I ain't never gonna put dirt on a—"

Ivy cups her hand over my mouth from behind and whips me around. Her eyes are wide. She tips her head toward the new people who arrived with Anna. She gestures in the no-word code. They think I don't know what it means, but I do.

Anna walks away to distract the newcomers from seein' what her mother's 'bout to do.

"Shhh! Keep your mouth shut, Catie. You have to learn to follow instructions. Disobedience and defiance will not be tolerated. You deserve punishment and are going inside the coffin, maybe forever!"

I'm not sure how to feel. To hear the other kids tell it, they say they were afraid, and they cried. Some of the kids said they screamed while others kicked to get out. They all said they hated bein' locked inside. Some swore it was almost impossible to breathe.

I climb up a rickety stepladder. The inside is covered with pretty satin. As I step into the casket, Ivy says, "If you'd only do what you were told, you wouldn't have to go into this coffin. You brought this on yourself, Catie. This is your fault. I hope this will remind you to mind…or else. You remember what your Great Grandpa Dean said. Now you think about that while you rest in this box of death." She glares, squintin' her eyes, and then she smiles.

Her smile is sick. She's nuts and should be in the loony bin.

"Remember, sweetie, your mommy is in a coffin. Just like this. She's six feet under the ground. A place where she can *never* get out." As she closes the lid, her last words are, "I wonder how long your air will last?"

The light begins to disappear.

I lift my arms to stop them from closin' the lid. One of the grown-ups takes his cane and smacks both of my arms so hard that it knocks them back into the casket. They slam the lid closed — the lock clicks.

275

All I can feel is the sting in my arms. I din't want to cry. I din't want to give them their way. I lie still. Alone. My arms throb.

When I open my eyes, it's pitch black as if my eyes are still closed —not even a seam of light. How long will I be able to breathe? I feel the satin all around me. Soft. Smooth. Cool to the touch. I stroke the cloth. It feels so pretty. I like silky things.

Funny enough, this casket isn't bad, after all. It's comfy, almost like a bed. The satin feels so good on my skin, 'specially my stingin' arms. I like the quiet and bein' alone, away from these creeps. I'm not afraid. I feel peaceful. Somehow I know Mommy heard my prayers 'bout the baby.

I decide to think about fun things, just like Peanut taught me. Barbie does it all the time. She always has a smile on her face. I remember fun times with Mommy and my family. No matter whatever happened, Mommy always protected me and kept me safe. I love my Mommy memories…

All five of us kids run down the stairs to play in our basement. We decide to put on a circus. Charley wants to be a lion or a tiger. He practices his roar while we chatter our ideas of a tight-rope act. I giggle inside the casket.

Catherine
February 1996

The images of Dean's eyes at the baby's grave loom as I recall the memory. His eyes are as black, black as sin, just like the night I remembered. I can't seem to get the haunting images out of my mind even months after the memory came back. Darkness swallowed everything around us, minus the small beams coming from their flashlights. There was a noise of a distant engine. My eyes darted in that direction, seeing the headlights come up the country road. Dean and the others clicked off their lights. We stood in pure darkness— waiting to leave the scene of their dirty deeds.

The memory falls over me like a heavy blanket. The baby. Whose baby was it that lay in the depth of the secret grave? Shame slams at my heart. How can I live with this?

Oppressing thoughts weigh heavy and leave me feeling hopeless. *Will I ever get over this? Will I ever recover or feel normal? What kind of a person could ever recuperate from such evil?*

Accusing thoughts stab at my mind. *A heartless, stone-cold soul.*

Is that me? Am I heartless?

I invite numbness to punch through with force to quench my unbearable emotions. At last, relief comes, as I can no longer feel. It seems to me I fail either way. I either fail to feel or become heartless. I hate myself. I grabbed a handful of hair and tug.

I need to feel but can't stand the pain, the shame, and the reality. *Am I going crazy?*

Marion
February 1996

I swallow a quick gulp of much-needed hot coffee. I worked late last night—too late. Fatigue lines my eyes. I push my sleepiness aside and circle several positive matches from the newspaper. *Am I acting crazy or desperate looking at these dating advertisements?* On a yellow notepad, I scribe notations of the contact information and details for each candidate who sounds appealing.

After I have finished, I fold the newspaper and hide it underneath a stack of books, not sure if I want anyone to know what I am doing. I am somewhat embarrassed, although being alone has proven to be worse.

Watching the clock, I pull out Catherine's file. It amazes me how fast time has passed. I scan the year; 1992—Catherine's first session. Our appointments started weekly, moving to bimonthly, and an occasional monthly session following our trip to Kentucky. I encouraged consistency while trusting God and Catherine to determine the necessary time needed to process the memories revealed in each session. I have agreed to continue at Catherine's pace. She has much to resolve.

I record February-1996 on the top of the legal pad to begin an assessment. My evaluations show: Catherine is handling the process of counseling quite well, with normal fluctuation of emotions with her recall of memories. I discussed my concerns with Catherine about her father's questionable awareness or lack of knowledge concerning the abuse of his children. She speculates her father must have been in denial or minimized the chaos in their family. She believes he felt financially trapped in the marriage. He worked long hours to provide but never seemed to get ahead. He needed a mother for his children. At that time, governmental financial assistance for single parents did not exist. Men were expected to provide for their families, and her father did not earn enough money to afford a full-time live-in nanny. In addition, in the 1960s, divorce was difficult. Such a proceeding meant a court case to prove your grounds for the dissolution of the matrimony. Per Catherine, her father could not afford either. He worked most of the time and barely made enough money to pay the bills and keep food on the table for a family of seven.

Catherine is focused and determined to bring light to the lies and replace them with God's truths. With each truth, she has received healing. Catherine has always functioned well and has been a gifted survivor. She works at a job she enjoys. She has finished college, as well as completed several specialized counseling courses. She's a natural at counseling as she has a heart for people. Her health is well, maintaining a high level of exercise, outdoor activity, and proper nutrition. Catherine practices self-control but is challenged during the holidays and at trauma anniversaries with sugar cravings.

I relate to the emotional eating. I have kept twenty pounds off but seem to have plateaued at my present weight. There is no question as to why. I have mind battles when it comes to my eating. I rationalize, justify, minimize, and do all the things I know are self-sabotaging. Conviction sounds within my mind indicating I need to practice what I preach. Pushing my thoughts aside, I continue reading her assessment and make additional notes.

I have researched the subject of satanic ritual abuse. It appears there are thousands of reports of occult victims within the United States as well as worldwide, with projections of numerous unreported accounts from individuals who are reluctant to come forward. Strangely, many, if not most of the cases, which have made it into the court system are reportedly dismissed. Last year, in 1995 alone, 12,000 allegations of satanic ritual abuse claims were reported, yet resulted in no cases brought forth to trial.

Catherine's memories confirm a network of community involvement: policemen, a doctor, nurses, even a judge, along with various individuals of significant influence—all connected to the occult. She resided in some podunk little town. I shudder to think of how well-linked the occult is in some of the major cities in the United States.

As I read these reports, there is a consistency to minimize or completely excuse the satanic involvement. From what I have surmised, there are numerous semantics and the covering up of facts.

Physical, sexual, and psychological abuse involving children are happening every day. Pedophilia is apparent. The signs are right before our very eyes. Yet, people deny the evidence, the crime, and deny it because it makes them uncomfortable. It is easier to dismiss the truth than to battle the war. My heart aches for Catherine and the many children who have and are still falling victims to such perversions.

The research goes so far as to categorize various types of satanic abuse, one which was called pseudo-satanism. This particular group sexually abused children using the trappings of satanic rituals, claiming demonic powers to manipulate, terrify, and control their victims. However, because the accused said they did not actually believe in such things; it was ruled not to be *true* satanic ritual abuse.

Such rulings are unscrupulous and very convenient for the abusers. Satan, the father of lies, is up to his work again. Lies on top of lies. I discern bribable legal representation and a corrupt court system all over these cases. I find myself enraged.

Catherine has kept her childhood secrets hidden for so very long. She fears the occult, their actions, and their threats to murder her family. I can understand why Catherine has fears and doubts about the law and is uncertain if it can or will protect her.

She often questions, 'what good will it do?' It has been decades, and Catherine suspects her abusers—Dean, Buck, and Ivy—are deceased, and have been for a long time. Anna and her daughters' existence are questionable.

There is more to be unburied. Although memories are coming back with ease, most are painful. Even faced with these extra challenges of unfolding her past and solving the mystery of the recurring nightmare, Catherine and Hunter are successfully settling into a loving, committed marriage. They have experienced the normal turbulence found in all relationships and have overcome the challenges thus far. Catherine and Hunter have a growing faith and a strong determination to have a successful marriage.

I continue to coach her on the daily necessity of examining her thoughts, rebuking the lies, and proclaiming aloud God's word and truth. Catherine is compliant to memorize scriptures that describe herself as a child of God—her sole identity.

Confirmed by what I have read, most occult methods of abuse were designed to destroy the victim's identity and purpose.

This information brings light to Catherine's vacillation to fully accept her identity as a child of God. If only I can help her comprehend that God created her in his image. She is beautifully and wonderfully made, the Lord's beloved precious daughter. My heart feels saddened for Catherine. She carries such a heavy burden of shame, which is instrumental in her feelings of unworthiness.

I sign and date the chart. Before closing the file, I make one last entry. Catherine has a heightened affection for dogs. I assess it is because she feels responsible for her pup, Happy's death. Somehow loving other dogs soothes the guilt she carries.

As I stack today's client files on top of the books, I notice the hidden want ads are a tad exposed. I push the newspaper deeper under the books to conceal my secret. Just then, there is a small knock on the door.

Catherine is here for her appointment. Sadness wreathes her face. I welcome her with a big hug and offer her a coffee. She makes herself comfortable, and we begin our session.

Catherine blinks to fight back her tears. "I feel so alone at times, *especially* when working through the abuse. I don't have anyone to talk with—except you."

She sighs, shifting her position. "Hunter tries, but I wish I had a friend who understood, someone I could talk with, in between our appointments. Maybe I'm just looking for validation, someone to say that they know what I'm feeling or understand what happened to me. I'm probably just asking for too much; it's not like it's a *common subject*. But it should be."

Catherine's anger appears to rise, like mercury in a thermometer. "I don't understand with all the evil in the world why people don't talk about child molestation associated with the satanic occult. It seems most people don't want to believe that such atrocities are real, or they choose to pretend that it doesn't exist. Heck, all you have to do is look in the phone book under churches. The *Church of Satan* is listed right there in the Yellow Pages."

I rest my elbows on my desk. "You are right, Catherine. People do not want to believe in Satan or that these types of crimes against humanity...children exist, at least not in their world, because it propels them out of their comfort zones. They are afraid because they do not know how to resolve the issue. *Satanists* have been around since the fall of Lucifer. It is unfathomable to understand why someone—anyone, would want to follow or worship the devil, but yet, people do."

She raises her hands. "What are people thinking? I mean, really? In October, you can go into any veterinary clinic and see signs posted saying, 'keep your pets inside—especially black cats!' That screams the occult and sacrifices. I can't believe people write it off as kids just making harmful pranks. Torturing and killing an innocent animal is NOT a prank." Catherine shakes her head. "Or what about brutal murders and mutilations? They rationalize it away as mental illness. But what's behind the mental illness?"

With each example, Catherine's voice grows higher and louder. Her hands shoot off in different directions. I listen and encourage her to express her anger and frustration.

"And missing children, or an onslaught of missing boys, from three to nine years old, sexually abused and murdered by some guy who says he hears voices in his head telling him to kill them?" She pounds her fist into the accent pillow. "All that is dismissed by simply saying the man is a serial killer, as if that somehow explains the evil."

Catherine stands and shakes her fists in the air. "Wake up people. It's demonic! It's evil at work! Stop pretending Satan isn't real. Talk about having a major elephant in the room. How can people be so deceived?" She falls back onto the cushions looking frustrated and exhausted.

"Catherine, Satan's most strategic lie—was and is—convincing the world he does not exist. People are too frightened to admit the reality of the demonic. Imagine the shock if they knew the massive numbers of individuals involved in the occult."

I shrug my shoulders and tilt my head to make my point. "It could be the person next door. A man or woman you see at a department store. A stranger with whom you might have a friendly conversation. Someone you would easily overlook in a crowd.

"Influencing the world of his non-existence is a powerful deception. Strategically, many of Satan's followers promote the lie, saying he does not exist, yet they follow him." My voice drips with sarcasm.

Catherine sits, her back rigid, and her voice assertive. "I know for a fact, firsthand, people who have worshiped the devil and called upon him for power. I have experienced their sicko warped need for power. As a child, I was overpowered by dirty old men. They used, abused, and treated me like a piece of meat served on a platter to satisfy their appetites of perversion. Such acts were promoted by the occult like it was a badge of honor."

Catherine's anger makes the veins on her forehead bulge. "Satan is nothing more than a cheap counterfeiter. Whatever God ordains, the devil comes up with his twisted, vile version. Like the Ten Commandments. Anna and her evil bunch demanded breaking every commandment, twisting it into a sick initiation requirement to be a part of the occult. And after having done so, they defined themselves proudly as *true members*."

I reach out to touch Catherine's hand to calm her and affirm her righteous anger. "God knows what you have gone through. His word warns us about Satan in John 8:44. 'When he speaks a lie, he speaks from his own resources, for he is a liar and the father of lies.' Satan is a liar, a thief, a deceiver, and our adversary.

"Unfortunately, Catherine, you know this truth all too well, in a much deeper way than most. I am so sorry. Even though others *may never understand your story*, you have an intimate experiential knowledge of God's love, mercy, and provision—of which many only dream."

My words seem to comfort her, but it takes some time for her emotions to calm.

Catherine's shoulders soften. "You're right. It is a bittersweet reality I'm learning to appreciate. I amaze myself at how I can go from forgiveness into such rage and back to frustration. I feel like such a hot mess."

"Life and its emotions can feel like a tempest. We must learn to turn to God during the most raging storms for his will, peace, and direction."

I offer her a glass of water. "Shall we move on?"

She nods, then looks up with a question. "During one of my sessions, the Lord said something to me, but I'm not sure exactly what it means. I heard him say he had made propitiation and restitution for me. What does propitiation mean?"

I lean back in my chair. "I will try to keep my answer simple but clear. The act of propitiation in Jesus's case was death on a cross. He paid the penalty for all sins, choices, and decisions that separate us from God. His action or atonement bought us restitution and a way to be reconciled to Father God, our Lord. So, when you believed and asked for forgiveness and invited Jesus into your heart, you were restored into the family of God, as his child, and as the bride of Christ."

"Hmm…Propitiation, paying the penalty. I don't recall ever hearing that term. Restitution was what I thought, but I don't think I could've said it quite as eloquently." Catherine digs for her pen to write my words in her journal.

"Marion, I recognize the lies in my mind more quickly than before. And when I speak the truth, my emotions calm, making it easier to make wise choices. I feel freer in that regard. You were right. This has been a process—a long journey."

I nod. "Yes, it has been. God is using this counseling to bring you the truth, truth that is setting you free. I am pleased with what you have overcome. The Lord has taken what was intended for destruction and used it to strengthen you. You, my dear, are a miracle."

CHAPTER THIRTY-ONE

Catie
Summer 1964

I t's a miracle that this devil-bunch are lettin' us go with them to play in the water. We walk to the local lake, which also has a dam. From someone who's as rotten as Buck, his sayin's can be funny sometimes. He calls this place the 'dam lake.'

I've brought my bug jar, tucked into the waistband of my pedal pushers, in hopes of catchin' somethin'. The sun has set, but the sky's still light enough to walk around. There's a pretty big group of grown-ups who seem to be in a big hurry to get somewhere. But not me and the other kids. We lolly-gag behind. We walk near the stream-bed that leads to the lake. Granny Poison Ivy calls it the swampy area, but we love it, 'cuz it's a great spot to find frogs and water bugs.

Dean musta told one of the women to stay behind. I'm guessin' that's why she isn't movin' more than an eyeshot in front of us. She seems okay with our pace and doesn't mind when we stop here and there to see what we might find. We hope to catch a pet frog or toad.

Dean, Buck, and the others are so far ahead that we can't see or hear them. The sound of the water from the dam makes it hard to even hear the people next to you. The lady tells us, real nice-like, "You-ens need to pick up yer speed since we're losin' daylight."

We decide to make a game of it. We line up and run in a horizontal line, holdin' hands, like in a Red Rover game, and to keep the faster runners from winnin'. It's so much fun. We all laugh and occasionally gasp for air 'cuz we're runnin' so fast.

The landscape changes, so we slow our speed. We skip around an outcroppin' of itchy picker-bushes to find the small openin' that leads eventually to the lake. It isn't easy to see unless you're lookin' for this particular spot. Not many people know 'bout this hidden place, only Dean, Ivy, and Buck. They live nearby and know all the ins and outs of these trails.

As we continue down the path, the light becomes dull, and the sky begins to settle into twilight. When I'm at home, this is the time when the streetlights come on, but out in the country, they don't have any lights. It's gettin' dark and spooky, makin' it hard to see. It makes me nervous. Charley hangs on tight to my hand, and I hold onto the back of Gilbert's shirt.

Not too far ahead, I can see the dim light of some small flashlights. I'm happy to see the grown-ups, 'cuz I wasn't sure how us kids would ever find our way out with the nighttime comin' on so fast. It gets super dark at this country lake.

We prance up to see the adults standin' right next to the water. Large rocks jut out into the lake. Most of this area has bushes right up to the shoreline. There's a small eddy with calm and still water clingin' around the boulders. It's a shallow area, 'bout twenty feet in size, somethin' I know 'cuz we come here to play. We're not supposed to get in the water, but we do. We've been warned to be careful 'cuz right off the shallow end is a deep drop-off and a fast current. But only if the dam's open.

Charley and me stop, but Gilbert moves ahead to see what the commotion is with all the adults. As we approach, they turn around. With one finger over their mouths, they gesture, shhh. We know to be quiet.

I have no idea why we're hidin', it's dark, nobody can see us unless they see the flashlights.

I squint. Some of the men are comin' out of the water. Their clothes are soaked and stuck to their bodies. A couple of the ladies wade behind the men. They're wet, but only up to their thighs. Charley and me find it funny and giggle. It sure is fun to watch the grown-ups take a dip in our favorite little swimmin' hole.

I wiggle my way between the adults to the front to see if I can go in for a splash with the grown-ups. I stop at the edge of the shore. The water is real cloudy—stirred up. It's dark, but somethin's out there.

Dean sprints up right next to me. He shines his flashlight ahead. I freeze. Can't catch my breath.

Oh no! What have they done? Bodies—floatin' face down. Adults? Kids? Or both?

Devil Dean jerks me around. I tremble. He bends and whispers, "If you tell anybody, you'll be sorry! You understand? I'll start with your baby brother. The one you dote after all the time."

I nod, lettin' him know I heard. Right then, I swear I'll never swim here again.

I've been held under the water many times in those horse troughs. They'd keep you down till you can't fight anymore. When you think you're gonna die, they pull you up, just long enough to suck in a big breath, only to be plunged back under again. With each panicked breath, they would scream threats at me like, 'You deserve to die. I'm going to kill you. Say goodbye. You're finished.' I never knew if they meant it or not.

Is this how these people died? Did they hold them under the water? I stare at the lifeless people floatin' facedown, like life rafts. Except there's no life in them. I can't stand the sight. *It takes my breath. I panic.*

Shakin' in fear, I push myself into the bushes. I move as far away from Dean and Buck as I can. Deeper and deeper, I crawl into the shrubs. Eventually, I turn to see how far I've gone.

A flashlight moves in my direction. They must be lookin' for me. I see a little girl already hidin.' She has thick, shiny golden hair that flows over her shoulders, a bit longer in the back. Such a cute face with small features and aquamarine eyes like my sisters.

The girl's hand shakes as she puts her finger to her lips. We both sit quietly. We stare at one another till we hear Buck, Dean, and the adults start to move out. We see the flickerin' flashlights again. The sky is gettin' darker.

On all fours, we sneak out of the bushes and join in line behind the devil people. I find Charley and Gilbert. We put our hands on the waist of the person in front and follow along. Dean's in the lead with the only lit flashlight. He told the others to shut theirs off. He says it will appear he's alone if someone notices the light.

The tall grass and weeds brush against my legs makin' me itch. A small section of trail sets back along the road. Whenever a car comes past, Dean shuts off the light. We stop dead in our tracks and wait silently. Buck comes up on the tail end of the group to make sure we're all here.

I named the kid in the bushes, Thumbelina. She looks like she's about three years old, but when I asked, she held up five fingers. One of my hands holds onto Charley's waist, and I grip the little girl with the other, pullin' her close so I can keep a good eye on both of them. Together we keep pace with the line. She's quite the talker. Good thing the water's loud, so Dean or Buck can't hear her chatter. It's obvious who's talkin', 'cuz she has a lisp and a stutter.

"Where did you come from?" I whisper.

"I-I'm a-always a-around. I've seen y-you before. I'm just really g-good at hidin'. GI Joes says I'm stupid' cuz of m-m-my funny talking. I stutter a-a-a little bit. B-b-but that's o-o-okay. I'll show him s-s-someday. I'm gonna figure o-o-out how to get a-a-away from here."

"Do you know any of the other kids? I don't think I've seen you before."

"Yep. I know G-gilbert, B-barbie, G.I Joe, but I a-a-already told you a-a-about him thinking I'm s-stupid. I a-a-also know Ice Man, L-lilly, and P-peanut, n-now you and Ch-charley." She swishes her head. "I've seen y-you before. Yep! I've seen y-you b-both."

She rattles on non-stop. She seems either excited or nervous. She must like dresses, like me. Her dress looks like a doll could wear it.

"I stay o-out of the way. Th-they for-g-get I'm around, s-some-t-times. I've saved myself a-alot of problems b-by learning to hide. B-but maybe w-we could p-play sometime? If I come o-out of hiding. I know Anna-banana b-brings you here a-a-alot."

I repeat Thumbelina's words, "Anna-banana. Anna-banana." Charley and me laugh. I like hearin' Thumbelina make fun of Anna.

When we finally arrive back at Poison Ivy's farmhouse, Charley and me collapse on the couch. He falls right to sleep, but I only pretend to sleep. I pray they'll leave us alone.

Anna comes in through the back door to pick us up. Dean tells her that I saw the bodies. He reassures her I won't say anythin'.

"She knows better," he says, standin' over me. "Hey, brat, get your ass up and get the hell out of here. Your *wicked stepmother* is here to get you."

He bellows one of his devilish laughs. I jump up, probably too fast, givin' away that I wasn't sleepin'. Charley stirs, all foggy-eyed. He blinks at Anna. Once it hits him that Anna's here, he darts to the door, rocket-fast.

Anna glares daggers at Dean and only shakes her head. He's mean to everyone, even her. It seems he's always tryin' to stir up a hornet's nest.

As I try to move by, he reaches out and grabs me by my hair and jerks me close to his face and grumbles, "Remember what I said about your precious, Charley?"

He yanks harder on my hair. I wince but obediently nod yes. He releases his grip, with a shove that knocks me onto my knees. Dean leans forward and laughs. He enjoys hurtin' me.

As I get up to walk away, he kicks me in my bottom, knockin' me *hard* onto the floor. My face burns as it skids across the carpet. *It takes my breath. I panic.* I gasp, and with my face still on the floor, I look to my right to see Thumbelina hidin' under the side table. Seein' her calms me. She smiles and puts her finger to her lips. She doesn't want them to know she's here. I hide my face from Dean and smile at her.

I've learned not to show any fear. I stand up and walk away. I don't look back.

In the back seat of the car, I send a message to Mommy in heaven. *Please help Charley and me, and fast, 'cuz I don't think I can take much more.*

Marion
April 1996

"Hello, Hunter. Please, come in and make yourself comfortable. May I get you a beverage to drink? Coffee, tea, water?"

"No, thank you. I don't think I could drink much more. I just finished an iced tea in the car."

Hunter looks well put-together in his tan tweed blazer, white shirt, and brown slacks. I study his eyes, wondering if he is still losing as much sleep as the last time we met. He brushes a few flakes of sleet off his coat before hanging it on the rack. "This will probably be the last of this weather. I smell Spring in the air."

"Yes, I am hoping for some warmer weather myself. 'April showers bring May flowers.' I am hoping to start my gardening soon."

"I agree." Hunter takes a seat and opens his briefcase, taking out a blue ink pen and a legal-size writing tablet.

"Thank you for coming in, Hunter. I thought it would be advantageous for us to talk. Although Catherine is making excellent progress in the recall of her past trauma, I am sure it must be challenging to maneuver through the many struggles her memories generate."

"You have no idea." He wrings his hands, followed by a continual twisting of his wedding band. "I don't get it. How does this stuff happen to children without people knowing?"

"I have asked myself the same question. Your wife lived in a very small town, and she said most of the rituals took place in out of the way rural areas. As far as the children involved, some were frightened foster children, and the abducted children; they may have been taken from other towns or states. Catherine was so young, and she has limited recall but enough to remember being blackmailed. Fear is a powerful weapon. It was out of fear: fear for her brother, fear for her family, and fear for her very life that she suppressed these memories and never told anyone, up until now. With God's mercy and grace, she will find the truth and answers she seeks."

He leans back and rests an ankle on his opposite knee. "I suppose you're right, Marion, but I feel at a loss." He wrings his hands. "I mean, at times, I have no idea how to handle the nightmares, the middle of the night screams, and the many things that trigger her. For example: if Catherine feels that she's not protected. She probably already told you about my family and how they avoid confrontation. Oh, and the *drama*, as Catherine would call it, with my younger sister." He shrugs.

"Yes, she has expressed her feelings about the way your family relates. We have addressed conflict resolution. Family origins, traditions, and habits can have a positive influence as well as negative ones." I offer a soft smile of compassion.

"However, you and Catherine are a family now. It is up to you as a couple to establish what and how you want to communicate. The key is cultivating a desire and willingness to be open and honest with one another, especially about your needs to successfully maneuver within your marriage."

Hunter wipes his brow. He sucks in a deep breath as if he is getting ready to plunge into the deep end of a swimming pool, then slowly exhales.

"Marion, I have to admit for most of my adult life I have done well and have felt pretty good about myself. I graduated from college with an engineering degree and made it through the Vietnam War. I moved back to Colorado and have always secured employment that propelled me forward. I have a flourishing business now. One I love, which is a bonus. I'm involved in our church and serve on several ministry boards. I look at myself as successful, except for when it comes to Catherine." He slowly shakes his head.

"You said…except for with Catherine? Tell me, how are you feeling about the marriage and the challenges you are facing?"

He looks up at the ceiling. "Like I'm drowning. I love Catherine with all my heart, and I have strong feelings about what she has gone through. Sometimes, I get so angry at what has happened to her—and her brother. Well, her whole family. They've been through a lot—too much. They've overcome more than most families. I'm guessing that's why they're so close. As for me, I don't like the feelings that come up within me when dealing with what Catherine remembers. Her childhood, I mean the timeframe with Anna. It was such a battle. A battle no one should have to fight, especially an innocent little kid."

"And what feelings are those?" I study his face.

Hunter rubs his chin, concentrating on my question. I hand him a list of emotions to help him identify what he is feeling. He studies the sheet.

"Well, the word that jumps off the page is *inadequate*. I'm in new territory. Marriage, in general, is challenging. And when you add Catherine's issues, it complicates the normal stress. I'm not saying it's all Catherine. As you know, she's a fighter. One thing about her is she is tenacious. She doesn't back down from much. I love that about her, but I also hate it because it makes me feel…umm…."

"Hunter, Catherine became a fighter out of necessity. God has used her unfortunate past for good. She is a strong communicator but does not do well with unresolved conflict or hidden issues."

"Yes. Believe me, I know. She calls it 'the elephant in the room'. Something her grandmother taught her. Trust me, we have discussed this more than once. However, I come from a family who sweeps their issues under the rug. And wouldn't you know it, God made my wife a rug shaker." He laughs.

"Catherine looks at her need to resolve conflict as a gift. I suspect that particular need was and is stimulated from the years of suppression. Although that coping mechanism was essential for a time, she is still living with the pain of her past. It is a stressful commitment to exhume the hidden wrongs and abomination of her lost years. She knows she must seek the truth to find freedom."

Hunter pinches the bridge of his nose. "I'm trying to understand her constant need to hammer out disagreements or disputes. Catherine's comfortable with confrontation. Resolving issues puts her at ease. However, if you come from the ostrich family, as she calls it, well, her need to resolve everything is a pain in the...well, you know." He cracks a big smile.

"I am sure any husband would feel inadequate, frightened, and even overwhelmed by yours and Catherine's situation."

"I'm disappointed in myself. I want to be Catherine's knight in shining armor." He sighs. "It's hard to admit that I'm not. I guess that's why I busy myself with things that I know I'm good at doing. It makes me feel purposeful."

He scans the list of emotions again, then looks up. "I like to feel important—valued. Maybe I want to be the hero, so to speak. But when it comes to dealing with the sexual exploitation and satanic ritual abuse..." He chokes on his words. "...she was only a little girl." He throws his hands up into the air. "I feel helpless, inadequate, and worthless—especially when Catherine is having one of her nightmares. She panics and starts screaming at the top of her lungs."

He shakes his head and rubs his palms down the top of his thighs. "It jolts me awake. Talk about a bolt of fear. I catapult out of bed, grab her, call out her name, and try to wake her.

"Sometimes I have to shake her." He lifts his hands and mimics his words. "She says she gets stuck in the dream and can't rouse herself. When she finally comes out of it, her breathing is heavy, often gasping for air. Her face has the expression of pure terror. I do what I can, but honestly, I'm uncertain how to deal with this, other than pray."

He leans forward and rests his chin into the palm of his hand with an elbow on his knee. "I depend upon you and Catherine to work through these issues. I want to help, but I'm not sure how. What do you suggest?" he asks with great concern.

"Hunter, the best thing you can offer is love, support, and honesty. When you are afraid, it would be best to tell Catherine. When you feel inadequate, tell her. When you feel—whatever you feel, share it with her. It is about overcoming your challenges *together*. For better for worse, in sickness and in health, until death do you part."

I steeple my hands against my mouth and watch him nod in agreement.

"It is a partnership, Hunter. Marriage is about a union. Catherine needs to know you are together. When you are away and focused on your own interests, the things you say that make you *feel* good about yourself; your very absence leaves Catherine feeling alone and lonely. The particular words your wife used to describe her feelings were abandoned and unimportant." I take out the release form from her file and show it to Hunter. "She has given me permission to share with you any information I believe would benefit you, her, and your marriage."

"Yes, I know, she told me before I came here. Catherine happens to be excellent at verbally expressing her emotions. Still, my whole life, I've stuffed my feelings and pretended everything was okay. I'm just now admitting this to myself. I'm not even sure if I know what I'm feeling when I'm feeling it."

I point to the list of emotions. "Take this with you. Your homework is to ask yourself what you are feeling a couple of times a day. Use this list to identify and describe your emotions. Then ask yourself, when was the first time you have ever felt this way and why? Share your findings with Catherine."

"I'll give it a shot." He tucks the paper inside his writing tablet.

"Life is not easy, Hunter, but most of the hard hurdles are worth it on the other side. The two shall become one…" I pause. "You both have brought your past wounds and victories into your marriage. Whether we want to admit it or not, our past has shaped us. Together you will work through your backgrounds in hopes of a victorious future."

"Yes, a successful marriage is something I want. I have to admit, being single all those years, I've brought some bad habits into our lives." He bites the corner of his lip. "I was lonely and only imagined what marriage would look like together. It was more of a fantasy and not very realistic. What I know about relationships, I learned from what I saw, mostly on the streets, if you know what I mean. I watched my good friends marry and then get divorced. There were always two sides to every story, both seemingly justified. I figured whatever was wrong with them was also wrong with me. I wasn't any different, so I waited to marry later in life. It takes much more than what I'd ever imagined to be married." He slides to the edge of the love seat.

Hunter gathers his notes and pen, sliding them into his briefcase. "Thank you, Marion, for your honesty and wise words."

I escort Hunter to the door and stand at the entry stoop as he walks away. It is a bright and sunny Spring day.

Catherine
May 1996

It's a bright and sunny Saturday morning. May's weather is often iffy in Colorado. Hunter and I have made arrangements to take a group of young adults, mostly guys, from our church on a mountain adventure. I'm excited to spend the morning outside and watch my husband teach the art of rock climbing. He's as graceful as a ballerina when he moves from one handhold and foothold on to the next.

Hunter says it's all about the balance and engineering, as each move takes you higher on the cliff face. Finding the exact route is like a huge math problem, and that is one of the things he loves about the sport.

It will be nice to have some time together, even if it's with others.

We load the car with all the ropes, harnesses, carabiners, and numerous pieces of protections for the climb. Hunter and I scurry around the garage, making sure we have all the necessary supplies.

"So sweetheart, with all these newbies, what's the plan on how you want to run today's activities?" I ask.

"I'll run a top-robe off an easy route…a 5.4 if we can find one."

"Will they be able to climb at that level?"

"Sure, that will be easy. It doesn't get much easier. You can help by assisting the guys into the harnesses and tying a figure eight on the rope to lock them in safely."

Hunter puts the last duffel bag into the back of the SUV. I smile as I watch his biceps flex.

"Hey, Catherine, after I've placed the top rope, I'll probably ask you to be the first to climb, and I'll have you on belay. It will build these guys' confidence to see you hustle up the rock face." He smiles with pride.

"Sure, that will be fun."

"And depending on the time…um…what time do we have to be back to meet up with your friend Karin tonight?"

"Oh, that's right, Karin is coming. I'm grateful she offered to show us how to do spiritual housecleaning…"

Hunter pipes in, "I bet you are. I would hate to be woken up in the middle of the night, seeing demonic spirits. I'm glad that's one of your gifts and not mine." He gives a last look-over at the equipment before closing the hatch.

"I would say it has its advantages, but being startled in the dead of night isn't one of them." I bite my lower lip. "Karin said she would be here around 6:30."

"Okay, that gives us plenty of time, but I may lead two top ropes and have you belay the second line just to make sure we're back home in plenty of time—"

The phone rings. Hunter picks up the garage phone receiver.

"Hello…" As he listens, his face pales. His eyebrows raise high, and his Adam's apple bobs as he swallows hard. After a few uh-huh's, and several okay's, he hangs up the phone and turns immediately to me, eyes wide.

"Catherine, it was Harriet. Something is wrong with her! She said she's lying on the floor in pain and is unable to drive herself to the emergency room. She asked me to take her. I can hear in her voice that she's in a bad way." He looks at the truck and back to me. "One of us will have to go…ahh…and it looks like it can't be me. You've never climbed lead or set up a top row. Sorry, honey, but you're going to have to go and help Harriet."

"Me? I doubt if she'll want me to come. Did you tell her what we were doing? Can she call a friend?" I wasn't even sure why I'd asked the questions. I had overheard the conversation, so I knew he hadn't asked her anything.

"I'm sure me showing up isn't going to go over well. It will probably make Harriet feel worse." I say, followed by a frustrated sigh.

Hunter shrugs. "It's not like I have a choice; all of these people are depending on me. Most of them have probably already left their homes and are en route to our meeting point."

My husband stares at me with a pleading look. "Will you go?"

I lower my head and mumble. "Yah."

Hunter drives away, and I hustle to get into my car and head over to Harriet's house. When I arrive, the front door is unlocked, so I go inside and find Harriet lying on the floor in pain, just as Hunter had described.

"Oh my goodness, something must be really wrong. Where does it hurt?" My concerns heighten.

Harriet looks up and scowls as if she is in agony. "I can't say for sure because it hurts from my hips to my ribs. I need to get to the emergency room."

I kneel next to her and quickly take her pulse. Her heart is racing at 96 beats per minute…probably due to the pain.

Within minutes I have Harriet in the front passenger seat, reclined, and we are on our way to the hospital. I take the shortest and fastest route. She moans and thrashes side to side. I reach out and pat her hand to encourage her.

"Harriet, you're going to be okay. We are only about ten or so minutes away from the hospital, and there is an excellent team of doctors who will be able to care for you." I squeeze her fingers for assurance.

I try to focus and keep my eyes on the road but glance over to check on how she's doing. Her face is still scrunched up, but now tears are running down her cheeks.

"I'm sorry, Harriet, you must be in terrible pain. I'm driving as quickly as I can."

Harriet's response surprises me. "I'm not crying because I'm in pain, although it hurts more than I'd like. I'm crying because of you. That you came to help me instead of Hunter."

Her words sting. I keep my eyes on the road and explain. "Harriet, Hunter would've come if he could've. We had a group of people from our church that we'd committed to taking rock climbing this morning. Most of the guys were probably already en route to the meeting point. It was too late to cancel, so I stayed behind to take you to the emergency room. Hunter wasn't able to come, or he would have."

"I know, Catherine, I know." She wipes the tears from her eyes. "After the way I've treated you all these years, I can't believe you were willing to help me." She sniffles. "I'm sorry for the way I've acted. It was just that my sister, Lee, was divorced and now single, and Hunter and I had never married. I used to say no one in the Stone family ever marries."

I hand Harriet a tissue out of the glove box.

"When I found out Hunter was engaged...somehow, it made me being single more difficult. I suppose I was jealous."

I'm taken aback by her confession. I try to process and understand her feelings. Although I don't know her story or why she isn't married, I do understand loneliness.

"Harriet, all my sisters live out of state. I don't have any family here other than Hunter. When Hunter and I married, I was so excited to have a sister-in-law in nearby. I wanted a close relationship, you know, to be family."

Harriet mumbles through her pain. "I just wasn't ready for Hunter to get married. I didn't handle the adjustment well."

"And I don't handle unresolved issues very well myself." I shrug. "I know I can be blunt, to the point, and aggressive when it comes to unsettled disputes. I find it healthier to get it out into the air and deal with the problem."

I pause and decide to tell it like it is and how I feel. "Hunter tells me your family avoids confrontation and sees it as a negative. I'm sorry if I've offended you. One of the things you have probably noticed about me is that I engage if I feel attacked, especially with intent. I have a close family, and that is what I want with Hunter and your family."

"The truth is I felt like you were taking my brother away." Harriet sniffles, then wipes her nose.

"I'm not sure how to respond to your words. However, I think a better way to look at the situations is, it's an opportunity to have another sister."

As timing would have it, right then, I pull up to the double glass doors of the emergency room. I put the car in park and scurry out to get a wheelchair.

We wait all day before Harriet receives treatment. The doctors were unable to diagnose a problem. The tests they ran were inconclusive. They said her abdominal pain could have been a number of things: kidney stones, intestinal spasms, extreme gas, as well as female issues. They gave her a prescription for the pain.

Harriet is wiped out from the discomfort, and our drive to her house is quiet. She dozes off most of the way.

I click the garage door opener and pull in. Hunter's not home. My plans for the day were less physical, but I'm exhausted from sitting in the hospital all day.

I watch the clock, wondering if Hunter's okay. I thought he'd be back long before me. Finally, the door creaks as it opens; my watch reads 5:45 p.m. when Hunter hustles into the house.

"Wow…what took so long? Are you okay? Did anyone get hurt?" I fire questions at Hunter.

"Everything's great. We had a great time. It just took longer than I thought without you being there to help." He looks at his watch. "I'd better get into the shower before your friend gets here. I'll tell you all about it later." Hunter starts up the stairs.

"Uh! Your sister is fine. We were at the hospital *all day*."

"Cool. I'm glad she's good. What did the doctors say?" he shouts from the bedroom.

"They didn't say. The doctor explained her abdominal pain could be a variety of things. It sounded like a bunch of guesses but no diagnosis," I shout back.

I scan the floor and notice the dirt and leaves that Hunter tracked into the house. *Why doesn't he wipe his feet before coming into the house?*

After making sure our home is neat and tidy, I go upstairs into the bathroom to tell him about our day and the conversation I had with Harriet while he showers and gets freshened.

The doorbell chimes. I scurry to answer the door. A quick peek out the window, and I see Karin, a college friend. I was expecting her to arrive around 6:30. I glance at my watch; she's early.

I swing open the door; my arms stretched out for a good-to-see-you hug.

"Hey, Karin, Come in."

"Hope I'm not too early?" Her soft brown eyes sparkle with eagerness.

"Your timing is perfect." I chuckle. "Come on into the kitchen. I'll get you something to drink." Karin's long tight brown curls bounce with every step.

As we turn the corner, we see Hunter standing in the kitchen, pouring a glass of iced tea.

"Hi, Karin. Iced tea okay?" He lifts the glass.

"Sounds delicious. Thanks, Hunter." She smiles and reaches for the beverage.

Hunter pours two more glasses for us.

We scoot out the stools and take seats at the island. For a brief time, the three of us engage in the usual small talk, catching up on the latest in our lives.

Karin knows my history. I've told her all about my nightmare and the progress I've made with recovering memories. I update her on being awakened by the manifestation of demonic spirits in the middle of the night. "It's unnerving and disturbing, seeing such an evil presence. And especially being jolted awake out of a dead sleep. It reminds me of my childhood with Anna. I know it's a gift, but at times it feels the opposite."

"Catherine, the discerning of spirits is truly a gift." She points to a list of verses she has brought along. Her finger rests on 1 Corinthians 12:10. "I believe the Lord has blessed you with this gift to prepare, protect, and provide answers."

Hunter takes a sip of tea and nods in agreement.

Karin looks distracted, fidgeting with a button on her sweater. She removes her wrap but still looks uncomfortable. *Maybe the wool is itchy. Or perhaps she's too warm. What if it's something else? Oh, stop.* There I go with my wandering mind, always questioning everything.

Karin has spiritual gifts that give her a more profound sensitivity to her surroundings. One gift is supernatural knowledge—God telling her things she has no way of knowing.

Karin reaches in her bag and removes more papers. "Are you guys ready to get started?"

"I'm more than ready," I say, cutting my eyes at Hunter.

Hunter holds up his glass. "Ready here."

Karin straightens her papers. "First, I thought we would read over some scripture that supports the dedication of your home to the Lord, followed by what I refer to as spiritual house cleansing."

Karin reads through the extensive list, and we follow along. She emphasizes several verses to prepare us for the process. There are two columns listing the verses.

Genesis 28:18	Leviticus 8:12-30
Exodus 28:41, 29:7	James 4:7-8
Genesis 13:14-17	Luke 10:19
Mark 16:15-19	1 Corinthians 12:8-10
Matthew 18:19-22	2 Corinthians 2:14; 10:3-6
1 Kings 1:16	

Karin continues with her teaching. "Throughout the Bible, it was common to dedicate and anoint both people and various things, such as homes, land, and territory unto the Lord. The applying of oil and the dedication of belongings is a simple way to set a person or specific things aside to be used for God and his service."

Hunter and I are excited to dedicate our home. Based on several verses, Karin instructs us to apply olive oil on the sashes of the front and back doors.

She sets her Bible on the countertop and gulps down her last few swallows of tea.

"Catherine and Hunter, when performing a spiritual house cleansing we must make sure your home is absent of anything that would give the demonic a legal right to be here."

"You mean like sin? Right? I've also heard that unforgiveness can be a big open door." I raise my brows, and Karin nods to affirm.

"I've racked my brain trying to figure out if there is anyone I haven't forgiven."

I think of Harriet and how many times I have forgiven her. After today's conversation, it's easier to extend forgiveness. I send up a quick prayer. *Lord, bless and bring healing to Harriet.*

I turn to Hunter, and he says, "I've done the same. Both Catherine and I are puzzled as to how these demons are getting access into our home."

I add, "We can't seem to put our finger on what it could be. It's tormenting, and I can't afford to lose any more sleep. I mean, *we* can't afford to lose any more sleep." I look at Hunter and offer him an apologetic smile.

Karin motions us into the first room in our house. "That's why we are doing this, to figure out what open doors or portals are giving the demonic spirits legal permission to be here. Sometimes we are unaware of what gives the authorization. I assure you, with the Lord's leading, we will find the answers."

We walk and pray through the entire house, taking turns, praying and asking the Lord to show us why demons are waking me.

It goes smoothly—until we reach the office.

Karin appears edgy. She bites her lower lip and scrunches up her face. "I sense something is off. There's a cold presence in this room. Something in here is dark. Deceiving. Leading to death."

She pulls her sweater back on and tugs it closed.

I nod, agreeing with Karin. "Normally this room is warm, even hot with the setting sun, but you're right, it feels cold in here—icy cold. I turn to Hunter. "Do you feel that? Or am I just getting the heebie-jeebies?"

Hunter cocks his head and shrugs his shoulders as if not feeling anything odd. He says nothing, only shuffles his feet. I chalk off his edginess to this being a new spiritual experience.

Karin closes her eyes and prays quietly, asking the Lord to lead her. She also has the ability to identify the presence of spirits—angelic and demonic. The spiritual gift is real. I've experienced it for myself.

"Hey, Karin, do you think it could have anything to do with the séances Anna made my siblings and me do as kids? She did try to conjure up my mom. You know, talking to the dead? Could that be an open door?"

She shakes her head. "I'm not sensing that. Didn't you renounce and repent of that with Marion?"

"Yes, but I thought just maybe…guess I'm grasping at straws. I'm just looking for an answer."

"No…no." Karin pauses, moving over to the desk and computer.

"It's here." She rests her hands on the back of the office chair.

I'm eager to understand what she's saying. "What do you mean *it's* here?"

Hunter clears his throat. "I think I know what she means. I believe…uh…I am the…uh…open door."

CHAPTER THIRTY-TWO

Catherine
May 1996

K arin looks at Hunter and then at me. "Hunter, it sounds as if you are aware of an open door associated with the computer." She stammers, which is unlike Karin. "Uh, uh, I'll leave you and Catherine to discuss the matter. I can be available later. Feel free to give me a call. I have another appointment anyway, so I'll need to get going."

Another appointment? Why is Karin making excuses to leave?

Hunter looks away, avoiding all eye contact.

"Oh...uh...well, thank you for coming by to help Catherine and me," he mumbles. "We don't want to take up any more of your time. Well...especially with you having another meeting. Let me walk you to the door."

After the door shuts, Hunter walks into the living room with his shoulders slumped, and his head dropped. His eyes dart from me to the couch. He walks in that direction. I follow, and we take a seat. A familiar nervousness brews and stirs in my stomach—a fear-knot.

"Well, I'm sure you're wondering what I was talking about when I said I might be the open door."

"Yes." It's the only word I can muster. I cross my arms and legs and wait for Hunter's explanation. I have no idea what he wants to discuss, but I brace myself. *Why do I always expect the worst?*

Hunter scoots a little closer to me and reaches out to take my hand. Instinctively I tuck my hands under my arms, feeling a sudden chill. He rests his clasped hands in his lap.

"Do you remember before we got married, I had told you that being a bachelor. . ." There's a nervous twitch in his eye. He looks away. "Uh, well, I struggled with looking at men's magazines."

"Huh? What kind of men's magazines? You have a subscription to several. Rock climbers, mountain biking, hiking…"

"Uhh…I don't mean those types of magazines. I mean—x-rated magazines, with, uhh, women." He stares at the floor, wringing his hands.

"What! Women? That's what you're looking at when I come into the office, and you slam off the computer? Do you mean p-porn?" I choke on my words. "Why?"

"I've only looked one or two times. It was a bad habit from my bachelor days. I've been feeling a lot of stress lately and…" He looks away, biting his lip. "I guess I fell back into…that…uh…I knew it was wrong when I looked. It was stupid. I'm sorry. Why would I do such a thing when I have you at home and can see and be with you anytime I desire?"

He stole the words from my mouth.

"I promise I won't do it again. I realize it isn't what God wants in our marriage. Or in any relationship as far as that goes. Please forgive me, Catherine."

Emotions of betrayal swell. A full-on attack comes at me within my mind—*you are just plain not good enough. My husband would rather look at some airbrushed model, a woman who doesn't even look like a real woman. He's no different than Edward. Self-focused, selfish. It's all about him. He only cares about what he is feeling. Stress huh?*

I think out loud. "Stress? Is your excuse…STRESS? I can't believe this! You betray me with some fantasy photos and justify it with *stress*. What? Did it ever cross your mind that I might have stress in my life too?"

"Yes, I'm sorry. I know you are stressed out, as well."

"How about *unnecessary* stress? Like you, opening the door to perverse spirits by looking up those porn sites on your computer. Don't you think it stresses me to be awakened in the middle of the night with some ugly demonic spirit staring me in the face? I have enough issues with not sleeping well, and you bring this on me?" Tears well up from my anger.

"Catherine, up until tonight, I didn't know evil spirits were attached to pornography. I promise it was only a few times. I didn't think it was a big deal."

He lifts his hands, his palms forward. "Hey, it's not just me looking at this stuff. So many men do this. And I'm nothing compared to most men."

"How dare you minimize this! You are *not* other men. You are *my husband!* I didn't expect such trashy behavior from you. If it was no big deal, then why did you hide it? Why'd you click off the computer?" I stand, jutting my finger in his face. "I'll tell you why, because you knew it was wrong. I'm supposed to be the *only woman* in your life."

His face hardens. "Catherine, please don't make a mountain out of a molehill. I just looked at a couple of photos. It's not like I had an affair." Defensiveness reeks from his words.

"It isn't? I know what men do when they look at those pictures. Don't play me a fool, Hunter. Only a couple of times? Hah. I don't believe you for a minute. Don't you dare add insult to injury by lying to me. If you are going to 'fess up, then at least be honest. Completely honest! Don't minimize your choices. I know better." My teeth and hands clench.

The thoughts of Hunter lusting at photos batters my heart. I slump on the couch, feeling beaten emotionally. Betrayed. Rejected. Not valued. And now I've been disregarded.

Hunter sits very still. "I think we should talk about this later. You're escalating the issue. I told you I was sorry. I promised I wouldn't do it again. We are both upset, and I don't want to say anything more. Especially something I may regret. Let's table the discussion for later." Hunter gets up and quickly walks out of the room.

And to think earlier, I was rattled about the dirt he brought into the house on his shoes. But that's nothing compared to the filth he has brought in on this computer—into our home and into our marriage.

CHAPTER THIRTY-THREE

Catherine
October 1996

Months upon months have passed, and the chill of autumn has set into the season. A similar coldness has settled into our marriage, the disgusting effects of Hunter's indiscretions—*filthy porn*.

I find myself praying for God to protect Hunter from the evils attached to porn and all its lust and temptation. "Lord, please put a hedge of protection around my husband and our marriage. Shield us from the wedge of distrust and betrayal that split marriages apart. I ask for your mercy and direction. I don't know what to do. I need your help. In Jesus' name, Amen."

My nerves are on edge. I feel like I'm always walking on eggshells. I'm uncomfortable in my own home. My stomach drops when I walk by the computer. All too often, Hunter seems to be just finishing up whenever I approach his desk. Click. He shuts off his computer.

I live with suspicion, skeptical of my husband's honesty, or better said, lack of honesty. And I'm tired, tired of the heartache that has moved into our marriage. My eyes look dark and sad, regardless of how much makeup I apply.

We make excuses for the void between us. However, with our busy schedules, time flies. We're ships passing in the night, so-to-speak. The disappointment rips at my heart. I miss Hunter.

No excuses. We simply aren't taking the time to be together, even if it's just cuddling during a movie or having a conversation over breakfast. Those moments have disappeared. I hate the distance. Hunter puts his head in the sand and pretends he doesn't understand when I bring it up. He merely plays dumb, if you ask me. Anything to avoid confrontation. All I can do is pray, and that is becoming difficult because I'm losing heart.

"What do you mean, you never see me? I see you almost every night before bed. Most of the guys I know have it worse— they have kids. They have to schedule a date with their wives," Hunter says defensively.

"That may be true, but I'm not talking about your guy friends. I'm talking about you—us. What I'm trying to say is that I miss you. It seems to me when we are home; you're always in the office on your computer."

"Yeah, maybe, but it's when you're making dinner," he grunts.

I glare. I hate the computer, along with the sick feeling that rises each time I pass the office. He's busy tapping away at the keys and always working on *something*. Something other than me.

"What now, Catherine? Do you want me to stand in the kitchen with you now? I can't be everything to you. Why are you so insecure?" His eyes narrow, and his brow furrows.

"I'm not insecure. Can't I want to spend time with you? Why don't you want to spend time with me? Why is *everything else* always a priority? If you're not at a men's Bible study, it's a meeting with the Christian businessmen's group leaders. Oh, and don't let me forget the science group, the car group, or you're hiking, rock climbing, or camping with one of your buddies."

Frustration eats at me. I square my shoulders and plant my hands on my hips. "I'm tired of getting leftovers. When you're home, you're too tired and half-present. I feel like the shoemaker's wife. Everyone has the best of shoes, and I'm left barefoot." I stare, waiting for his response.

Hunter rolls his eyes and takes in a long breath, letting it out slowly. "Tell me what you want. I'll do it. It seems like I always fail you. Name it—I'll do it," he says with gritted teeth.

"Not like that, you won't." I point my finger at him. "You're angry. Why? About what? How can you possibly be angry about me wanting to spend more time with you? Really? And now you're trying to put a guilt trip on me? The fact that you don't want to spend time with me is hurtful. Sure, you can force yourself to do anything, but your heart isn't in it. Don't you understand that I can see that?"

I lean in, demanding an answer. He doesn't speak.

"Hunter, all I'm asking for is some intimacy with you. And I'm not talking about sex. I want the tenderness we use to have before our life spun out. Like before…when, you actually noticed if I walked into a room and you'd send me a smile, even if you were busy. When you would make a date to be with me. When I felt like…you loved me." My voice softens. "Don't you? Don't you love me anymore?"

"I'm here, aren't I?" His eyes looked tired, rimmed in red. "I feel so torn; everyone always wants something."

"Maybe you should consider giving something up? Something, other than me."

"Like what?" he snarls.

"How about one of the men's groups or the—"

Hunter cuts me off. "Has it ever occurred to you that I might enjoy those groups?" He puffs. "I love you, Catherine. I do, but I can't meet all your needs. You need to ask God to fill whatever it is you're yearning for because I don't know what more I can do. No matter what I do, it's never enough."

He starts to walk out of the room, then stops short and turns. "I'm going to change out of my suit. Is that all right with you?" he barks. The sarcasm drips from his question.

I say nothing, only shake my head in disappointment and frustration. The harshness, in his words, break my heart. My emotions hammer, nailing lies into my mind. Rejected. Not valued. Tossed aside. It is evident that I'm not Hunter's priority. My heart aches. I pull out a pan to make dinner. Not that I have an appetite.

Dinner is tense, with simple one-word answers. *Why do I even bother to have a conversation?*

Hunter finally talks, but his words are full of excuses and blame-shifting. "You need to understand that I need time to ponder conflict, unlike *you* who act like a Schnauzer, nipping at my heels, demanding we talk and resolve our challenges immediately. It's just too much, Catherine."

I retort, "Well, the way I was raised, when there's conflict, you focus on communication, meaning you give or get more information to resolve the problem. You're not supposed to go to bed, angry. Isn't that what the Bible says?" My comments point out the obvious. We're madder than hornets in a disturbed nest.

"I don't like it when you choose to act like the ostrich family, always sticking your head in the sand. You're always stuffing your feelings and your thoughts. I think you use this, 'I need to ponder...'" I exaggerate each word, "is an excuse, because you never come back to talk."

He pushes his chair out and throws his napkin on the table. "I need to leave for my meeting." He walks out of the house in a huff.

My heart is heavy from our fight. I trudge up the stairs toward the bedroom, thinking a hot bath may be the solution to relieve my tension. As I pass the office, I remember I have yet to review my notes from my last workshop. Sitting down at the desk, I click on the mouse to look for my Word doc. My eye catches on the history tab.

Do I dare?

Remembering the steps Marion had told me about, I make several clicks, and each click reveals more than I'm prepared to see.

My heart drops, along with my mouth. My world implodes. I sit, frozen, and stare. Unable to control my shaking. It all comes crashing in like shards of glass.

Again!

The pictures blur through my tears. Too many to count. Too many pages. Of women. Erotic women. Dressed in nearly nothing. Poses that make me shudder. I run to the bathroom—my stomach heaves.

Marion
October 1996

A hard knock echoes off the office door. Catherine bursts through the doorway. "Marion, I appreciate you seeing me so late tonight. I didn't know who else to turn to." Her hands are shaking, her eyes red and puffy.

Even more worrying is the fact that Catherine's face is void of makeup. She is wearing sweatpants and an old sweatshirt beneath her jacket. I have never before seen Catherine in public without wearing makeup or dressed in proper attire. I realize I am staring, actually more like gawking, so I force my eyes to look at the file on my desk.

"I was just finishing rescheduling my last client when you phoned." I sign and date my last entry and set it to the side. Composing myself, I look up at Catherine. "What has happened? You do not look like yourself. Is everything okay?"

Catherine stands, her hair is disheveled, and she is as white as a ghost.

"I don't know what to do. Hunter and I got in a fight tonight, and he seemed so defensive and disdainful. Disdain towards myself that is." She takes a seat and begins to squeeze the throw pillow between her hands. She does not waste time before voicing her reason for being here.

"Bottom line, I checked the history on the computer. I was trying to figure out what Hunter was doing in the office for so long. He seems more interested in spending time there than spending time with me."

Her eyes brim with tears that spill over and stream down her blotchy face.

"Porn, Marion. Disgusting porn." She buries her face into her hands, allowing herself to grieve.

My eyes close. "Oh, Catherine, I am so sorry."

Catie
Summer 1964

Daddy buries his face in the newspaper and reads it every mornin', but this time he reads it out loud for all of us to hear. "Wow, Anna, have you heard about this? A few days ago, there was a family found drowned at the dam near your folk's house."

I jerk and look at Charley, who's playin' with his green army men. Charley looks back; his mouth drops open...

Daddy taps the newspaper. "Yes, it says right here, 'Family of five found drowned.' It appears they ran into rough water and lost their raft."

Anna speaks up, "Oh, how sad, five of them you say. They must have gotten too close to the rapids when the dam was open. Those currents are strong and will take you under quickly." She looks over at Charley and me. "You kids go outside and play. It's a nice day, and the sunshine will do you some good. Melinda and Shawnee, you go along and have some fun."

We all shuffle out the front door. I know what I saw at the dam, what we saw, but neither Charley or me say a word.

It feels like only a few minutes later, I scuttle across the yard in my play high heels and bust through the front door, runnin' straight for the bathroom. I don't know why I can't hold my pee like my sisters and the other neighborhood girls. I'm not suppose to wait till the last minute to go to the bathroom, but it always feels like the last minute, no matter when I go into the house.

I never peed the bed when Mommy was alive. But, now I do and almost every night. Somethin's wrong with me, but Anna and Dr. Noir say I'm fine. He told Daddy, my bladder was too small, but I'd grow out of it once I'm older.

Right in front of the doctor and Anna, I explained that my bladder wasn't too small when Mommy was livin'. I din't pee the bed then. I asked the doctor how come my bladder shrunk? Anna told me to shut up. She said I was bein' disrespectful questionin' the doctor's diagnosis, whatever that means.

Now Anna and Daddy have to wake me up to go to the bathroom before they go to bed, and I'm not allowed to drink after six o'clock. I'm thirsty every night at bedtime. Sometimes, I cheat and swallow some water after I brush my teeth.

Things have changed in our lives; my sisters used to be light sleepers, but now they appear dead to the world when Anna sneaks us out of the house. They seem extra sleepy the followin' mornin' too, or groggy as Carolyn puts it. I guess no one sleeps well anymore with Anna and all of her shenanigans.

I can't wait to get back outside. We've been playin' games and fishin' in the porch steps. I button the waist of my shorts as I walk out the front door. Charlotte's still readin' a book under the tree. Claudia and Carolyn are jumpin' rope. Melinda and Shawnee are playin' hopscotch on the front sidewalk. Charley's lowerin' somethin' into the fishin' hole that is in the middle stair of our front porch steps.

It's the first time we're alone since daddy read about the family. Charley whispers, "You hear those lies in the newspaper?"

"Yah, I heard." I check to make sure Melinda and Shawnee aren't listenin'. "You know they're all a bunch of big liars. But now I'm scared that the devil people have workers at the newspaper office too."

"Probably best to keep the secrets and just forget, right?" Charley looks at me through his bangs.

He hovers over the rotten gap, then drops one more thing into the open hole. "There's no real fish in these steps," he says. "But sometimes it's better to pretend. Right, Catie? So that's why I put my candy wrappers in the hole. Then some sticks. And two army men. Yipee…now we have something to catch!"

I nod and give him a big fake smile, hopin' to put the drownin's out of our minds.

Charley dangles the makeshift pole into the fishin' hole. He bobs the attached safety pin up and down. Sure enough, he catches one of the army men. We squeal in excitement.

"Now it's my turn. It's my turn!" I'm a little wobbly, 'cuz I'm wearin' my new play high heeled shoes from my eighth birthday this month. They're black with matchin' wide elastic bands on the toes and heels—really fancy shoes, but hard to walk in.

"Catie, why don't you take off those stilt shoes of yours? We're not playing circus, we're fishing."

"My high heels aren't circus tall. But I wish they were. You think Grandpa would make us some stilts?" I flip off my fancy shoes, makin' myself sure-footed. I'll be able to catch somethin' now for sure. I jab, swish, aim the pin for a catch, and then pull up on the pole. I've pinned me a dark red cinnamon candy wrapper. I sing out and dance around. "I caught one! I caught one! Look at me, Charley."

He doesn't even notice. My shoulders slump. Then, Daddy sticks his head out the door. "Lunch is ready."

I like it when Daddy makes lunch 'cuz he gives us choices: a half a sandwich, soup, and somethin' sweet like canned peaches. Anna only makes a can of watery soup with dry saltine crackers. Yuck.

Today we eat pears instead of peaches. I like both. As I'm carryin' my plate, bowl, and silverware into the kitchen, I ask Daddy, "Can we dance after lunch?"

"Sure, you kids can dance all you want."

"No, I mean, can I slow dance with you, Daddy?" I tilt my head, bat my eyelashes, and flirt with him. Lilly taught me how. It usually steals his heart and gets me what I want. "You know, slow dance to one of the records."

"What song would you like to dance to, Catie?"

Carolyn jumps up from the table. "Me too, Dad!"

Charlotte and Claudia chime in. "We want to dance too."

Charlotte pulls out a record and places it on the record player. It doesn't start, but makes a scratchy noise, 'cuz she didn't get the needle in the right place. Daddy walks over to help.

"Charlotte, look here, you have to put the handle right past the slight outer hump. See, right where the grooves begin," Daddy says.

She lowers the needle perfectly this time.

Music fills the air with one of Daddy's favorite singers, Johnny Mathis. I run over and step up onto Daddy's feet. He bends down. I take his palm and reach my other hand high, around his waist. Someday I'll be tall enough to reach his back, and eventually his shoulder. Charlotte and Claudia don't have to step on his feet. They're tall enough to dance with Daddy like real women. But I don't care. I like to glide around swayin' to the music. Daddy twirls me in circles, which is my favorite part. It's more like a ride. Charley loves it too.

Melinda and Shawnee wander into the room just when it's Charley's turn to dance.

Shawnee's eyes light up.

Melinda growls. "Boys aren't supposed to dance with boys. Charley's just a big ole sissy."

Daddy stops and turns toward her and speaks firmly. "Melinda! You never-mind, young lady. Practicing is how boys learn, so when they're men, they know exactly how to dance with their wife."

His voice softens as he turns back to Charley. "And Charley here, my little *McFudd*, is going to be quite the smooth dancer. His moves will be as smooth as Johnny Mathis' voice."

We all coo at Daddy's comment.

After we've all taken a turn dancin', Anna comes out of her room. She changes the mood from carefree fun to walkin' on eggshells. I hurry off into a small corner of the livin' room to play, in hopes of not bein' screamed at, slapped, or punished for the sake of Anna's entertainment.

I hate her. In fact, I hate everythin' about her, her kids, and her family. I know bein' a Christian now, I'm not supposed to hate, so I asked Jesus and the Holy Spirit to take my hate away, but it hasn't happened, so I think in my case, it might be okay.

I also ask the Lord to pull the roof off our house and take us out of here, away from Anna and her brats. So far, nothin's happened. Charley thinks I'm askin' for too much. I reason I'm not, 'cuz the last movie I saw with Mommy was the Ten Commandments. God saved all the people and even parted the Red Sea! So rippin' our roof off seems easy. He could do it in a jiffy.

Grandpa and Teenage Granny say God's time isn't our time. He must have a different clock. I hope he hurries up.

I question God, "Why can't I have a life like other kids?"

It's been way over two school years of livin' with Anna, and I don't know how much longer I can take her and her crazy devil family. No one ever talks about the stuff Anna, Dean, and Buck do to us in secret.

My memories of Mommy are startin' to disappear. I can't remember her face without lookin' at pictures. Her voice, her smell, are all fadin' away. It's hard to imagine what it was like to have a nice mommy anymore. I don't like to think about it, so I sit on the floor and play with our tinker toys, but we've lost some of the pieces, makin' it hard to make most things. I dump the container of Lincoln Logs onto the floor. I like playin' with both.

Daddy and Anna are sittin' in the dinin' room. Anna just finished her lunch. Daddy's readin' his newspaper, again. She's jabberin' on about somethin'. I can tell she's cross by her tone. Daddy excuses himself from the table and walks into the livin' room, where us kids are playin'. He sits on one of the comfortable chairs.

Anna doesn't like that Daddy got up and left. Her face is all snarled up and red. She must see him leavin' the table as an insult. Of course, she thinks everythin' is *always* 'bout her. I keep my head low, but still, keep an eye on her. Through my bangs, I watch her slip off her stiletto high-heels. She keeps a hold on one, tight in her hand. I tense up.

I shoot a look toward my sisters, playin' a game across the room on the coffee table. Their heads are down concentratin', I guess. I can't get their attention. Darn.

Anna stands up and moves fast, right toward Daddy. He doesn't see her comin'. I try to warn him. All I can stammer out is, "Daddy!"

Everythin' seems to happen in slow motion.

Anna draws her hand back like she's playin' baseball, then swings her shoe with the golf-tee heel pointin' straight towards Daddy's face.

SLAM!

I see it with my very own eyes. The heel goes straight through his cheek, and right inside his mouth!

Blood gushes!

I scream. I close my eyes and cover my face!

Carolyn told me later that I fainted. I don't remember what happened but I wish I could faint all the time, so I don't have to see all the ugly things Anna does.

I bet Anna has some Apache Indian blood in her. The sneaky kind. Like the western movies, I've watched with Grandpa and Daddy. Anna can sneak up, and you never even know she's there.

Her stare alone can wake you up out of a deep sleep. She wakes Charley and me that way. I'm afraid for Daddy. I wouldn't put it past her to sneak up on him in his sleep, with somethin' sharper than a high heel.

With Mommy gone, I don't know who to tell. Who can I ask 'bout these grown-up fights? And 'bout the devil stuff? Who's safe? It seems like Devil Dean, Buck, and Poison Ivy know everybody. They say they even know my school's principal. I believe 'em 'cuz, they know the two policemen who drive by our house, Mr. Judge, Dr. Noir, and his nurses, plus all those other adults who keep their names a secret. And now the newspaper people. They know everybody!

Mean Dean promises if I tell anyone—anythin' at all, he'll kill

Charley first, then the rest of my family. Even the person I tell. My tummy hurts just thinkin 'bout his threats.

I can talk with my sisters, but not 'bout the secret stuff. It would scare the dickens out of them. Charlotte and Carolyn say we should all gang up on Anna and beat the snot out of her. Claudia insists we should continue to pray. I'm not sure 'bout either plan. I don't know what to do.

I pray out loud. "Lord, what's takin' you so long? Get us out of here. Hurry! In Jesus' name, I pray. Amen."

CHAPTER THIRTY-FOUR

Marion
November 1996

Catherine and Hunter hurry into the office, arriving a few minutes late. Though both are dressed nicely, the current strain is plain on their faces. Hunter appears distracted and tense while Catherine's dark-circled eyes dart everywhere, and her fingers fidget constantly.

"Please, have a seat." The space between them seems as wide as the Grand Canyon, although only inches apart on the love seat. Catherine sets her gloves and scarf between them.

"Thank you for coming," I say, trying to start with some affirmation. "First, I'd like to say I am glad that Catherine's relationship with your sister is moving in a positive direction.

Catherine tells me you have seen her on a few occasions, and your sister is making an effort to be polite and kind."

Catherine and Hunter both nod but say nothing. Time to move along to the next subject.

"I am going to be frank. We are here to discuss an important yet uncomfortable topic. I recognize the heightened emotions between you, which I had expected. I am going to ask you to agree to some foundational rules. I have mentioned this subject before. This communication format is called Active Listening, Reflective Listening, or my favorite, Drive-through-talking."

"Yes, we have used it at home," Catherine says. She holds her body erect, her gaze straightforward.

Hunter nods. "Yes, I remember. We take turns talking, and neither of us can interrupt." His shoulders slump.

"Let us begin. First, I would like for you to explain what you are experiencing by using 'I' statements." I hand them an emotional word list.

"Using words from this list is intended to help you express what you are personally experiencing. Keep in mind emotions are neutral. Neutral means they are simply describing how you feel. It does not place blame, fault, or guilt on the other person. However, what you do with your emotions, such as a knee-jerk reaction or a well thought out response, is another thing altogether. Please refrain from using 'you' statements, as it may be seen as accusatory, therefore putting a person on the defense."

I make deliberate eye contact with both of them. After confirming I have their attention, I continue with a directional statement.

"The desire is to move toward resolving the issue." I pause. "Any questions?"

"Yes," Catherine says. "Who goes first?" Her jaw clenched, along with her hands.

I move my gaze to her husband.

"Hunter, would you be willing to take the lead? I would like to hear what has happened from your perspective. Please begin by using 'I' statements." I extend a soft, encouraging smile.

"Umm...well...I've been feeling..." He looks down at the

handout listing various emotions. "Pressured, stressed, inadequate, and at a loss on how to handle what we have been going through the last four years. Um...meaning, there has been a lot of adjustments. I've made a big mistake in bringing a bad habit into our marriage. I know it's wrong. And I feel bad afterward. It's stupid. I know." He shifts his feet.

"I'm not blaming Catherine. It isn't her fault. But what she's facing with her past stresses me out. I'm uncertain about how to help her. I haven't been feeling good about myself. I guess I just wanted to feel better. I thought marriage would be easier. And I'm lousy at dealing with failure. It appears that the things she's good at, I'm not."

I moisten my lips as I think. "Hunter, to which *things* are you referring?

"She's good with conflict and great with words. She has a way of saying things so clearly." He links his fingers together, followed by an awkward chuckle. "I stumble over my tongue. But Catherine is bold and not afraid to face hard things." He turns his gaze to her, offering a half-smile. "She's a fighter. I wasn't taught how to resolve conflict. I've always believed anger was bad. Like something was wrong with *me*." He taps his chest to make his point. His gaze shifts to the floor.

"I don't know how to share my emotions, especially anger. I try to stuff my frustrations and irritations, so when I am mad, I keep it to myself. It's not that I don't *feel*. I just don't know how to express what I'm feeling. Sometimes it just comes out, and more forceful than I intend. Often I see myself as a failure in this area." Hunter falls quiet, rubbing his eyes as if trying to erase the circumstances from his sight.

"Very good, Hunter. Thank you for being honest and willing to share. I appreciate how difficult it is for you to leave your comfort zone."

I shift in my chair, then address Catherine. "I would like for you to share what you heard your husband say, followed by 'I' statements of what has happened from your perspective."

Catherine replies, "I heard Hunter say he is feeling uncomfortable with emotions. Emotions he doesn't know how to discuss. He hasn't been feeling good about himself, so he has chosen to bring his old habit into our marriage. *A bad habit.* Porn! I hear excuses."

Hunter's back stiffens. He sits a little taller and begins to wring his hands.

"Catherine, I would like for you to move on to what emotions you are experiencing based on the choices Hunter has confessed."

Her lips tighten. She grabs the list of emotions from the cushion between them.

"Betrayed. Devastated. Loss of trust." Tears pool in her eyes. She blinks them away.

"Thank you, Catherine. Hunter, what would you like to say to your wife?"

He turns toward Catherine. She looks ahead, not acknowledging him.

"Sweetheart, what I heard you say, is that I've hurt you. I am so sorry. It was never my intent. I don't blame you for being upset, but I need you to trust me and know that I love you."

Her head swings around, and her words flash like flames. "What? You need me to trust you? How about you being trustworthy! You think saying, 'I'm sorry gets you off the hook, a free pass?"

"Whoa—whoa," I interject. "Let us focus on 'I' statements. What I am hearing is, Catherine is deeply hurt. Hunter, I believe you are sorry and want your wife to trust you again. However, this is going to take time to heal and restore. While you are composing yourselves, I would like to discuss a few things about marriage." I raise my voice slightly to maintain their attention.

"First of all, God designed intimacy in marriage. He wants the marriage bed to be pure, intimate—bonding married couples. The Lord bases marriage and intercourse upon love and giving, bringing the couple closer: body, soul, and spirit. A soul tie occurs when the marriage is consummated. The two become one. It is the glue—giving the relationship strength to weather life's challenges—*together*." I pause.

"The world has defiled God's design for marriage and intimacy and replaced it with superficial sex-based lust of taking and using. The world laughs at the thought of a couple being virgins until they are married. Nevertheless, there is a crucial reason as to why the Bible teaches this."

Hunter pulls out his writing tablet and pen. "This is something

I've never heard. I didn't have any sex education growing up. The only information I ever heard was from my mom." He laughs, shaking his head.

"I was walking home from elementary school and saw a square package on the sidewalk. I picked it up. It felt squishy and had a picture of a peacock on the outside. When I arrived home, I handed it to my mom and asked her what it was. Her face turned bright red. She struggled to reply but finally forced out the words. 'Son, it is peacock food.'" Hunter chuckles. "My mom tucked it into her apron pocket. End of discussion. End of my sexual education." He shrugs.

"As a man, I realized it was a condom." He bobs his head, like a schoolchild. "My parents are great people but shy. Hey, it was in the 1950s. People didn't talk about such things back then. I learned about sex off the streets from my buddies. And, like you said Marion, it was all lust-based." He offers a straight-lipped smile.

I continue speaking. "It is sad to say, but most people learn the same way. We are influenced by the world's ways all too much. However, if we think about it, God's design is to remain pure and wait for the biggest day in our lives." I lean forward toward Catherine and Hunter, carefully choosing my words.

"Imagine that you are together with your family, closest friends, and your cherished love—your fiancé," I say. "The wedding day finally arrives. You stand proud and make promising vows. The celebration of your life follows the covenantal ceremony. And then, the crescendo of the event is here." I watch their faces, then say in a soft voice, "It is your wedding night."

Neither Catherine nor Hunter move. "The consummation of the marriage bed leads you, the couple, to focus and imprint on giving your love to one another. Your hearts are intertwined. True intimacy—together."

This last part, I offer to them slowly, one point at a time. "The act of sexual intimacy—and the giving of pleasure to one another—is to be experienced exclusively with one another. Sacred to the marriage covenant and the marriage bed."

"Wow." Catherine's voice is a whisper. "God's way sounds so much better."

"Why isn't this being taught?" Hunter's face is lined with resentment and disappointment.

"It should be." Catherine's voice rises, firm.

"It is taught by some pastors. I have heard a teacher compare the imprinting process of a crane with that of a male having his first sexual experience. When these birds are born, they imprint on whatever creature they interact with after their birth, assuming it is their mother.

"When a young man is seeking sex the *world's* way, being lured by lust, he will try to manipulate any girl to accommodate him. His first experience, for example, may be in the back of a car, with steamy windows, making promises he does not intend to keep, convincing her it is okay to go further and further. He will say things like, 'No one is a virgin anymore.' 'Everyone is doing it.' 'After all, we are in love.'"

Hunter nods. "That's pretty much the ticket."

Catherine looks at Hunter, then to me. She shrugs and nods in agreement.

I continue to paint an unattractive but common scenario. "Finally, the boy persuades the girl to consent. He enters her, experiencing his first sexual encounter with a girl and an adrenaline rush, unlike anything he's known before. He imprints on lust, seduction, manipulation, taking, and using."

I pause to allow my description to sink into their minds before going on to explain and expose the traps of lust.

"This is the same man who will continue to chase after superficial sex, asking for outrageous acts to relive the adrenaline rush. He is the one who wants to '*do it*'." I make air quotes, emphasizing the slang and superficial use of the term. "He desires to have sex in an elevator or in an airplane, fulfilling his goal of becoming a proud member of the mile-high club. He is driven by the bondage of lust to seek out edgy fantasies of seduction, asking his partner to be a naughty nurse, cheerleader, or the exotic stranger he picks up in a bar."

Hunter chokes back a prideful chuckle. Catherine releases a sigh of disgust. Hunter picks the lint off his dress slacks to avoid Catherine's disdain and the heat of her judgment.

325

I interject to keep the subject on track and lead the couple to the reality of where such acts of sex lead.

"This man is not necessarily interested in the woman; he is interested in sex. The fantasy he may be acting out is to obtain the rush the craving provides. Pornography is a part of the fantasy and feeds the lust trap for men."

Catherine tosses her journal on the coffee table. "What is it with men? I feel like I'm reliving the same betrayal I suffered from Edward, my ex-husband. He didn't feel needed, so he justified his affairs. And now, Hunter. He isn't feeling good about himself, so he justifies porn and fantasy affairs." She crosses her arms across her chest.

Hunter pulls away. "I'm not like Edward. I'm not having an affair. I'd never cheat on you. How can you even compare the two of us? Talk about exaggeration." He furrows his brow.

"Okay, so I looked at a few pictures, a couple of times. I can stop. Please don't make this bigger than what it is. I told you I wouldn't do it anymore," he barks, his arms crossed.

The counseling session has shifted from what I intended, resolve, into more of a fight, and walking on eggshells.

Catie
Summer 1964

I'll be glad when I go back to school 'cuz it gives me a break from all the fightin' at my house. Seems like fussin' is a part of my everyday life. I always walk on eggshells around Anna. I never know what will set her off. She loves nothin' better than tantrums and throwin' anythin' she can get her hands on. I've learned to be quick and duck out of her way.

Today Anna threw the one thing that bothers me the most: Mommy's silver tea set. It sits on the buffet in the dinin' room, and every time I walk past, it reminds me of Mommy. It's beautiful, just like she was.

Anna hates it, 'cuz she *hates* Mommy. Every chance she gets, she throws the tea set up against the walls. But lately, she's been throwin' it through the front picture window.

Claudia says even the best silver can only take so much beatin' and bangin'. Most of the pieces now have dents and scratches, but still, the tea set is precious to us.

Charlotte says Anna throws it 'cuz she's violent. Carolyn agrees and says Anna's a complete nut case. All that's true, but I say she throws it through the glass picture window for a reason. She likes seein' the glass man. Whenever he comes over, Anna acts nice.

Today the glass man showed up right away. Every time he's here, we're *locked* outside to play. He stays after the glass is back in the window. Sometimes for hours, but he always leaves before Daddy gets home.

Dinner is soup and sandwiches since Anna had no time to cook a real dinner with the glass man bein' here all day. While we sit at the kitchen table, Charlotte peels the crust off her bread and sets it on her plate. Then out of nowhere, she blurts a question right in front of Daddy.

"Anna, what were you and the glass man doin' so long after the window was fixed?"

Anna dips her spoon in her soup, lifts it to her lips, and smiles. "Just being neighborly, Charlotte. That's what's called being polite. You offer up a cup of tea, coffee, and maybe some home-cooked muffins."

She picks up a saltine and dips it in her soup. "Being polite helps in getting good service and discounts. Next time," she pauses, slurping a spoonful of soup, "I'll let you girls come in and learn how to serve up some snacks."

Anna's quick with her tongue and can make up stories on the spot. More like believable lies, but I never believe her, 'cuz I know she's a good liar. Just like her family.

---

nother Sunday rolls around, and me and Charley have to go to Poison Ivy, Buck, and Mean Dean's house. They're all so hateful.

I don't care for goin' in the barn, but that's where they keep our bug jars. I tiptoe inside with the workbench in sight.

Mean Dean comes out from nowhere. WHAM—a sharp pain stabs the middle of my back. His giant-sized cowboy boot sends me flyin' across the ground, belly down. The dirt digs into my face. My elbows sting as the skin rips away, as I try to break the fall and stop myself from slidin'.

The evil in his deep, throaty chuckle echoes around me. He leans against the wooden stall in the barn and stares. He smiles as he watches me.

I grit my teeth to hide my pain. Seconds later, my eyes betray me with tears poolin'. The pain in the middle of my back throbs from his boot.

The wicked dark thing that lives inside of Devil Dean glares right at me. He and his followers all have those same black June-bug eyes. I might be lookin' at Satan himself.

I lay on the ground and suddenly remember what the preacher said, 'bout me havin' the Holy Spirit inside me, givin' me strength and power over the devil and his evil followers.

I push myself up and spin around. With a strong voice, not typical of me, I speak out—loud! I'm almost yellin'.

"You will pay for the evil you do. Someday, you will stand before God." I stack my hands on my hips, like a Miss Bossy. I like this new feelin'. I feel brave knowin' the Holy Spirit lives inside me.

Dean laughs. He seems entertained by my sudden spunk and spark. "Says who?" he asks. "Who am I going to stand—"

Without even givin' him a chance to continue, I interrupt him—on purpose.

"Jesus. That's who. He's my Savior. And he's gonna save me from you." I stab my finger directly at his face. "That's who! You are in big trouble, Dean. You will pay. You'll see, you will definitely pay!"

I speak proudly with my hands still restin' on my filthy knee-knocker pants. I no longer feel like a squirrel frozen in place, hopin' to go unnoticed.

Dean's anger rises. I can tell 'cuz his face burns red. He grabs me by the arm and jerks me close. His eyes narrow as he cocks his head. But I surprise him when I pull away. He pounces toward me in a false charge. He's like one of the bulls in the field. But I don't move. I stand firm and hold my ground. All the while, in my mind, I'm callin' out, *Jesus, Jesus, Jesus!*

"Aww, you think you're all grown up now? Even standing up to me, huh? I'll show you who's boss." Dean grabs me, digs his fingernails into both of my arms, and then throws me up over his shoulder.

My fists pound and beat at the old man's back. I fight as hard as I can to get out of his hold. Oh, how I wish I were bigger, stronger, like a grown-up, so I could beat the snot out of Dean. He carries me to the back of the barn.

With his jaw clenched, he mutters, "I'll show you who will pay. You'll see."

Dean thinks he's won, just 'cuz he overpowers me and has his way with me. I cry out from the deep pain. *It takes my breath. I panic.*

Lilly hears me and comes runnin'. Lilly speaks slowly, with the same sexy voice Anna uses when her men friends come to visit. Lilly sets her gaze on Dean like he's a chocolate cake.

"Hello, Dean." Lilly has a way of distractin' men. She captures Dean's attention givin' me some relief.

I move off to the side, leavin' her with Dean. I don't like the way Lilly acts with men. She makes me nervous. So much so, I can't breathe right. I don't like the feelin' when I panic, and it takes my breath.

I wander off in my mind, just like Peanut taught me. It's then I see Thumbelina hidin' behind the post. The tail of her pink dress skirt peeks out on the side, givin' away that she's there. I carefully belly crawl over to Thumbelina. She takes me to one of her hidin' places. She pulls back an old dirty board coverin' a hole that leads into a hidden closet in the stall. We curl up into the small space. I feel safe. The cracks in the barn wood allow me to look at Dean. I watch him in disgust. I don't understand how Lilly does what she does, but I thank Jesus for sendin' her to be my friend.

I also have a few more things I want to talk to God about. I squeeze up next to the wall and close my eyes real tight before I finish my prayer.

My grandparents and our preacher say your timin' is different from our timin', but that you always keep your promises. If that's so, Lord, can you send me one of your kind of watches or a clock? We need a new one anyway. The clock we have in the kitchen has a big crack in it, and you know who wrecked it. I'm only askin' 'cuz I want to be ready when you come and get me out of this mess. Umm...and thank you in advance, 'cuz I know I can count on you. In Jesus' name, Amen. P.S. Do you think you could speed it up?

CHAPTER THIRTY-FIVE

Marion
December 1996

I speed read my notes for a quick review. Catherine and Hunter attended a session on November 22nd, two weeks ago. She was quite disgusted with her husband. However, I encouraged the couple to work toward forgiveness and rebuilding trust.

We discussed God's design for marriage, which is founded on a covenant of committed love, loyalty, giving, and intimacy; whereas in contrast, the world promotes marriage defined by contracts of performance-based acceptance, as in prenuptial agreements.

I distinctly recall Hunter making direct eye contact with Catherine and stating that a prenup was something he would never ask for, being he did not believe in divorce. Both of them recognized these contractual agreements are superficial and based on distrust.

I assigned them to schedule a regular weekly meeting to honestly discuss their emotions and the fears they are facing in their marriage.

Pulling out a piece of lined paper, I print Catherine's name, then write December 6, 1996, at the top, ready to begin today's discussion. The room is quite warm and stuffy as the sun spears through the slats in the window shutters.

After I open in prayer, Catherine fans herself with her journal. I note her body language: pinched lips, eyebrows lowered and drawn together, and one leg bouncing nervously.

"Marion, you told Hunter and me to encourage, support, and uplift one another. I believe sometimes it's also about saying the hard stuff, which can mean pointing out the mistakes in each other's life, like Hunter with the computer. He makes excuses about needing to check his emails or researching some topic—blah, blah, blah." Catherine flutters her fingers through the air and rolls her eyes.

"I don't believe him for a minute. Talk about lures. The computer is full of enticements. Just one little click, and Hunter can find himself in a heap of trouble. All it takes is one of those pop-ups on the screen to grab his attention. And I mean grab his attention in the wrong way. Those ads are nothing more than deceitful temptations, snares, and trappings."

She shakes her head. "Of course, Hunter denies that he's constantly on the crazy screen. He minimizes, rationalizes, and justifies his hours of use. He has even gone as far as blaming me." She rolls her eyes. "Can you believe that?" Anger and resentment resonate in her tone. "He says, I stress him out, and being on the web relaxes him. Bull! It's nothing more than a wasted time grabber and a fake fix in fantasy land."

Catherine massages her temples. She rolls her neck side to side. She is not done.

"I've tried everything. I've gone to Hunter in love, gentleness, and respect. It isn't like I'm unwilling to admit my faults. I see conviction as a motivator to confess your issues and make changes. Unlike me,

332

Hunter sees those same conversations as condemnation. He resents my need to resolve issues and talk things out. He says it bothers him, but I can't live pretending everything's all right. And I can't seem to get that message through to him."

Catherine rakes her fingers through her hair. Small lines crease her eyes. I listen, allowing her to vent her frustrations and concerns, yet observing her focus is somewhat skewed. She is pointing the finger at Hunter and how he should change versus owning up to her issues and responsibilities. I wait, listen, and pray for the Lord to bring Catherine truth and balance.

She inhales. "I'm exhausted hearing how it's my fault because of how I present the issues. Hunter says, 'tell me *when* I do something so I can recognize it.' When I do, he yells at me to stop nagging, or he changes his excuse to 'you need to wait and approach me when I'm not angry or processing.' His blame-shifting then moves onto him saying that the problem is my tone. My attitude. My insecurities. And he says I don't appreciate all that he's given me. Somehow now he says it's because I'm ungrateful. Huh? Really?"

She cocks her head as if in disbelief. "It's not like he is the only one working. And when I get home, I'm still working. Cleaning. Cooking. Laundry. Ironing. I don't recall much praise for what I contribute. I suppose housework is expected. Last week, he even said, 'You need to appreciate the time I give you.'" She rolls her eyes. "What *time?*"

"Is his schedule still quite full?" I inquire, wondering if there has been any change.

"Yes. It's always full." Her lips pinch tight.

I want to reach over and gently shake her and say, Catherine, Catherine, Catherine, oh how I wish you would concentrate more on yourself and how to overcome your struggles and not dwell on Hunter and trying to fix him. I cannot say how many times I have reminded you to focus on his positive attributes and how he has supported you with your challenges. These are blessings in your relationship.

Instead, I interject, "I realize these circumstances are difficult for you, Hunter, and your marriage, however—"

Catherine continues, unaware I have spoken.

"I've been going to a recovery class at my church. I've been learning about the cycles of relapse. My take on this is when Hunter starts to feel inadequate; he fills his schedule with projects. Things he's good at, *of course*. However, my husband doesn't know when to quit. He has minimal margin in his life for *me*. He gets tired, overwhelmed, and frustrated, which leads to his short one-word answers, and there you go, we start arguing.

"It seems like he pulls away, distances, and isolates himself. That leaves me feeling rejected and abandoned. His avoidance makes me feel dismissed and unvalued." She looks down briefly and then continues to share her perceptions and her protest.

Lord, help Catherine and Hunter to remember that a soft heart brings a compassionate response versus defensive reactions. I pull out a photograph from her file. It is one of her wedding pictures with the two of them laughing in an embrace. I gently set it on the coffee table in her view. I say nothing but allow the photo to speak for itself.

Catherine cradles the image and studies each of their faces before turning it over to read the note she had penned.

"I remember giving you this. I also remember when this was taken." Her voice and shoulders soften. "Today, it feels like it was ages ago. You know, Marion, when I compare this picture to Hunter's last expression…umm…let's just say, it wasn't pretty.

I keep praying silently for the Lord to soften Catherine's heart and attitude.

She picks at the corners of the photo and is quiet for a couple of minutes before speaking. "I guess Hunter must feel inadequate, like a failure. The reason I say that is because anything I say he takes as a dig, a put-down, or some judgment. It makes me wonder if he feels rejected himself—the way I do. Funny how two people who love each other can feel so lonely living in the same house." She bites her lower lip and blinks back tears.

"Umm…well that's when I suspect he turns to the porn and entertains fantasies in his mind. He'd never admit it, but I think it has to do with trying to live up to some unrealistic image of being the man he wants to be, or better said, some superhero."

She sighs and places the photo back onto the coffee table.

"I'm growing in my understanding of cycles, and even under these circumstances, which I hate, I truly have compassion for his feelings of inadequacy. I know it's not all him. You, Marion, out of all people, know how I've struggled. I've shared with Hunter how I have to fight against feeling inadequate and unloved. The whole battle for the mind issue."

She presses her palms to her temples, demonstrating her frustration.

"Regardless of what I've learned, know, or experienced, he just plain doesn't want to listen. It's difficult for Hunter to receive and especially from me."

I intently listen and look for a precise moment to interject. *Lord, remind Catherine that trusting you with Hunter is the best path to follow. You will guide him to truth just as you have her. She does not have to fix him or be his savior. You alone are the Savior. Please calm her fears and give her peace about trusting you with Hunter.*

She dabs the corners of her eyes. "Hunter has some mindset or belief that being the man of the family somehow means that he has to have all the answers. I get the impression that if I know something—I mean anything that he doesn't know—it makes him feel weak. I can't seem to win. And I'm suspicious."

When she finally pauses, I take a deep breath.

"Catherine, understanding cycles is good. However, it is more important for Hunter to recognize his patterns with pornography. The first step of healing is coming out of denial, being honest with yourself. Has your husband mentioned that he is struggling with temptations? Are you suspicious of him falling back into looking at porn based on proof, or is it projection based on suspicion? Has he given you solid reasons to believe that there needs to be concern? Could a portion of this apprehension be filtered through *your* struggles with distrust?"

Catherine stiffens and sits erect. "I can't say for sure. When I check the computer, it's usually wiped clean, or only a few business sites logged on his history. I know he must be erasing stuff. He's on the computer way too often to have only a few sites listed. Or none. That in itself, makes me skeptical."

"Doubts in and of themselves can cause triggers. With that premise in mind, shall we focus on how you are doing with trusting? Trusting God with Hunter?"

"Some days are better than others. I battle with my thoughts and emotions. Doubt. Fear. Betrayal. Dishonesty. Secrets. All subjects that come knocking for regular visits. Oh yeah, not to forget resentment. I'm struggling with having to deal with this whole mess."

I raise my brows. "How are you processing those thoughts?"

She crinkles her nose at me and offers a playful smile before she continues. "I take the thoughts captive and remind myself of God's truth as written in the Bible. That's an ongoing work in progress. I'm not having a problem with that—my problem is I have the gnawing feeling Hunter is hiding the truth from me."

"Why do you think he is being dishonest?"

"I've been through this enough to recognize the signs. Although it was better for some time, his cycle of anger has returned. He looks for reasons to pick fights with me. It's as if he wants to be mad at me. And, again, I'm being awakened in the middle of the night with the presence of evil spirits in our room. I see them and often. It's disturbing having such things in the house again."

"Have you talked to your husband about this subject?"

"I've brought it up, but Hunter says what I'm discerning is from all the people we invite into our home." Catherine sighs. "I don't know about that, but I believe the Holy Spirit is showing me that he's looking at porn again."

Catherine sets her jaw and clenches her teeth. "And if he is, you better bet, I'll find out."

Catherine
December 1996

I set my jaw and clench my teeth, barely able to look at Hunter as he walks into the kitchen, holding his new calendar for next year.

"Hey Honey, we have a Christian Business board meeting coming up next quarter. I know it's not for a while, but I'm doing some preplanning. I was wondering if we could serve pizza or something like that for the group. It would be nice to serve a meal for the guys." Hunter places a quick kiss on my cheek.

I cringe and pull away, whirling with emotions, seething at what I have found. I stir the chili and check the cornbread in the oven. I bite my tongue to keep from spewing the hot, burning words battling within my mind. *Lord, help me.*

"What's wrong? Why'd you pull away?"

"I'm tired. I'm tired of all the extra meetings and boards you sit on. I'm tired of not being a part of your life. I'm tired of being second and not being valued. Everything always comes before me." I put my hand on my hip. "Everything!"

"Oh no, here we go again." Hunter leans up against the cupboard with his arms crossed.

"And…I'm sick and tired of the lies!" I spout.

I war against the thoughts of his betrayal. My anger rises, and numbness tries to invade. I push it away—but then disgust and mistrust bubble up. I glare at him.

"What are you talking about, what lies? Are you calling me a liar?" His face burns red.

"I mean when you make *everything* more of a priority than me and then offer empty promises…" I lean in to make a point. "Promises you don't keep. Saying cheap words of 'I love you,' yet your actions speak the opposite. Not to forget you hiding your *dark secrets*. If that's what you are referring to—then, yes! You are a liar!"

I squint my eyes at him, holding my position, with the hidden hope that Hunter will confess the truth with sincere sorrow. If only he would be honest and own up to his mistakes. Integrity with accountability is something I can respect. But his lying—no way! I hold my breath and wait.

"Catherine, now you wait a minute." He points his finger in my face. "You'd better stop right there. You are crossing a line calling me names and making unjust accusations." His shoulders square, and jaw sets.

"No! Hunter, *you* wait a minute." I point my finger back at him, accompanied by a few jabs for emphasis. "I'm not making false allegations. Don't you turn this around on me. I'm speaking fact."

The temperature in the kitchen seems as hot as inside the oven. Beads of sweat form on my upper lip. I swipe it off with the corner of a paper towel.

Hunter stomps out of the kitchen. "I'm going upstairs to change my clothes and give you some time to cool down. We can talk later," he hollers over his shoulder.

Adrenaline fills my veins. The trembling shakes me to my core. I refuse to buy into my husband's avoidance. I stomp behind him.

Hunter drops his briefcase in the office. I'm right on his heels. He turns on the computer and ignores my presence.

I nudge, no yank, the mouse out of his hand, and click on the history tab. Two clicks. Photos pop up. Photos he promised never to look at again.

Hunter's face pales.

"Um...those...um...those must be from before." He swivels in his chair and turns his back on the blaring and disgusting photos.

"Are you kidding me? You are going to lie straight to my face?" My eyes widen in amazement. "Just tell the truth, Hunter. I can't deal with all the lies. If you're honest, I—"

"I'm not lying!" he shouts.

I grab the mouse in a stranglehold. I can't believe Hunter is holding onto his lies. What is this? I feel like I'm living out a country/western song. The husband asks his wife who caught him cheating. 'Are you gonna believe me or yer lying eyes?' My anger percolates, ready to spew at having to prove my accusations.

Where is his conscience?

One-click. I point to the date.

Silence. He slumps. Caught. Red-handed.

"Sad. This is so sad, Hunter. We've come to this? I rarely see you, and when I do, you are wiped out and tired. You're never interested in us. The old saying is right, 'if you snack before meals, you lose your appetite.' Why do you insist on lusting at these fake airbrushed photos, having fantasy sex, when you can have a real intimate relationship with me? How am I supposed to feel when you prefer garbage to making love to me?"

Hunter sits quietly with his head down, resting it on his folded arms.

I wait.

Silence. His choice is void of an apology.

"Are you going to say anything?" My stomach flips. Familiar pangs beat within my cramping and twisting gut. His lies. His denial. The vivid proof of his betrayal illuminates the computer screen. *What is there to say?* My words die in my throat.

The allegations of the enemy toy with my mind, 'It will never be any different. Men are all the same. Not to be trusted.'

Hunter remains still. He continues to hide his face from me. Silence. The absence of words ratchet up the tension. His quietness and lack of responsibility or ownership stab and rip piercingly deep into my broken heart.

I hold back the floodgate of tears as a large lump grows in my throat. Emotions of disappointment drown me in sadness. I leave the room and stagger downstairs only to collapse on the couch, sinking deep into the cushions.

The words I desired to hear from my husband are never spoken— never verbalized—never proclaimed. I'm left alone only to question.

What's Hunter feeling, thinking, and believing? Is he choking on pride? Too proud to admit the truth—his lies? Is he sorry or just plain resentful?

My silent pleas have gone unspoken. I'm lost for words, unable to speak. I feel beaten by emotions: shame slaps me while humiliation haunts me.

Where are you, Lord?

Words bubble up within me. I hear a soft loving voice. 'You are children of the King of Kings. You are both my children, and I desire that you are loved, protected, and cherished. Stand firm on my truth and who I say you are, my daughter and my son.'

The Lord's words soothe and encourage me. I know I must stand for what is right, regardless of Hunter's choices. I must fight for myself, for him, and for our marriage. I won't enable him any longer or support his destructive cycle, with the many activities that merely stroke his ego. Something has to change. No, something *must* change!

The pastor's words from my recovery class flash through my mind. 'Doing the same thing over and over again and expecting a different result is the definition of insanity.' A quote from Einstein. The words confirm why I'm feeling like I'm going crazy. I must take a stand. Even if I must do it alone, I need to be the change in our lives.

I grip my pen and write a letter to the Christian Businessman Board.

Metro-Board Members,
I am writing this letter to formally resign from my position. I, in good conscience, can no longer sit on the board or support my husband's role in the Christian Business group for a variety of reasons, which I will explain...
When I finally finish, I close with...
In Honesty and Sincerity,
Catherine

The pen rolls from my hand across the coffee table as Hunter walks into the living room.

"What are you doing?" he mumbles with his head held low.

"I've decided I must take a stand for what I believe is right. I just finished writing a letter."

"To whom?" he asks, his head cocked.

"To the board members. I'm resigning from my board position

and have every intention to expose your imbalance in priorities and your indiscretions." *Your selfishness and nasty porn habit.*

"You what?" His eyes are wide. He takes a second look as if in disbelief.

"You heard me." I make firm eye contact. "I'm making a stand for what's right." *Even if you're still in denial and lying to yourself.* "I'm willing to read the letter to you first, so you are better prepared. That is, if you're interested in hearing what I have written." I motion toward the couch. "Have a seat."

Hunter's ghostly complexion returns. After reading the letter, Hunter stands and begins to pace.

"You can't do this!"

"Oh, yes I can."

"This is unbelievable. You are suffocating me." He throws his arms up. "I won't be forced into this. You're being used by Satan himself to destroy what God has called me to do. This is demonic." He points. "You are trying to ruin me."

My emotions burst into flames. "Don't you *ever* associate me with having anything to do with Satan and his minions!" I grit my teeth. "Don't you dare twist this and blame me for *you* not having *your* priorities straight. Do you think the board members would support what you've been doing? Would they affirm the smut you're looking at on the computer?" I squint in resentment.

His sarcasm slaps back. "You are so in the dark about men. I would bet they're doing the same thing. God just wired men differently. Something you obviously don't understand." Disdain drips off his words. "And if you think you're going to push me to quit my position on the Christian Businessman Board, so I have to be with you constantly, I'll leave before that ever happens."

His words are harsh. Hard. Threatening. Piercing.

An unexpected peacefulness envelops me. *'I am here.'* God's sweet words and presence calm my emotions. The numbness doesn't show up. God's tranquility embraces me. Words of sincerity come out of my mouth before I realize what I'm saying.

"If this ministry means more to you than me, if this role is more important to you than us, then I will respect your wishes. You are free to leave." My words hang heavy in the room.

Hunter tilts his head and raises his brow as if surprised.

"Um...ah...I mean it." He raises his voice in a threatening tone. "You will not control me!"

"I'm not controlling you, Hunter. I'm simply asking you to make a choice. The only thing I request is for you to make a final decision about leaving in the next three days. I don't wish to be dragged into some long, drawn-out emotional roller coaster."

"FINE!" He yells and stomps out of the room.

I jump to the echo of the garage door slamming.

Catie
Autumn 1964

A door slams in the distance, but we pay little attention. Claudia and Carolyn are sittin' with me on a bench at the back of the garage enjoyin' our weekend off from schoolwork. The rest of the girls are stretched out in the grass, except Charlotte, who's in the house. My mouth waters as I suck on a sweet cinnamon candy. I'm tempted to bite down, but resist, 'cuz I know it will last longer if I don't. I pat the three pieces tucked away in my front pocket. Claudia's tellin' one of her funny stories when Daddy clears his throat. The sound grabs our attention.

I guess he has been watchin' us for a while. His face is stern, and his jaw is clenched, along with those steely eyes, which tells me that we're in trouble. But I haven't quite figured out why. I smack on the cinnamon candy and wait.

His voice booms. "Open your mouths!"

Without question, we open our mouths, displayin' the dark red candies balanced on our tongues.

"Where did you get the candy?"

We're instantly quiet. We're busted—no excuses. I look for Claudia and Carolyn to come up with somethin' clever. No such luck.

Charley runs around the corner with one of his matchbox cars, racin' it through the air. Makin' a rumblin' sound of an engine, he squeals to a stop.

"Ertttt. Hey, you girls got any more candy?" He sticks out his little hand.

Daddy's eyes squint. "Yes, Claudia Lee, Carolyn Marie, Melinda Lynn, Catie Kay, and Shawnee Ann," Daddy pauses. "Do you girls have any more candy to give to Charley?"

Charley starts walkin' backward. He's caught on to the fact that we're in big trouble. Daddy called us out by our ages, oldest to the youngest. Uh oh! He only uses our middle names when we've really messed up.

"Well? Where did you get the candy?" He looks into each of our eyes, demandin' an answer.

Claudia's the first to speak. "The Little Store."

"You bought it? Who gave you the money?" He steps in closer. "Or did you steal it?"

Claudia keeps her head down and kicks her feet back and forth nervously.

"We didn't have any money."

"Claudia, Carolyn, Melinda, Catie, and Shawnee, we're going to The Little Store so you can tell the store owner exactly what the five of you have done. Got it?" He points his finger at us. "Now, march."

We hop up and stand to attention. All of us stare at our feet, and we don't dare look up. Like a brood of ducklin's followin' a Mallard, we follow Daddy. He marches us straight into the store and asks Mr. Tony, the owner, if he noticed any dark red, hard candy missin'.

The man knows right away what Daddy is referrin' to. He brings out the half-full bag of candy. The very sack we had torn into, leavin' a small hole as evidence.

I'm glad Daddy's doin' most of the talkin'. I think he feels sorry for Claudia. She's been bawlin' the whole time. I don't crack a tear, but Carolyn cracks a smile at Claudia for doin' all the blubberin'. Daddy makes us promise in front of Mr. Tony that we won't ever do it again. Melinda and Shawnee stand still and quiet.

The store owner says he thought he had mice after seein' small holes nibbled in a couple of the candy bags. "Any chance you were pilfering from this one?" He holds up a second bag, the root beer barrels, a delicious, brown-colored, hard candy. We all shake our heads no, boldly lyin' to the nice man's face. The lie comes out so easy. I feel lousy knowin' I'm not supposed to lie. I'm actin', just like Anna. I can tell the Holy Spirit is livin' inside me, 'cuz I can feel him in my chest. It aches.

Daddy hands the storeowner the money for both bags. He lets us know right away we can't have any of the candy. In fact, we're goin' to earn money to pay for the candy we've stolen. He tells us in front of Mr. Tony. As punishment, we will be sent to our rooms for three hours, followed by rakin' all the dead leaves in the yard.

As we leave, one by one, out of the creaky wooden screen door, Mr. Tony says, "May the Lord Jesus bless you and keep you and your children safe."

My heart jumps. *Is Mr. Tony, a Christian?*

I turn and skip back to the counter. "Mr. Tony. I got saved a while ago and was baptized in the river too! I have the Holy Spirit livin' in me 'cuz I'm a Christian now. Are you?"

His smile shows his crooked, yellow teeth. "Well, you sweet dear, I sure am."

Daddy interrupts. "Come on, Catie, leave Mr. Tony alone. We've taken up enough of his time."

It's been way over a whole two hours. I'm goin' crazy to get out of this bedroom and back to The Little Store. Since I now know that

Mr. Tony is a Christian grown-up, I'm hopin' I can tell him 'bout Anna, Dean, Buck, and Ivy.

Mr. Tony has Popeye-muscle arms—a strong man, much bigger than Dean. Daddy says he's Italian and probably part of the Mafia, whatever that is.

I asked Charlotte, and she says the Mafias are tough men who have a lot of business connections but sometimes do crimes, like thievin' and sellin' booze when you're not supposed to. So it sounds like Mr. Tony and his family have done some stealin' too. He might be the perfect man to tell 'bout me and Charley's problems. And he'll probably understand 'bout my stealin' and won't be too mad. I have my fingers crossed hopin' he has rough and tough friends and family. Maybe he can help me since God's clock seems to be broken.

I tiptoe to the top of the stairs and peek through the spindles. I quietly squeak out my request, almost in a whisper. "Daddy, can I come downstairs? I want—"

"Get your butt back in your room, young lady!"

"But, I need to talk to Mr.…."

"I don't want to hear any if's, and's, or but's about it. Go—now!"

I sneak back into the room, not wantin' to wake Carolyn or Melinda. I tear a piece of paper off of my big yellow writin' tablet. I take my pencil and write Daddy a letter.

> Dear DAddy,
> I Am sorry. I promise not to do it AgAin. I forgot to tell Mr. Tony I Am sorry. Can I come out of my room so I cAn go to The Little Store, by myself, to sAy it to his fAce? I Am sorry And need to Ask him to forgive me.
>
> Answer Yes [Jor No[J
>
> I love you DAddy.
> Peanut CAtie XOXOXO

I fold the paper into a square. I grab our fishin' pole and stick the safety pin through the top of my letter, then cast it over the stair railin'. Daddy's sittin' on the couch below. I make small swings back and forth in front of his face. I jiggle it a little, like Granny Grunt and Grandpa taught me, to attract the fish. He bites. Daddy takes the note off the hook and reads it. I reel my pole back and wait.

"Catie, come on down here." He says soft, but firm.

I fly down the stairs. "Yes, Daddy?"

"What are your sisters doing?"

"They're sleepin'. I cross my fingers on both hands behind my back. Daddy's quiet, just starin' at my note. I cross my legs for extra luck.

"Do you really want to go over to apologize to Mr. Tony? Or is this an excuse to get out of your room?"

"Yes. I need to talk to him. And this isn't an excuse to get out of my room. I'll go back into my room after I tell him I'm sorry."

"Okay, let's go." He stands and takes my hand.

"No, Daddy. I have to go by myself; otherwise, Mr. Tony will think you made me say it. It's just right across the street, just kitty-corner from our house. You can watch me walk over. Why don't you write him a note, sayin' it's okay for me to be there? I need to go by myself. I can buy somethin' like bread if you want."

"We don't need any bread, but I'll write a note, so he knows you have my permission to be there. You come right back. And don't you think for a minute that you're not going right back upstairs when you get home. You hear me, young lady?" He lifts his right eyebrow.

"Yes, Daddy."

The store's screen door creaks as it opens. I poke my head inside and look to see if anyone's around. I have to tell someone before it's too late. I call out, "Mr. Tony, are you here?"

CHAPTER THIRTY-SIX

Catie
Autumn 1964

I shuffle my feet across the wood floor inside The Little Store. It looks like no one is around. The place is dead quiet. I mosey closer to the register. Silence.

Crash!

I jump at the sound of somethin' fallin' and hittin' the ground. I stand frozen, like a squirrel. *Who's in here?*

"Mr. Tony? Mr. Tony, are you here?" My voice cracks.

I tiptoe toward the noise. I'm in luck. Mr. Tony is dustin' off some canned goods.

"Excuse me, Mr. Tony."

He looks my way. "Well, if it isn't, Miss Catie."

He throws his dustin' cloth over his shoulder and walks me toward the cash register area. I hand him the crumpled note from Daddy.

"My daddy knows I'm here. I came to say I'm sorry. I know stealin's wrong, and I am sorry for stealin' your candy. Will you... please...forgive me?"

I rub my sweaty hands against the sides of my slacks.

He sets down his dustin' cloth.

"Well, yes, of course, Miss Catie, I forgive you. It takes a lot of courage to admit when you've done wrong. I'm proud of you for understanding that what you did was disobedient to your parents and God. I appreciate you asking for forgiveness. You're a sweet little girl."

He fluffs up the hair on the top of my head.

"Umm, I'm a sweet girl with a sweet tooth."

I look up at him with my best puppy-dog-eyes and then eyeball the penny candy, but only for a second. I shuffle my feet.

"Umm..."

Askin' him to forgive me was easy. Easier than I thought. Now what? Ugh!

The thought of tellin' him 'bout the devil worshipers makes me nervous. I'm sweatin' like a stuck pig, as Grandpa would say. I'm not sure what that really means, but I'm so jumpy the hair at the back of my neck feels drippy wet.

"What? Cat got your tongue?" Mr. Tony lifts his eyebrows.

I pinch my thigh. *Spit it out. Do it! Do it!*

"Uhh..., Mr. Tony, you're a Christian man...and seem to understand the difference between right and wrong. Right? You know, 'bout people sinnin' and all? Right?"

He nods, tiltin' his head.

"What would you do if you had *a friend* who had some grown-ups doin' nasty and evil things to her and her brother? I mean really bad, more than double-dog bad. Or double-devil bad, if that's a word."

He scratches the bald spot on the top of his head.

"What do you mean? A crime? Like breaking the law?"

"Not sure. Is it a crime to hit and hurt little kids and do things to them that grown-ups shouldn't do? Mean things?" I bite the end of my fingernail and look up at Mr. Tony. "Is it a crime to be a witch? Or to be meaner than a rattlesnake?"

"Well, hmm, Catie. Have you talked to your parents about this?" He wrinkles his forehead as if he's thinkin' real hard.

"No. I haven't talked to my daddy 'bout it, 'cuz it's 'bout *my friend*. She doesn't want me to tell my parents."

I start fidgetin', 'cuz I know it's wrong to lie, and I'm doin' it again. I bite the corner of my upper lip.

"Umm...I promised her I wouldn't tell."

I scratch my burnin' ears.

"Mr. Tony, if *you* had this problem, who would *you* tell?" I move closer. "Your family?" I don't wait for an answer. I just keep on flappin' my jaws. "Would your kin beat up these bad people so my friends don't get hurt anymore?"

I lean in and look straight into his eyes. I ask in a hushed whisper, "Are you in the Mafia?"

Mr. Tony lets out a loud chuckle. He bends over and holds his big belly that's almost as big as the fake Santa Claus who works downtown at the department store.

Is he makin' fun of me? I squeeze my brows together into a frown. I'm as serious as a heart attack, as my Teenage Granny would say. I stomp my foot.

Mr. Tony lets out one word. "Oh!" His lips form a circle and stay in the same position as he comes around the cash register counter. He bends down on one knee and puts his arm around my shoulder.

"I'm sorry, Catie. I was taken aback when you asked about the Mafia. It's obvious you have an excellent imagination."

He's fightin' back a grin. I ignore it 'cuz I need answers. I need help to save Charley, my family, and me.

"What would you do, Mr. Tony? Who should I tell to help my friends? And they have to be a Christian."

His face turns serious. "I would call the police if it were crucial. You know, life or death?" He crinkles his eyebrows together and looks hard and long at my face.

I open my mouth to tell Mr. Tony that it's worse than life and death, but just then, the bell on the store's screen door jingles.

Tony speaks up, "Catie, this might be the man you need to talk with about your friend. Have you ever met, Policeman Doug? He patrols this area and always drives by or comes into my store."

I slowly turn. My tummy stirs. I scurry behind Mr. Tony and then peek my head out from around him. It's a policeman all right, the blonde one, the one I've seen way too many times with Mean Dean and Buck. I never knew his name before.

We look at each other, both glarin'.

"You guys know each other?"

Yes, Mr. Tony. I've seen Policeman *Doug* before. Many times."

I say his name, extra-long. I know it bothers him that, now, I know his real name, 'cuz it goes against Dean's rule of not knowin' anyone's name.

"Catie, do you want to tell him about your friend?"

"NO! He's not a Christian. My friend wouldn't want him to know. Only Christians that are in the Mafia."

The dirty-devil-policeman starts laughin' like it's all a joke.

I turn to Mr. Tony. "Thank you for forgivin' me. I need to go home now."

His face looks confused as he scratches his head again. I walk out, wavin' goodbye. The screen door slams behind me.

I stop just around the corner to spy and listen to what they're sayin'. Regardless of the shivery autumn air, I'm sweatin'. The policeman asks questions.

"So what's going on with the little girl? Christians in the Mafia, huh?"

"She was just havin' some fun. Quite the imagination, I'd say."

"So, what does she want to talk to a policeman about? What did she tell you?"

"Nothing really, but you don't qualify," Mr. Tony snickers.

"Hey, man, I'm a law enforcer and a Christian."

"She must've heard about how you carry on over at Pete's bar. I'd question your faith too."

They both break out into laughter. I hear the floor creak.

"Tony, hey man, do you have a pack of cigarettes, Pall Malls, before I take off?"

I run as fast as I can across the street to my house. When I'm in my yard, I look back over my shoulder to see if Policeman Doug is on my trail.

What if he tells Anna and her family? What if they kill Charley? Or worse, my whole family?

I dart into the livin' room. Daddy's still sittin' on the couch.

"I did it, Daddy. I asked Mr. Tony for forgiveness for stealin' his candy," I say while catchin' my breath. "Now, can I start my punishment of cleanin' up the yard?"

Daddy looks up with a slight smile. "I'll gather the rakes, but you, young lady, have another 30 minutes in your room."

I walk by our big livin' room window on my way to the stairs. I notice Policeman Doug comin' out of the door at The Little Store. He's smokin' a cigarette. The devil-cop stops and begins lookin' around. He looks my way. Uh oh! He points and shakes his fist. *At me?*

I run from the window and fly up the stairs to my room. I hide under my bed covers and pray. "Jesus, I haven't got my clock yet, but I know you hear my prayers. Please hurry. Come and save me and my family."

Marion
December 1996

F at snowflakes flutter past my office window, covering every surface with a sheen of white. Whether a sleek park bench or a rusted trashcan, each item is transformed.

I walk over to the office cabinet, reach in, and pull out Catherine's file to review my notes prior to her afternoon appointment. My attention is drawn to her name. Catherine Williams is typed on the index tab with Hunter's last name, Stone, added in blue ink, written in cursive.

A brief smile flashes across my face as I recall the joy I felt so long ago when I penned her married name on the tab. My smile fades, and my joy transforms into a serious concern.

I rehash Catherine's recent narrative of the pornography challenges with Hunter. She is desperate, in search of solutions, real solutions without bandages or compromises to bring the necessary changes into her life—their lives. I scan the pages of notes. Our December 6th session ended with Catherine sharing a time where she had to face a similar dilemma in her childhood as Catie.

Ironically, history appears to be repeating itself. Catherine, like Catie, is desperate to resolve the pain and despair in her life. Both determined to tell their secrets and expose the hidden darkness—both willing to risk the high stakes of loss, both lament in a heart-rending cry for help.

As for me, they rip heavy on my heart.

"Lord, I am willing, I am here, but I depend upon you to deliver the answers, the healing, and the cleansing—whiter than snow. Bring victory to your daughter."

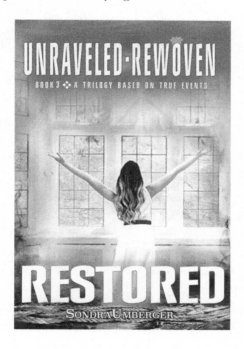

A novel based on true events. CATHERINE—with well-guarded boundaries nailed into place is determined never to be mistreated or deceived again by any man. Separated and on her own, she keeps HUNTER, her husband at a distance, demanding that he faces his demons of addiction.

Christian counselor, MARION, encourages Catherine, also known as CATIE, to unlock the black box of her hidden childhood secrets, known as her 'lost years'. Frightened and fragmented, only seeing pieces to the puzzle, she perseveres. Images appear. Secrets revealed. Questions are answered as the recollections unravel. Catherine experiences God's provision, protection, and exercises the unique gifts he gave her as a child.

A time—meant to be silenced.
◆ As darkness is uncloaked, a spiritual battle erupts. Is it all too much?
◆ Will they overcome the formidable odds stacked against them?
◆ Will Catherine trust an invisible God and a husband whose betrayal amplifies her brokenness?
The unspoken—is exposed.

What others are saying:
When all feels lost, discover hope, healing, and redemption—**A PAGE TURNER**.
~*Genevra Bonati, Author*

A captivating novel based on actual events. Determined and combating evil with faith-based principles, confrontations ignite, and spiritual weapons discharge, leading to victory! A story of sexual addiction that exposes the hidden lies of many. **Offers hope and restoration**.
~ *J. C. Richards, Author*

ABOUT THE AUTHOR

Sondra Umberger, Christian counselor, an ordained minister, and President of Healing Hearts Ministry, Inc., and Connecting to Christ, offers faith-based materials and counsel on how to prevail through the challenges and struggles of life. Sondra instructs on a variety of topics, including confronting and overcoming abuse.

Sondra loves to laugh and enjoys outdoor activities and adventures with her husband in the vast playground of Colorado.

 www.ConnectingToChrist.com

 Facebook.com/SondraUmbergerAuthor

PRAYER

Unraveled-Rewoven is a trilogy inspired by true events. I understand the accounts are challenging, having your eyes opened to the darkness. Nevertheless, as you turn the pages, my desire and prayers are that you will find the truth, hope, and healing, as Catherine found through her faith and trust in Jesus Christ.

I am supplying a prayer for those who desire to invite the Lord into their lives.

Dear Father God,

I realize I have made many mistakes, knowingly and unknowingly. I admit my sins brought death and destruction into my life and into my relationship with others and with you, Lord. I do not have the answers on how to change my heart or my path in life. But I believe you do and that you are the answer.

Your word says in John 3:16 that you loved the world so much that you gave your son, Jesus Christ, to pay for our sins and that whoever believes in him would not perish but that you, Lord, would give them eternal life. As best as I can, I now place my trust in you. I am grateful that you have promised to receive me despite my many sins and failures. Father, I take you at your word.

Lord, I confess I have sinned and need your forgiveness. I believe you sent your Son, Jesus Christ, to die in my place, paying the penalty for my wrongdoings. I believe he died on a cross and rose from the dead. I admit, sometimes I doubt, help me with my unbelief. I ask you to please fill my emptiness with the Holy Spirit and make me whole. Teach me your ways and show me how to have an intimate and growing relationship with you. Thank you for all you have done. I surrender my life to you. Thank you for hearing this prayer. In Jesus' Name. Amen.

If you prayed this prayer and would like to know what steps to take next to grow in your faith or have questions, you may contact me at ConnectingToChristWebsite@gmail.com

Blessings,
Sondra Umberger

AFTERWORD

Unraveled-Rewoven
Book One: ROBBED-Innocence Stolen
Book Two: RIPPED-Lies Exposed
Book Three: RESTORED-Truth Unfolds

Author: *Sondra Umberger*

Author's purpose:

This trilogy, based on actual events, is a story of survival and victory.

I have written Unraveled-Rewoven to motivate and inspire you, the reader, to understand that you can be an overcomer and victor in Christ. I encourage you to conquer your conflicts and challenges by examining and applying Biblical truths and Christian principles. Although your struggles may differ from the story's characters, the answer is the same, Jesus.

As you journey into your faith, seek the truth. Take hold of the promises, the power, and the authority given to you as a child of God, to bring victory into the battles you face.

Connecting To Christ

Published by Connecting to Christ
www.ConnectingToChrist.com

ACKNOWLEDGEMENTS

My deepest gratitude to my husband, Thomas, whose loyal support and understanding helped me fulfill this goal. His continual encouragement made this trilogy come to fruition.

My sincere appreciation and gratitude for Debbi Wise and Gigi Gray for being my writing partners. Thank you for the many hours you spent reading and critiquing these books as the accounts came to life on paper. I love the laughter and time we spend together, giving input and hand-holding through times of fatigue and feeling overwhelmed. You are both such an inspiration to me. Thank you.

Thank you, Chris Richards, for believing in me and the story I had to tell. I appreciate your skillset and the time you invested with me from day one at the coffee shop. Expressed gratitude for sharing your expertise and insights into the world of writing and publishing.

Beta group: MaryJean Cipro, Nicole Adrain Cyler, Tracy King, Roy Richards, and Tom Umberger. Thank you for taking the time to read this trilogy. I appreciate your feedback, suggestions, and encouragement to have this story published. Your inspiring support motivated my completion of these books.

Thank you, Marlene Bagnull, for responding to my email and sending your book: Writing His Answer, as a gift. Your response and invitation to attend the CCWC (Colorado Christian Writers Conference) years ago was the beginning of my journey to becoming an author. Your continued support and encouragement to urge Christian writers to use their voices, via words, to tell a broken world of the good news of Jesus is making a difference.

———————

Thank you, Bob Tamasey, for investing the time to proofread this trilogy. Your support, encouragement, and creative feedback are much appreciated.

———————

My heartfelt thanks to book cover designer: Keno McCloskey. Your artistic and creative ability captured the essence of this trilogy. Your talent shines through each book's cover and reflects the story before the books are even opened. I can't thank you enough for your commitment and perseverance to create truly stunning works of art.

———————

My sincere gratitude and appreciation to Debbie Maxwell Allen for your diligence, perseverance, and the efforts you invested in editing and formatting. Your encouragement and hand-holding was a huge blessing to me. I can't thank you enough.